NIGHT WITCH IN BERLIN

Joanna Brady

CONTENTS

Library of Congress Cataloging-in-Publication Data

Author website: https://joannabradysite.com/

Brady, Joanna
Night Witch in Berlin / Joanna Brady – 1st ed.

1. Cold War fiction
2. Russian night witches fiction
3. WWII women flyers fiction
4. Russian Women fiction
5. Historical romance WWII fiction
6. Espionage in Berlin post WWII fiction
7. Novels set in Berlin

For my family.
And for brave women everywhere.

"These women feared nothing. They came night after night...they wouldn't give us any sleep at all."
Hauptmann Johannes "Mackey" Steinhoff, Commander of II/JG 52, Knight's Cross of the Iron Cross with Oak Leaves and Swords

Commandment #1 (of 12): "Be proud you are a woman."
Marina Raskova, pioneering Russian aviatrix, founder and leader of the all-female Soviet fighting forces, World War II.

GUIDE TO CONTENTS

AUTHOR'S NOTE

I was inspired to write this book in 2014 while sitting in traffic and first heard the Russian Night Witches referenced in passing on NPR. My interest led me to three books in particular: *A Dance With Death* by the late Anne Noggle, *Wings, Women & War*, by Reina Pennington, and *Night Witches* by Bruce Myles. There were also innumerable newspaper articles and documentaries about these incredible women.

It occurred to me that to place such a gutsy woman in post-war Berlin as a spy would be an interesting subject for a story. The result was *Night Witch in Berlin*, a tale that shifts from Moscow and Ukraine to East Germany, London, and finally, to Key West in the U.S.

For the conditions that prevailed when a million and half victorious Red Army soldiers stormed Berlin in 1945, I refer the reader to *A Woman in Berlin – Eight Weeks in the Conquered City* a poignant memoir published anonymously in 1959 by German journalist Marta Hillers, who suffered the fate of over 100,000 German women after the Battle for Berlin. Her identity was revealed much later.

Stalin sent over 800,000 women to war, including snipers, gunners, nurses and tank drivers. The Night Witches were only one small group. Yet, in an effort to repopulate the country after WWII (called The Great Patriotic War by Russians), 456 jobs were made unavailable to women in Russia, 'to protect their reproductive organs from danger.' Flying a plane was one of them. In the light of what the bright, brave Night Witches went through, this ban was beyond risible. Women who flew innumerable dangerous missions during the conflict were denied the opportunity to continue in their field of expertise—a misogynist move only lifted in 2019, when more opportunities, like flying, were opened up to women. At this time of writing, the BBC reports that women have recently been allowed to drive trams. The ban on 79 other jobs continues.

While biographies of some Night Witches exist, I chose a fictional composite of many rather than one in particular. And while I've tried to stay true to people and places, I did invent where required: The main Kommandatura office was in Berlin-Dahlem on Kaiserswerther Straße, but the branch near the Adlon Hotel was my own invention. There was no Drummond Hill air base outside of London; no Karl Marx military airport outside Moscow, or People's Gliding School in that city. And to my knowledge, no Marching Saints dance hall in Berlin.

There were a lot of moving parts to this story. I am not a historian who writes novels; I'm a writer passionate about history, particularly World War II. Any inaccuracies in interpreting historical events are my own.

Stories of women who triumph over adversity are of particular interest to me. My first book, *The Woman at the Light* was about a woman lighthouse keeper in the Florida Keys in a secret miscegenative relationship. For *Night Witch in Berlin*, my canvas was much broader.

I wish to thank all the beta readers who encouraged me along the way in the writing of this book; in particular, my son Terry, and husband Walter Schmida, who each read it numerous times. Thanks to Kevin and Dorothy Schmida for their moral support. I'd like to thank June and Capt. Jerry Gerard for technical advice, reader friends Katherine and Bradley Brown in Toronto, and in Key West and Fort Lauderdale, writer Lew Weinstein and Pat Lenny. Also in Key West, writer Patty Patten Tiffany and Ruth Reiter. New York writer, Judi Winters, and Doris Montag of London, Ontario. In Berlin, good friend Achim Grunwald was an invaluable resource. Russian-born Elena Southcott in Key West helped me with Russian translation. A special thanks to my wonderful computer guru, Thomas Livingston; my editor, Alison McCabe in San Francisco, Elena Karoumpali in Greece who designed the beautiful cover, and to all my friends at the Key West Writers Guild, as well as my friends in France. Without all their constructive criticism, this book would have fallen short. Lastly, I'd like to thank my readers and Key West book sellers, whose gentle reminders encouraged me to complete the novel.

My humble thanks go to the Florida Keys Council of the Arts who awarded me a grant in 2015 to continue the work, and the Anne McKee Artists Fund in Key West, who awarded me funds to finish it in 2020.

Lastly, if you've enjoyed *Night Witch in Berlin*, I have a self-serving request. Ratings and/or reviews on Goodreads or Amazon are greatly appreciated! Many thanks.

Key West, February, 2021

PROLOGUE

H itler's Wehrmacht once considered our all-female night bombing regiment Stalin's practical joke, an embarrassing nuisance. Now they are no longer amused. It's humiliating for them to be bombed by Russian women, most of us still in our teens.

The sleep-deprived Nazi troops are expecting us. They call us *Nachthexen*—night witches—and anyone who manages to down one of our bombers gets awarded an Iron Cross and two thousand marks. We venture into every sortie in terror, hoping that God—if there is one as some claim—will spare us yet again.

There are no surprises. It's always the same, because our routine is efficient. Night after freezing night, our squadron approaches a target from an elevation of about 4,500 feet. In my flimsy Polikarpov Po-2, I throttle back to idle, descend quickly, and glide in, quiet as a whisper, with lights off. A sister plane flying a few minutes behind me in formation will cooperate over the target, charging like an enraged bull to destroy the broad searchlights and draw fire away from me and my navigator, Rufina.

Timing is crucial. As we circle the target, Rufina will drop the flares with their mini parachutes. Once the plane behind us succeeds in distracting the enemy, it will quickly escape in the opposite direction to avoid the anti-aircraft ground fire. When the target appears, I'll position us to drop our deadly payload by gliding in silence, banking slightly into a turn as I side-slip down into the dark abyss. Then I'll level over the target when my altimeter reads six hundred feet, no lower or I'll risk damage to my own plane from the blast.

After Rufina unleashes the bombs I'll reignite the engine, and we in turn will become the decoy, flying into the blinding lights while my sister aircraft repeats what we've done. Out of bombs, both planes will high-tail it back to base, and two more planes flying a few minutes behind us will take our places.

This is how it will play out. Most nights it works well.

We're ten minutes to target. Rufina has been shouting above the din through our intercom to relieve the tension.

"Getting colder," she yells to be heard over the wind and the noisy engine. "I don't think I'll ever be warm again."

She says virtually the same thing on every sortie. We're both shivering, though we try to put it out of our minds and work through the frigid air slamming our bones. No possible way to add heat to our Po-2 cockpit, open to the elements of the merciless Russian winter.

This sortie is our fourth of the night, and there will be a good many more—some nights as many as eighteen. Because our planes are so small, they cannot hold large bombs and must be constantly reloaded. As Rufina referenced, the cold *is* unbearable, minus 20 Celsius. Biting wind easily permeates the scarves we've wound around our faces. Frost decorates our goggles like finely powdered sugar. Our feet, plunged into men's boots and stuffed with newspaper at the toes, are numb, even with two layers of heavy wool socks. After the Germans, frostbite is our worst enemy.

Our payload weighs down the aircraft. Cheaply

knocked together from plywood and canvas, the Po-2 is a tandem biplane trainer, neither designed nor equipped to fly combat missions. The control panels are bare bones and weakly lit, with no radio communication to base. To lighten weight, we have no parachutes, so each sortie is like flying a trapeze without a net. We communicate to our partner by shouting through a primitive rubber tube connected to a microphone and an earpiece. Our engine is so noisy, the enemy calls the Po-2 the *Nähmaschine*—the sewing machine.

Before take-off, Rufina brought up one of her anxieties about her family: "I dreamt of my parents again last night, Kira—this time they died of starvation and exposure. It was so real, Kira."

I can sympathize. Rufina speaks frequently about her parents and her beloved fiancé, Micha. Her bad dreams stem from fatal reality. Leningrad, her parents' city, is still under siege; the population is starving and dying from cold. Micha is probably fighting near the Finnish border and also in constant danger. The news she hears from him is usually a month or so old. Now, heading for our target, she seems despondent, and I worry that her mind is elsewhere. I focus on the target as I visualize our descent.

"Compass heading!" I shout over the din to keep her alert.

Our mission is the destruction of railway cars next to a Nazi encampment in the Caucasus on the Southern front. The supply route to an enemy-held position in the Kerch Peninsula rich in oil reserves, precious reserves Hitler needs to fuel his war. It's closely guarded by German artillery and anti-aircraft weapons. In the air, it's defended by Messerschmitt 109 and Focke-Wulf Fw190 fighter planes.

By flying in low we avoid the German planes, but this tactic leaves us vulnerable to antiaircraft attacks from the ground. It's a fine balance, a potentially fatal trade-off.

"Seven minutes to target," Rufina calls back to me.

I keep asking her for compass readings to take her mind off her parents. All business now, she reads them off. Finally, she announces, "Four minutes."

"Get ready to blast Herr Hitler's troops to hell," I shout. My usual rallying cry.

This part never gets easier. Our nerves are on edge. Determined and disciplined, we lend ourselves to the task with grit and single-mindedness, motivated by our hatred for the enemy.

As we move in closer to the German bivouac, fear grips me like a vise, and I know Rufina is feeling the same terror rush. My pulse is pounding, my mouth is dry, throat parched, and breathing shallow. Extremities are devoid of sensation. Because our bombings are exclusively at night, circadian rhythms of our body clocks are completely disrupted and we're always tired, averaging only about two to four hours sleep. Adrenalin keeps our minds alert, but it is sometimes a struggle to keep my thinking clear and my judgment sharp. While I study the movement of clouds that could help or hinder us if they allow moonlight to wink through, Rufina curses the Nazis—and the mothers who brought them into the world. One of her coping skills.

"One minute to go!" she shouts.

Nervous silence now as we focus on finding railway

cars and the network of tracks in the dark, our target clumsily concealed by the enemy with light-colored tarpaulin blending with the surround of snow.

Our sister plane jolts the slumbering Germans awake as the pilot steers into the searchlights. Time to lower altitude. I throttle the engine to idle.

We glide in toward the encampment in silence, lights extinguished. Rufina prepares to toss the flares to mark the target, followed by our bombs. Before she can carry through, a Focke-Wulf appears, flying straight at us. As it passes alongside, the scrim of cloud blocking the moonlight moves away, exposing us. The pilot's face is taut as he shoots; a stuttering, deafening sound that rattles our bones and nearly shatters our ear drums.

I dive quickly to dodge him and perform the necessary sideslip, altering the trajectory of our Po-2 as I tilt to one side. The Focke-Wulf is a real fighter plane, the pride of Göring's powerful Luftwaffe, sleek and swift, but our diminutive size is an advantage against more sophisticated aircraft. The Po-2 may be small and slow, but it has easier maneuverability and can fly very low. When I re-ignite my engine, I can execute a fast turnaround and descend sharply, while he must make a wide circle to come in for the kill. If he follows me down to the lower altitudes, he risks stalling his plane and crashing.

The Luftwaffe pilot manages to get off several shots. The tattoo of his bullets roars in our ears like cacophonous drums. I'm frantic about our fuel tank. A lucky shot could turn my aircraft into a mini-inferno in seconds. I dive lower till I am directly under him, too low for him to descend; too awkwardly positioned for him to get a clear shot.

"He'll be back!" I shout. "I'll go down to the tree line and make a sharp turn back. Toss the flares and unload fast, so we can get out of here! Ready?"

Rufina says nothing.

"Dammit! Flares, Rufina! Now!"

Our bombs are attached to racks located just below the plane's wings. If I land without unloading them, I'll blow us up. My fuel gauge tells me we can't fly much longer; we have to dump our payload.

Rufina does nothing about the flares. And I can't see the targets in the dark without them.

"Rufina?" I scream in desperation. I risk a half-turn to glance over my shoulder. In the moonlight I see her leaning sideways, rivulets of blood streaming down her face, soaking her scarf as they bubble from a wound in her forehead. Her leather helmet is twisted to one side, and the bloodied scarf and goggles have wrangled their way down to her lower face. Eyes wide open in surprise, her expression is a mask of horror and disbelief.

"Oh, shit! Shit, shit, Rufina! No!"

No time to lose. Despite the cold, a sweaty terror arouses me. It's up to me now. As I register the carnage, I become a wild, avenging angel, spurred by fury. I release my safety harness. Like a contortionist, I spread myself across the seat, lean backwards and toss the flares to light up the railway cars; I make the required turn, then I reach down with my free hand to pull the wires beside Rufina's right leg and release the payload, narrowly missing a towering pine bough as I fight to keep control of the shuddering plane.

The train cars I hit are crucibles of death, carrying

arms and explosives, and despite my sorrow at losing Rufina, I yelp with elation at the fiery inferno I create. Time to escape this pandemonium while I can. I have to hurry. Through the smoke and burning particles in the air, my heart nearly stops as the Focke-Wulf reappears through the fog of debris. I make another sharp turn to outmaneuver him, and drop to a lower altitude. With thunderous popping sounds from his guns, noise from the sirens, and the flak from antiaircraft shooting at my companion planes all screaming in my ears, I head for base in what has become an airborne coffin. Seeking other prey, the Focke-Wulf fades back. My sister decoy plane has survived and is following me closely.

Allowing myself to tremble, I take a deep breath and slowly release it. I fight for control of my adrenalin rush, and numbness settles over me. I've survived to fight another bombing; a baby step toward winning the war.

Finally, the scenario of what I've just been through hits me like an express train.

"Oh Rufina," I moan aloud. "I'm so sorry." My eyes tear up and the words catch in my throat. "So very sorry." Hiccupping sobs, I allow my eyes to release the tears, blurring my vision as they escape my goggles, freezing on my eyelids and cheeks.

"How many more of these can I get through alive?" I cry out to nobody in particular. Verbalizing all my terrors aloud, I ramble on to keep myself from sliding into a restless sleep despite the sharp bite of the cold. Without help from a navigator, I stumble my way through the night sky hoping my fuel holds up as I search for our base, darkened to camouflage against German raids.

There'll be no input from Rufina. She continues to

stare ahead, silent forever.

She was nineteen years old.

CHAPTER 1

East Berlin, 1947

I was at my desk, evaluating the résumé of a former Nazi guard from a "special transit camp"—euphemism for a depot where Jews, Slavs, gypsies, homosexuals, and other people deemed undesirable by the Third Reich were locked up until shipped East. He'd checked "Communist" in the affiliation box of the Fragebogen form, so I stamped "approved" over the top. If I didn't, someone higher up would.

Every day, our department screened hundreds of dossiers for former Nazis applying for work in East Berlin. While some of Hitler's cronies were prized—the engineers, physics professors, mathematicians, or applicants from any of the purely scientific professions—trained guards who were healthy and wanted to work for us Russians were also in demand.

So many German soldiers were still in POW camps in the Soviet Union, we usually had to scrape the bottom of the barrel to get trained, qualified personnel. Or able-bodied men, free of serious injuries. As unwilling guests of our camps in the East, many of our Nazi candidates had learned Russian. These would inevitably end up as functionaries or constables in our newly formed East German secret police, Kommissariat-5, or K-5, a group that was currently shaping up to be an organization as brutal as our Russian NKVD.

The strident voice of Inna Ivanova Gradska, my boss's secretary, pierced through my thoughts: "Kira, Comrade Petrov wants you in his office. Now."

"What does he want?"

"You'll have to go in and find out," she snapped. "And he doesn't like to be kept waiting."

I'd sensed her edgy animosity toward me since day one. As she applied fresh lipstick at her desk, I reflected how she wielded a lot of power for a clerk. She was about my age, a tiny girl, pretty and feminine, with creamy ivory skin and sleek dark hair. Only in her sharp blue almond-shaped eyes and her steely controlled voice did her self-confidence and assertiveness reveal a sharp, more brittle side. Senior Lieutenant Petrov brought her with him from Moscow where she worked as his assistant throughout the war. I wasn't certain what their relationship was, but nothing surprised me.

Though my job was humdrum, I never felt the luxury of being able to relax. A summons from a superior could mean anything in these unstable times. In some ways, such a directive might be as dangerous as night bombing Nazi troops. Having lived under Stalin, I knew the best strategy was always to keep my head down, my ears open, and my mouth shut. As I walked up the two flights and down the long hallway to Petrov's office, a familiar sense of dread stirred somewhere in my gut. I'd done my best to escape his notice since the quick handshake on my arrival.

Was I to be censured? A quick examination of conscience produced a pleasurable memory: my recent trip to an allied conference just outside of London where I'd spoken at length with an American pilot at Drummond Hill, a British military air base.

London

It had taken place a few weeks earlier. Our delegation was touring a makeshift museum set up in a hangar. On display was a welter of confiscated enemy weaponry and aircraft commandeered immediately postwar. A small collection of Focke-Wulf Fw190 and Messerschmitt 109 fighter planes—grisly souvenirs of the horrors we'd been through—brought back dark memories that reached out and grabbed me in their clutches. In my nightmares, I still saw those deadly machines coming at me in the Crimean moonlight.

I froze. The sight of one battered, worse-for-wear Focke-Wulf Fw190, riddled with bullet holes, produced an unexpected physical and emotional reaction: shallow breathing in my chest, a feeling of nausea. My pulse quickened, and I felt my spirit leave my body. Rufina, drenched in blood, was leaning to the side of the back seat of the cockpit. Reaching out to me; words choking her throat. I didn't stop to reason why she'd be seated in an enemy plane. Alone, I fled the area. Panicked, I blindly made my way through heavy rain, taking refuge in a nearby viewing gallery at the terminal building. My mind was in turmoil, much as it was the disastrous night I lost my navigator. The horror of that sortie repeated itself in quick snapshots as I questioned my sanity.

For some time, I stood in the gallery of the terminal taking deep breaths to recover my composure. Through the huge glass panes, I took in the aircraft arriving on the airfield landing strips, and slowly my calm returned. Using all the mental exercises I'd used to relax in combat, I brought my vitals back under control.

After a while, I became absorbed by the sight of the silvery Allied military aircraft glistening in the morning drizzle as they zeroed in on puddled runways. With longing, I focused on a Spitfire as it pierced through the clouds like a glittering needle, leveling wings and lowering flaps.

The reflection of a man behind me appearing in the glass took me by surprise. Curious, I turned to face him. He hobbled toward me, relying on a cane. A gold oak leaf on his collar identified him as a major in the U.S. Army Air Corps. He came closer, and I saw that a patch covered his left eye. Taking stock of my fur hat with its red star and my shabby raincoat, he glowered at me and pointed to a sign on a wall.

"Sorry, Miss. This area is restricted to Authorized Personnel."

I'd seen the sign when I took refuge there and knew I wasn't welcome, but I ignored it. Instead of challenging his authority with my credentials, I gave him my most charming smile and shrugged.

"English—*nyet*."

A lie. My knowledge of English was actually good. At university, alongside our Russian textbooks and engineering manuals, some reference material was written in German; some in English. I'd had to take a course in both. I read English perfectly, and could write it, though for lack of practice I did not speak it well.

He spoke in the slow way people speak to foreigners. "You're with the Russian delegation?"

I nodded. "*Da. Russki.*"

"No English at all?"

I shook my head.

"*Parlez-vous français?*" he asked hopefully. I shook my head again. Another lie. I had taken four years of French in gymnasium.

"Okay, then. *Sprechen-Sie Deutsch?*"

We couldn't go on like this, so I nodded. My German was fluent, and living in Berlin, it was getting better every day. Ironic, I thought, that our lingua franca had to be the language of our common foe during the war. I hastened to assure him that my grasp of the language was poor: "*Ja. Deutsch. Aber nicht sehr gut.*"

"*Wie ich!*" His was poor, too, he assured me. "Listen," he said less affably, in stilted German, "You aren't supposed to be here. This area is restricted to Authorized Personnel. You'll have to leave."

I allowed my disappointment to show, pouting my lips.

He was quiet for a moment. I had no desire to go back out in the rain, now teeming in torrents from a dull gray sky. Would he march me out? I thought I saw the trace of a smile being repressed.

War has a way of accelerating the aging process, making us all appear old beyond our years, but he was young. Mid-to-late thirties perhaps. Hard to tell. His officer's cap hid most of his dark hair, except for the thick thatch that fanned across his forehead. No visible scarring from burns. The smile told me that whatever his injuries were, he had managed to keep his teeth —well-cared-for American teeth. I considered his limp. Amputations were commonplace. Had he kept his legs?

His feet?

"You interested in planes?" he asked in German, dialing down his rudeness.

About this at least, I could be honest. I nodded. "Very much."

"Do you fly? Pilot?" He pointed at the sky, then flapped his hands to indicate wings.

I had to laugh; yet a bitter taste filled my mouth. I shook my head. "*Nyet. Nein.* I am …office clerk."

"You Russians bring office clerks to these conferences?" Without waiting for an answer, he pointed to himself. "*Kampfpilot*," he said. "When they let me fly."

So, a fighter pilot. That immediately endeared him to me.

Indicating the few American planes parked on the airfield, he added. "I've flown most of these during the war; and then some."

As he appraised me, he appeared to like what he saw.

"Vick Moran, U.S. Army Air Corps."

He had a reassuring handshake that warmed my chilled hand. I didn't want to let go. Our initial animosity had waned.

"Voronova. Kira Voronova."

"You look familiar."

My name had resonated and he was trying to place where. "Have you been in films? You're a movie star?"

A line if I ever heard one. I shook my head and smiled. "*Nyet.*"

Crew members from one of the planes trailed in from the airfield and the last one left the door wide open, admitting a blast of cold damp air.

Seeing me shiver, he asked, "How would you like some coffee? Real coffee? There's a canteen down the hall. We can warm up. They won't challenge you if you're with me."

I was delighted at this change of mood, his friendliness. While his German wasn't as good as mine, it was fluent. We were able to talk.

The leader of our delegation, Comrade Leonid Skuratov, wouldn't have been happy to see me in the company of an American officer. But, I reasoned, I could tell him I thought the American might share usable information. Intelligence was currency now.

The door read "Officers' Mess." Inside, the room was more than half-full of military officers from both sides of the ocean. It was an impersonal, utilitarian space, except for a congenial area near the lighted fireplace. He led me to a cozy spot facing the fire; then headed for a counter where he ordered two mugs of coffee and, refusing help, hobbled back with a small tray holding them, along with sugar and cream, placing them on a small table in front of us.

"After your delegation leaves, it's back to tea." He made a face. "Their ersatz coffee here is usually too weak and awful to be drinkable. But this is the real thing."

My first sip assured me that it was, and my eyes closed with pleasure at this unique treat to my senses. I hadn't had real coffee with thick cream and sugar since before the war. A Proustian moment. The rich flavor brought back memories of long-ago afternoons with Maxim after class. The love-making . . .

The Mess was furnished with shabby, crackled black

leather club chairs with armrests well-worn from sharp elbows, seats sculpted to the shape of emaciated buttocks. Inviting and comfortable. The walls had probably been institutional white at one time. Now they were pale tan, stained from years of nicotine assault.

A large official photo of England's King George VI in full regalia, the embodiment of royal dignity, loomed above the bar. On a perpendicular wall, a well-pock-marked dartboard bore the face of Adolf Hitler, his eyes, nose, and signature mustache destroyed with accuracy spurred by loathing.

Artwork was supplied by posters of planes and pilots dating from early aviation days. Black and white newspaper pictures of English war heroes, either alive or encased in a Union Jack-draped coffin in front of a plane or church, were tacked onto a bulletin board on another wall. Curls of smoke rose from languid cigarettes in ashtrays. Scents of coffee, beer, and damp wool from fusty wet uniforms mingled to permeate the air, and the susurrus of English conversations enfolded me, offering comfort and congeniality. Despite the fact that I was surrounded by strangers, I was more relaxed than I'd been in a long time.

I liked the English. I thought of England as a little island with enormous courage, and I admired how they'd defended themselves against the Nazis in the face of overwhelming odds. Though we were not allies at the time, Churchill's ". . . *we will never surrender*" speech after Dunkirk had inspired us Russians; Maxim and I had listened to it on the radio on one of our lazy afternoons in bed.

It would be a full year before yet another radio speech

moved us to take up arms: the speech by Molotov announcing that Hitler had broken our treaty and invaded us. We were at war. Almost overnight, we'd become allies of the British.

Our friendship was not to last. With the war over, Churchill, as Leader of the Opposition, was delivering speeches proclaiming that an Iron Curtain existed between the U.S.S.R. and the West. Discord loomed as a new brutal regime rose from the ashes of an enfeebled East Germany. I could only listen to the slow drums of a cold war with dread.

But none of that concerned me at the moment. I was enjoying the coffee and the company, and happy to be in England, away from the gritty ruins of Berlin. After the chilly visitors' gallery, the Mess was hot and dry. I shrugged out of my army issue overcoat and removed my hat.

"Here, let me take that," Major Moran said. He draped the coat over a chair alongside his own. It was only then, as he sat down across from me that his jaw dropped.

"Holy shit," he said in English. "Ho-ly shit!"

I could easily relate to this reaction. On the left-hand side of my tunic were seven rows of ribbons and bars I'd earned for combat duty. On the right, medals of honor and distinction: my Gold Star Hero of the Soviet Union medallion, the nation's highest honor, Order of Lenin, and the Order of the Red Star, among others. A well-polished cluster.

He leaned in to examine the medals closely and snapped his fingers. "You're that Russian woman pilot. The famous Night Witch."

"One of the Night Witches," I quickly corrected him. "There were usually eighty in our regiment, forty two-person crews."

"The krauts called you ladies *Nachthexen*."

Nachthexen. Yes. Night witches. I bristled at the silly moniker the Nazis gave us. Their pilots were mystified at our agility when we glided down to drop bombs. Awed by how easily we could outmaneuver their fancy, powerful aircraft, they attributed it to something otherworldly. I had to smile. There was nothing magical or paranormal about us. Our planes were just small and slow; easy to move around.

An American Army Air Corps officer seated a few tables away recognized me.

"Captain Voronova! I'd heard you might be here with the Soviet delegation."

He walked over to our table and extended his hand. "Colonel Francis Marcus, U.S. Army Air Corps. We met at the Potsdam Conference in '45. An honor to see you again, Captain."

He was speaking English, so to keep up my deception I had to pretend I understood little of what he said. Major Moran translated it into labored German.

I'd created a needless complication. I should have just admitted I could read the sign on the wall and was fluent in English. I couldn't remember meeting Marcus in '45. I hoped we'd shared no conversation in English at Potsdam. I shook his hand and nodded, mumbling something in German.

Dazzling our allies was the reason I was included at conferences. First of all, I was pretty; I'd been told that often enough. I was tall, and a poor wartime diet kept my figure slim, though I managed to retain my natural curves. With my deep hazel-green eyes and my natural blonde hair coiled into a braided crown, I did attract attention.

More importantly, with the addition of a brilliant display of medals pinned to my uniform, I'd become an attractive public relations ploy, a fine way to show off the Soviet Union's unique combat women. Being used in this way was painful to me. My medals—once markers of heroic sorties—were now merely ornamental. Trimmings on a Christmas tree.

In reality, except on these outings where I would interact with foreigners, my bravery was largely forgotten now that the war was over. My piloting skills no longer required, I was reduced to being decorative. With my education, my flying skills and experience, why was I rubber-stamping forms at a desk in a dreary office in Berlin? Here in London, I sensed a shift in attitude. As people like Colonel Marcus fawned over me and my accomplishments, I could feel embers of my self-esteem reigniting. I was enjoying myself.

"I've been reading about you, Captain," Colonel Marcus continued. "Impressive. Nine hundred and forty-two sorties to your credit. Eighteen in one night—in the freezing cold of Russian winters." He shook his head in disbelief. "And flying those open bi-plane crates—Po-2s, for Christ's sake!" He turned to explain to Major Moran, "Little Polikarpov trainers equipped with bombs. Imagine." He grimaced. "Designed back in 1928! Amazing."

Conversations died around us as officers seated nearby began to eavesdrop.

It was rare for anyone outside our Motherland to acknowledge what female combat pilots accomplished during our night raids. Few foreigners had even heard of the 588th night bombers, or our other two female flying regiments. No other country had sent women in air combat. Ever.

"If those stats are right," Marcus said, "You're a legend, like Marina Raskova. You should be entombed next to Lenin on Red Square."

This was over the top. "Please. Tell the Colonel I don't plan that far ahead," I told Major Moran—who was still translating.

I was surprised Marcus had heard of Marina Raskova, Russia's answer to Amelia Earhart. She was a unique, charismatic navigator, famous for her long-distance flights, and it was she who'd begged Stalin to let her organize female flying units. The women in my regiment regarded Raskova with awe. She was attractive, brave, and innovative. A true leader. When she lost her life, at the age of thirty-one attempting an emergency landing near Stalingrad, the rest of the country grieved along with us. Raskova was honored in many ways: streets and a ship were named after her, her image was on stamps and posters—and her ashes were placed in the bricks of the Kremlin in Red Square. But few people outside the Soviet Union knew about her.

As he prepared to go back to his table, Colonel Marcus glanced at my companion. "Major," he said with a nod. Moran struggled to his feet to salute him, knocking over his cane. Marcus gestured for him to remain seated. "At ease, Major."

After Marcus left, Moran said with reproach, "And I believed you when you told me you were an office clerk!"

"I didn't lie to you, Major. That's all I am now." I shrugged. "The war is over."

"So they say," he said, taking a sip of his coffee. "More coffee? If you're hungry they'll toast one of those doughy English crumpet things for you. They're not bad with strawberry jam or marmalade."

I couldn't get enough of the coffee, but passed on the crumpets.

"So, they gave you an office job, too, huh?" he said.

"Yes. I'm afraid so."

"I know what it means to be grounded." He lifted his cane in disgust. "We put our asses on the line; they give us a bunch of medals, then tell us to go fly a desk."

He didn't explain his injuries and I didn't press for explanations. I was not about to boast that I, and I alone among my regiment, had never been injured. Shot down, yes, a couple of times, emergency landings in gusty winds and ice, but never seriously hurt. No fractures. No burns. Always able to get out and hobble away with no more than a sprained ankle, a touch of whiplash, or a few lacerations—a feat regarded by my colleagues as nothing short of miraculous. My nickname was "*Povezlo*," meaning "Lucky."

Like any good Communist I was not religious. No scapulars or St. Christopher medals for me. Just Maxim's little metal airplane pin, my good luck charm; I'd carried it in my pocket for years.

"Kira," Major Moran said, interrupting my thoughts. "Maybe we can find more real coffee somewhere. Tomorrow perhaps?"

A spark of interest ignited in the hypothalamic part of my brain. He wanted to see me again. I had to acknowledge that our casual meeting awakened something in me. Something long dead. With regret, I shook my head.

"We're leaving London first thing in the morning."

"For Moscow?"

"No. Berlin." I paused, adding the obvious, "*East* Berlin."

"I'm stationed in Berlin, too," he chuckled. "*West* Berlin."

"So, we're neighbors."

"Yes, neighbors," he said with a slight grimace. "For now."

Through a door left ajar, I saw our group leader, Comrade Skuratov, seeking me out. On a wild impulse, I scribbled my phone number on Moran's cigarette pack before reaching for my coat.

"Call me," I said as I turned to go. "We'll find that coffee in Berlin."

A mad gesture, fueled by curiosity. Nothing more ... when I glanced back at him from the door, I thought I saw him smiling at someone else in the room.

CHAPTER 2

"Enjoying your work here, Comrade?"

Senior Lieutenant Vasily Petrov's voice snapped me back to the present. He was a large, burly man with hairy knuckles and tufts of dark hair peeking out of his ears. Pocked remnants of teenage acne scarring and miniscule broken capillaries combined to give his complexion a rough and ruddy hue, while medial drifting of his yellowing lower teeth jammed them together at the front, like slabs of ice in a spring debacle. It was hard to guess his age—somewhere in his mid to late forties was my guess. He had a full head of dark hair veering into a well-defined widow's peak, sleekly combed back with brilliantine. A perpetual five o'clock shadow was creeping over his broad face despite the early hour. He invited me to sit.

Prior to this meeting, I had met Petrov when I first arrived; we'd exchanged scarcely more than a few words. With nothing to base any kind of familiarity, I proceeded with caution.

His question caught me off guard, so I took a moment to answer it.

Enjoying my work? I had to still my pent-up frustration and anger; quieting my urge to cry out: *Well, what do you think? No, I'm not enjoying it at all! I hate every boring minute of it. What I want is to fly planes again; to design and test new equipment; to instruct pilots; take to the skies so I can improve my own flying skills on sophisticated planes. Not stamp documents in this dreary shithole!*

"Yes, sir, of course," I replied.

He was peering at me with calculating unblinking eyes, a falcon eyeing prey. I knew Petrov had served in Intelligence through the Great Patriotic War—an NKVD desk job in Moscow his wife's family connections in the Party finagled for him. Supervising bone-crushing interrogations of accused dissidents in Moscow's Lubyanka prison had been part of his work. Bloody scenes I shuddered to visualize.

"With your background, I imagine you're frustrated with the work we have you doing in Berlin," he began smoothly.

He was inviting me to complain; a cute, transparent NKVD ploy.

"It's . . . interesting. Quite interesting, finding out who was in cahoots with Hitler, seeing how they whitewash their applications—" I responded cheerfully, venturing a smile. "There are no Nazis left in Germany, of course; only KPD—the Germans who were Communists before the war."

"Yes," he harrumphed, amused at the irony. "We had no idea we were so numerous!"

Few of our applicants would admit they'd ever supported Hitler. A needless prevarication, since brutal fascists were welcome in certain jobs. Petrov returned my smile, offering me French brandy and a cigarette. I shook my head. I needed to stay alert.

"Quite right about that," he said, pouring himself a morning eye-opener. "They've all shredded their Nazi party membership cards. But the reasons these retreads want to work with us are less than ideological. They're all desperate. They were promised a thousand years of prosperity; now they sell their souls for an extra book of rations."

He sat back in his chair. "What we're doing in this office, the Americans, British, and the French are doing over there." He indicated West Berlin with a wave of his hand. "They're fussier than we are, though. Unless they're valuable, Nazis can't get hired in the West. Communists aren't welcome, either. The busiest people in Berlin these days are forgers."

We knew most Germans preferred to work for the Americans, but not everyone could afford a forger to falsify papers. It was easier to get jobs with us Russians in a hurry; important when you were hungry. All applicants had to do was write 'Communist' in the box that asked for Party affiliation and we'd sign them up.

"The Americans keep turning up Nazi dossiers to be shredded or pulped by Hitler's regime," I offered. Although I socialized little with colleagues, I was adept at picking up interesting bits of information around the office. "They're sifting through piles of them, hoping for persons of interest."

"Yes. They pretend to search out the big fish—the war criminals. Make an example of them. But the ratline is alive and thriving, and the well-off guilty are already hiding out in other countries. The smart ones. They saw the defeat coming. Planned for it well before the end."

"The Nuremberg trials . . ."

"Show trials! Everyone knew the outcome in advance. They rooted out a handful to appease the revanchist masses. A public relations display." He poured himself another drink. "What they're after are the valued ones, just as we are."

He took a swig of his brandy. "The Nazi scientists. They're the prizes we all,want." He waved his hand in disgust. "All those gas van drivers, prison guards, janitors, waiters, entertainers, and factory workers? Grunt work. Yes, we need them, too, don't get me wrong—but they're jobs anybody can do. When it comes to big game, the Americans are winning. It's all about money. They have an endless supply of it."

"We've plucked some engineers, physicists, and chemists from the slush pile," I said defensively.

"Not enough," he said. "I rely on you clerks to find the good ones before they do."

You clerks. Yes, get used to it, Kira, I told myself. *That's all you are now. A clerk.* I swallowed hard, stemming the anger in my chest.

"We do our best, sir."

His expression darkened. "Imagine. My predecessor let Wernher von Braun and his team get away."

I nodded. Von Braun had invented the dreaded V-2 rocket for the Nazis—a deadly weapon to replace the V-1 'doodlebug' flying bomb that terrorized England during the Blitz. He was a coveted asset, now happily on the American Government's payroll living in the U.S.

"The Americans recruited von Braun and his people long before we Soviets got here. They didn't even wait till the war was over." I ventured.

His eyes flashed with anger. "Be sure and tell that to anyone who asks you."

"Of course."

He grew quiet, staring into space, brooding.

A chance to gather my own thoughts. I had grown

weary of war, intrigue, and the fear of purges I'd grown up with; the stress it wrought on ordinary citizens. I could feel beads of sweat gathering under my clothing despite the chill of the room. I eyed the door, longing to escape his scrutiny, waiting impatiently for words of dismissal.

My goals had changed so much. During the war, I was proactive, driven, ambitious, and hard-working. A leader. I derived satisfaction from a job well-done; from bombing the powerful German Wehrmacht and keeping their troops from getting any sleep. Now, it was I who was sleepless, visited by nightmares from things I'd seen and endured. Things I'd done.

I'd had to suppress my urge to lead. And beyond that, in Russian-occupied East Berlin I was making my way through a labyrinth designed by yet another forceful regime. New, but with all the trappings of the old. I had grown vulnerable and protective of myself; beginning to understand the reality of things with new clarity— like my place as a woman in the post war era. The enforced inferiority *vis à vis* men who served the USSR.

"Tell me, Comrade Voronova, what do you think of Americans?"

His question caught me off-guard. "I know little about Americans. I've only met a few."

He said nothing, so I added, "They were our allies, helped us win the war. "

"Allies. Yes. Yes, they were. Times change, though, Comrade. Wars create strange bedfellows, as the saying goes. Affiliations switch. Our enemies become our friends; and our friends? Wartime friendships are tenuous."

In no hurry, Petrov flicked a growing length of ash into an ashtray. His cigarettes were American—black market, like everything else in Berlin.

He continued to pontificate through a wreath of noxious grey smoke: "Throughout our lives, Comrade, circumstances bring us together with other people. Self-interest forges bonds with them. But when we no longer find their presence useful, it's time to cut ties. *To everything there is a season,*" as our God-fearing friends are fond of quoting."

A crass way of framing it, but I nodded. Everyone knew we were locked in a cold war. I just wanted this pompous, preachy tirade to be over.

"So it is with nations, Comrade," he droned on. "We accommodate ourselves to those we need while we need them."

Finally, he did get to the point: "It's my understanding, Comrade Voronova, that you spent time with an American officer in London last week."

So, I *had* been reported. The air in the room grew dense. I sensed a lack of oxygen, and my heart began to pound.

"At Drummond Hill Field? Yes, I did. I ran into the terminal to get out of the rain. I was observing the Allies' planes in their viewing gallery to note what they're flying now. Something to pass the time between meetings and the tour."

"Go on."

"An American officer showed me to a canteen where I could warm up and he offered me a cup of coffee. That's all."

"How well did you get to know this man?"

"Not well at all. We spoke in German. He'd learned it from a German grandmother in a place called Pennsylvania, but didn't speak it well. He did tell me his name..."

"Victor Moran," he said. "They don't use patronymics."

"Yes, that's it. Moran. A major in the U.S. Army Air Corps."

"Correct," he said.

"A fighter pilot during the war. He walked with a limp, using a cane; had a patch over one eye. I don't know what his injuries were."

Petrov donned his reading glasses and crushed out his cigarette in the ashtray as he removed another one from the pack.

"How old are you, Comrade Voronova?"

"Twenty-four, sir."

He opened a folder on his desk and consulted a sheet of paper. "Yes. Twenty-four. Engineering degree, Moscow State University; a trained night bomber pilot,deputy squadron commander in the 588th, later called the 45th Guards Bomber Regiment . . . you fought in combat for three years . . . trained pilots while finishing your degree . . ." He turned the page. "Recipient of the Gold Star, Hero of the Soviet Union, Order of the Red Star, Order of the Red Banner, Order of Lenin . . ." There was a pause. He glanced up with a trace of awe in his eyes. "Remarkable. And you made it to rank of Captain."

It *was* remarkable. More remarkable still was that I outranked him; yet he was my boss.

He read on: "You've had an interesting personal life, as

well. Marriage, motherhood . . . *some tragedy*—"

"Yes. Correct." I swallowed hard.

My pain of the past five or so years—wounds that re-fused to heal—all of it reduced to *some tragedy*. He put down my dossier. It was impossible to read his expression.

"With all you've experienced, surely you're not so je-june, so naïve as to accept people at face value?"

"Sir?" What the hell was he getting at? I braced myself.

He opened the top drawer of his desk and extracted another file folder. "Comrade Voronova, Major Moran is as able to walk as you or I. He sees perfectly. There's nothing in his file to indicate that he has ever been ser-iously wounded in action. It was an act to solicit your sympathy. Does that surprise you?"

It did, but I was too taken aback to answer.

"Yes. Moran attended a prestigious university called Massachusetts Institute of Technology and became an aeronautical engineer before he enlisted in the U.S. Army Air Corps. His wife was British."

Wife? I had to ask. "Was?"

"Yes. She and their twin daughters were killed in the London Blitz. Like you, Moran has good reason to hate Nazis, and his superiors make good use of that, along with his talents. He's one of the top operatives in Ameri-can Army Intelligence in West Berlin. A seasoned flyer. Code name, Osprey." He looked up and faced me, his ex-pression condescending. "I'm afraid you've been played, Comrade Voronova."

"I see," I said. A new flush of heat was spreading its way across my face.

"I'm not sure you do. This man deliberately sought you out. I'm curious about why he would do that."

I recalled the American's boyish, vulnerable demeanor; his limp, the cane—trappings that tugged at my war-weary reserves of sympathy. I relived our confrontation in the gallery and the smooth transition to an invitation for coffee, Major Moran's keen blue eye, the one not covered by the patch, perusing me.

"The bastard," I said under my breath.

"Did Major Moran want to see you again?"

"He didn't indicate that he did. He was interested in my combat medals and ribbons, knew I was a 'night witch.' I told him I worked in East Berlin when he said he was in the American Zone—"

"What else?"

"Nothing else. Our chat was short. Very general."

Petrov rose and began pacing. "Voronova, you can be of considerable use to the Party here. I know you're a pilot. But we have plenty of underemployed fliers these days. Men, with families to take care of. We've been waiting to find you something worthy of your talents. You're a smart, educated girl."

Girl? That's all I was to him. A smart girl, overly educated. Not a pilot, nor even an adult. *Yes,* I seethed, *I am smart.* Smart enough to recognize bullshit. They had no plans for me—nor for any of my flying sisterhood. The war was over, and we who had fought hard to defend Russia could be scrapped, like the Po-2s we'd flown.

"I want you to learn English, Comrade Voronova."

I was about to tell him that I had studied English in university. But something stopped me. Through some glitch, my language skills had apparently not made it into my file.

"We have a contact in the American Zone who'll teach you," he continued. "The sooner you're fluent, the more important you'll be to us. Your lessons are also your cover for going to the American Zone—and from there you can easily travel into the British Zone. And the French Zone when it opens up."

My mind was reeling.

"They say English is easy to learn. I want you to mingle over there. With your looks, that shouldn't be hard. Socialize. Get to know Americans and British. Go to parties. They have an active social life in the West. In particular, find Major Moran—run into him 'accidentally'—and use him to obtain information."

I caught my breath. "You're telling me to spy?"

"We call it engaging in 'Intelligence,' not spying. Your meeting was no accident. He chose you to fraternize with. He had a reason to do that, Comrade. Pretty girls in Berlin are hardly a novelty."

Petrov had a point. Why indeed had the American bothered wasting time with me?

Steepling his fingers, he was off on another tangent. "The occupied zones are full of opportunistic German women—sixteen females for every ten men. Some have children or ailing parents. They're starving—few can live on the paltry rations we allot them, and they'll do anything to survive."

He said this as if it were unseemly to persist in remaining alive.

"Americans! They've never known a hungry day," he

continued with disdain. "They've plenty of everything; enough for soldiers to eat and drink their fill, pay for sex, and sell their PX goods on the black market."

I'd heard that often enough about American servicemen. They were able to barter and sell anything, earning obscene profits to send home. A pack of Lucky Strikes costing just five American cents at the PX could be sold on the street in Potsdam, outside the Brandenburg Gate near the ruined Reichstag, or in front of Zoo Station, for close to a hundred dollars. Enough to bed a lot of pretty girls. The black market was as lucrative as prostitution, and the two went together.

"For a few cigarettes or chocolate candy bars—trifles —the Americans in this city have what they want whenever they want it," Petrov added. Was he envious? Despite his scorn, the fancy watch he wore and his American cigarettes marked him as a consumer who supported the system.

"For the American major to seek you out, he had something in mind; to get information about us, our plans here in Germany."

"But—that's ridiculous. I know nothing that could be of value to our enemies," I protested.

"He doesn't know that."

Petrov was right. I'd been played. I scolded myself for having been seduced so cheaply; with a cup of coffee. Foolishly, I'd assumed that the American found me interesting for my own sake.

"What do you want me to do?"

He referred back to the photo in Moran's folder. "A good-looking man. If I'm correct about his motives, he'll be in touch to win you over. Don't appear eager. Accept his little gifts. Have fun with your nylon stockings and your chocolate. You're an adult; I'll leave it to you how you choose to amuse yourself. Take it to the limit if that's your pleasure. Am I being clear?" His eyes narrowed balefully. "Just never lose sight of which side you're on."

CHAPTER 3

I knew perfectly well which side I was on, which side I had fought for. I was the daughter of Communists and had, throughout childhood, been a member of Komsomol—the Communist youth organization in Russia. I'd been fiercely loyal to Russia.

What Petrov suggested was a sharp departure from anything I'd been trained to do; well above my pay grade. I knew nothing about Intelligence work, how it was done. What if I failed? At the moment, I was treading water just to survive. What if I bungled something and caused an incident? I saw myself lined up against a wall before a firing squad. Or poisoned. A real fear. My friend Zinaida's father had been executed for writing a satirical poem. Petrov's proposal—no, Petrov's command, for that's what it was—filled me with malaise.

To refuse wasn't an option, but in a moment of clarity and courage, I was bright enough to recognize it as an opportunity. A chance to work out some kind of deal to my advantage.

Sitting straight in my chair, I said, "I'm hardly a good candidate for spy work, sir. The reason I chose to re-enlist was my interest in aviation. I miss taking to the air. I'd like to fly again."

He stared hard at me, cigarette smoke streaming through his nose. We were silent for a minute or so. Had I pushed too far?

"Well, there is something you might aspire to here, *if* you gather useful Intelligence."

I held my breath.

"General Belenko and I are receiving requests from younger troops in Berlin who want to fly. Most are men. But increasingly, enlisted women are also asking for basic flight training. It occurs to me that a female instructor might be ideal for these girls."

I brightened. Instructing women would be right up my alley. "When would this happen?"

"Well, of course, nothing is etched in stone as yet. It's still only an idea. But it's a good one. I'm sure I can convince General Belenko to promote you. It could happen as early as, say, six or so months, perhaps a year."

I could wait a year. "I serve the Soviet Union," I said. The standard reply. "I'll be ready if the American Major makes a move. And I look forward to hearing more about the instructing position."

A moment of silence passed between us. It was difficult to guess what he was thinking as he appraised me through the hazy swirl of his smoke, now being formed into rings as he shaped his mouth into an 'O' like a fish. Since he glossed over the list of medals I'd earned, it was a good time to remind him of my qualifications.

"I'm an excellent pilot, sir. And I've been an instructor. You saw the medals I earned. I would be able to contribute much to serving the Motherland in the position you describe."

"Of course. Yes. You served our country well. And it's good that you'll continue to do so. You could become useful to our Government here, depending how you do with this assignment."

Before I could comment, he added, "By the way, this directive—your involvement in Intelligence—didn't originate with me. It came down from General Belenko."

General Dmitri Petrovich Belenko was Petrov's boss. From his office in Karlshorst, he headed all our Intelligence in East Berlin. A dynamic and decisive man in his early forties, he had a reputation for being ruthless. He'd ordered the execution of several people involved in a child prostitution ring exploiting DP orphans, and the word was he came down hard on black marketers. What I questioned was how he treated spies who didn't deliver.

"Good." Petrov nodded. "Then it's settled. Expect to hear from our contact, a translator in the U.S. Zone with teaching experience. By the way, we'll be feeding you disinformation to offer Moran. To mislead him. He'll be doing the same with you. You'll have to learn the difference between truth and propaganda. Sometimes it will be obvious, but not always.

"One other thing, Voronova. This American major has many talents. It has occurred to me that he'd be a valuable asset to bring to our side."

Now we're getting somewhere, I thought. The reason for all this. I was to be used as a honey trap. His remark, delivered casually, was the true purpose of our meeting. Alarm bells went off in my head. Listening and squinting through peepholes was one thing; but turning someone's allegiance away from their country, especially an American military officer, was quite another. A gargantuan task, unless blackmail could be used.

"We're hoping that you can persuade him to consider what we could offer. If not...well, we won't discuss other means. Not right now."

Other means? Gathering *Kompromat*, details that could be used to embarrass, was certainly one. Moran no longer had a wife, but something treasonous on any senior officer could be trumped up to frame him in some way. Abduction, a snatch on the street was another possibility. And there were other, more nefarious ways of getting him to our side.

Did Petrov honestly believe I'd be able to charm him into working for us? It was ludicrous. It would take more than a pretty face to turn the man's head so radically.

"You'll check in with me every few weeks, Captain Voronova. More often if you have something important to report."

"Will I need to go to a school of some kind to be trained for all this?" I asked, still bewildered.

He laughed for the first time, exposing his large nicotine-stained teeth. "A school for spies? No, we have nothing so structured here in Germany. Not yet, anyway. We're not asking you to join the NKVD or the K-5. At least, not yet. We already have experienced spies in place in all the western sectors."

Spies in place? This produced a new fear. Did he mean that Erich Mielke's infamous K-5 secret police would be looking over my shoulder even as I was spying? What if I failed? I glanced up at a photo of Stalin on the wall. Our leader glowered back, his menacing eyes boring through me. *I'll be watching you*, he seemed to say.

"Our real spies—who work at it full time—have stringent training," said Petrov. "Your orders will be much more amusing. For now."

That assurance, at least, was a relief. I had little inkling of spycraft, but I knew it was detailed, tedious work; work that could involve getting one's hands dirty. Not anything I aspired to.

"Will I know who and where the real spies are?"

"No. Except on a need to know basis. And I don't have to tell you that we've never had this little talk." Petrov busied himself at his desk, a signal that the meeting was over.

I remained for a moment, dazed by what had just occurred. He glanced at me.

"That will be all for now, Voronova. Dismissed."

My interview with Petrov prompted a bout of soul-searching. As I navigated the maze of cubicles to my desk, I thought back to my mindset as the night-bombing warrior I'd been just a few years before.

In combat, I routinely killed the enemy, training myself not to view Nazis as real people. Their troops on the ground, running for cover or hurrying to antiaircraft guns, were like ants attacking a sugar bowl, and after a while I observed them with cold passivity. I never knew how many died at my hands; how many of our explosives raked their flesh, maimed their bodies, burned and killed them, creating widows and orphans. It was part of our training to be single-minded. We were there to do a job, and we did it. We took no joy in killing faceless Nazis.

This was different. What Petrov had hinted at was

the possible abduction—a kidnapping of someone I had met. Someone who had a face. A fellow pilot, someone I liked enough to share my phone number with.

Despite his ruse in London and my vexation over it, I had no reason to hate Americans in general. Yes, they were loud and brash and richer than everyone else. Their sense of entitlement was a source of envy and anger. But they were there when we needed their help against Hitler. It was too bad that they were now part of the Western Bloc, disagreeing with our ideology and vision for Europe. But that didn't mean we should turn against them as individuals.

My independent spirit rebelled at a man like Petrov dangling such a job offer as enticement. He'd guessed I was fixated on returning to the sky and was banking on my desperation.

Still, I was shrewd enough to see this assignment as a happy weekend escape. Quite apart from the promise of a possible promotion, I was excited to be going over to the American Zone. Taking more English lessons would be easy, not work. And there was the prospect of meeting Major Moran again. His sense of humor, charm, and his breezy American style had appealed to me. It could be fun.

Alone at my desk, I thought again about Petrov's dossier on me, the entry, *'some tragedy"*. In two words, he summed up the turbulent episodes of my life. Thoughts drifted again to my time in the Red Army. Could I ever be able to take my mind off it? Or get a good night's sleep without reliving fear?

CHAPTER 4

I 'd never been to Berlin before the war, but I had seen pictures of it on deckle-edged sepia postcards with other keepsakes in a dresser at my parents' apartment in Moscow. I was awed by the messages of enthusiasm scrawled in faded ink by peripatetic friends who'd moved there in the 1930s, deeming Germany safer than risking the purges of Stalin's Russia.

By all accounts, Berlin was once one of the most beautiful cities in Europe. During the heady days of Hindenburg's Weimar Republic, with the Great War over, a spirit of dynamism, gaiety, and naughtiness dominated the German capital, piercing through the hyper-inflation of post WWI economic problems. Though ideologically Communist, my parents' friends refused to delve into negative territory in their messages. Rather, they stressed Berlin's cultural soul and its lively pulse.

But the next war—a mere twenty-one years after the war to end all wars—changed everything. The bombed-out Berlin I entered with my Red Army regiment in early May of 1945 was a destroyed, defeated city still holding its breath for the next onslaught, unable to grasp that the cataclysm had finally been brought to an end. Unrecognizable from the postcards of memory, the cityscape had been rearranged into a gray and desolate apocalyptic hell on earth, devoid of any distinguishable shape or hope. After intense bombing by the RAF and the Americans, and especially the damage inflicted by the brutal arrival of 6,300 Russian tanks as we took the city, Berlin was finally in tatters.

In the aftermath of the conflagration, its structures lay crumpled and shredded. Despondent people scurried around like ants, carrying signs in search of relatives. Disoriented orphan children of all ages wandered the streets searching for someone, anyone, to care about them. Many of these lost children had been living in German pockets of Eastern Europe, like Danzieg and Sudetenland. With parents murdered by partisan nationals after the war for their support of Hitler, they were left on their own and turned feral and tough surviving their trek to Berlin. Innocence lost, they grew up overnight.

Despite the stream of refugees, the population of the city, nearly four and a half million before the war, was less than three million when our regiment flew in, most of the survivors women, old men, and Hitler youth too young to serve in the *Wehrmacht*. There was little food to be had, and the population was in misery.

When I felt too deeply about the suffering of surviving Germans, I'd recall what the Nazis did to my people, fertilizing our country with bones of slaughtered Russians. It quashed any feelings of pity. The war, our Great Patriotic War, had hardened me.

My regiment, the 588th, was disbanded shortly after the triumphal, brutal entrance of our tanks into Berlin. My tour of duty up, I welcomed the chance to return to Moscow after the Potsdam Conference a few months later, to pick up the thread of my disrupted engineering studies at Moscow State University.

"Why return to Moscow?" asked my commanding officer, Colonel Tamara Drobovitch. "With your talents, there are opportunities you could explore here in Berlin."

I scanned the pile of ash around me. "The war is over," I said. "We've liberated Russia, Belarus, Poland . . . we've conquered Berlin. I'll be staying until the Conference in August. But I think we're done here. There'll be changes in Russia now, too. And its infrastructure is largely intact compared to Germany's. It will be a better place to live."

"You think you will be happier there?" There was doubt in her voice. I'd known her for a few years, since my training days at Engels, and could read what she was really saying.

"Isn't that what we fought for?" I asked. "Peace. An easing of the way things were in our Motherland? Besides, I want to finish university."

She smiled but said nothing for a long moment.

"Good luck," she whispered finally.

She did not add, *"You'll need it."* But I heard her.

Moscow
Autumn, 1945 – Spring, 1947

And so, I joined the throng of veterans returning to Moscow in the autumn of 1945 to complete my engineering degree; but after graduation in the spring two years later, post-war life in the Soviet Union was not what I expected. To encourage repopulation, women were being discouraged from working outside the home. There was little or no thanks for the gelid winter sorties I'd gone through; the risks to my life; the enemy destruction I'd brought about. Medals I'd garnered in combat were rusting somewhere in a box. I was just another unemployed civilian. A female civilian.

Memories of things I wanted to forget persisted during the day, while ghosts from the past haunted my nights. Maxim was gone, and the pain of his loss was almost impossible to bear. Sleep did not come easily. There were nights when I woke up after an hour or two, trembling and sweating, screaming in terror. My heart beat so fast I thought it would explode into a bloodied crater, like chest wounds I'd seen in the war.

And always, there was Rufina. My memories of her continued to haunt me with pain, guilt, and affection.

To recapture the rhythm of my old life, I tried to work through the difficulties of resettling. I contacted surviving sisters from my regiment, but they had scattered, and those I did find—while friendly—were trying to forget the war, get married, and have babies. Things I was not ready to do again. Might never do again. The sisterhood had made a pact to meet again twice a year. That was all.

Zinaida had remained in Moscow. She'd been the closest person to a sister in my life, but the ties of our relationship, so close and nurturing in our childhood, had frayed. Too much had happened. We saw each other, but not often enough. Lunches in the beginning; then it became a hurried coffee. A note once in a while. And finally, just a signed card on my birthday.

My dreams of meaningful work were fading. After struggling to earn it, my degree, I discovered, was worthless. As I suspected, the good jobs were being given to approved men released from the army—most of them experienced engineers. I felt displaced, and I missed the buzz of taking to the skies. Missed being in charge of a plane and its ground crew; the challenge and the terror that life had been. I was even nostalgic about sporting the polished medals on my chest, once displayed with pride.

Underscoring all this was a gnawing suspicion that the peacetime Russia I'd hoped for wasn't going to materialize. People still disappeared with no explanation. Everyone still spoke in whispers. German troops had been stopped short of entering Moscow, and it wasn't bombed as badly as Berlin, but it hadn't escaped unscathed. Familiar buildings were gone; many of those remaining showed signs of damage. People were despondent. Overwhelmed with discouragement, I began to think Colonel Drobovitch was right. Perhaps I'd been precipitous in my decision to return to the Rodina of my youth. An idealized Russia which had never really existed. If it ever did, it wouldn't be in my lifetime.

In a rash moment, early in the spring of 1947, I decided to re-up, hoping the Red Army would put my skills and education to use in aviation design or test-flying new planes. Instead, they sent me to Berlin, where I was assigned work in the Intelligence Unit at the East Berlin Soviet Kommandatura.

"Berlin?" echoed my father when I told him. "How can you live among those people after what they did to us? And why go back to that terrible place? A destroyed city where nothing works—I've seen the newsreels. You think Moscow is bad? Berlin is a ruin. A disaster. You'll be miserable."

"I'm miserable here, Papa. I know what to expect of Berlin; I was there when we took the city. But being part of its restructuring may be the way to put the past behind me—"

"You can't escape the past," he scoffed. "Nor should you ever forget it."

I tried every day to forget it. True, I was struggling with what the Germans had inflicted on us. And I still grappled with the sadness the war had visited on me and my family. But deep down, there was more to it than that.

The truth was, as time went on, I was having more and more apprehensions about the way our Soviet government still treated our people. Nothing had changed since the purges began in the 1930s. I wanted to believe in the ideals of true Communism again, the way I had when I was younger, an enthusiastic zealot attending Komsomol meetings. I still loved my country, but having come of age in Stalin's Russia around adults who communicated through whispers, I was wary of those who now governed her. A stint in Berlin might be what I needed to reset my thinking. And perhaps it would lead to a good career. Women were being encouraged to work in East Germany. They needed us to help rebuild.

"I want to think of the future, Papa," I told my father. "We're going to reconstruct Berlin, make it ours. I'm an engineer now. I'll be doing something important."

My father, a survivor of Stalin's NKVD prisons, merely exclaimed, "What an idealist you are! Have you learned nothing?"

CHAPTER 5

It was my father's arrest and the ruin subsequently suffered by my family that crushed any shred of idealism I had nurtured growing up.

Papa was a cautious man, a brilliant lawyer forced by the Party into accepting a judgeship. As part of the *Intelligentsia*—Stalin's favorite scapegoat—he was particularly vulnerable. Mindful of political traps, especially after the fate of my friend Zinaida's father, Papa took on only easy cases dealing with domestic and family issues. By keeping them to a minimum, he could still teach law part-time at the Moscow State University. And the more time he spent there, the less time he needed to preside on the bench. It was a way to navigate a tangled system fraught with dangers, while enjoying the trappings of being a well-regarded jurist; a dance he carefully choreographed around the puddles of bureaucracy.

As clever as my father was, he was not above making a mistake. When a colleague asked him to take on a criminal case because his wife was dying, my father agreed to it as a favor. The case was the trial of one Ivan Rysakov, the People's Commissar of Petroleum. He had embezzled over forty million rubles and was caught red-handed. My father judged him guilty and sentenced him to the standard eight years of hard labor. What he didn't know was that Rysakov was married to the sister of a top Party leader who had Stalin's ear.

Retribution was swift. The day after sentencing, our household was awakened at two o'clock in the morning by a loud pounding on our door:

"Open up! Police. NKVD."

I'd been sound asleep, dreaming of Maxim. We had been secret lovers for several months and he was always on my mind. Terror gripped me as my brother Yuri and I peeked out from our rooms. What could the People's Commissariat for Internal Affairs want with us?

The pounding continued until my mother opened the door and three uniformed men barged in. The leader of the trio, a squat, fat man with missing front teeth, saw my grandfather, my Dedushka—who'd lived with us since the passing of my grandmother —bedded down on the living room couch.

Grabbing him by his night shirt, he shouted, "Sergei Dmitrievich Voronov, we have a warrant for your arrest. Get dressed. It is in your interest to come quietly."

Dedushka, half asleep and confused, thought he was back at the collective farm in Ukraine being arrested for aiding and abetting the Kulaks—once prosperous farmers who had resisted collectivization and continued to be troublesome. He began to cry.

"Please, I'm innocent. Have mercy, Excellency. I'm not a *podkulachnik*. I don't even know any Kulaks!"

My father, half dressed, opened my parents' bedroom door. "*I* am Sergei Dmitrievich Voronov."

"Please, spare me," Dedushka continued to beg, recalling arrests for unfulfilled quotas, thefts of a little corn or a handful of wheat; or for no reason at all.

"Not you, old man," the fat man said, realizing his mistake. Then he punched my grandfather in the face and shoved him back down on the couch.

My father struggled to control his anger. "I'm the one you want. Leave my father-in-law alone. What am I accused of? Read me the charges."

The leader read off a list of charges under the catchall, Section 58 1(b). If the government wanted you to be incarcerated, they would draw on this broad part of the legal code for a crime to apply to you.

Dedushka still cried as blood trickled down his cheek.

"It's all right, Dedushka," my father said kindly. "It's me they want."

"Come with us, Sergei Dmitrievich Voronov. Bring nothing with you. All you need will be provided."

My father, ever dignified, told them he would finish dressing. As they waited, their eyes swept the apartment with a practiced eye. Would they report on how well we lived? Give our apartment to one of Stalin's friends? I was no longer the naïve girl I had been before Zinaida's father was arrested. I now expected the worst.

My mother was sobbing and protesting, "It has to be a mistake!" she wailed. "My husband has done nothing. You have the wrong man."

"*Zatknis!* Shut up," said the man who hit Dedushka.

Yuri spoke then:

"Where are you taking my father?"

"To Butyrki."

It was the prison where *intelligentsia* were normally taken for questioning.

Finally, Papa put on his overcoat. He turned to us and said, "All of you, go back to sleep. It's some clerical error. Everything will be fine."

My mother persisted. "My husband is a respected judge, a long-standing member of the Communist Party; he's a professor at the university, a dedicated leader of—"

"Anna, please. Don't worry," my father reassured her. "It's a misunderstanding. They've taken me for someone else. Stay strong. I'll be home soon."

He gave me and Yuri a quick kiss on the cheeks. Then he kissed my mother, taking a minute to bury his face in her neck and hair as he murmured something to her. They hauled my father away in handcuffs like a common criminal and frog-marched him out the door, leaving us all in a state of shock.

"At least he isn't going to Lubyanka," said Yuri. It was where career criminals and *politicheskiy zaklyuchennyy*, political prisoners, were incarcerated.

"Maybe they're treated better at Butyrki, Mama?" I suggested.

"Zinaida's father was first taken there!" she said tearfully. "After booking him, they sent him to Lubyanka to be tortured. A quick show trial, and then a public execution."

"But Zinaida's father provoked Stalin by writing that inflammatory poem," I protested. "Papa has done nothing; just doing his job."

She lowered her voice. "And that matters? Stalin is paranoid; he can't believe anyone can be trusted. I'm lucky they haven't arrested me for some imaginary offense, like not reporting the egregious crimes of my husband."

At the mention of Stalin, Dedushka, who we thought suffered from mild dementia, glared at my mother.

"Enough, Anna! Be quiet." His voice was clear and low. "You'll get us all in trouble. Never, ever speak of our leader like that again!"

We all stared, shocked at his lucidity. Mama was startled at first, then leaned into him and moaned, "Oh, Papa, what are we going to do?"

He patted her and muttered, "It's happening all over

again. Like in Ukraine."

After that night I could never see our present government the same way.

So my father was wrong. I was not an idealist. Nor was I naïve. Still, because I was young, hope was what motivated me. With the move to Berlin looming, I forced myself to recapture those early postcards and their cheerful greetings from the beautiful, fun-filled German capital. I believed I'd help revive the city as part of the teams in charge of restoring its former elegance and grandeur—a fine city again.

I fully understood the peculiar complexity of the political situation there, that half the city was occupied by the United States, England, and France. This would slow our progress, but the situation wouldn't remain like that for long.

We Russians would soon rule all of Berlin. We'd rebirth it as a communist bastion of the new order under the Soviet Union, a crown jewel to be proud of.

CHAPTER 6

S uch was my conflicted but hopeful thinking when I arrived in Berlin that second time in the early spring of 1947. But my position had nothing to do with either engineering or flying. Instead, I was assigned a mind-numbing desk job—a position I despised from day one—sorting job applications for Comrade Vasily Ivanovich Petrov.

The job candidates, former Nazis all, had already been investigated and triaged by the time their documents hit my desk. I was to sort one pile with rejects and bounce a rubber stamp on others destined for departments requiring personnel. Because we needed to increase our workforce in a hurry, many a blind eye was turned as our stamps sanctified de-Nazification papers with a single imprimatur, sins washed away. Washing was a good analogy. The process was referred to as a *Persilschein*, named for a well-known detergent. It was beyond boring. Why had I bothered to attend university?

Immediately after this disappointment, I went through a succession of lodgings that were either filthy, charred from the bombs and fires, or freezing, with no promise of heat. Some were on streets still blocked by rubble, or too far to walk or cycle to my office in the Kommandatura. Others were located in dangerous areas where destitute displaced persons, referred to as DPs, would mug or kill for a crust of bread. In certain neighborhoods, the combined stench of burnt-out buildings, trash, human waste, and bodies sepulchered in basements lingered enough to make me retch.

I was about to despair when, at lunch in the Kommandatura's makeshift canteen one day, a familiar female voice rang out from the background hum of male brouhaha:

"Comrade Voronova? Kira! Over here!"

Standing by a table waving at me was Galina Budanova, the brilliant pilot who'd replaced Rufina as my navigator on the night she was killed. She hadn't changed much: still stick-thin, flat-chested, slightly coltish--more handsome than pretty, with straight soot-black hair and dark eyes that I recalled could smolder in righteous anger with little provocation. She had still not tamed her thick arched eyebrows that nearly met in a unibrow.

Galina was with two other girls I recognized from my old squadron. One was navigator Elena Kaloshina, whose blonde elegance and delicate prettiness still stood out, despite the ugly drabness of her uniform. With her straight white teeth, she continued to dazzle with the same ready smile, a smile I'd often seen turn flirtatious.

Contentedly zaftig Luba Golyakova rounded out the trio. My cheerful armaments mechanic, she'd occupied the same dorm as I did at Engels Aviation Institute near Saratov Oblast. If anything, Luba was rounder than before—an anomaly among our rationed Russian countrymen.

Three friendly faces. Living reminders of our training camp on the Volga River. Delighted, I veered toward them and plunked my tray on the table. Hugs and feminine shrieks of friendly greetings over, I sat down and basked in the joy of renewing old friendships.

"I am so happy to see you! I'd no idea any of you were in Berlin. You're all working here at the Kommandatura?"

"I've been here about six months," said Galina. I caught a whiff of nicotine off her clothing. Her fingers were still yellowed by her nervous fondness for cigarettes. "I'm a driver for one of our big shots, General Ilyich Vorobyev. At his beck and call most of the time. But he's decent enough. Gives me time off for lunch."

The other two had stayed on since the conquest in April of 1945.

"They have me doing translation and general office work," Elena volunteered. She lowered her voice: "I'm bored to death."

I was relieved to see Elena in Berlin. When I last saw her, she was being housed in our brig at Engels, preparing to go before a military tribunal with a gulag or prison sentence hanging over her head.

I glanced at Luba. Her fingernails were as broken and grubby as I remembered. Poor Luba. She'd been a medical student at Moscow State University until her mother, a war widow who took in washing, was arrested for repeating political gossip about a customer with contacts in the Party. A harmless enough crime; but she served a prison sentence, and it stamped her as an enemy of the people, changing the lives of her family. Luba had been forced to quit university and work to help her parents and siblings. I was happy she'd landed in Berlin. She'd seen me through a bad chapter of my life at Engels, and I remained grateful to her.

"What are you up to, Luba?"

"What else?" She flashed her coarse, roughened hands. "I'm still a mechanic. At one of our military airports.

Right now I'm on continuation training."

"You were on the same maintenance team as Zinaida. Do you keep in touch?"

"Zinaida Sebrova? We did for a while. But last year she stopped writing. I think she's living with a man."

Given that my contact with Zinaida had also become sporadic, this didn't surprise me. But it bothered me that she hadn't shared her new situation.

"I haven't heard either. We've been friends since we were small children. Our parents were friends, and we lived in the same complex." I stopped short of saying it was Patriarshy Ponds, a prime residential area, afraid it would mark me as an elite—*Intelligensia* in Stalinese. "We've grown apart, I guess. For a while, we used to get together in Moscow. But then less and less."

"A shame when that happens." Galina interjected. "I've tried to stay in touch with our sisterhood from Engels. But people tend to move around, or they're busy working just to get by."

"Do you have a good place to live?" Elena asked.

"No," I admitted.

"Hey, you're in luck!"

The girls lived in a boarding house with an opening for another roommate.

"It's a terrific flat on Französische Straße," said Galina. "We walk to work in about twenty minutes. The meals are sparse, but edible. Most of the time."

"The street is cleared, not much rubble left," added Luba. "And there's a telephone we can use for a couple of marks a month. Our landlady finally got it to work."

"A telephone?" A working phone in a private apartment in ruined Berlin was nothing short of miraculous.

"Yes. The place is run by a German war widow, Frau Hilde Schuman. A Russian officer she lived with after the conquest had it installed. He left it for her when he returned to Russia. Anyway, a room has just become available, if you're interested."

Interested? I was over the moon. "Does she have heat?" I asked hopefully.

Lack of fuel was a huge problem. Even with people willing to work the mines and coal fields in the north, there were no means of getting it to the cities.

"We have to use coal when we boil our drinking water," said Elena. "But Frau Schuman pleads with us to go easy on heating it for bathing. She says cold water baths are healthier."

" '*Baden mit kühl Wasser sind mehr gesund*'," added Galina, nose slightly in the air, mimicking their landlady's German, and her toplofty attitude.

"The flat is usually—well, not warm—but not freezing," said Luba, always conciliatory. "It's been a cold winter. But by June, it should warm up, and that won't be an issue."

"It's on the cool side," Elena agreed. "You'll want to keep your cardigan handy."

"But," added Galina. "It's nothing compared to the open cockpit of a Po-2 on a winter night in the Crimea!" A hoot of guffaws all around. Everything was relative.

Elena said, "Here in the center of Berlin, utilities like the electricity and water supply work most of the time now. Our flat is huge, part of what was once a mansion. You'll have your own room, and she has a real kitchen with an ice box. And a gas stove for cooking. Before the war, it must have been a pretty nice place."

"Yes," said Luba. "Very bourgeois. High ceilings, wood paneling. She even has a toilet and a bathing room right in the flat—not across the hall. We don't share it with anybody."

Only a Russian forced to live with a dozen or so complete strangers in the crowded apartments of Moscow could appreciate such luxury.

"The place is immaculate," Galina said. "Frau Schuman is an obsessive German Hausfrau. All spit and polish. She should have been in the army."

"Perhaps she was," I said wryly.

Clearly, I'd seen too many news photos of camp liberations. I conjured up the vision of a hefty Aryan blonde woman in a prison guard's uniform, armed with a whip and a pistol, leading a fierce drooling dog through a concentration camp. The Ilsa Koch cliché. Then I chided myself for accepting such a banal stereotype. Time to accept people as individuals. Even Germans.

"She's tolerable," laughed Luba. "She was pressured by the Soviet military housing authority to take us in. We buy food so she can prepare it for us. She serves us a pretty scant breakfast, and the evening meal is a simple supper. She calls it *abend essen*. It's never enough."

"Yes," interjected Galina. "What we'd call *zakuski*. Light food. Small portions. She's not much of a cook. Her own rations provide her with only about 1,500 calories a day, sometimes less, so she welcomes our contributions—depends on them, in fact."

"She has a huge chip on her shoulder," offered Elena. "Deferential enough, but don't trust her. She despises us

Russians. Complains sometimes that when they divided the city, her building landed on the wrong side of the demarcation line. She thinks she should be in the British sector."

I nodded. Although it was the British and American Allies who'd bombed Berlin, most of its citizens still preferred the West. They hated us Russians; hardly surprising, after our fierce arrival and occupation. Many of our soldiers arrived immediately after liberating concentration camps, which had only deepened their ferocity. When the tank assault began, the Red Army shelled everything and everyone in their path, destroying whatever the bombers had not, as though by flattening Berlin they could vaporize the memory of Hitler forever. They saw Berlin as a symbol, the epicenter of Nazism, blaming it for everything. For Berliners, the sight of our troops entering the city in April, 1945 was their worst nightmare come true.

Personally, even two years later I didn't relish the thought of living with a German, but I was ready to put past hostilities out of my mind for practical reasons. I needed a place to live, and was happy to find a clean Berlin apartment.

"Can I visit the flat today?"

Galina hastily scribbled a map on a scrap of paper. "Follow these directions and you'll find it. There's no longer a number in the address. Look for a pair of baroque cherubs on the frieze over a deep blue door. Forget maps from before the war. They're useless."

She was right about that. The signs identifying streets were either destroyed or still buried in the mess. Few landmarks had survived. It was disorienting for Berliners; for foreigners, it was far worse. Many—even those who, like ourselves, were once pilots and navigators—had to carry compasses to orient ourselves. We were often forced to ask directions from gangs of *Trümmerfrauen*, the rubble women passing bricks from destroyed structures to each other as part of clean-up chains. They hated us so much they sometimes gave us wrong directions to send us off on a wild goose chase.

"Is the area safe?" I asked. Crime was rampant. "I've heard women are still being assaulted. And there are articles about attacks by hungry people begging. Packs of young boys flash-grabbing purses. Even cannibalism. Bodies have been found on the street with parts carved away."

Galina made light of my fears. "I've heard those stories. But I've never seen any carved-up people." She grinned. "If you do stumble over someone like that, be sure to take his watch!"

"And his wallet," chimed in Luba as she dissolved with laughter.

Then, serious again, "No place in the world is completely safe, Kira," continued Galina. "Stay in uniform as much as possible; don't go out at night, and you'll be fine. A lot safer than flying sorties over German-occupied Russia in a rickety Po-2! Just use common sense. She yawned and dismissed the subject with, "Anyway, Kira, those carved bodies—if they do exist— are Germans. Don't waste your sympathy. They didn't waste theirs on anyone else."

Such was our state of mind.

CHAPTER 7

As I walked through Frau Schuman's neighborhood I could tell it had once been grand. One of the sculptured stone cherubs over the front door of her Gründerzeit building had lost its nose; the other had a missing wing. Yet, the neo-baroque façade still managed to retain a genteel shabbiness, recalling the opulent lifestyle of turn-of-the-century upper class Berliners, wealthy Junkers, fallen on hard times.

In the faded "Belle Epoque" entryway, the least slam of a door sent nuggets of plaster, marble, and torn bits of flocked wallpaper tumbling from walls and moldings. A welter of gritty particles littered the foyer.

The once graceful mansion had been divided into eight apartments, probably in the 1920s. There were empty slanted spaces next to doors in the dilapidated marble hallways where mezuzahs had been attached. Testaments to "Final Solution" horror stories now surfacing on a daily basis.

As my eyes swept over the seediness of the staircase with its missing and broken balusters—the war-scarred decay of it—I mused how our two countries had shared much over the centuries. Yes, the average German regarded us ordinary Russians as a backward, ignorant people, *Untermenschen,* intellectually inferior Slavs. But at a more rarefied level, our histories were somewhat commingled, influenced by royal intermarriage and mutual appreciation of each other's arts, culture, political writings, and music. Unfortunately, all it took were a few brutal dictators, deluded royals, and a popular desire for sweeping changes to alter the playing field in the early to mid twentieth century to cover over any mutual ground we enjoyed. Bitter memories of World War I and the more recent Great Patriotic War would scar our generation and those to come indelibly, like a tattoo on baby tender skin.

Frau Schuman's apartment was located on the third floor. The elevator, I'd been warned, did not work. Breathless from the walk up, I arrived right on time and she opened the door promptly after one knock.

I had only a vague idea what to expect meeting Frau Schuman. Clichéd Ilsa Koch image aside, I'd imagined an elderly *Hausfrau*—perhaps a dumpy, white-haired granny. I was admitted instead by a slim, still pretty woman in her early forties, with ramrod-straight posture and a deft sense of style. Curly blonde hair beginning to thread with gray complimented the icy blue of her penetrating eyes, which were elaborately made up. She had delicate features, and her pale, flawless skin stretched tautly over her high cheek bones. She wore a simple black day dress set off by a colorful scarf. Extending her hand, she offered me a brittle smile.

"*Wilkommen*," she said in a cool voice. "The others assure me you will be a good tenant." More of a warning than a compliment.

Inside the apartment, the wood floors varied in color, and I inferred she'd once had loose rugs, probably oriental. Bare light bulbs dangled forlornly in place of elaborate chandeliers and crystal wall sconces; phantom outlines from missing artwork marked the walls, reminding me of the absent mezuzahs; and there was scarcely any furniture. The apartment lacked warmth and cheer, but as the girls promised, it was spotless, and

—unlike many places—had the fresh pine smell of being well-scrubbed and sanitized.

"I wasn't always poor," she told me in her lofty *Hochdeutsch* as she took me through. "My maiden name was Von Hayek. The Von indicates noble lineage. An old family."

I was tempted to point out that in Russia her aristocratic background would impress no one; could, in fact, put her on Stalin's hit list. But it appeared more important to Frau Schuman to be judged by past affluence than by her reduced circumstances. To that end, she played her role of chatelaine with the sassy hauteur jocularly referred to as Berlin *schnauze*; an attitude peculiar to that city. So I let it pass.

Pointing to her diploma from Freie Universität on a wall, she informed me that she had three degrees in Egyptology and had worked as an archaeologist in Egypt prior to her marriage.

"Everything changed with the war," she continued. "My husband was a doctor, sent to the Russian front in '43. He was killed in a night bombing in the Crimea."

This brought me up short. The bomb that plunged her into widowhood could well have been dropped by any one of us in the 588th. I made a mental note to avoid references to where and when I'd served. Living with her would require putting past hostilities aside. A mutual tolerance. As tempted as I was to point out that her husband's troops were the invaders who deserved what they got, I focused on the here and now: The flat, and the room.

"After he was reported dead, I trained myself to be a seamstress." Frau Schuman sighed. "Better to be a well-fed seamstress renting rooms to Russians than a starving archaeologist, *nicht wahr*?"

I nodded. While she loathed us, she knew she could suffer worse fate than hosting a few Russian women. As Red Army officers, we could easily make her life miserable if we had a mind to. A stay in jail could be a complaint away, and would certainly take her down a peg. But there was no point. We needed to get along.

"With this new communist government, I don't have any say when it comes to my *own* home," she couldn't resist lamenting as she led me to the room I would occupy. "I'm merely a steward, a custodian now."

Even two years after the conquest, she was having trouble accepting the concept that there was no such thing as one's *own* home. At least, not on this side of the demarcation line. I avoided mentioning to her that once we Russians took over the Allied-occupied zones, it would no longer matter which side of the line she lived on.

"A custodian! That's all I am," she repeated. "Ach. Had it not been for that fool Hitler. Always with him it was the Jews; the Jews, the Jews, the Jews! I had nothing against Jews myself. My husband and I bought this building from a Jew. We got it cheap because he was no longer allowed to own property. A terrific deal, we got. Afterward, we rented an apartment to him. And he was a good tenant; always paid the rent on time. No, I had no problem with Jews."

I stared at her, glad that Galina was not within earshot. Clearly, Frau Schuman saw no irony in such an inequitable situation. I opened my mouth to tell her what I thought of her 'business deal,' but then recognized the wisdom of shutting up until I saw the accommodation.

Her reference to Hitler being a fool was doubtless to impress me. Nobody admitted to having supported the Führer now. Even as she'd said it, I could visualize her shouting "*Sieg Heil*" at rallies in the Sportspalast; waving a swastika from her balcony as the Nazi troops paraded by. When it came to Frau Schuman, my imagination ran wild. I had to stop placing her in cliché wartime scenarios.

With its distinctly masculine feel and musky scent, the virtually bare "furnished" bedroom she showed me was even more cheerless than the other rooms. It had once been wallpapered and partly paneled with fine cabinet-quality wood, but the wallpaper was water-stained and peeling, and sections of the wood panels had been removed, probably to fuel the porcelain fireplace in her living room. There was a cot, a floor lamp with a faded fringed shade, a cheaply made dresser, and a small desk. My guess was that it had once been her husband's study, but a pile of books on the floor— mostly Russian classics—indicated that someone Russian might have recently used it. This was confirmed when I saw a photo on the desk: the "*gnädige Frau*" posing on the arm of one of our generals, all smiles and coy looks of affection.

Still, after the nasty places I'd been to in awful locations, the room was palatial. "This is perfect," I announced, noting the decorative touches it needed. "I'll take it."

Back in the kitchen, she took a set of keys from a drawer. "The apartment has fallen on hard times," she complained. "This war changed my life completely. I suppose you'll say—like your Russian girlfriends—that my home could have had a direct hit, with me in it. True, but why did any of it happen?"

She searched my face for the answer, or at least some spark of sympathy. When none was forthcoming she continued: "Everyone says I'm lucky. Some of my friends have had to make a living picking up cigarette butts and re-rolling the tobacco in papers to sell on the black market." She shook her head. "Imagine. Smart women with respectable professions. Lawyers, accountants, business owners. Reduced to that, just to eat and pay for a place to live! I know of one woman who eats mushrooms she scrapes off filthy walls in damp basements."

A frown of disgust tugged at my mouth.

"Yes," she agreed. "Awful."

As she led me through the rest of the apartment, I learned that the burning of her grandmother's fine antiques for firewood was another bitter pill she ruminated on:

"I tried to sell them on the black market, but no buyers. Biedermeier pieces, in the family for generations. Biedermeier! Can you imagine? Worth a fortune. And the French furniture from my husband's family—some were 16th century pieces—museum quality. All up in flames, just to keep from freezing."

"At least you're alive," I murmured.

"Alive, yes. That's all. Alive, but without my things. Our things are what define us."

There was nothing to be gained by antagonizing the embittered Frau Schuman. I gave her my first month's rent, and she handed me the keys.

"I'll let myself out," I said, preparing to leave. "I'll move in tomorrow, if that's acceptable."

"Fine," she said with a curt nod as she emptied the contents of a laundry basket into the kitchen sink for washing. "Tomorrow, then. I may be out, but you have your keys. We eat dinner at eighteen hours sharp. I'll expect your food contributions every Friday. Rent on the first of every month, in advance. *Auf Wiedersehen.*"

At that moment, I heard Galina and Elena at the door, the sounds of my native language a welcome diversion. Luba was a few minutes behind them.

"Kira! Have you seen the room?" Galina called out when she saw me.

I dangled my keys. "Yes. I'm in!" I murmured with a grin. "I was about to leave. You can help me move in tomorrow."

"Don't go yet. This calls for a drink," said Galina, producing a bottle of wine given her by her boss, General Vorobyev, for overtime work.

"*Vashe zrodovye!* Welcome home!" said Luba as they hugged me. "It will be like being back at our dorm in Engels."

At that moment, it did feel like home. My Red Army Air Corps friends were now my tribe, my new family. I didn't know what lay ahead, but I was young and optimistic, and for the moment, determined to seize the day.

As we clinked glasses, Elena held her finger to her mouth to caution me. "A word to the wise," she confided in a low voice. "Be careful. Her spoken Russian isn't good, but she can understand it. And she hates us enough as it is."

"I don't know what *her* problem is," whispered Galina, with undisguised bitterness. "I lost fifteen members of my family, shot in ravines or starved in camps. All she lost was a husband."

"And her city," I said. Half her country, I could have added.

"And her precious antiques," added Elena wickedly.

The girls invited me to their rooms, to catch up and show me around. They removed their uniforms and changed into warmer clothing. As they'd predicted, the flat was chilly. Each of their rooms was the diminutive size of the one I was assigned. It seems we were living in the former servants' wing of the building. Frau Schuman had closed off larger rooms, including a seedy white and gold paneled ballroom, to retain heat in our living/sleeping areas.

Family photos, colorful posters, mementos reminding the girls of happier times, brightened their walls. It cheered me how they'd managed to create coziness in the snug privacy of their cocoons.

Elena had hung a framed newspaper clipping that described an ice skating championship she'd won in Moscow. Attired as a graceful swan skimming across an ice rink with a handsome partner, she was an ethereal vision.

"My fiancé," she explained wistfully. "Killed at the front. We had hoped to skate professionally after the war."

Luba's walls were covered with baby pictures of her nieces and nephews. There was a photo of a family reunion featuring men in uniform, and other family images that reminded her of happier times. She was not sure if any of her brothers had survived the war. So often our men went off to the front and were never heard from again.

Entering Galina's room, I felt an immediate chill unrelated to room temperature. Her sorrow and anger flooded the space, where she had tacked up photos of her deceased parents and relatives, the many dead marked with an X. She had also included a feature article from *Pravda* showing her village in ruins, and one featuring a mass grave where some of her own family were tossed—a noir mnemonic to keep her raging anger alive. Prominently displayed was the photo of a man in uniform, her fiancé—his whereabouts unknown. I remembered her telling me that he was a prisoner of war, but being Jewish, the Nazis probably had special plans for him.

"So, Kira," said Elena as we settled down with our wine in her room. "I'll bet you were surprised to see me in Berlin?"

"The last time I saw you, you were headed for a work camp in Siberia," I admitted.

"Yes. I was convicted. They sentenced me to ten years."

"What? I didn't know that," Luba said; she had just entered Elena's room.

Elena handed her a glass of wine. "You didn't know you were sharing quarters with a convicted felon, Luba? I'm an underwear criminal."

"What actually happened?" asked Luba. "The details were kept under wraps. Your trial was secret."

Elena sighed. "It was a stupid thing to do. I was cleaning out a cupboard and found a parachute left by male pilots before we arrived in Engels. I opened it up and ran the silk through my hands. Real, soft silk. On my day off I made several pair of the loveliest, silky panties."

"Good for you," Luba said. "That droopy men's underwear they issued us was terrible."

"Yes," agreed Galina, her nose crinkling with disgust. "Here, we volunteered to fight and they prepared nothing for us—men's boots, men's uniforms. All too big. Nothing fit. That was bad enough. But the underwear!" She rolled her eyes.

I had to agree. That was the worst. The very act of donning men's underwear was enough to feel our femininity slip into neutral.

"Those panties felt so nice next to my skin!" said Elena. "When I got caught, they took them all away. Put me in the Guard House for three days."

Some of us visited her there. Little bigger than a telephone booth, it was designed so prisoners could only stand still, a cabin so small she had little room to bend or lie down. To use the commode, a male guard would follow her out and watch her closely. A further humiliation.

"Ten years was the sentence they handed down—the maximum penalty for stealing and destroying government property—to be served after my deployment."

"But you're here now," I said. "How did you manage that?"

"Yes, I'm here. I speak perfect German—my mother was a German professor—so they offered me a job at the Kommandatura. They were short of translators, so they were happy to use me."

"So, you had a choice?" I clarified. "Berlin, or prison for ten years?"

"You call that a choice? I'm in exile. I'll spend the rest of my life here."

CHAPTER 8

Moscow, 1941

While I had little or no sympathy for Frau Schuman when she recounted how she lost control of her building under the new Communist regime, I understood how she felt. I empathized with her loss of home ownership, intuiting her loss of one of our most basic needs: Our privacy.

There was no such thing as privacy in the Soviet Union, though it was a long time before I was aware that lack of it was the norm for most Russians. It took my father's arrest to drive that message home.

As we feared, the elegance and quietude of our living conditions in Patriarshy Ponds was not lost on the scruffy NKVD officers who arrested my father. We were notified soon afterward of a decision by our local Housing Authority: With the head of our family gone, our apartment had a surplus of square footage for the number of persons living there—we were allowed nine square meters each—and additional tenants would be assigned to our home. We were to expect a family of four to move in shortly.

"This must mean Papa's not coming back," I wailed miserably to my mother, who was biting her lip hard enough to draw blood.

"Strangers in our home! He'll be furious," she murmured, rejecting my interpretation.

"We should complain to the Authority."

"Don't be foolish. If we draw attention to how big our apartment is, they'll send us even more."

Neither of us was prepared for Nadia Harlamova. A few days after they'd dragged my father away, I came home from school and there she was, making herself at home in our apartment. She had let herself in with a key given her by the Authority and had brewed herself some tea. An empty glass next to Dedushka's favorite chair indicated she'd already introduced herself to my grandfather and shared her tea with him.

"Could you and your mother move your stuff out of my bedroom when she gets home? I'd like to finish moving in." It was said pleasantly, but her eyes challenged me.

She was a flamboyant kind of woman, with long dyed black hair teased into curls. Her brightly-colored print dress clung to her body like a sports car on a hairpin curve, hugging her in all the right places. Nadia's best feature was her flirtatious dark eyes veiled by long, fringe-like eyelashes.

She had two teen-aged boys in tow. Boris, about my age, worked in an armaments factory. A sullen, dark-eyed boy with acne and slicked black hair, he had a sensual way of appraising me that aroused my anger and indignation. I disliked him on sight. A slightly younger boy, Anton, was still a student, pale and blue-eyed; younger, but taller. Pleasant enough. My guess was they had different fathers.

Her request stoked an ember of resentment into fury. "*Your* bedroom?" I shouted. "How dare you barge in here? This isn't a hotel. It's a private home. Please leave at once."

"Leave? Dearie, if you don't like it, *you* can leave. This is my home now."

Nadia held up her door key and gave me a haughty look as her voice became menacing. "You people! *Intel-*

ligensia. Bah. You're so spoilt. There are people in this city living ten or twelve strangers to an apartment not nearly this size. Your own kitchen and bathroom? Unbelievable. And you've had it to yourselves for all these years. It's a scandal."

She was right about that. After I was born, my father, then a young lawyer, had taken on the case of a man employed by the Housing Authority whose wife had been arrested for shoplifting at GUM, the Government-owned department store on Red Square. By some miracle he had gotten her off with a light sentence, and in lieu of a fee, was given the privilege of jumping the queue to move into the exclusive Patriarshy Ponds. The man had since died, but through a mysterious boondoggle, we'd never had to give up exclusive occupation of our apartment. Until now.

Our domestic peace and privacy was all about to unravel with the Harlamovas' arrival. We eventually accommodated ourselves to living with the family, but things were never quite the same for us afterward.

Before we knew it, Nadia had taken charge of the kitchen like an extended family member, insisting on cooking for us all. My mother, who'd always said she could not share a kitchen with anyone, would arrive home, limp after a fifteen-hour shift at the hospital, and put up no resistance to the delicious meals Nadia would lay out on the table. Mama contributed our rations, but mostly Nadia declined them. She always had plenty of food. Good food, even luxury items. It was like eating at a restaurant every night.

Without shame we let Nadia insinuate her way into our family. Our initial confrontation was forgotten when she began to feed us, offered to do our hair—she worked as a hairdresser at a nearby salon—and pitched in to help us with chores like laundry and mending. Nadia could be entertaining; she claimed to have psychic powers and was a wiz with tarot cards. Often she'd inquire about my father, and was always ready with a sympathetic ear to our problems.

Dedushka, who I thought was suffering from dementia, appeared bewitched by her. He'd never set foot in my babushka's kitchen in Ukraine, but he was soon working alongside Nadia. Our kitchen had come alive. She put him to work peeling vegetables while she orchestrated dinner. He taught her to dance Ukrainian folk dances; she taught him a dance called a Czardas she learned from her Hungarian mother, and they would sing folk songs off key together. At sixty-eight, Dedushka was full of energy and enjoying life again.

Life is full of trade-offs. We'd evolved into a strange ménage.

CHAPTER 9

Berlin, 1947

Our Berlin ménage was equally odd. Most of the time, Frau Schuman assumed an air of tolerance toward us. We knew she hated us. Yet, I guessed that sometimes she felt a conflicted kind of neediness to connect. Having us around kept loneliness at bay.

A few days passed after my interview with Petrov. Rubber stamping applications at my desk, I awaited word—with some angst—from the mysterious English teacher in the West. I needed to pretend that I'd never studied English; that I was learning it for the first time. My contact—would he or she be one of the spies Petrov referred to, reporting all my movements to him? If so, perhaps my forays into the West would not be as amusing as I hoped.

At quitting time one day, I headed for the small grocery store near Frau Schuman's where I was registered. I put the collar of my coat up and, face buried down into the scratchy wool of my army overcoat against a strong early March wind, I stepped with the usual caution over the clutter of detritus on sidewalks. A long queue of shivering Berliners clutching ration books in frostbitten hands was ahead of me. They stomped, feet in place, to keep warm in the clutch of bitter cold.

As a Russian officer, I didn't need to join the queue; I was off rations. I elbowed my way to the head of the line and showed my credentials with a list of food items I wanted, ahead of a young German woman with a baby, next in line. She said nothing, but eyeing the red star on my fur hat, she glared at me through large hostile eyes, her skin waxen and taut over hollow cheeks. A common feature among the hungry.

I generally avoided eye contact with German people, but as the store clerk collected my provisions from the sparsely stocked shelves, I glanced at the young mother, and for the first time since my arrival I felt a stir of genuine pity. Rosy from either cold or fever, her infant in arms was whimpering, too apathetic to summon a healthy, demanding howl. A sharp ache in my heart turned my thoughts to my own son, Pavel.

"How old is he—or is it a she?" I asked in German.

"A girl," she replied, appraising me. "She's ten months old. Russian father."

I knew the answer, but asked anyway. "One of our soldiers?"

"One? There were seven that time." Then, she tapped her swollen belly. "This one—another Russian. And yes, it's still happening."

I peered more closely at her babe in arms. The poor child looked only six or seven months.

"How old are you?" I asked her.

"Seventeen."

I lowered my eyes and silently replayed the mantra drilled into us post war: *Don't waste your sympathy on the Germans. Don't befriend them and don't fraternize. They deserve what they got. They asked for it. Don't forget, they supported Hitler.*

But, I reflected, it wasn't young girls who had chosen to break treaties or invade us. They didn't bomb us, occupy us, imprison us, decimate our population or throw the world into chaos. They were but the ones left to pay the price.

I took my two bags of groceries from the clerk and paid her in occupation marks.

"What's your name?" I asked the young mother.

She hesitated. "Steffi. Steffi Bauman."

"Do you have a husband?"

She stared at me, incredulous. "How would I have a husband? The Führer sent all our boys to the front. Now they're still POWs in the East. Look around you!" Her voice was rising. "All we have here are old men and Hitler youth. And your Ivans, those assholes who rape us and leave us with the clap and babies we can't raise. With all the Jews gone, there are hardly any German clinics left, and now we're being butchered by your Russian quacks."

People around us were staring. Out of the corner of my eye, I saw an old woman behind the girl tug at her sleeve to keep her quiet.

I bristled with indignation. "We have many good doctors," I said, thinking of my mother, an overworked pediatrician. "Most of our physicians here are caring people. And well-qualified."

She lowered her voice and indicated her pregnant belly. "I hate this baby. I don't want it. But I'll never go to one of your doctors to get rid of it. I know girls who've died at Russian clinics."

It was entirely possible. The lack of medications and antibiotics would most certainly reflect in both maternal and infant mortality rates. And our doctors were overwhelmed with the lingering work load they faced with our troops.

She wasn't done.

"Your soldiers!" she huffed. "They're savages. Age meant nothing. My eleven-year-old sister, my mother, and my grandmother? She tried to fight them off and they shot her. Sixty-three years old." She turned away, tears gathering in her eyes.

Picking up my groceries, I swept past her without another word and she took my place in line. It would be useless to explain how Hitler's troops had done the same to our women.

Once outside, I walked only about thirty feet when an inner voice nagged at me, propelling me back in the direction of the store. I stood out front and waited until Steffi Bauman came out with a weightless little cloth bag hanging from her free arm.

"Fraülein Bauman," I called out.

She examined me with apprehension. Would there be repercussions for what she'd shouted in the store? I approached her and set my bags down on a bench out front.

"Here," I said, reaching into one. I took out my cloth-wrapped butter and three small tins of meat, slipping them into her half empty bag. Then I reached into the other and withdrew an onion, a turnip, and a small packet of flour, three potatoes, and a can of milk.

"Take these." I said. "Can you manage? Will your bag be too heavy?"

"Nein, nein!" Her face was glowing like a child on Christmas morning.

"Would you like me to walk you home?" I asked. "I could carry the baby."

The truth was that my arms ached to cuddle her little one and rock her in my arms. I was even willing to give up some of my provisions for the privilege.

"Nein, danke. I live not far from here."

"I shop here after work a few days a week," I said. "If you come around at this hour, maybe I can help you sometimes. I'm not on rations."

Her eyes challenged me suspiciously, "Are you a lesbian?"

"No. Why? Do you think Russians only give food for special favors?"

"I'm sorry. It's just that I have had attention from women like that."

"Perhaps they too only wanted to help. Anyway, I assure you I have no ulterior motives." Noting her roughened red hands, I removed a pair of my gloves. "Here. Put these on."

Her eyes lit up and she smiled. "Danke! Thank you so much. You're a kind person—for a Russian."

"You're welcome." I returned her back-handed compliment in kind: "You may be German, but you're still a human being."

CHAPTER 10

Like my comrades, I harbored profound hatred against the Germans, whom I blamed for the deaths of roughly twenty million of our people, but I tried to direct my animosity at those responsible for the war: those inhuman Nazi leaders who were dead, in custody, or in hiding.

My meeting with the young girl, Steffi Bauman, burdened with precipitous unwanted motherhood, affected me, awakening my maternal feelings. I knew she had to have conflicted feelings about her children, despite how they were conceived. I'd wanted nothing more than to take the infant from her, to hold her baby close and keep her safe. Despite her insolence, I even felt maternal about Steffi, who was only seven years younger than I was.

In his scrutiny of my dossier, Petrov had not specifically referenced my infant son. Yet, my baby had been a huge part of my life. I still thought of him every day.

Like Steffi's child, Pavel had not been planned, but my baby had been conceived in love when Maxim and I spent a memorable afternoon at my parents' home together.

Steffi's babies—both of them—had come about as a result of brutal assaults by invading strangers in ruins of buildings. Bitter memories, impossible to erase. The flashbacks of those terrible attacks had to be enclosed forever in her mind, like flies trapped in amber.

Still ruminating on our encounter that evening, I was seated with my room-mates at the table for Frau

Schuman's usual *Abendessen.* The homey clatter of plates and flatware in the kitchen promised much, but as usual, produced little that was edible. As the girls warned me, cooking was not the gnädige Frau's forte.

Because we were beginning to socialize on weekends, I thought it was time to tell my friends that for an undetermined period I'd be going to the American Zone to learn English.

"Hmmph," said Elena, naked envy darting from her eyes as Frau Schuman served our usual watery soup. "How come they picked you?"

I shrugged. "I don't know."

"Nobody will ever offer me something like that. I'm still a dangerous enemy of the people. It's what I get for turning a parachute into panties!"

Over the main course, a mysterious casserole made with tinned SPAM meat mixed with boiled onion and turnip, served with a small mound of overcooked spaetzle dumplings, Galina turned to me.

"Okay, Kira, so why did they single you out?

Luba was less circumspect: "Are you sleeping with Petrov?"

"Don't be ridiculous!" I admonished her. "Have you ever seen him?"

"He may not be your type, but maybe he's sweet on you."

I waved away any possibility of that, and changed the subject. Without reflecting, between the casserole and a lumpy pudding concocted with molasses and corn starch, I told the girls about Steffi Bauman, unmindful of what their reaction would be.

They all but gasped, but said nothing until Frau Schuman was back in the kitchen.

"You're making friends with Germans?" Galina hissed as she held my gaze.

"We're not exactly friends, but I hate knowing that babies—yes, even German babies—are starving when we have so much delicious food."

I indicated our plates with a sardonic smile, expecting to elicit a laugh from them at the paucity of our own meal. My attempt at levity fell flat. Nobody cracked a smile.

Usually, as we dawdled over dessert pretending to eat it, Galina would share titillating morsels of gossip with us, things she'd overhear as the driver for a high ranking military officer. Tonight, she was subdued.

Finally, she said, "In the car today the general hinted to another officer that we are planting personnel to spy on the Western powers. Not official spies—personnel who go back and forth and keep their eyes and ears open." She looked at me expectantly.

The other two glanced at each other, then at me.

"What is that supposed to mean?" I challenged.

"Nothing," said Galina. "Probably nothing."

Instead of lounging in Frau Schuman's sitting room with our tea listening to jazz on RIAS—Radio in the American Sector—as we usually did, we all retired directly to our rooms after dinner. I wished I'd kept quiet about Steffi Bauman. I had miscalculated the depth and pervasion of their animus toward ordinary German citizenry.

Later, in my bed, I reflected on their barrage of questions, my uneasiness in answering them, and the need to get along and cohabit with people who were not, in fact, related to me. Like we had to do with Nadia and her sons.

Yes, we were all part of a sisterhood and we loved each other. They were good friends who shared many of my wartime moments, but not necessarily my values or experiences. In the end we were from disparate backgrounds and each had our own secrets.

My stomach growled from hunger. Frau Schuman's awful cooking made me appreciate Nadia's. Thinking back to her delectable creations in Moscow, I recalled with nostalgia one evening in particular which would always stand out in my mind . . .

Moscow, 1940

Nadia had prepared an elaborate dinner and was upbeat.

"I made beet soup, potato purée, pork shashlik, and for dessert, my specialty: *palacsinta royale*, crepes filled with walnuts and chocolate sauce. Bring your glasses to the table; we'll have vodka between courses. My boys aren't home yet, but let's start."

"We haven't had pork for ages. What's the occasion?" asked my delighted brother Yuri. At fifteen, he was experiencing a teen growth spurt, and couldn't get enough of her sumptuous meat dishes.

"Occasion? Do we need an occasion? We're here; we're alive!" Nadia exclaimed with élan. "What more is there to celebrate?" Raising her glass, she toasted our good health: "*Za vashe zdorovye!*"

A feeling of shared conviviality filled the room as we raved about her culinary talents. My grandfather kept beaming at her with affection, and Nadia basked in his praise.

As we were about to devour her superb palacsinta, a scratching sound at the door startled us. Someone was feeling around for the hall light switch; or perhaps breaking into our apartment. We all sat dead still, nervous as cats.

It wasn't the NKVD. They'd announce themselves with pounding and shouting. Break down the door, if necessary. It couldn't be the Housing Authority to tell us yet another family would be moving in. Too late in the day. Nadia ran to the kitchen and brought out a frying pan and a butcher knife. As the rest of us sat riveted to our chairs, she stood in front of the door and waited, muscles of both arms taut from the weight of the pan. Then she motioned to Yuri, whom she'd armed with the knife.

We listened as a key turned in the lock. The door slowly opened and a thin, pale, ragged-looking man with a gray beard, wearing an ill-fitting overcoat and a surprised expression, stood in the doorway. He gaped at the fierce woman wielding a pan. Taking a step back, his arms flew in front of his face in a well-practiced protective gesture against attack. I heard my mother's intake of breath.

"Sergei? Oh, my God, Sergei! Is it you?"

She waved Nadia away as my father stumbled into the room and the rest of us just stood there, our mouths agape.

CHAPTER 11

Berlin, 1947

An envelope is delivered to my desk. I glance around the office; no one else has gotten one. It's an invitation, hand-written on the personal stationery of Mrs. Beatrix Belenko, wife of General Dmitri Belenko. My presence is requested at a cocktail party to be held at the Belenko home in our Russian Zone on Saturday at 17:30. Civilian semi-formal attire is requested for the ladies.

Instead of pleasure, I'm beset with anxiety. "Semi-formal"? I'd arrived in Berlin with a small suitcase containing cheap toiletries, two pairs of serviceable walking shoes, thick cotton stockings, several changes of plain cotton underwear, a light summer uniform, three pullovers, two cardigans, and a couple of blouses and skirts for times when civilian clothing was called for. I have nothing to wear to this event, and there are no stores in the ruins of Berlin where I can buy anything fancy. Not that I have the resources to buy anything elegant, even if there were.

I have trouble concentrating on my work. I picture myself in my army uniform at the party, taken for someone's *aide de camp*—a courier who dropped in to deliver something—surrounded by women in elegant clothes and glittering jewelry,

The more I think about it, the more stressed I feel. I do breathing exercises to relieve my anxiety, the ones I practiced in the air on our night raids. Leaving the office, I'm so distracted I'm nearly knocked over by a cyclist whose view is obstructed by a pile of debris being sorted by raggedy Trümmerfrauen. The women see me, and unimpressed by my medals, laugh at my near accident.

I'll be scorned the same way by guests at the party. Nobody will bother to talk to me; they'll be too busy snickering at me in my shapeless uniform, thick stockings and clunky shoes.

By the time I get home, I'm sweating despite the cold.

My room-mates at Frau Schuman's had forgiven my softening attitude toward Germans and we were sisters again. I convinced them that Steffi Bauman and her two unwanted Russian babies did, after all, deserve some pity. As women they had to sympathize with her plight.

When I came in, Elena sensed I was fretting about something. Over a glass of hot tea, I confided my fears. What I didn't mention was that a prospective flying instructor position might be riding on how I dressed and behaved at this affair. I was sure that the invitation was Petrov's doing, a chance to observe me in social situations.

"This whole thing has made me so nervous, Elena. More than I ever was before sorties during the war, if you can believe it. It's crazy. All because I have nothing to wear."

"It's just a party, for heaven's sake," she said soothingly. "I can't believe you're letting it get to you. You of all people! You never let the German Luftwaffe faze you. And now you're afraid of what people will think?"

"You're right. I've lost my sense of what's important."

Even as I said it, I realized it was time to rid myself of the fear I'd allowed to consume my mind; to put things in perspective. I straightened my posture. I was again

Captain Kira Voronova, a Red Army officer in charge of her life who took to the skies with guts and grit—not some silly wimp who went to pieces over not having something fussy to wear.

"I'll help you," said Elena. "Come on. I have just the thing."

She opened the armoire she shared with Luba.

"You and I are about the same size." Holding up a well-cut dress, she let its black chiffon fabric fan into a soft billow. "I bought it from a German bar girl for five cigarettes. Isn't it a honey?"

It was. I lost no time trying it on. As Elena fussed over the details of straightening and zipping, I surveyed myself in Frau Schuman's full-length chevalier mirror and felt a surge of femininity I hadn't experienced in a long time.

A woman I didn't recognize stared back. Pretty and confident. I loved the dress, with its bold décolletage, the cocktail length, and the decisive, saucy slash that opened to show off my legs when I walked. The delicate fabric of the bodice had glittery diamanté adornments sewn into swirling patterns. A chic creation. Expensive looking.

"Are you sure you want to lend it to me?"

"Of course. I know you'll be careful with it."

Luba walked in at this moment, eating an apple. "Well, aren't we all dressed up!" Then peering down at my sensible brown oxfords, she added, "I hope those aren't the only shoes you have. Where're you going?"

Frau Schuman happened to pass by Elena's bedroom and she looked approvingly at the dress. "Nice. Are you attending a reception?" she asked me.

"A cocktail party at the home of General Belenko," I said. "He's the—"

"I know who he is," she said eagerly, cutting me off. "I met him once, when I was with Oleg. He's very important. So, you know the Belenkos! You're good friends?"

She was so impressed, I didn't disavow her assumption. Let her think I regularly hobnobbed with top Russian brass.

"You will eat well," she said. "The food and drinks they serve at these affairs is sometimes contributed by the other occupying powers. Champagne. Foie gras, good scotch whiskey."

Staring down at my feet, she declared, "You can't wear those ugly shoes with that dress."

With that, she fetched some black prewar sling-back beaded sandals and a small matching evening bag from her armoire. Warming to the occasion, her usual diffidence faded and she was all smiles.

"And you must do something with your hair! It's so . . ." She stopped short of telling me I resembled a Slavic peasant. Before I could protest, she unpinned my hair and unraveled my braids. Then she offered to wash it and set it in soft waves, a fashionable, more Western European style, on the evening of the party.

"Well. That was out of character," whispered Elena after she left. "She certainly became ingratiating after you mentioned Belenko. She's envious of you, going to that affair. I doubt she gets out much. She's angling for something."

"You think she wishes she were going?" I would have

been more than happy to let her go in my place.

"Absolutely. What she wants is to land another officer to support her like the last one did. That Russian general, Oleg. He kept her for a while before he went back to Russia. There are sure to be candidates for his replacement at the Belenkos' party."

After the conquest, some German women managed to find Russian officers to provide them with food and protect them from marauding drunken troops. Apparently, she was one of the lucky ones.

I tried on Frau Schuman's shoes. They were about half a size too tight and had high heels. I walked back and forth across the room, managing well enough without falling, but I knew I'd have blisters by the time I left the gathering. Comfort would have to be sacrificed for appearance.

"This party sounds pretty exclusive," said Luba. "How did you get invited?"

"I have no idea," I said evasively. "They probably picked my name from a hat."

My friends weren't buying it, but they said nothing more.

I could hardly have explained that Petrov wanted me to mix with the Americans and the British. If, as Petrov claimed, the directive for me to gather intelligence had originated with General Belenko, this invitation was likely so Belenko could size me up.

"Are they going to ask you to fly again?" Elena persisted. Like me, she was bored at work and wanted to take to the air again.

"I don't know, Elena. They've said nothing to me. I

doubt they'd want to see me back in a cockpit."

"Well, keep me in mind if they change their mind."

"Of course." I stood in front of the mirror. "Do you think this was the last dress that poor bar girl had left to sell? She must have been desperate to have parted with it so cheaply. A few cigarettes."

"Don't worry about her. She'll manage okay," said Elena. "A girl's got to eat. And those few cigarettes will keep her eating for a while in this cigarette economy."

Wistfully, she watched me do a saucy pirouette in the mirror. "You're lucky to have somewhere to wear it. I bought that dress months ago and haven't had a chance to show it off. I wish I could get invited to parties."

Elena, we all suspected, had a man in her life, but she was being quite secretive, always meeting him outside the apartment. She sometimes closeted herself in the room where the phone was kept for a private conversation, and once I thought I heard her speaking English in muffled tones. We'd all inferred he was married with a wife here in Berlin, which meant he must be a high-ranking officer. If Elena were the 'other woman' living in the shadows, he couldn't be seen with her.

"Don't feel bad. They don't invite me either," pouted Luba as she appraised me with envy. "And I've never even had a real boyfriend. I wish I could meet a nice, single Russian officer. One who can dance."

"So do I," I said. "There are so many women around and not enough good men who aren't already taken."

Elena sighed. "The nicest ones are always taken. I'll probably die an old maid, my virginity intact."

This brought loud guffaws from Luba and me, who

knew from Elena's vodka-induced boasts that her pretty face had led her into several romantic interludes in her native Leningrad, not all of them chaste. We didn't even mention her present love interest.

"Well, maybe not quite intact," she laughed. "But we were so young before the war, we didn't get much chance to do normal things. As an enemy of the people, I can't return to Russia to meet anyone. The acceptable Russian fellows we meet here? They like *Schatzies.* And some of those girls are so pretty." Then she added. "Anyway, Kira, enjoy the dress. But remember us if you happen to meet any presentable men at the party; you know the phone number to give them. Tell them our names—not Frau Schuman's!"

"Right," Luba interjected. "And don't keep them for yourself."

Caught up in the moment, she lent me her grandmother's pearl earrings—a sweet gesture I appreciated. They were Luba's only family heirloom.

"Here. These earrings are worth much more than Frau Schuman's shoes. Don't lose them!"

CHAPTER 12

*T*he night is long and restless. In my head, I rehearse conversations I anticipate at the Belenkos'. Will I say the right thing? Will there be spies? How will I recognize them?

I toss and turn. As I am about to drift off to sleep, I hear the roar of an enemy plane in my ears, the shrapnel penetrating my fuselage.

A Focke-Wulf is flying straight at me. I see the pilot's face, filled with hate. He begins shooting. On the ground later at our makeshift base, Rufina's body is covered with a rough blanket, half her cranium missing. The fatal hole in her forehead. Zinaida and Luba cursing with rage and tears.

I stomp in place to keep my feet from freezing as Commander Tamara Drobovitch chooses another navigator for my next sortie. Galina, an experienced pilot who can also navigate, is the logical replacement. She has lost her pilot to serious injuries on an earlier sortie.

No time to mourn Rufina. My hands shake from fear and cold. It could so easily have been me. I'm swamped with guilt. Had I banked the plane a fraction more, would it have made a difference? A slight correction to the right? I'll never know. Watching my plane being refueled and rearmed, I dread my return to the sky. Next time I might not be so lucky. Then I am airborne again, the faint scent of Rufina's blood in my nostrils— this time with Galina.

Rufina's face looms, staring at me, accusingly. Why didn't I keep her alive? Why am I going out to parties when she is not?

Another night with only intermittent bouts of sleep.

Another night of wrestling with memories from the past. The next day, I'm exhausted; remnants of last night's dreams are still bouncing around in my head.

Nightmares have killed my appetite. Frau Schuman has hung used tea bags for re-use on a small clothesline in the kitchen—a money-saving hack she read about somewhere. As all my scary memories re-play in vivid detail, I sip a breakfast of watery tea. I have no desire for food, especially not the stale *Pfannkuchen* pastry she lays out.

At the sounds of my room-mates wakening, I shake off the past and focus on the future. The near future: the party at Belenkos' home this evening.

◆ ◆ ◆

Beatrix Belenko turned out to be a lissome, stunning blonde with sculpted features, a shapely figure, and a winning smile framing very white teeth. I'd heard a lot about her. There was a self-possessed charisma in her manner, smooth, poised, and outgoing. With practiced ease and confidence, she commanded the large living room where she received her guests. I guessed her to be in her early 30s, about ten years younger than her husband.

Grace and charm aside, the single most extraordinary thing about her was that while her Russian was perfect, she was actually German. I knew this beforehand. The gossip mills had all speculated how General Belenko had managed to remain married to a German woman throughout the war without incurring the wrath of Russian authorities, especially Stalin. High-ranking generals had been executed for less. Stranger still was that she was even here, in Berlin. None of the other Russian officers brought their wives to Germany. Our leaders had no doubt welcomed her presence because her glamorous appearance had value as a public relations tool. Frau Belenko chose to speak to me in German with a hint of Berlin accent.

"So, you're the amazing woman combat pilot," was the first thing she said.

"Not so amazing," I replied modestly. "And I'm one of many. There were eighty women in my particular regiment, the 588th." Accepting a fluted glass of pre-war champagne from a proffered tray, I continued, "But yes, we were combat pilots—night bombers." I took a small sip of my drink.

"The famous 588th regiment. They called you Nachthexen, *ja*? You were fairly numerous, but I understand you were the most decorated pilot in your regiment, Captain Voronova. Very impressive."

"I'm merely the most decorated who survived to tell about it. Many of my comrades were not so fortunate. We lost nearly thirty women who earned posthumous medals. Many others were badly injured." I bit into a foie gras canapé, the pleasure from its silky texture and taste absorbing a little of the pain I felt remembering my sisters-in-arms.

"Such brave ladies," she said, with unabashed admiration. "Our country has paid an incalculable price for victory, has it not?"

That she referred to Russia in such a proprietary way

surprised me, particularly since she was speaking German.

"Yes, we did. So many deaths. In so many families—including my own."

"I'm sorry." She remained quiet for a moment, waiting for me to elaborate. When I did not, she asked. "How long were you in active service, Captain?"

"Nearly three years."

I had to smile. I liked that she addressed me as Captain. It had been a long time since anyone had. The leveler patronymic "Comrade" had widely replaced earned titles of respect.

"Such an unusual thing for Stalin to do, wasn't it, sending women into combat," she mused. "We were the only country who did that."

I grew wary. *An attempt to get me to say something negative about Stalin?*

"It was voluntary; we all enlisted. We were interested in aviation and we wanted to fly, to protect our country from—" I almost said 'the Germans'—"From the menace of war."

"Enlisted. Yes," she said, ignoring my gaffe. "Commendable. So young and eager, and so willing to lay down your lives. I can't tell you how much I admire you for the role you played. I've done nothing so heroic. I was a film star prior to the war."

Another known fact about her. There had been whispers about what kind of films she'd been in when she was young and hungry, before she broke into stardom. But by the time she met General Belenko she was a well-established mainstream actor.

What did she think of us? Did she share the German view that Russia was a challenge to conquer because of our land mass, weather, population numbers, and the size of our armies; but that except for the genteel few who contributed to culture, we did not measure up to codes set down by the master race?

To avoid her scrutiny, I cast my eyes around the room. Although they could have chosen to live in one of the well-preserved villas with large properties closer to his Karlshorst office, the Belenkos lived in Mitte Berlin near Alexanderplatz in two apartments they'd combined. It occupied the ground floor of one of the few intact buildings left in the center of the city. An oasis of civilization amidst the rubble, it was furnished comfortably, boasting a massive grand piano, valuable artwork, and elegant crystal chandeliers. I heard one guest say the furnishings and art had been seized from villas of prominent Nazis; in all probability, originally looted by the Gestapo from ransacked Jewish residences.

Junior-ranking military personnel, recruited for the occasion, served guests champagne, chilled vodka, and hors d'oeuvres—a bewildering display of gourmet offerings considering how difficult it was to obtain such rare provisions. Frau Schuman mentioned they'd be donated by the American, British and French contingents of West Berlin—a display of mutual friendship that was fast disappearing.

There was a sprawl of about fifty or so guests, mostly Russians. A handful of German men in civilian dress were in attendance and I speculated who they might be. A number of Americans and British, dressed smartly in officers' uniforms, clustered in groups to speak English. And French was being spoken in a couple of other pockets of the crowd. One of the Americans was playing wartime hits at the piano. Songs made popular by British songstress, Vera Lynn.

Odd that Beatrix Belenko had singled me out from this throng for a lengthy chat, I thought. I suspected she knew of my assignment and was aware of the real reason her husband and Petrov added me to her guest list.

"You've created a lovely home," I said, to keep the conversation going.

"Thank you," she said, flashing her salon-manicured nails as she took a dainty sip from her champagne flute. "Yes, we finally found a decent place to live and furnishings for it. We have a nanny, a lovely Swiss woman. Now I'm looking for a good school that's still intact."

"So, you have children?"

Her face lit up. "Yes. A girl, Liesel. She's five. And a four-year-old son, Joachim. We call him Achim."

My son—my sweet Pavel—would be almost four now, too. I thought of the last time I saw him, cuddled in my father's arms as I boarded the train for Engels. I had been home to give birth and my maternity leave was up. I recalled the foreboding I felt. How I'd wanted to dash away with him, hide somewhere, keep him safe, wartime duty be damned.

"There's no place for our children to play," she fretted, intruding my reverie. "I'm from Berlin. When I was a child, the parks and streets here were lovely. So green, and the stately old trees we had everywhere! A beautiful city, especially in the spring, with all the flowers. But now, since the war, I worry about the toxic air. Our grasses and trees are still scorched. The earth has been poisoned. I worry about our water. And all the unexploded bombs. They could go off any time."

I said nothing. After 75,000 tons of bombs from British and American planes, and the destruction we Russians caused with tanks afterward, the apocalyptic horror we created spoke for itself.

"The air quality here now is so awful, Achim has developed asthma. Liesel has allergies. It's a terrible place to raise children."

I agreed. It wasn't healthy for anyone.

"It's certainly not the city I once knew. In the '30s, Berlin offered so much to do, such a lot of entertainment." She smiled as she reminisced. "To be young, and German, and in Berlin during the Weimar Republic— *wünderbar*. Even if you were broke, it was fun. A latter day Babylon!"

I had wanted to idealize the city once, too. The postcards from my parents' apartment depicting Berlin still occupied my thoughts; joyous paeans to the city. What Frau Belenko was neglecting to mention were the extreme poverty, hyperinflation, and unemployment that plagued the city after the Great War. That Germany was a country crippled by war reparations and political discontent, giving Hitler a lame excuse to lash out.

"I used to know Berlin so well. Now I can't locate streets," she lamented. "I can't even be sure where my family home was."

"You still have family here?"

At the mention of family, a wave of emotion stripped away her sophisticated veneer, filling her eyes; vulnerability surfaced in raw grief. Her voice cracked when she finally spoke.

"Had. They all died in the war. The bombings. . ." She turned away.

And at that moment, I decided I liked her. She might be beautiful and important, but she could feel a deep sense of loss as I did. Losses had been unspeakable on both sides.

"That's very sad," I said, and steered the conversation to more pleasant thoughts. "You were in many films before you married?"

Happy to leave the subject of war aside, she named some of the motion pictures she'd starred in. I'd seen a couple of them, early ones, and while they had little artistic merit her compelling camera presence was undeniable. She'd been an exquisite beauty. The faint lines beginning to appear on her face notwithstanding, she still was.

"Before the war, Germany had a thriving film industry," she said. "The first cinema in the world was not far from here, the Berlin Winter Garten, near Potsdamer Platz. Built in the 19th century; but it was destroyed during the War."

"I didn't know that. I thought the Americans . . . Hollywood . . ."

She waved dismissively as she scoffed: "*Nein, nein*. It was us. The Germans. We were the leading film makers in the world. I was under contract with UFA Studios in Babelsberg. Great directors were here then. Billy Wilder, Fritz Lang, Josef von Sternberg . . . and actors! Peter Lorre. Marlene Dietrich, oh, so many. I knew most of them well." Her face clouded. "But then the Nazis cracked down on film people who were Jewish, and wanted the others to do only propaganda films. In the end, about fifteen hundred of them left for the United States. Such an exodus of talent! Germany's film industry will never be the same."

"Hitler made sure Leni Riefenstahl remained."

"Yes, he kept Leni, of course. She wasn't Jewish. And Leni thrived on the sight of throngs of troops goose-stepping past the Führer—propaganda documentaries."

We chatted about how Beatrix met her husband when he was teaching Russian Literature as an exchange professor at the university here, until our conversation was interrupted by a handsome man in a well-pressed uniform, four stars on his shoulder boards and gold embroidered leaves decorating his collar. I recognized him at once from photos and my arm almost rose automatically to salute him.

"Ah, there you are, darling," he said, putting his arm around her shoulders.

The frisson his touch and endearment sparked showed immediately on her face as she registered a tender smile.

"*Liebchen!* Darling, this is Captain Kira Voronova, one of the famous Nachthexen . . . the female night bomber pilots we spoke of?" She turned to me. "My husband, General Dmitri Belenko."

"Captain Voronova. Of course," he said in Russian as he clicked his heels and offered me a curt bow. His glacial blue eyes never left mine. "An honor. You're quite famous. We're proud of you and your fellow women pilots."

I was melting from the heat of embarrassment at such praise. He appraised me curiously, a scientist examining a new species. Like a pinned butterfly, I wished someone else would join us and release me so I could fly away. The feeling of relaxed rapprochement I'd managed to establish with Beatrix dissqlved. Now I was feeling edgy, worried that I'd say the wrong thing, or sneeze and spill my drink on his dazzling polished boots. Or something equally stupid that would show me for the inept Russian bumpkin I was.

I'd been pressured into taking on new duties at the General's instigation, but now I asked myself how he'd deal with me if I failed to meet his expectations. I thought of his execution orders; of the power he had. And the blood drained from my face. Fear was no stranger to me. It was there every time I got into a plane during combat, but that had been righteous fear of the enemy. This was different. It was fear of failure, and its consequences. Fear of someone who could direct my life. Or destroy it.

"I've wanted to meet you for some time, Captain," Belenko said smoothly. "I don't feel that our Russian women pilots receive enough recognition. We should do something about that."

I glanced sidelong at him, imagining what inglorious acts he had committed on the climb to his present position. Did he get his own hands bloodied, or merely sign the orders? He was tall, fit, and attractive. I tried to picture him interrogating prisoners without breaking a sweat, and my mind brimmed with questions. How many executions had he been responsible for? How had he proven his loyalty to Stalin and the Communist party? He must have worked hard to ensure his German wife was tolerated. She had to be his Achilles' heel.

Beatrix remained an enigma. It intrigued me how she

had begun our conversation speaking of Russia as our homeland, but switched to "we" and "us" when she spoke about Germany's film industry. Now she was speaking Russian, and the "we" and "us" were Soviets.

How much did she know about her husband's work? From her demeanor around him, my guess was that she didn't permit herself to see beyond his mask of attentive husband and indulgent father. One never knew.

"I, too, was a pilot in the Red Army Air Corps," Belenko said, his steady, authoritative voice piercing my thoughts. "We may have been occupying the same skies at the same time."

"My husband is being modest," said Beatrix. "He is a Hero of the Soviet Union, among other honors. Look at all his medals!"

I had to smile. Yes, he sported an impressive array, but I had earned just as many. I only said, "It was a crowded sky in those days, General."

"It certainly was. A crowded sky."

"We can only hope it will not be so again," I added.

Over his shoulder, I saw Petrov had arrived, with Inna Gradska a few steps behind. Were they together? I was surprised that a secretary would be invited to the party when my Red Army aviator friends were not. He was observing us with an approving smile as he glad-handed fellow officers scattered around his path.

"We were saying only this morning that we should have you come to dinner some time," remarked Beatrix.

Her husband's eyes met mine again. "Yes, absolutely. We'll do that. My secretary will contact you."

Oh, no, I thought, foreseeing myself in another awkward social situation, blurting out things that might embarrass myself. I was uncomfortable enough having to attend this party. Now they were talking about dinner?

To my relief, other guests gravitated to them, fawning and fussing with introductions. The general and his wife assumed the role of a royal couple receiving at court, serene and elegant, sure of their glamour, good looks, and ability to charm. My cue to move on.

Before I did, Beatrix introduced me to several high-ranking male officers, and I noted their names for Galina, Elena, and Luba.

A handsome British RAF officer who spoke excellent Russian took an interest in me, introducing himself as Colonel Stephen Carter.

"So you're one of those Russian women pilots," he said. "Where do you live?" An odd question, but I told him which neighborhood, and then he asked, "Might you be a room-mate of Elena Kaloshina's?"

"You know Elena?"

"Yes. We've met." He didn't indicate where, but his smile told all. Carter introduced me to his wife, a cool British beauty in her early forties who spoke only English and appeared uncomfortable. Clearly, she did not wish to be there. She was attractive, but older and not as pretty as Elena.

Before I could find out more, a middle-aged Russian Senior Lieutenant named Igor Fomichov muscled the Carters out of the way and touted out the usual banal pick-up lines. Fomichov had a wife in Moscow, but did not let that govern his behavior. Alcohol heavy on his breath, he became annoying and attentive, invading my comfort zone as he gripped my arm whenever he addressed me. I entertained the wicked thought of matching him up with Frau Schuman before I remembered how kind she'd been about doing my hair and lending me her shoes. Fomichov was beginning a discourse on the Battle of the Kerch Peninsula when an attractive red-headed woman appeared at my side.

"Could I interrupt?" she asked in Russian. She shot Fomichov an apologetic smile. "Sorry. I must borrow Comrade Voronova for a few minutes."

Ignoring Fomichov's disgruntled glare, she led me away by the elbow.

"Thank you," I said. "He was becoming a nuisance."

"Yes, I thought you needed rescuing."

I examined her closely. With her curly red hair and blue eyes, she reminded me a lot of my old friend, Zinaida Sebrova. This endeared her to me immediately.

"And you are?"

"Angela Taylor. British, but I work as a civilian translator in the American Zone."

"The American Zone? A translator. You're my English teacher! Senior Lieutenant Petrov didn't tell me your name."

"Not many people on this side know it. I'm a bit of an enigma around here. I don't get over to this Zone much."

"You have an English name," I noted. "Yet your Russian is perfect."

"White Russian parents. Our *byvshy* name was Tarasov. My parents fled St. Petersburg to London after the Revolution. Here in the East, our comrades are willing to overlook my parents' imperial leanings. At least for the moment."

I detected a trace of bitterness in the way she spoke.

"As long as I'm employed by the Americans, I'm useful to the Soviet Union."

So, she had no illusions. I liked that. She not only resembled Zinaida, she was straightforward like her. An endearing trait; one that could be dangerous.

"We should talk about your English lessons."

To escape the background noise of the party—getting louder as liquor consumption increased—Angela led me to a quiet corner near the vestibule where we could chat in private. Even her inscrutable smile reminded me of Zinaida's—back in the days when as children she still smiled—before things fell apart for both of us.

Interrupting my thoughts, Angela said, "Okay. About what I'll be teaching you: the English you learn from me will give you a British inflection, one the Americans will find charming. Though you'll always retain a Russian accent."

"American or British, it makes no difference. When can we start?"

"Next Friday. Are you at the Central Kommandatura on Kaiserswerther Straße in Berlin-Dahlem?"

"No, I work in the East, out of a smaller building, not far from the ruins of the Adlon Hotel, near Pariser Platz."

"Where do you live?"

"Near there. In a boarding house on Französische Straße."

"I know the area. So, come over after you leave work. From your place, you'll be crossing the line at the Brandenburg Gate. That'll put you in the British Zone. I'll be waiting for you at the Gate at 16:00 this first time. After that, here's my address, with directions." She handed over a card already written out. "It's an easy walk from there to my place in the American Zone. Plan to stay overnight at my apartment. I have a tiny place, but I can put you up on my couch."

Accommodation was not something I'd considered.

She explained: "It would be unsafe for you to go home alone after dark. The men in this town continue to hunt down women in packs, like wolves." She rolled her eyes.

"Still? I thought it was safer now."

"It's not as bad as it was right after the war ended, but yes, it still goes on. Don't take chances—wear your uniform and you're less likely to be bothered."

"I hate to impose on you," I said.

"Not to worry. I'll be happy to have the company. Have you ever studied English before?"

I had to be consistent with my lies. "No. Never."

"It's not hard to learn. The grammar is a cinch. But all foreigners have trouble with the pronunciation and the accent. That only comes with practice. You'll get lots of that in West Berlin. We'll make it fun. Spend an hour or two on grammar, converse a bit, and go out later, maybe to one of the new bars opening in the Bizone. Comrade Petrov wants you to mingle; get to know people who can help with your assignment—whatever that is—so the more exposure the better."

"Did he tell you what it is? My assignment?"

"No. And I don't want to know. Safer that way."

Her answer was quick, like she'd had it prepared.

CHAPTER 13

Angela and I chatted for a while, straining to keep our voices low while still speaking over the noise of the party. Once we'd established the parameters of what my instruction would be, she allowed herself to be distracted by casual conversation with other people, mostly Americans she knew, who stopped to greet her.

That was okay with me as I was off track in the conversation. Angela's resemblance to Zinaida continued to distract me, teasing my memory and bringing up remembrances of my old friend.

I recalled how when I thought everything was fine—even after our favorite math teacher did not turn up at school and was replaced the next day with someone of lesser ability—Zinaida was ahead of me. She had guessed first that he'd been taken away, a victim of the purges and the gulag system. It was the fate of many people our families knew.

Our parents had been pressured to join the Communist Party, but Zinaida's father resisted. Like Angela's parents, he was a White Russian with ancestral ties to the tsarist regime. A satirist whose poems could be mordant and acerbic, he was also a professor of philosophy at Moscow State University and an outspoken critic of Stalin. I'd known her father all my life and was fond of him. He was like an uncle to me.

Remembering him brought me back to the night Zinaida arrived at our apartment frightened: "I must talk to your father," she said. There were tears in her eyes, and her eyelashes were coated with frost from the cold.

I ushered Zinaida into Papa's study. My father bade her to enter and closed the door before I could follow her inside. Feeling excluded, I went into the kitchen and complained to my mother, who was tidying up after dinner.

"Quiet," she admonished in a low voice as she handed me a tea towel. "Sometimes, the less you know, the better. And you must learn to shut up, Kira. These are dangerous times. A loose tongue can get you thrown into prison. Or shot." She reinforced her warning with a proverb: *Boltun nakhodka dlya shpiona*. A chatterbox is a treasure for a spy. It occurred to me for the first time that I'd been so wrapped up in myself, my flying lessons, my schoolwork, and the powerful force of my teenaged hormones, I was the only one who hadn't intuited the political reality of the times we were living in; hadn't understood the dangers around us.

Despite the distractions from other guests, Angela was still focused on our new relationship. She interrupted my thoughts, picking up on our previous conversation:

"There's fun to be had in Berlin. Plenty of parties and dances in the American Zone. Do you like to dance?"

I nodded. "It's been a while, though. There weren't many occasions to celebrate during the war, nor even since the war ended."

"Not to worry. As they say, it's like riding a bicycle."

I hoped she was right. It would be fun to dance and enjoy life again.

Zinaida and I had taken ballet at the government-sponsored children's classes taught at the Bolshoi. But after her father's execution by firing squad for writing the poem about Stalin, that came to an end. She and her family were declared *personae non grata*, enemies of the state, forced to leave Patriarshy Ponds. Their new status denied her and her siblings opportunities to continue their education in academe or the arts. Though a brilliant student on track for a career in microbiology like her mother, Zinaida had to drop out of school and take a job in an armaments factory. When she left without saying good-bye, it was as though someone had removed one of my limbs, leaving me with phantom pain.

My brother Yuri, who'd harbored a crush on her, was shocked. "We'll never see Zinaida again?"

I shook my head. "No. They've lost their apartment. It shows you--no one is safe. We have to be careful from now on."

Angela's voice again pulled me firmly back to the present.

"Some of the American soldiers are colored, from the South of the United States. They play a kind of fast jazz music they call Dixieland, and everyone dances these crazy new steps. I'm still learning them. Girls are always welcome, especially if they're pretty. The American soldiers—they call them G.I.s—they'll be more than happy to teach you ..."

She stopped talking long enough to look me over, taking in Elena's dress.

"You certainly pass the 'pretty' test. And that's a lovely frock. Do you have other party clothes?"

"No. I had to borrow this one."

"Well, not to worry. You're a bit taller than I am, but about the same size. I can lend you clothes to wear. I have access to their PX, and they sometimes stock nice things. It's easy to meet men over there. Put a smile on your face, and learn to speak with your eyes." The serious expression she wore morphed into a flirtatious one as she smiled and hooded her eyes into a saucy look.

"That shouldn't be too difficult," I said, tossing her a smile that was a creditable imitation of hers.

We both dissolved into laughter. "You learn fast," she said with a mischievous wink.

She was fun. We would get along fine. I was assessing how long I would have to keep up the pretense. "I hope I can learn to speak English quickly."

I glanced back at General Belenko, the specter of failure and its consequences gnawing at me.

Angela said, "How fast you learn depends on how motivated you are. It's not a difficult language. Not like Russian or German. You're a bright person; they tell me you're an engineer. The key is practice. Motivation is important, too, of course."

I nodded. Fear was also a great motivator. So was ambition. And I was spurred by plenty of both.

CHAPTER 14

Engels, USSR, 1942

M y friendship with Zinaida could have died out after she moved away but for a chance meeting on the Moscow subway a few years later. I had joined the Red Army Air Corps as a pilot in the 588th. Zinaida was still working in the Tula Arms factory. While she was not allowed to further her education enough for a pilot's license, I convinced her to see if our Air Corps could use her in armaments. Over a glass of tea, I talked her into joining up.

"It might help rehabilitate your family if you serve," I said. "They might not consider you an enemy of the people. It would help your sister, and perhaps open up opportunities for you after the war."

She was accepted into our squadron as a mechanic, arming our small planes with bombs and refueling them after each sortie. A tough, demanding job.

We had no idea what we were getting into. Our rigorous basic training at Engels Aviation Institute was a fourteen-hour-a-day eye opener for us; a glimpse of reality that hit us like a torrent of ice water. We trained for three months. And what followed was three years of hell we'd never forget.

While our early friendship had been the impetus for our reunion at Engels, it was through our army sisterhood that Zinaida and I became closer, confiding secrets, and keeping a protective eye out for each other. I even told her that Maxim and I had eloped before he left for the front. Something I'd told nobody else—not my parents; not the army; not even my brother Yuri.

CHAPTER 15

Berlin, 1947

I was pleased to be meeting Angela beforehand. Ours would be an informal, comfortable kind of student-teacher relationship. Over the din of the party, she said, "I understand you were a pilot for the Red Army?"

"Yes. A night bomber for three years during the war."

"I'm amazed they found so many women willing to do that. You were always motivated to fly?"

"Yes. As a kid, I was really interested in stars and galaxies, and the idea that people might be living on the moon. I wondered what they'd be like, and if they could speak Russian. I was sure that one day we'd hurtle into the air and land up there."

"We might do that yet," she said, taking a sip of her drink.

I hesitated about questioning Angela much about her job in the West. Petrov hinted her work was sensitive. She really worked for us, but was employed by the United States. Yet, she was British. With connections in three Zones, I was curious about her true allegiance.

She wasn't about to tell me. Our conversation was all about me. But I couldn't resist tapping her for information.

"Angela, do you happen to know a man named Vick Moran? He's a major in the U.S. Army Air Corps in the American Zone."

She ran his name through the files of her memory. "Should I? I suppose I might. I know a lot of American men. Oh, wait. Vick Moran. Of course. Also known as Viktor Moranov. He had a Russian father, or grand-father. Yes. Actually, he was here, at the party. Just for about five minutes or so. He brought some bourbon as a contribution from the American contingent. You must have just missed him."

Moranov? A Russian background? This threw me. That Moran would be on such cozy terms with our side was a surprise. It occurred to me he was already working for us as a double agent. But if that were the case, where did I come in?

A man in a British officer's uniform tapped Angela on the shoulder and she turned her attention to him, speaking rapid fire English. The look she gave him was the flirtatious one. Time for me to move on and mingle.

CHAPTER 16

My head was still buzzing with the revelation I'd missed Moran. Still, it told me that he was around. He hadn't called me, but if it was this easy running into him here in the East, I was sure I'd have no trouble tracking him down on his home turf.

Hoping to please Petrov by socializing, I excused myself to chat with a few other people. I strolled over to a painting being admired by a Russian couple.

"I tell you, it's an Otto Dix," said the officer, a Russian who sounded German—probably from the Kaliningrad Oblast area.

"No, you're wrong. It's unsigned, but I'm sure it's a George Grosz," declared the woman at his side. She turned to me. "What do you think, Comrade?"

Think? I wasn't familiar with either artist. I was about to apologize for my ignorance of Weimar art, but instead announced with authority, "Why, you're right, of course; it's a George Grosz; anyone can see that." Then I ambled away.

"You see?" I heard her say. "I was right."

This party was turning out to be more amusing than I'd anticipated. I suppressed the urge to laugh. Was it so easy to lie to people? To convince them of something, as long as you averred it with authority? Goebbels would certainly have said so; most of Hitler's half-baked ideas he propagated were founded on falsehoods.

I made my way to where a curvaceous Inna Gradska, Petrov's secretary, sheathed in a powder blue cocktail dress, was holding court with two British officers.

About to join them, I heard them speaking English. Inna, intent on the point she was making, ignored that I was close by, so I kept going. Where had she learned to speak English with such confidence?

I joined in here and there, meeting other couples and a few men who were on their own. With my roommates in mind, I approached a group of several young Russian officers commenting on the bourbon they were trying for the first time, and asked if they'd like to meet some nice Russian girls.

"Why?" asked one. "I have my choice of beautiful Schatzies. A Russian girl? It would be like dating my sister." They all laughed at that, and one man hooted, "But I wouldn't mind going out with you, *Daragaya*!"

I moved on. Igor Fomichov was soon all over me again. At one point, I noted a look of determined clarity in his eyes that belied his apparent drunkenness, and it occurred to me that his behavior was a bit over the top.

"You know, my little *latoshka*," he said sotto voce, "it would be in your interest to see me again."

"What is that supposed to mean?"

"What do you think it means?"

"Do you always talk in riddles, or is it the vodka?"

He said nothing, but continuing to hold my gaze, he poured his drink into the soil of a potted *monstera deliciosa* plant Beatrix had growing in one of the windows.

"Appearances can be deceiving," he said.

Who the hell was he?

"Give me your phone number," he said, an order—not a request.

The energy of the party had begun to wane, and people

were disappearing. I weighed my choices. If he were important or resourceful, he could easily find out my number in the files. If he couldn't, then he probably wasn't worth spending time with. I gave him a false number and made a mental note to find out more about him.

He promised to call me the next day.

As the party broke up, Angela took me aside and whispered in my ear. "Kira, a word of caution. You're being watched. Don't worry. It's routine. Just be careful. Be careful about everything. When you leave, hang on to your handbag. This Zone is very dangerous. See you next week."

And with a wink and a smile, she disappeared into the night on the arm of a British officer.

CHAPTER 17

T he cab fare to the party was higher than expected, and I worried I'd come up short if I took another taxi home. Yet, it was far to walk. As I debated my options outside, Igor Fomichov, puffing a cigar, sidled up to me.

"Come with me, *Daragaya*. I have a car with a driver. I'll drop you off."

"I don't have far to go."

"Get in," he said. With his driver present, he was behaving like a drunk again.

The last thing I wanted was a wrestling match with any Russian officer, drunk or pretending to be, but in spite of his strange behavior and our conversation at the party, I decided to take my chances.

An unwise decision. He began subtly, slipping his hand onto my knee. When I pushed it away, he tried fondling my breast. In between these annoying maneuvers, he took puffs of his cigar, allowing sparks to escape, and fouling the air inside the vehicle. Worried that he would burn holes in Elena's dress, I moved as far as I could to the car door. By the time we reached the intersection of Unter den Linden and Friedrichstraße, I'd had more than enough, and over Fomichov's protests I told the driver to stop.

After a curt "good night," at which I avoided a slobbering kiss, I set out to walk the rest of the way. The evening air was clear and fresh, and I took deep breaths to clear my lungs of the offending smoke. From where I'd gotten off, it was a short walk to the apartment on

Französische Straße. I could easily have done it in comfortable shoes, but in Frau Schuman's killer heels, every step was crippling, so my progress was slow. To make matters worse, the temperature was dropping.

Thoughts of Fomichov were darting in and out of my mind. Was I being played again? Tested by Petrov? And was Fomichov part of that? Angela's parting remark about being watched gnawed at me. My head was still buzzing over having missed Vick Moran. Strange how he had made a quick appearance at that party, and left so early. I also thought about my upcoming lessons—my goal was now to become fluent enough to speak easily with Brits and Americans, at least as well as Inna Gradska.

I let these ramblings take over my mind as I strolled along, making the mistake of letting my attention wander. A cardinal sin no former bomber pilot should ever have made.

There were few street lamps; and no one out walking or socializing. The early spring weather was volatile, with warm days and cold nights. A bare dusting of light snow earlier had coated the ground like finely sifted crystals, and the chill was condensing my breath. The hoary sheen of frost visible in the moonlight made walking in the stilettos treacherous. Charred ruins of buildings, their emptiness spooky and discomfiting, echoed my eerily deflected steps. Sounds only got louder as I made my way. Or was it someone else's footfalls? I strained to listen.

I stopped, and what I took for an echo also stopped. I recognized a foreboding that saved me so often in the air when a quick glance over my shoulder revealed a

Luftwaffe fighter at four o'clock. My own inner voice was warning me. As pilots, we'd all been equipped with a knife, a pistol, and a cyanide pill in case we were taken prisoner. Carrying my landlady's ridiculously small evening bag, I couldn't bring my gun, and now the soldier in me was regretting it. But I did have my knife. I kept walking. My building was within sight. I quickened my step. A cloud had edged its way over the pale moon, and the street was even dimmer now. Fear crept over me, an emotion all too familiar. Men talking, a muffled laugh. Voices speaking in Russian glanced off the derelict buildings.

With no warning, a soldier jumped out at me from an alleyway. He was followed by three others, low-ranking drunken men in Red Army uniforms. They surrounded me, making lewd remarks.

"A pretty one," said the most aggressive as he tried to kiss me. "*Schöne frau! Komm mit uns.*"

"Get away from me, you idiot!" I shouted in Russian as I wrenched my head and shoved him away.

"Whoa," he exclaimed in surprise. "Hey Boris, this one knows Russian!"

"Then tell her we hope she's a good fuck!" called out one of his buddies.

"You fool!" I yelled. I was frightened, but I wasn't about to show it. "I *am* Russian. I'm a Russian officer. Captain Kira Voronova of the USSR Army Air Corps." To insert gravitas, I added, "Hero of the Soviet Union."

"Hear that? She's a Russian officer!" another soldier mocked in the broad accent of a Caucasus peasant. He raised his voice to a falsetto meant to imitate me. "A hero of the Soviet Union!"

They all laughed, but one of them appeared nervous. "Did you say Voronova?" he asked in a Moscow accent.

I was kicking at his friend's shins. "You assholes! I'm a personal friend of General Belenko's. I demand your names and serial numbers at once."

At this, Muscovite buttoned up his pants. "Nikita, stop. She could be Belenko's girlfriend. Leave it. There's lots of other bitches around." He began backing into the nearest alley. "Come on. Let's find some Schatzies."

But the other man and his friends were determined. I was low-lying fruit. Why look for other women? They jammed me against a wall, opening my coat to grab at my breasts, pulling up my dress, tearing at my garters, and reaching to yank down my underwear as I dug my nails into their hands and faces.

I screamed every obscenity I'd ever heard from male pilots. I pulled my knife from my pocket, and my blade landed a deep slice down the face of the one called Nikita.

"You bitch!" he screamed, and his fist made contact with my cheek, just under my eye. Paralyzed with pain, I teetered, then lost my balance, and went down hard to the ground. He quickly disarmed me. Then, continuing to curse, he grabbed me by the hair and anchored me to the icy concrete while the two others held me down by the arms. A wave of panic. I reeled with pain and desperation. My struggle was coming to an end.

Behind me, the distant rumble of a car engine—I turned my head and the outline of a large vehicle appeared, lights blazing as it came to a stop. It looked official, a Horch perhaps, imposing, the kind of automobile military brass used. The door opened on the driver's side and slammed shut. Someone else had arrived in the darkness. Not another one! His face was largely hidden by his hat and the collar of his coat. A tall figure in silhouette, his presence was rimmed by the car's headlights behind him.

The first name that came to me was Igor Fomichov. It had to be him.

Without a word, he lifted the two drunken hooligans holding down my arms by their necks, and smashed their heads together. Then he turned to the remaining one, the soldier called Nikita, and brought his fist down on his face, already bloodied from my knife. There was a crack as it landed; I couldn't discern whether it was his nose or jaw. Over Nikita's howl of pain, my Good Samaritan then turned to me and asked in Russian if I was all right. Though pain was blasting through my cheekbone where Nikita's fist had landed, I said I was fine.

He pulled me to my feet. "Go home. Right now. You shouldn't be out alone."

I still couldn't see his face.

"Go!" he repeated. "I'll cover you."

Humiliated and trembling with shock, I murmured my thanks through grateful tears. I pulled up my torn underwear. One of Luba's earrings had been ripped from my ear, and I felt a sticky trickle of blood on my neck. There was a rip in Elena's dress and the heel of one of Frau Schuman's shoes had come loose. I managed to find my handbag, pulled myself together, and hobbled home, leaving my savior to deal with the assailants.

I was a sight as I leaned into the door of the apartment: my hair was a mess, my make-up smeared; my cheek beginning to swell. My ear was painful and still bleeding. I couldn't bear to face Elena and my landlady in the damaged dress and shoes; or telling Luba I'd lost an earring.

In the living room, Frau Schuman and the girls were doing needlework, sipping chamomile, and calmly listening to American jazz on her radio. I stepped inside, shaking and crying all at once. Galina saw me first; she jumped up from her chair and took me in her arms.

"Kira! Darling, what happened? Are you okay? Are you hurt?"

The others also sprang to their feet and fussed over me as I collapsed into a chair.

Luba put a glass of boiling hot tea in my hand, waving away my apologies over the earring. Elena covered my shoulders with a warm woolen shawl. I was feeling disoriented, and a blurred kaleidoscope of images rapidly shuffled together. Irrationally, thoughts of my family ran through my head. I whispered to my mother, my father. My hands shook as I gripped the hot tea and my teeth chattered against the glass. I conjured visions of my brother Yuri; Maxim, and our son. The bleeding from my ear lobe reminded me of Rufina, her blood spewing from the bullet hole in her forehead. Vaguely, I was aware that I was hallucinating. With the equanimity of a fire-eater, I gulped down the tea, allowing its heat to scald my mouth and inner core as it flowed through me.

"She's in shock," announced Frau Schuman. "I've seen this before." She removed my shoes and discreetly examined the loose heel of her sandal.

I began to sob then, and the girls hovered over me like mothering wrens, soothing me and offering comfort.

"We must notify the police at once," declared Luba.

Frau Schuman just looked at her with withering scorn.

CHAPTER 18

I stopped shaking, and gradually I calmed down.

"So," said our landlady, "even Russian girls are not safe from beasts on the street. Those pigs! Where did your army find such louts? Were they raised by wolves?"

Frau Schuman shook her head as she took a deep breath. "In '45 they raped any woman who had a pulse. And for all I know, some who had none."

She took my glass and topped it up. "When your Russian tanks rolled in, it was chaos. Men everywhere, over a million of them, wandering the streets looking for women, alcohol, and food—in that order. Looting stores and homes. They were wild with victory, yelling and grabbing whatever they could."

Steffi Bauer's brief narrative notwithstanding, none of us had heard a first hand account of how it had been for German women when our troops arrived. The few of us who were here then had been in denial; selective about what stories we chose to believe. It was hard to accept that the brave men who'd fought to save us from the Nazi fascists were capable of such appalling herd behavior. They could have been our fiancés or brothers . . . our fathers.

"Some of them barged in here," our landlady went on. "The barracks they'd been assigned were overflowing and they had no place to camp. All my female relatives had been bombed out and took refuge in my apartment. Your troops forced their way in and had their way with us—me, my sisters and nieces. Over and over. Rough, dirty, disgusting soldiers. Then a bunch of them decided they liked my place. They moved in; squatted here.

"They had no manners; no scruples; no cultural refinement. They turned my home into a pigsty, a bordello, dragging women and girls in here off the street —screaming, terrified girls. I could do nothing to help them. The pigs told their friends and more men came . . . so many. A nightmare. We were raped repeatedly. Every day. Every night."

She was getting angrier and tears were spilling from her eyes. "Your Mongolian peasants were the worst. They didn't know how to flush a toilet. Or even what a toilet was for. They wanted to use it to cool wine. They would shit on the floor. Pee against the walls. Disgusting. Some of them rode horses, and they would traipse horse manure into my apartment on their boots. It would end up in our beds. The stench! Like a barn. A lot of soldiers had the clap, and some of those poor girls got diseased or pregnant. Or both. Brutal animals," she spat. "It took me months to clean away their dirt and stink after they left."

She had been bottling up her rage and hate, and now it flowed like an unstoppable rush of toxic lava.

Galina closed her eyes. I knew she could justifiably list crimes the Nazi troops had perpetuated on Russians in general, and her Russian Jewish family and friends in particular. But even for Galina, this was a horror story and she remained quiet. I could picture it happening.

"Women are always spoils of war," Luba said. "It's just the way it is."

"Yes," added Elena lamely. "Your troops treated our women the same way."

Galina made no attempt to defend the indefensible. "How did you get rid of them?" she asked dully.

"It went on for eight or nine weeks," Frau Schuman said, "until they called the savages home to Russia. But some of those apes are still here, as Captain Voronova found out this evening."

She continued on, citing horror stories. Not things I wanted to hear after my own ordeal. The girls were quiet after that. We all knew it was true—not only in Berlin, but all over Germany. And not just Russian troops. I'd heard about atrocities on German women by the French, the British, and the Americans, but not on such a large scale, or in such detail. Our victorious Red Army troops had been like voracious locusts descending on a corn field.

"At least those early ones brought food," she said finally. "They knew we were hungry. They wanted us to be grateful to them, so they were looting grocery stores —stepping over bodies of people who'd worked there. The first days, they stopped at the bakeries and grabbed all the bread to bring along. Even pastries."

Putting aside her anger, she savored that memory. "We ate well then."

"What was your role in the bordello, Frau Schuman?" Luba asked, her impudence returning. Though our landlady was sharing her traumatic experience with them, my roommates couldn't forget she was German.

"I wasn't the madam, if that's what you're implying. I was assaulted like all the others. I'm saying we ate well while they were here. That's all. They looted wherever they could. We made the best of a bad situation. Anything to stay alive."

"So, you cooperated?" probed Elena.

A naïve question. We all knew that faced with a similar situation, our self-preservation instincts would have kicked in, exactly the same way. There was nothing a woman could do to stave off a bunch of wild, sex-starved armed soldiers. Steffi Bauman said they shot her grandmother for resisting.

Frau Schuman was fuming as she turned on Elena. "You're not listening! Your side won the war. Death and destruction were all around us. Our men weren't here to protect us; they were dead, or still rotting in your prison camps. We were starving; in a terrible way!"

Her voice rose with outrage at our lack of sympathy. "Those men—*ja*, they were assholes—but they were a source of supplies: they brought flour, coal, candles, liquor, cigarettes—whatever they could steal. Who are *you* to judge me for making use of what they gave us? You weren't here. You don't know what we had to put up with. The price we women were paying. You dare to suggest we spread our legs for them *willingly*?"

"Well, I'm thinking about the siege of Leningrad by your Nazi troops," countered Elena. "You say you endured it for two months? That went on in Leningrad for twenty-nine months, during the fiercest winter on record, with people scrounging for food ... the siege took the lives of one and a half million people, 800,000 of them civilians!"

Elena's reference to the siege put me in mind of the letter I wrote to Rufina's parents, informing them of her death. It had come back from Leningrad stamped "deceased." Rufina's nightmares had come to pass.

Frau Schuman wasn't going to be silenced by Elena. She had no interest in a suffering Leningrad, only what Berlin had gone through. Her own ordeal.

"They looted the liquor stores and got drunk," she continued. "Then they were insatiable, with no respect for our bodies." Fresh tears stole down her cheeks as each painful memory intruded, some so awful she chose not to share them.

She admitted that she lost no time in figuring out the best strategy for a pretty German woman: find a strong man, an officer with authority, and hook up with him for protection. Frau Schuman had certainly hit the jackpot—a Russian general, no less—to take care of her.

"*Danke Gott*, I met Oleg," she said. "He was from Leningrad, a general. Well-educated. Cultured. I...loved him. He made them clean up and sent them packing. He and I were together for eight months. Then he too was called back to Russia."

Hands shaking, she wiped her eyes and turning her attention to me, smoothed my hair. She saw me as a fellow victim.

"How many of them were there tonight?"

"Four," I said through my chattering teeth. "Then, one of them left, but the others ... they didn't succeed. A man stopped to help. A Russian. He pulled them off me."

Frau Schuman nodded. "You were lucky. If you'd been a German woman, he would've gotten in line with the rest."

Lucky? Luck was relative. *Povezlo* may have been my nickname at Engels, but after tonight, I felt it was a misnomer. I'd been a strong leader, survived the war, won all those medals, only to be attacked by Russian men— my own countrymen—in peacetime. In the end, I was just another helpless woman unable to defend herself, and that label frustrated me. The *only* lucky thing that evening was my Good Samaritan showing up when he did.

But was it luck? Who was he? I thought of Angela's whisper: *You are being watched.* It crossed my mind that Petrov assigned someone to follow me. I'd thought of being watched as a negative thing; now I saw it as protection.

"You're going to have a black eye," announced Frau Schuman as she put a cold compress on my eye and cheek. "But that's better than getting the clap or having a Russian brat to get rid of, like I did."

"You got pregnant?" asked Luba.

"I guess the last thing you wanted was a Russian baby," said Galina.

"The last thing I wanted was *any* baby," was the gnädige frau's retort.

She turned her back on them, focusing on me. "Your ear lobe will heal up. At least they didn't break your teeth. You're still pretty. Come, I'll boil water for a hot bath."

A *hot* bath? It was a special occasion.

I eased myself into the water. Aching from bruises, my stinging knees raw and bleeding, I began to cry again, sobbing into a towel Frau Schuman handed me.

"I almost forgot." she said in a soothing tone. "Someone called you. A man speaking German."

"Did he leave his name?"

"Yes. Moran. Victor Moran."

My heart started with excitement. "Oh! Did he leave his number?"

"No, I asked him for it, but he said he couldn't be

reached and hung up. He'll call again, he said."

CHAPTER 19

After a few days, I'd more or less recovered from my trauma. Some might have taken longer to get over such an attack, but the war had toughened me. Like a drumbeat in my head was the mantra that no matter what fate sent my way, at least I had survived. It was time to move on.

I *was* lucky after all. Someone had come along to help and I was at least spared the horrors of a gang rape. The experience taught me two valuable lessons: never go out alone at night in Berlin, and never leave the house without a pistol.

It was, in the end, a reality check. The soldiers' behavior brought me down to earth, reminding me of gender inequality.

Engels, 1943

In the army, I'd fought with the valor of a man, but was not treated like one. I never would be. A lasting lesson driven home to me by a Russian officer at Engels, Major Anatoly Sinyakov.

As night bombers in active service in the Crimea, we lived in constant gut-piercing fear. Our schedules were grueling. Only heavy fog would ground us. We flew multiple sorties every night in biting, freezing weather. With each sortie we knew we might not get through the night alive. The rigors of training, the terrible hours, cold, fatigue, stress, and lack of good food were to take their toll. They wore me down and finally brought me to my knees.

At my friend Zinaida's nagging, I consulted Dr. Kamaneva, the doctor at our base.

"I wish I had some penicillin, or that new miracle drug, streptomycin, for you," she said. "I only have aspirin to bring down the fever." She rummaged through a cupboard and handed me a vial of pills. "Hot tea, soup. Lots of fluids. Stay warm. And rest whenever you can."

I would have laughed had I been feeling better. There was no way to stay warm flying a PO-2 at night; no place to pee on the plane if I was drinking a lot of fluids. And rest? To coddle myself meant shifting the burden of my missions to other pilots, so I continued to work through the chills and bone-rattling malaise until I was sent to an army field hospital, where I was told I had double pneumonia.

My commanding officer forbade me to participate in any more missions until further notice. Then, to my dismay, I was ordered home to Moscow to rest up. Not a recommendation, it was an order; one I had no choice but to obey. Resigned, I began to pack.

As I was about to leave for the train station, a letter from Maxim changed my recalcitrance to joy.

"Maxim will be in Moscow, too!" I told Zinaida as I read it.

Zinaida was still the only soul to whom I'd confided that Maxim and I had eloped before he left for the front.

"He says he'll be there the week after next on a special assignment, as personal pilot to a high-ranking Party member. He'll arrive a week after I do."

"Oh, Kira. That's fantastic news." She squeezed my

hand. "It'll be like a honeymoon!"

There was no better remedy for my exhaustion. Although we'd been lovers for a while, Maxim and I had never spent a whole night together. Sick as I was, I was ecstatic at the prospect of flying into my secret husband's arms.

"We'll be together as much as we can. I'm going to tell my parents that we're married. It's time."

"It's great that you've found someone you care for, Kira. I'm anxious to meet this handsome Maxim of yours."

"You will, Zinaida. Soon. Hopefully, soon."

Luba came running in when she heard the news.

"You're in luck, Kira! I just refueled a plane being repositioned. A Major Anatoly Sinyakov and his junior officer are to leave shortly for Moscow. Ask the major to let you fly with them. You'll be home by the end of the day."

Recalling the terrible nine-day train trip getting to Engels from Moscow, I dashed over to the waiting Il-2 and introduced myself. A young man was checking controls in preparation for take-off. He identified himself as Corporal Roman Ageikin.

"You want Major Sinyakov to take *you* on this plane?" he scoffed. "Do you know him?"

I shook my head. I did not.

"The major doesn't approve of women in combat. Says they get in the way. That women should be home raising kids. And he thinks it's unlucky to allow a woman on his plane."

Anger flushed from the tip of my spine to the roots of

my hair. "But I have orders! A doctor's orders. I need to get to Moscow in a hurry. If I take the train, it could take days."

"Hey, I'm not sayin' he's right," Corporal Ageikin said, wiping his hands on a rag. "But most of the men—most Russian *people*—feel the same." He began to clean the window on the pilot's side. "I know, I know, you're a decorated Night Witch and all that, and you're doin' somethin' important, but that's the way it is."

He turned to face me, his expression one of sympathy.

"Y'know, when my sister joined the army as a nurse at the front, her fiancé broke off with her. His mother said his sisters would never find husbands because of her disgrace."

"That's crazy," I said. It was the first time I'd heard such nonsense, but not to be the last. "Why? That's the most..."

"Listen Captain," he cut me off as he cleaned the back windows. "I know what the major will say. He won't take you. He outranks you, so it's his prerogative."

Major Sinyakov arrived, an imposing figure in his early forties with a bushy mustache like Stalin's, obviously in a hurry. I quickly explained my predicament.

He tossed his duffel bag into the storage area of the plane and with a wave of his hand, dismissed me like a pesky fly. "We're already full," he said. "Besides, women bring bad luck."

Roman Ageikin shot me an "I told you so" smile.

I couldn't believe it. Did male pilots believe we'd conjure some kind of spell on their planes? I stared at him. "Major, I have pneumonia and have been ordered home to Moscow. The way the military sidelines train cars for troop transport, if I take the train, it could take nine or ten days. On your plane, I could be home at the end of the day. Surely, you wouldn't deny me passage to Moscow when I'm so ill?"

"I told you. We're already full," he retorted as he got into the pilot's seat of his near-empty plane. "And if you're sick, all the more reason. We don't want to catch whatever you've got." With that, he put on his earphones to shut me out.

"I thought we were fighting the same war," I snapped.

He removed his earphones. "What did you say, Comrade?" he snarled.

Standing behind me, Roman Ageikin muttered in my ear, "Be quiet, Captain. Salute him."

Seething with fury, I was about to sass him again, but Ageikin's warning triggered a mental picture of Elena suffering in the guardhouse.

"What did you say?" Sinyakov repeated, louder this time.

I raised my hand in a weak salute and calling up to him in the cockpit, I said, "I serve the Soviet Union. Sir."

With that, I turned on my heel, eyes blazing, and stomped away.

Unlike the train to Engels from Moscow, packed with other girls singing and playing cards and laughing, this time I was traveling alone, without cheerful sociability and brouhaha. Physically, I was feverish and listless, miserable, cold, and unable to focus on the gray, dreary countryside we passed through. I even lacked the focus to read. I shifted uncomfortably in my oversized boots and clothing, ran my hand through my shorn hair, and lapsed into brooding at the unfairness of my situation.

As I dozed off and on, sitting upright on the hard wooden seat of the train, the long trip, lack of decent food, and boredom added to my despair. The windows were coated with frost and coal dust. Nights were long, and the lights and heat in the coach were erratic. Several times we were sidetracked to allow troop trains access, adding to our travel time as we waited for other trains. Fear of being strafed by German bombers was a constant, and every time a plane flew overhead I clenched my teeth and planned how I would dive for cover.

Inwardly, I could only rage against Major Sinyakov. For a brief time, I shared a bench with a soldier named Leonid who, it turned out, was under his command.

"I know Major Sinyakov well," said the young man cheerfully. "He's a mean son of a bitch. You don't want to cross him."

I nodded with a sigh. Thank goodness I'd never have anything to do with him again. Or so I thought.

CHAPTER 20

Berlin, 1947

"**M**y God, what happened to you?" Angela said when she saw my black eye. As promised, she was waiting outside Brandenburg Gate.

"Four men jumped me after the Belenko party. Russian soldiers."

"Bloody hell! Did they rape you?"

"No. I got away."

I waved away her concern. I didn't want to relive the painful memory of it.

Today, determined to put my recent night of terror behind me and brave any army of men, I wore my uniform, medals in full view. I had my overnight bag in hand and my pistol was within easy reach in my large army-issue handbag.

Entering West Berlin required no passes at that time. There were guards, but they didn't have much to do. Thousands of East Berliners worked in the Western zones every day. No frisking, no hassles. There was talk in my office predicting things would not remain so lax. Too many young engineers, health care workers, teachers, and technicians—people needed to rebuild the East—were leaving in the morning and not returning. The idea of a wall to demarcate the East from the Western occupied zones in Berlin sometimes came up, but was usually dismissed as impractical.

Angela's apartment was in the block of the American sector bordering the British, an easy walk that took us through part of the Tiergarten. Berlin's largest park patiently awaited the renaissance of its scorched trees, and here and there the shrubbery was showing faint signs of hope.

Her place was a tiny third floor studio apartment featuring a kitchenette, and a bathroom with shower, so small you could hardly turn around in it—private living quarters carved out of a large, older home, perhaps for a servant. Devoid of clutter, it was decorated with feminine touches like a crocheted rose-colored afghan, museum posters of Degas ballerinas, and framed photos of family. An enlarged picture of a pretty, smiling girl vaguely resembling Angela, stood out from the others. Angela had already organized our English course material on her kitchen table.

Over a welcoming cup of coffee, real PX coffee, we went over a few city maps and she gave me a guide the U.S. Army provided their personnel; invaluable in helping me find my way around. There were so many things about West Berlin I was ignorant of. It was like being in a different country.

Finally, I asked her what was on my mind.

"Um, Angela, that U.S. officer we spoke of at the party— you said you knew him. Vick Moran?"

"Yes?" She was smiling. "What about him?"

"I uh, I wondered if you'd seen him lately."

"No. Not for a couple of weeks. He may be away. He's a busy bloke. What's your interest in him?"

"None, really," I shrugged, regretting my question. "It's . . . he's the only person I know on this side. I might have told you, we met in London. I just thought . . ."

"He's handsome, isn't he?" She was still smiling. I

hoped she had no personal interest in him.

"Is he?" I was backpedaling. "I wouldn't know. He was wearing an eye patch when I met him."

"He's good-looking, in an American sort of way. He certainly has no trouble attracting girls." She paused. I didn't follow up this comment with one of my own, so she began our lesson.

As expected, the early lessons were boring. I had read dry, esoteric engineering manuals in advanced English; now I had to act unaccustomed to the Roman alphabet. To validate my charade, I made a show of struggling to learn my ABCs like any toddler.

Expressing myself in English was quite another matter. As Angela pointed out, while English grammar is relatively simple, for foreigners the pronunciation is not. My struggle with that was genuine, something I knew I could only improve by practicing with English speakers. Angela kept her corrections to a minimum so as not to intimidate me. She taught me the basics about names for family members and relationships. She familiarized me with simple forms for several common verbs. And to encourage conversation, she asked me questions about various things like my work and my family.

"Were you an only child?" she asked in Russian.

"No. I had a brother."

She asked me the same question in English, taught me how to answer, then switched back to Russian. "Tell me about your brother. Does he fly, too?"

I wasn't expecting to talk about Yuri. I caught my breath. "No," I said. Her question set in motion a whole new range of memories.

It was still difficult to talk about Yuri—in any language. I'd worried about my brother day and night while he was in basic training. He was only seventeen. I wrote to him often, whenever I wrote to Maxim. Letters from both were sporadic, reporting old news by the time they arrived, always careful not to give away their location. Sometimes several would come at once.

Mail from servicemen—reassuring hen-scratchings scribbled in a hurry to assure families they were safe— might be read quite a while after the authors had been killed, often reaching their family's hands well after the tragic telegrams from the Department of War. Mama had no illusions about their veracity. I often found her in the kitchen crying quietly over a letter from my brother.

When Yuri was sent to Stalingrad, another city on the bank of the Volga River, we were all vastly relieved. Stalingrad was considered safer than areas near Moscow or Leningrad. He would be one of the lucky ones. We thought.

Convinced that Yuri was relatively secure there, I found the courage to tell my parents that I too had signed up and would soon be leaving. But I lacked the moral steel to tell them I'd eloped with Maxim, my flying instructor.

"Stalingrad?" exclaimed Angela, breaking into my narrative. "Safe?"

"Yes. That's what we thought."

"The bloodiest battle on the Eastern front?"

"The bloodiest in the history of warfare, as it turns out."

"Unbelievable, the carnage. . ."

"At one point, the life expectancy of a Russian soldier in Stalingrad was only one day. We lost so many."

"German soldiers fared even worse!" she exclaimed.

"A disaster for both sides," I agreed. "Two million total casualties."

"Yes. And your brother?"

"Yuri was killed," I said, my voice struggling with emotion.

"I'm so sorry, Kira."

"It was supposed to be safe. The city wasn't strategically important. Sending in the 6th Army was one of Hitler's more erratic decisions. Some thought he attacked it for its propaganda value—the city was named to honor Stalin."

"Hardly a valid reason!"

We were quiet for a bit. Then Angela said, "With half a million German soldiers wiped out in one battle, it's small wonder there's such a shortage of men here. War screws up the normal ratios of a population."

True, I thought, remembering Steffi Bauman's remonstration in the store. And all the desperate women in Berlin doing what they had to do to survive. To feed their children and care for aging parents.

"Yes," I said. "And the numbers in this war have been staggering. It was common hearsay that for Stalin, 'a single death is a tragedy. A million deaths, a statistic.' "

The quote defined our glorious leader's thinking, but I still wasn't sure where I stood with Angela, so I said nothing more. We might eventually become friends, but as Petrov said, friendships were not always to be trusted.

Angela shook her head sadly. "The war must have been hard on your parents."

"Yes. They suffered listening to radio reports. By then, I regretted signing up, but it was too late. The Army owned me."

I thought back to everyday life during that awful period. Göring's Luftwaffe bombings of granaries in our cities and crops in the fields left us with serious food shortages; shelves were emptying, queues for food were forming, and we were put on strict rations. Still, the battle for Stalingrad raged on for six months. Fortunately, Hitler could not supply his ground forces there by air indefinitely.

"At least the Russian victory in Stalingrad marked the turning point of the war on the Eastern Front," remarked Angela.

"Yes, there was that."

A small consolation. I was not home with my parents when the official letter came. My beloved, sweet brother Yuri had been reduced—in Stalin's words—to a statistic.

"I know how it feels to lose a sibling," murmured Angela.

I waited for her to explain. But she quickly switched off. Reaching for the pitcher of water she'd supplied, she refilled our glasses as we took a brief break in silence. Then she rustled about, sharpening pencils, and positioned them by our places.

"Shall we go on to the next lesson?" she inquired as she opened a book.

I nodded. It was time to turn the page, move ahead. To

stop dwelling on the past. And to learn English.

CHAPTER 21

A ngela thrived on getting out and partying. Caught up in the convivial scene of the American Zone, she loved places where she could dance to popular music of the day. Though we were the same age, I had trouble keeping up with her.

My colloquial English was improving and I was steadily building a vocabulary geared to social situations. Angela offered encouragement, marveling how fast I was learning.

"My English student, Kira Voronova," she'd say with pride as she introduced me to people. "You wouldn't believe how smart she is. A few months ago, she didn't know a word of English!"

Still living my white lie, I would blush with embarrassment at her praise.

By the time spring melded into summer, we'd become friends. Yet, I still found her to be an enigma. She was a party girl, yes; but sometimes she would have a look of extreme sadness, and oftentimes she lapsed into silence. At the clubs we went to, she appeared to be seeking something or someone, but I never felt quite close enough to her to ask why she seemed depressed. In my search for Vick Moran, I was sometimes in the same kind of mood, scanning every place we went, always without success.

Angela's moodiness didn't slow her down. She was eager to check out new dance halls and night clubs. By mid May, a big one with a New Orleans theme opened its doors. It was on the Spree River in a converted brick warehouse.

"*The Marching Saints,* it's called," said Angela. "Dixie-land-style jazz, performed in a crude jerry-built structure."

There were many such empty buildings put up by the Nazis for arms storage. Before the Americans arrived in July, 1945, our Russian troops would already have cleared out the weaponry and shipped it to the U.S.S.R. Anything of value became part of our "Strip it and ship it" program. Looting on a gargantuan scale. We had dismantled entire factories and sent them by rail to Russia.

"Now it's owned by a Czech with British citizenship. An enterprising bloke—financed it by selling shares to American G.I.s. Those soldiers in the Bizone don't know what to do with all the money they rake in."

The unprepossessing industrial exterior of The Marching Saints belied the amount of space inside. The interior was vast and barn-like, sparsely furnished with battered chairs and scarred tables salvaged from war debris. It was reasonably clean, if a bit dingy, and the music was new to me, featuring as it did a lively quintet of drums, trumpet, a sax, bass, and a trombone. Even the musicians, with their various shades of dusky complexions, seemed exotic.

"Isn't this fun?" said Angela. She was in a happy mood.

I nodded. It was a good place to seek out Vick Moran, who'd apparently disappeared—no sighting of him since I'd begun coming to the Bizone. The place was noisy and smoky, filled with military men looking for a good time, and plenty of girls ready to accommodate them. While women did outnumber men in the city overall, such was not the case in this corner of Berlin catering to American G.I.s.

"Find some soldier to buy you dinner," Angela suggested. "I hear they have good bratwurst and sauerkraut; order it with *Kartoffle Salat*, that lovely German potato salad. And one of those hot white radishes. Or go American and get a burger and coleslaw."

I wasn't sure what burgers were. Watching food being served with heavy German ale in mismatched chipped steins, I was tempted. I hadn't eaten since lunch-time; a bratwurst might go down well.

"I doubt if this jazz group will play all night," she said. "If it's like the other clubs, they'll take a break and let the long-haired musicians have a go."

This meant an alternate group made up of unemployed classically trained Europeans would play slower numbers at intervals. Mostly dance tunes by Duke Ellington, Harry James, and Glenn Miller. A lot of Glenn Miller.

Angela was about to say more when an American soldier led her away to the dance floor. She waved to me before getting lost in the throng, and I waved back. Wandering over to the bar, I wriggled up on a stool.

"*Bon soir Mademoiselle*," said a voice behind me. I looked into the flirtatious brown eyes of a man I hadn't seen at clubs before. He was great-looking, medium height, with good strong features and auburn hair. His uniform had the French tricolor sewed to his sleeve.

"*Bon soir*," I replied.

"*Vous me permettez?*" Without waiting for me to nod my assent, he sat down on the barstool next to me.

When I indicated that I didn't speak his language, he

switched to broken English, and introduced himself as Marcel Levy. He offered me a cigarette—a Gitane—and I noted how stained his fingers were from nicotine. I passed on the Gitane.

"Where are you from?" I asked.

"Paris." He drew on his cigarette. "In Le Marais. The 4th *arrondissement*."

Levy asked me my name, why I was in the American Sector, and what kind of work I did.

"I stamp job applications all day," I said, hoping he'd find that too boring to pursue.

Instead, he raised his eyebrows in surprised interest.

"That's intriguing."

"No. It's actually very dull work."

"You must come across the names of many Nazi applicants."

"Well, they write Communist on their Fragenbogen."

He smiled. "We both know better."

"Of course. Yes, they're mostly Nazis."

Something told me I'd said too much. His face was alive with interest.

"I imagine you'd have access to a lot of their files."

This was beyond casual conversation. He was prying and I felt uneasy.

We briefly carried on a cat-and-mouse talk about Nazis. He kept bringing up depressing atrocities of the past, ghosts I wanted to forget. When I changed the subject, Levy referred back to my work. I clammed up.

"Listen," he finally said, "I know people who'd welcome information you have. They'd be willing to pay . . ."

"That's confidential information," I snapped. I turned away, feigning interest in the music. My eyes scanned the room for anyone watching me.

After a couple more attempts, he handed me a card. "In case you ever want to talk about it."

I put the card in my purse before excusing myself. "I'll think about it," I said.

I strolled away, aimlessly making my way through the crowd past the dance floor to get away from him. It was almost funny. I'd always claimed my job was so menial I had no information to sell. But in these times, every scrap of Intelligence had value to someone.

As I perused the animated space, the British and Americans dancing and enjoying themselves, I sensed a relaxed breeziness. Something I found enviable.

These Westerners had been raised feeling free, and took that freedom for granted.

They'd never watched friends or relatives shipped to a gulag for some imagined infraction; never stood by helplessly while people close to them were ordered to stand before a show trial or a firing squad; never known the tortures of the NKVD. And they didn't feel the need to speak in whispers for fear of secret police listening.

Had I ever been carefree like them? Perhaps. A long time ago, before my father's arrest. That single invasion of our home had destroyed my innocence and shaken my beliefs.

It was a warm, steamy evening in the dimly lit space. Candles stuck in cheap wine bottles on tables and along walls supplemented the feeble electric lighting. My eyes were stinging from the cigarette smoke that fogged the room. I felt very alone for a few moments, but it didn't take long for me to be discovered. Before I knew it, several men were asking me to dance. Amid the dazzle of congeniality around me, I thought I saw Inna Gradska, all dressed up and nicely coiffed, leaving on the arm of a British officer. Could it be her? I remembered her speaking English at Belenkos' party. What was she doing in the West? I tried to catch her eye, but either she hadn't caught sight of me or didn't want me to see her. She quickly disappeared.

I ordered another drink and wandered around the crowded room, keeping my eyes peeled for Vick Moran. So far, my quarry still eluded me. I'd been unable to deliver on my assignment.

If Petrov and his cronies gave up on me they might take matters into their own hands. A disaster from my point of view. Not only would I lose my weekend privileges, I might be punished for my failure. And I could say goodbye to the instructor's job.

Past the bar in the semi-darkness, at the far end of the room, a U.S. major was talking to other officers at his table. Moran! Elated to have found him at last, I rushed over as fast as I could move in Angela's high heels. Reaching out, I touched his shoulder.

"So this is where you've been hiding out," I said flirtatiously in my accented English.

Slowly, he turned to face me. "Hi," he drawled. "You lookin' for someone in particular? Or just lookin' for a good time?"

I gasped as I came face to face with a man I didn't know. My face reddened. "Oh. I thought you were someone else."

"Anyone I know?"

"Uh, Moran? Major Vick Moran."

"Don't know him," he said. "Buy you a drink?"

"I … I already have one. My mistake. I'm sorry."

He was on his feet. "I'm not. Would you like to dance? My name's Phil. Phil McKay."

It was the least I could do. I was feeling ridiculous. He didn't even resemble Moran up close. But it was easy to understand my mistake from a distance in the smoky room. Same shaped head, same coloring, same rank identification on his uniform.

I put down my drink. He led me to the floor, and we danced a couple of times, one fast and one slow. During the slow one, he held me too close and let his hand wander down my back almost to the base of my spine. I squirmed uncomfortably.

Finally, he guided me to his table, offered me a seat, and in front of his friends asked me, "So, babe, what do you charge?"

The heat rose from the depths of my chest and covered my face in a full blush. He'd taken me for a working girl. Or at least a hungry German girl. Just another Schatzie. Excusing myself, I immediately got up and made to return to the bar.

"I'll go as high as six cigarettes," he called out as I strode away from his table.

Without a word, I searched the room for Angela, feeling like a piece of meat with a price propped in front of me. I made a mental note to ask her for some good snappy English responses for such situations.

"So, what did you think?" asked Angela later as she

held a pillow under her chin to slip it into a pillowcase for the guest couch. "Did you have fun? I saw you on the dance floor."

"Yes," I replied, straightening the sheets. "Though without much English, it felt a bit like I was on the outside looking in. And my dancing is awful."

Angela nodded. "Well, you're bound to feel that way at first. But we'll get you speaking good English soon enough. Don't worry about the steps. We can practice here together."

"I did dance a couple of times," I admitted. "Badly. Once with a rather rude American officer who propositioned me."

"Yes, you have to expect that. Most of them are good chaps, though."

"I also met a Frenchman, a Marcel Levy. We had a drink together."

"Oh, I know him. He's a suspicious character. Military. He's here in advance of opening up the French Zone next year. Always hanging around, asking questions, listening to people's conversations. He has to be a spy. Jewish, I'm guessing. Probably something to do with Palestine. I'd stay away from him."

She didn't say for whom he might be spying. But Levy had shown far too much interest in what I did at the Kommandatura. I thought of his offer to pay for information. Spying had become a cottage industry, with as many spies in Berlin as there were people being spied on.

"Then I danced with a couple of British fellows," I said. "A man named Derek Price. And another one, Liam Flanigan."

"Both disreputable," she said dismissively, heading to the kitchen sink to brush her teeth. "Derek Price? He's involved in running prostitutes. Scum. Flanigan? A trouble-maker. He's not even English. He's part of that rag-tag Irish group, the IRA. Believe me, you can do better. I'll introduce you to some real charmers." This was delivered with a mischievous wink.

"Of course, I don't know Petrov's plans," Angela added, waving her toothbrush. "If all he wants you to do is mix with people from the occupied zones and learn English, I guess it doesn't matter who you dance with. Enjoy yourself."

It seemed like an invitation to leak information despite her earlier protest that my assignment didn't interest her, but I said nothing.

Perhaps because I hadn't been able to find him, the anticipation of confronting Vick Moran was building. No closer to spotting him, I speculated how long Petrov would wait for a report.

That night I had trouble sleeping. The stimulation, the men I'd met, the music at the smoky dance hall, and memories of the past were all skittering around my mind.

I thought of how cheap the American major, Phil McKay, had made me feel. Well, what did I expect? Going out every night, hanging around bars seeking out a man. Even if it was a particular man. Recalling McKay's offer, I found myself blushing. So this was how the Schatzies felt. I was only worth six cigarettes. Not even half a pack.

CHAPTER 22

Berlin, June,1947

A couple of weeks later, while I was getting some shoes re-soled at a cobbler's near Alexanderplatz, I saw Beatrix Belenko emerging from a newly opened shop that carried children's clothing. The weather had turned cool for early June, and she was sheathed in a tailored amethyst-colored tweed suit, standing out like a glittering geode against the gray, fragmented city. Her golden blonde hair was freshly coiffed and her nails perfectly manicured. With her dazzling smile, smart clothes, and a Russian sable stole, she might have been on a fashionable avenue in Paris or New York.

"Captain! Captain Voronova," she called. "What a surprise. Lovely to see you!"

"Frau Belenko," I replied.

"Oh, please, do call me Beatrix."

"Kira," I responded to invite reciprocity.

She was holding her son by the hand while her daughter helped carry their lighter packages. "I was about to take the children for Himbeersaft, that raspberry drink they're so fond of, at the new Konditorei around the corner." She turned to her children. "Liesel, Achim, this is Captain Voronova."

The Belenko children were sweet and well-mannered. Liesel acknowledged our introduction with a shy smile and slight bow of her head, while Achim held out his dimpled hand with an endearing grin. My heart leapt when I saw her son. This is what Pavel would be like now; no longer a toddler, but not yet ready for kindergarten. I could hardly take my eyes off her little boy. I wanted to bypass his proffered handshake and hug him. Hold him safe. Instead, I took his hand in mine and held it, reluctant to let it go.

"Would you care to join us, Kira? I'm having coffee. My treat."

Real coffee was expensive, as were pastry shops. I glanced at my wristwatch, which Angela had gotten me at the American PX. I had time before returning to my desk.

"That would be nice," I said. "Thank you."

As we walked to the Konditorei, Beatrix talked non-stop. "That rubble heap on the street near the corner? It used to be a cabaret featuring fabulous entertainers before the war. I once saw Josephine Baker perform there. A beautiful black American woman. She wore nothing but a belt of gilded bananas. A lovely voice, she had. Such a talent! Marlene Dietrich performed there too. A unique woman—a legend. I knew her."

From her vivid descriptions and name dropping, ghosts of the fun-loving Weimar Republic rose eerily from the cold grey ash.

"Two buildings down, there was a dress shop. Chez Gigi. She carried lovely silk lingerie from Paris. So soft, with such pretty lace. You'd have loved that store, Kira. And over there," she pointed at another pile of rubble and debris. "That was where I used to have my hair styled years ago. Fritz used to do it. Until they took him away. . ." Her voice faded.

I didn't ask what happened to Fritz.

Beatrix was a different creature, on a loftier plain than other women I knew who, like me, struggled to ration water to wash their hair once a week. The puff of a light breeze swirled the aromatic drift of her tangy French perfume in my direction. It was as close as I would ever come to inhaling it.

"As the wife of a General, I should feel safe in Berlin," she sighed, removing her fur stole as we sat down at a table inside the Konditorei. "But I don't. Being German complicates things. Our troops—we know what they did to the women here in 1945—when I'm on my own, they take me for a *Schatzie* bar girl. Whistling. Calling out."

I knew what she meant. And how she felt.

"Berlin certainly isn't where I want my children to grow up. Not now," she continued as we ordered our coffee and Himbeersaft. "But I worry about moving back to Russia, too. They despise Germans. And my children are half German."

"They're also half Russian."

"Yes. That will help, of course. But still... I'm not sure I . . ." She didn't finish her thought.

The Konditorei was scented with the nostalgic aromas of vanilla and cinnamon, chocolate, and coffee; heavenly. She took a sip of her *Kapuziner,* an Austrian version of cappuccino topped with plenty of cream, creating a white mustache I found endearing on such an exquisitely elegant face. Watching her children enjoy their Himbersaft, she lowered her voice:

"I love children. We had hoped to have a big family, Dmitri and I; we've been trying, but it hasn't worked out. And now, living in Germany, it's not the best place for a baby, anyway."

I was surprised that she shared such a confidence with

me.

Little Liesel reached for a serviette to wipe the cream from her mother's upper lip, and they both giggled as she planted a kiss on her daughter's cheek. I enjoyed watching Beatrix interact with Liesel and Achim. She was a good mother, loving and patient; never raising her voice. But I sensed that behind the face she presented to the public, her happy, optimistic smiles hid a great number of secret emotions. In this post-bellum horror, no one could be happy. The past was bitter. The present was ugly; and a better future too far off to console us.

"Kira, you're not quite as tall as I am, but you're about my size. Would you be offended if I offered you some clothes? You're young and single; you must need pretty things for socializing. I have so many outfits from before the war I barely have room to store them."

Offended? I'd been embarrassed having to borrow clothing for evenings out with Angela. And Beatrix had put it to me in such a charming way—as if I'd be doing her a favor taking things off her hands. So, no, I did not feel offended.

"Won't you need them yourself?"

She shook her head with a wistful sigh. "No. I go out so little now. The studio wanted me to look good while I was promoting my films, so, in those days I shopped on the Ku'damm; sometimes at the Ka-de-We on Wittenberg Platz, or at Wertheim over on Leipziger Platz. I loved clothes, and I often went on shopping sprees in Paris and London. Rome. Even Beverly Hills in America. I went to a lot of parties then."

I could visualize her stepping out of taxis or limos at

fine hotels, laden down with hat boxes and packages, enlisting the help of doormen or bellhops to carry them.

"The dresses may be a little *démodées*," she admitted. "Out of style. But most are classics you can up-date with the right accessories or by adjusting the hems. I see in fashion magazines that Dior is lowering hemlines this year. He calls it the 'New Look.'"

"I know a good seamstress," I replied, thinking of Frau Schuman.

She patted my hand. "Excellent. Come to my house to-morrow for lunch and slip them on."

That was how the next day, I found myself having lunch at the Belenko apartment with my new friend. She prepared us a simple omelet. Then, I gratefully tried on a dizzying number of dresses, suits, slacks, sports-wear, and silk blouses she'd laid out. As soon as I picked one dress up, she would reach into her closet and take out a smart hat to go with it. One after another, I slipped them on and off, appraising myself in her full-length mirror while she stood behind me. She either smiled or frowned, clucking approval or shaking her head.

Where fashion was concerned, I was a case of arrested development. I'd had no time or money for feminine things in Moscow, which were hard to come by in any case. The heady elated feelings surging through me as I tried on her apparel were like those of a teen-age girl awakening to the sparks of nascent feminine power. Some outfits, I sensed, were perfect. In them, I moved differently, swayed more seductively, carried myself with ease and comfort. Some things hugged my ample breasts, and I held myself in a posture that emphasized them. Although I wasn't up on style or who was who in the fashion world, I noted that most of her labels bore familiar French names. Even maternity clothes she'd placed in a separate pile to be donated to refugees bore what I assumed were designer labels.

"You wear clothes beautifully!" Beatrix cooed repeatedly. "Such a lovely figure you have. You should have been a model. So natural . . . You remind me of Ingrid Bergman. I knew her, you know. You look fantastic in that. Here, try this one." And she'd reach over for yet another outfit.

As an afterthought, she added some silky underwear, lacy and sexy, to the pile. Brassieres and panties, even sleepwear. They were still in their original packages.

"Oh, I couldn't. " I said, blushing. "I have no use for such . . ."

But she added them anyway. "You may have occasion to thank me for these," she said with a wink. "I was a lingerie model for a while and these were given to me as samples by the manufacturer. I never wore them. After I got pregnant, they were the wrong size."

I was learning that you couldn't argue with Beatrix. By the time I left her home, I was laden down with enough clothing to last me for years, and couldn't wait to show my haul to the girls. At last, I was in a position to lend clothes to them on evenings out, especially Elena, whose dress I had managed to ruin.

Thinking of Steffi Bauman's burgeoning belly, I asked Beatrix for the maternity clothes she'd put aside.

"Yes, please take them, if you know someone who can wear them. I don't think I'll be using them," she said regretfully. She added them to the pile.

Beatrix called me a taxi which she paid for, and gave

me a sisterly hug as she saw me out. "Thank you so much for helping me clear out my cupboards!" she exclaimed.

"I should be paying you something for all these beautiful things."

She merely scoffed. "Your friendship is payment enough."

That evening, I stopped for groceries on my way home. To my disappointment, there was no sign of Steffi Bauman, normally there around that time, so I left the maternity clothes with Trudi, the clerk who usually waited on me. She promised to make sure Steffi got them, along with a few select items of food that I paid for and left in an extra cloth bag I had.

A pregnancy was no time to be hungry.

CHAPTER 23

Moscow, 1943

After the ordeal of flying in the early months I was expecting Pavel, I knew what Steffi was going through.

During the war, when I was always hungry, food dominated my thoughts, especially when I was pregnant. On sorties, it took my mind off the stress of the moment to focus on good things to eat. We'd seek shelter from a snowfall in a sleeping bag under the wing of our Po-2s on a makeshift air base—usually a frozen cow pasture or wheat field.

While eating a supper of nearly frozen black bread with a scant slice of hard sausage, I'd picture myself dining in fine restaurants, sipping champagne with my fill of smoked salmon. When my stomach cried out for more food, thoughts of tasty meats and mouth-watering rich cheeses served with fragrant rye bread, fresh from the oven, crept into my mind. I was desperate for the texture and scent of ripe fruit and crisp green vegetables. And sweets—my favorite comfort food. My mind clutched memories of silky chocolate and my baba's Raspberry Cream Pudding. I imagined waking up to the smell of coffee—real coffee with rich cream, and of course sugar, perhaps with a warm croissant and Scottish marmalade.

I hadn't planned to start a family, of course. Not while there was a war going on around me. Pavel's conception occurred the time I was sent home ill with pneumonia from the front . . .

◆ ◆ ◆

My mother had warned me in a letter that my grandfather—yes, the grandfather we'd considered afflicted with some form of dementia—was now sharing a bed with our bodacious flat-mate, Nadia Harlamova, and was looking and acting twenty years younger.

I'd been shocked at first, but when I shared this news with Zinaida, we had a good laugh. Why not, if it rejuvenated him and made him happy? It was better than the couch.

When I finally arrived home from the front, sick with pneumonia, my parents were still at work. The apartment was quiet—until I heard someone giggle and the sounds of love-making from Nadia's bedroom.

Dedushka, I thought—*you old rascal!*

With so little privacy in living conditions in Moscow, the sounds of sex in progress were run-of-the-mill, something that called for theatrical throat clearing; a subtle message to the lovebirds to carry on undisturbed.

As sick as I was, I went into the kitchen to make tea and was pleasantly shocked to see a plethora of food items scattered on the kitchen table. Many of them were luxury foods I'd not seen since before the war. Putting them away on the bottom shelf of Nadia's side of the pantry was Dedushka, who peered up at me in surprise.

"Kira, sweetheart, oh my little *myah sladkaya!*" he said, struggling to straighten up and stand tall. "I didn't know you were coming home."

I was confused. "Dedushka!" I exclaimed as I helped him up and kissed him. "You're here in the kitchen. I thought you were in with Nadia?"

"Oh no, that's her lover, Vladimir Petrochenkaya."

"Vladimir *Nikolayevich* Petrochenkaya?"

While at the front, I'd been out of the loop, but I still recognized the name at once. He was none other than the Secretary of the District Communist Party. "The Secretary? He's Nadia's lover?"

"Oh, yes," said Dedushka. "Has been for years. He's the one who arranged to get your father out of prison. He did it for Nadia."

"Nadia?" I could feel my jaw drop. "She was responsible for getting Papa out of Lubyanka?"

"Yes. Just in time, too. Sergei was about to be shipped off to a work camp in Siberia. She loves our family. And Petrochenkaya is quite smitten with her. Has been for a long time. He also got her into this apartment. Nadia thinks he's Anton's father."

I blinked at this. Anton was now sixteen. "It's gone on that long?"

"Yes. He can't give her any money, but he has access to food and medicine. All this food he brings . . ." Here Dedushka lowered his voice. "Much more than we can eat. She sells some of it on the black market. Vodka, too; he keeps us well-supplied."

"Does he know that you and Nadia are . . . together?"

"Yes, he tells me to keep her bed warm for him. He doesn't think I can do much else." Dedushka winked wickedly at me. "He doesn't know!"

I was having trouble following the machinations of

this *ménage à trois* and wondered if my parents had any idea of what was going on virtually under their noses.

"What about his wife?" Photos of them as a couple had appeared in Pravda.

"I've never tried *her*."

"Dedushka!" I was blushing.

"His wife is all wrapped up in that sickly son of theirs. If she does know about Nadia, I doubt she'd say anything. She's intimidated by her husband."

The rutting and grunting sounds from Nadia's bedroom were getting louder and I was embarrassed. Despite my fever, I had to ask: "Shouldn't we go outside or something? Maybe go for a walk? What if he comes out of the bedroom?"

"No, no," said Dedushka as he turned back to putting the groceries away. "He's fine with it. I stay here until he leaves. It won't be long now. They've been in there quite a while."

About five minutes later, the bedroom door opened. Sounds of laughter from Nadia; a deep male voice blended with hers. A discussion about their next rendezvous then took place as he consulted a pocket diary. Intimate sounds followed, probably from quiet groping or fondling; another titter from Nadia. The outside door closed.

Nadia headed for the kitchen. "Oh, that man!" she moaned to no one in particular. "He wears me out. It's never enough for him."

She appeared in the kitchen and her eyes grew wide when she saw me standing there. "Kira!" she shrieked. "Oh, Kira, it's so good to see you!"

She took me into her arms and hugged me, almost lifting me off the floor.

"You feel so hot. Are you not well?"

"No," I said. I was feeling terrible and wanted to get to bed.

"Well, some good food will make you feel better."

She turned toward the panoply of food items spread out on the table. "Look at all the tasty things Vladimir brought me! He's a dear sweet man."

"He's certainly generous," Dedushka said, eyeing a jar of smoked herring.

The discovery that Nadia was Vladimir Petrochenkaya's mistress should have shocked me, and would have a short time before, but war and hunger do strange things to people, altering the way they think.

I lowered my voice to a whisper, ever mindful of someone listening.

"Dedushka tells me you were responsible for getting my father out of prison."

Nadia glared at Dedushka as she whispered back. "He wasn't supposed to tell anyone."

"So, when Papa arrived that night after dinner . . . the frying pan, the carving knife . . .?"

"That was such fun," she said with a grin. "You know how I like to tell fortunes. Vlad told me when your father was going to be released, so I kept reading the cards for your mother to lift her spirits—all good things she didn't believe. Like not to give up hope; that he would be released soon.

"After Vlad got him out of prison and he came home, she thought I had special powers to see the future. Now she thinks I'm a genius!"

I smiled as I recalled the charade with the cast iron pan when my father appeared at the door, the cheerful tarot card expectations Nadia had given my mother when Mama thought her world would collapse.

"My mother hasn't guessed it was you who got Papa released?"

"No. I didn't want your parents to know. I still don't. They'd probably want me to solicit Vlad's help in getting some of their friends out of prison, and I don't want to push him too far. It's better to keep these things quiet." She quoted a Hungarian proverb that said the fewer who know a secret, the better.

Nadia grinned at me. "Now, let's have some champagne to celebrate your arrival. Vlad brought some French Camembert cheese and British water crackers, good black country-style bread, even Spanish black olives!"

At that moment, I warmed to Nadia's heart of gold. The knowledge that she'd arranged my father's release from prison—saved his life—was enough to endear her to me forever. As for Dedushka . . . well, she had done wonders for him, too, the intimate details of which were complicated.

I was beginning to consider her an integral part of the family unit. Like an eccentric auntie, perhaps. I accepted the champagne and, virtually starving after my train trip from Engels, I put my weariness aside and dug into the black bread, the cheese, and the olives, without a thought to their source.

My hunger satisfied, my other basic human need surfaced: the urge to satisfy my longings for my beloved

Maxim at our imminent reunion. I needed to focus on getting well before he arrived.

CHAPTER 24

S teffi knew when I did my shopping. At the store, I always bought extra supplies of milk, tinned meat, fish, root vegetables, and bread rolls, and waited outside the entrance.

It had been a couple of weeks since our last shopping forays had coincided, and I'd begun to worry about her.

Finally, I saw her at the grocery store, wearing one of Beatrix's prettiest maternity dresses. She beamed when she saw me, and had her bag open even before I greeted her.

"Fraulein Voronova, I'm so glad to see you," she said, jiggling her baby. "I've been home sick and couldn't get over. My mother had to shop for me. Thank you so much for the clothes you dropped off. They're beautiful."

"I've told you that I'll help you whenever I can," I said, placing food items in her bag. Too hungry to wait politely till she got home, she crammed a chunk from one of the bread rolls into her mouth. After she swallowed, she said: "Yes, you have. But I didn't believe you. I don't trust . . . anybody."

She had been about to say Russians.

"How are you managing?" I asked.

Steffi took another bite and looked tentatively at me. She wanted to tell me something.

"What's wrong, Steffi?"

"Please say you won't be angry if I tell you something."

"I don't know how I'll feel until you tell me."

"It's something I did a couple of weeks ago. A silly thing."

I waited, and she continued, "I could be in trouble. I was out with some friends and there was a threat from an unexploded bomb. We all rushed to the nearest U-bahn station to take shelter."

I had an ominous feeling about what she would say next. "And? What happened?"

"There was a photo of your Stalin on the wall in the shelter."

"Yes, his posters are everywhere in the East. So what?"

"He has a dour, mean-looking mouth."

That was true enough. I thought the same thing each time I passed his towering image hanging near the ruins of the burnt-out Adlon Hotel on the way to Angela's apartment.

"One of my friends said she never saw photos of him looking happy. So, I took an eyebrow pencil from my purse and drew him a big smile."

I caught my breath. "Oh, Steffi. You didn't!"

"I did."

Her expression was so defiant that I would have burst out laughing had I not known the possible consequences of her vandalism. Any disrespect of Stalin was flirting with danger. I thought of the execution of Zinaida's father over a poem. Steffi's punishment could be equally draconian.

"Did anyone see you?"

Steffi shrugged. "Some people at the shelter."

"Any Russians?"

"I don't know. Someone passed around a bottle of vodka and it put me in a defiant mood. It was just for fun. Some of the people laughed."

I worried about those who had not.

In her innocence, Steffi was more concerned about what I would think of this silly peccadillo than of any possible punishment. In an ideal world, that's all it would be—a foolish prank meriting a reprimand—but not in a Communist state. The dark world I lived in took a dim view of such stunts. She had no idea.

"Steffi, listen to me. Avoid being seen around your neighborhood for a while. Especially if you see anyone who might be Russian."

Steffi scoffed as she patted her belly. "Your advice is a little late, isn't it? You think I don't steer clear of Russians? Believe me, I've become an expert at ducking them. Anyway, I have to go."

Then, with a tentative smile and a quick *"Danke,"* she took the groceries I'd given her and waving in my direction, disappeared into the evening.

Vodka? They weren't Germans.

CHAPTER 25

West Berlin, 1947

Angela and I had slipped into an easy relationship, reviewing words I'd already learned at each lesson in a relaxed, unstructured way. She took me with her to run errands; to shop at the PX. We went to private parties, or for coffee with friends. I was meeting English-speaking people everywhere we went. And English was coming fast and easily to me.

But my main purpose of going to the West continued to gnaw at me. Still no sign of the man Petrov wanted me to spy on. Vick Moran. Where the hell was he? The man was keeping a low profile. I asked about him whenever I met Americans, but few admitted they knew him. None of those who did had any idea of his whereabouts. At least they said they didn't.

Ruminating on my quest one evening at The Marching Saints, I ran into Igor Fomichov. He had just ordered a drink.

"Ah, it's you, *daragaya*," he greeted me, but he wasn't smiling. "You do get around. I didn't expect you here in the West."

"I could say the same thing about you."

"A cute trick you played on me at Belenkos' party with your false number."

"False number? I don't know what you're talking about."

"Yes, you do."

"You were drunk. Perhaps you misunderstood me."

"I don't think so." He brought his face close to mine with a baleful glare. "You were the one who wrote it down."

He certainly was sober this time. Wanting to make our conversation less confrontational, I was about to ask him if he had been my Good Samaritan the night I was attacked. A logical question since he'd been in the vicinity. He moved closer and I was about to push him out of my personal space when someone he knew stopped and spoke to him in English. He answered in kind with what I was beginning to recognize as an American accent.

Fomichov didn't introduce me, and in fact, became so involved in the conversation that he appeared to forget I was there and strolled away with his interlocutor, leaving his drink untouched.

I got up and left in case he returned.

Although Petrov had not called me in for briefings, I knew he soon would, and felt pressured to deliver some kind of information about Moran. Someone had to know where he was. I was even tempted to ask Petrov about involving some of our trained spies working in West Berlin to help locate him. It occurred to me that Fomichov might be one of them, and we might end up working together to track down Moran. Not something I would look forward to.

"Do you remember your first plane trip?" Angela asked

one day as an English lesson opener.

"Yes, of course. I was only ten years old. In Ukraine, the summer of 1933. My brother Yuri and I were visiting our grandparents there. My mother's side of the family. They worked on a small collective farm."

"They owned the farm?"

"It had been theirs before the State collectivized it. They were kept on to work it."

Angela's probing questions often stimulated my memory, bringing past events sharply into focus. I thought back to that heady summer of discovery in Ukraine. Yuri and I were so innocent then. Our parents had sheltered us from the bitter truth, and we'd no idea our beloved Baba and Dedushka had survived a planned, manmade famine, a *holodomor*—literally, death by starvation. Part of a brutal ethnic cleansing orchestrated by Stalin.

"By August, a week before our return to Moscow, Yuri and I were as bored as two Muscovite kids could be when stuck on a farm. The skyline of Moscow with its spectacular view of the Kremlin fortress, the broad vistas of Red Square, and the colorful onion domes of St. Basil's Cathedral stirred our souls far more than wheat fields in Ukraine. We envied our friends back in Moscow enrolled in summer programs for children—parties, picnics, and puppet shows in the parks.

"Baba gave us pails to pick raspberries. We were engrossed in what we were doing, so at first we didn't hear the sound of a low-flying plane growing louder. All the birdsong and the chirps and buzzing from insects in the field were soon blotted out by the roar of its motor.

"We'd never seen an aircraft land. So of course we

gazed at it in awe as it circled the wheat field, coming so close we saw the pilot's face. He leveled the plane and landed it, scattering a blizzard of ripening grain in all directions. We stared, young kids slack-jawed at the wonder of it. He taxied his plane to a full stop and turned off the engine. Then he flung open the cockpit door, raised his goggles, and glanced around. When he lit a cigarette his hands were trembling. He looked over and saw us watching him.

" 'Hey, you kids,' he shouted in Russian. 'What do you call this place?'

"So rattled were we by this bizarre apparition, we forgot the name of the village and shook our heads. He said, 'Where is the nearest big town? Do you know the name of it?'

"When we didn't answer, his voice grew louder: 'Are you deaf? *Vy govorite po russki?*' Do you speak Russian? Stunned, we stood there, mute, and he muttered: 'Shit. Just my luck.'

"I recovered first. I said, 'Hermanivka is our village. The nearest big town is called Prolisky.'

"Yuri pointed northwest. 'No, Litky is closer.'

" 'So you *can* speak Russian!' the pilot said. 'Good. Are your parents at home?'

" 'Our grandmother is here,' we told him. 'But she doesn't know much Russian—'

" 'Fine,' he said, tucking a map under his arm. 'I must talk to her.'

"I watched him shyly as my brother and I led the way to the farmhouse. He was wearing a leather helmet buckled under his chin and a fleece-lined flight jacket.

The hot sun bore down onto a little metal pin attached to his jacket, a silver airplane. I couldn't take my eyes off it.

"We skipped ahead of him toward the kitchen door at the back of the house. This was the most exhilarating thing that had happened to us all summer. By far. Baba had seen the plane and met us at the door. Dedushka was working in a neighboring field that day.

" 'What's going on?' my grandmother demanded. She was wary of strangers, always afraid the local Soviet authorities were spying on them. Perhaps inspecting the fields so they could report on my grandparents' performance.

" 'A man in an airplane,' I told her. 'He flew down from the sky. He only speaks Russian and he wants to know where the nearest town is.'

"The pilot removed his leather helmet and I noted how his thick blond hair was damp from the heat. Our new friend bowed politely, speaking slowly so she'd understand his Russian. He said, 'Good day, Madam. My name is Maxim Alexandrovich Dubkov. I'm a member of the Voronezh Flying Club, and I've drifted off course. I need to find an airfield with a telephone, so I can call my club and tell them where I am.'

"Yuri and I translated for her. My grandmother answered haltingly: 'You need go Dvirkivschyna. The Agriculture Overseers have crop dusters. Perhaps have telephone. No telephone here.'

"He shrugged out of his jacket; his shirt was drenched with sweat. Then he laid the map out on the kitchen table, and with a pencil stub, Baba circled Dvirkivschyna, and traced the way. He studied the route she gave him. 'Yes, yes. I see where I went wrong.' He bowed again and thanked Baba as he took his map and folded it so he could read the route at a glance. Then his eyes were drawn to the stove where a pot of my grandmother's borscht was bubbling and I saw him suck in his nostrils.

" 'Sorry to disturb your midday meal,' he said. 'Could I trouble you for a drink of water?' Baba indicated the kitchen pump, and pointed to the glasses on the shelf. Noting the longing in his eyes, she asked, 'You eat?'

" 'Not since early this morning,' he told her.

"She didn't hesitate. Pointing to a seat at the kitchen table, she ordered him to sit.

"As we all sat down to eat, Baba ladled most of her share into Mr. Dubkov's dish, leaving her bowl almost empty. She'd relinquished her portion in case he was from the regional Party.

"I couldn't take my eyes off Mr. Dubkov. I thought he was handsome. He was in his early twenties, but to me he was very old. Not as old as my parents, but he was an adult. I told him I wanted to fly when I grew up.

" 'Good,' he said. 'Maybe you will fly someday. How old are you?'

"I told him I was ten.

" 'Ten?' he said. 'Well then, in six years you can join a flying club and they'll teach you to glide in the air, like a bird. Would you like that?'

"I couldn't believe it, Angela. I stared at him, astonished. 'Six years? I could fly in six years?'

" 'Yes,' he said, 'you could. But only if you are attentive in school. You must work hard at maths and science.' He smiled for my grandmother's benefit. 'And geography, so you don't get lost, like I did.'

"The subjects he mentioned were not ones I enjoyed, but in that moment, I became aware that flying was the only thing I wanted to do.

"When it came time for him to leave, Mr. Dubkov made use of the outhouse, then returned to the kitchen to thank my grandmother for her hospitality. She gave him a dry smile and offered him a few apricots to take with him on his journey. He pocketed them, stooping down to take her hand and give her a hug.

"Leaving the kitchen, he lit another cigarette, and re-placed his flight helmet. It was Yuri's turn to help Baba clear the table, so I was free to walk him back to his plane. As we reached the aircraft, I had a wild idea. 'Mr. Dubkov,' could you please take me up in your airplane? Please?'

"He adjusted his goggles and put his jacket back on. 'No. Of course not.' He patted my head. 'But ask me in six years. I'll be happy to take you up then.'

" 'I'll be flying myself by then,' I said boldly. 'You said so.'

"At that, he laughed out loud. 'Yes, I did say that, *la-toshka.*'

" 'Please, oh please,' I said, my hands together in prayer, begging. I had never wanted anything so badly, Angela!

"He stared at me for a long moment. Finally, he crouched down to my level:

'I should have my head examined, but go ask your grandmother. If your babushka gives you permission, I'll take you up. Twenty minutes or so. No more!'

"I told Baba that the pilot had initiated the invitation. Her answer was predictable: 'Out of the question! I'm surprised you would ask such a thing. And more surprised that he'd suggest it. He should know better.'

"My mind was whirring. I skulked out of the farmhouse; then, with fierce determination I ran back to Mr. Dubkov. 'She said it was fine, as long as I don't stay up too long.'"

Angela laughed. "Oh, my—you were naughty Kira! Telling fibs like that."

"Yes, I could be."

"So then, what happened?"

"He put a cushion on the rear seat to elevate me, he harnessed me in, and slipped an extra leather helmet he had onto my head, snapping it closed. He fitted me with a pair of goggles. Then he lost no time slipping into the pilot's seat and switching on the ignition.

"The engine started up with a roar. It was a tiny biplane with an open cockpit, no bigger than the Po-2 I would fly much later in the Red Army. As we took off, my heart was racing. We were airborne in a few minutes and I was on top of the world. As we flew through clouds, it struck me for the first time—they were amorphous vapor, devoid of any shape. I'd thought they were dense, like pierogies or cushiony white mattresses in the sky that we could sink into."

Angela smiled. "I thought that too, when I was little."

"Looking below, the tops of trees were smudged in painterly tints of green daubed onto an artist's palette. Rivers became silvery ribbons looping down from hills to irrigate fertile plains of golden wheat."

"A poetic description."

"It was a poetic moment. For the first time, I understood birds in flight. My spirits soared as we rose up even higher. The sensation of freedom sluiced through me, fully—like wading naked into water; the most glorious feeling in the world. My pulse was racing. It was over all too soon.

"When we were on the ground back in the wheat field, he said, 'So, I'll see you in six years, eaglet.' Then, as an afterthought, he took the little airplane pin from his jacket lapel and fastened it to my shirt. 'Here. This'll remind you of your first trip into the sky.' Then, he kissed me on the forehead, his mustache tickling my skin. Little did I know then that…"

"That?" Angela seized on my pause. "That what?"

"That I would marry him someday."

"Marry him?" Angela gasped. "I want to hear all about that!"

"That's another story," I said laughing. "For another time."

CHAPTER 26

While I spent my weekends in West Berlin, still searching for Victor Moran, subtle changes were taking place at our Französische Straße boarding house. Sometimes, the only people at the dinner table were Frau Schuman, Luba, and myself, and I was missing Galina's gossip and Elena's funny stories. Both girls had begun to get busy around the same time.

Galina was on call for General Ilyich Vorobyev, ordered to drive him and his wife to social events after hours, so that often occupied her. She said her spare time was now taken up with studying to qualify for the Aeroflot exam. We assumed she was at the Kommandatura library to immerse herself without distraction.

Elena, though, had no such preoccupation, and she worked regular hours, so we had our own ideas of how she spent her time. When she did turn up for dinner, we would tease her with, "Ah, you're gracing us with your presence this evening. So, when are you going to tell us about him?" Or, "Big date tonight? Who's the lucky man?"

"What man?" Elena scoffed one evening. "What are you talking about? I go out with friends. Girls from my office. No one you'd know."

She always managed to mention something to distract us. "I might take up skating again when the summer's over. There's a good artificial rink in the *Eisstadion*, and this winter they're planning to reopen the outdoor rink in Alexanderplatz. The skating federation says I could still compete. Perhaps for East Germany, when it officially becomes a country."

"So there's no man in your life?" pressed Luba.

"When there is, you'll be the first to know."

"I'm sure that with Fraulein Elena's good looks, she has many beaux," Frau Schuman interjected in a rare complimentary comment. Then, predictably, she added "Do any of them have older brothers?"

"I'll be sure to ask them, if I ever meet any," Elena said, winking at me.

Soon, Luba joined a Red Army soccer league, and even she was out a good deal of the time.

We continued to overhear Elena speaking on the phone in muffled tones in what sounded like English. Unfortunately, she continued to keep her conversations behind closed doors. Having met Stephen Carter at the Belenkos', I pictured him at the other end of the line. Or had she met someone else?

"Okay, American or British?" I asked her once after she completed a call.

"Oh, for heaven's sake! There's no privacy in this place," she complained. She never answered my question.

Galina rode Elena mercilessly. "Why are you being so secretive? Is he married, with a wife back in Washington. Or is it London?"

"It's none of your business," Elena retorted with an edge to her voice.

I said nothing about having met Stephen Carter's wife at the Belenkos' party. I was waiting for Elena to confirm who the man in her life was. Since she was not about to tell us, we finally dropped it. But I always watched for Elena in the night clubs I went to with Angela in the West, ready with teasing remarks.

CHAPTER 27

Berlin, Summer, 1947

That summer, I lived for Fridays. As it got hotter and the sun beat down on me in my uniform, I couldn't wait until I could reach Angela's to change into something cool. The only shadow cast on my walk over to the West was when I passed under the giant image of a scowling Stalin that loomed near the Adlon Hotel before I crossed the demarcation line. Even in the heat, I'd feel a chill when I peered up at his disdainful mien, sensing his disapproval.

I could certainly relate to Steffi's desire to draw him a smile. A happy clown smile, maybe. I would imagine myself climbing up there with a ladder and some red paint. I might even be tempted to give him a red knob of a nose.

As time went on, my visits with Angela in the West were too much fun to let anything bother me much. I'd walk jauntily along the Unter den Linden toward West Berlin, humming a Glenn Miller tune, excited to be heading to the Bizone. As soon as I crossed over I would feel a heady sense of liberation; the giddy knowledge that from there I could direct my feet in any direction and feel the relief of having crossed the line unchallenged one more time; a breath of air that felt free, if not fresh. The specter of being watched by spies haunted me still, but with my new zest for life and adventure, I was putting my fears behind me.

I now had a key to Angela's apartment and would make myself at home until she returned from work, often with treats for our tea. I loved her tiny quarters, envied the fact that she did not have to share it with a surly landlady or inquisitive room-mates.

My English lessons were fun. I'd intuited that the key to any culture was linguistic savvy. Knowing the language of people we Russians regarded as adversaries—people who couldn't be bothered to study ours—gave us a distinct advantage over them.

Our entertainment after hours at the clubs was a bonus. I was young, and I was having a good time—a novelty after the bleak war years. At each cabaret or club I went to with Angela, I danced and flirted with American officers, always on the lookout for my prey. When I'd ask American officers if they knew Moran, they'd clam up if they guessed I was Russian. I switched to telling them I was Polish until one of them began to speak to me in that language. He quickly dumped me.

Petrov had begun to ask for debriefing sessions every few weeks. At first, he was indulgent, but I sensed a growing impatience with my lack of results. Major Vick Moran had simply disappeared from the scene. I wondered if he'd been assigned to another country, or something more sinister. Either of these scenarios would bring my happy time in the West to an abrupt halt.

"Perhaps he's no longer stationed in Berlin?" I suggested to Petrov on one occasion.

"He still reports to Berlin Intelligence, at least on paper. They may have him on a temporary assignment somewhere. Stay alert. Sometimes information can come in unexpected ways. Comrade Taylor is pleased with your progress in English, by the way."

Of course. Angela would be talking to him about me, sending him report cards. When she asked me probing questions, even innocuous ones, I was never lulled into letting down my guard. It was possible she was also gathering information—for whom I wasn't sure. Yes, we were both Russians, but our backgrounds were diverse. Her parents were White Russian émigrés, now British citizens. She worked for the Americans, but was not forthcoming about her true political views. I was a Red, a Russian Communist since childhood. She *appeared* to favor the Communists, but I knew little about her. I trusted no one.

Once, after Angela had been whisked onto the floor at 'The Marching Saints', a husky, attractive American approached me in the dim light of the bar.

"Dance, Schatzie?"

"Sure."

I didn't correct him. Let him think I was German. The way he was appraising me, I guessed that he too would proposition me. I speculated how many cigarettes I'd be worth this time.

As he slid his arm around my waist and we strolled into a better lighted area, I realized I knew who he was: Colonel Francis Marcus, from the Officers' Mess in London, the American officer I'd met when I had coffee with Vick Moran. With my hair down, and wearing Angela's make-up and fashionable civilian clothes, he didn't recognize me. I could hardly contain my excitement. Meeting him could be helpful.

"You from East or West Berlin, honey?" he asked, firm grip around my waist.

"Does it matter?" I asked.

He shrugged. "No. Both sides are krauts. I mean, Germans. Pretty dress."

"Thank you." After a few minutes of swaying to Glenn Miller and hearing him hum in my ear, I asked, "Do you know Major Vick Moran?"

"Vick? Yeah, I do. He's in my unit. You know Vick?"

"Yes, I met him some time ago. He was supposed to call me, but he never did." I affected a girlish pout.

"Don't take it personally, Sweetie. He's been away. Istanbul. Well, Incirlik, near Istanbul. Anyway," he said, holding me a little closer, "He probably forgot. He knows a lot of Schatzies."

His lazy, drink-driven smile told me he had imbibed more than he should. He had no memory of meeting me in Potsdam; forgotten we met again in London; didn't remember showering me with compliments in the Officer's Mess.

"I'm not a Schatzie."

"Oh? The blonde hair—what're you, Polish?" He fondled my unbraided hair, which was loose, tousled, flowing down past my shoulders.

I shook my head. "Russian."

He was taken aback, then said: "You're pretty, for a Russian. I always think of Russian women as flat-faced crones with metal teeth, plowing fields in *babushkas*."

His rudeness took my breath away. I bristled, thinking of my chic, sophisticated mother and all her attractive urbane friends in the Moscow medical community. The many pretty women in my regiment, the photo of Elena skimming the ice in her elegant swan outfit. Was that the perception of Russians in the West—our women were ugly and our men rapists, unable to use a lavatory properly? I could feel his bourbon breath on my cheek as he grazed it with his lips. I pulled myself back to avoid any further intimacy, but his arm tightened even more around my waist, and I felt his arousal.

Then, a moment of clarity. His grip relaxed, arousal gone. "Have we met before?" he demanded.

"Why? Do I look familiar?"

"Yeah. You do."

He said nothing more, but I sensed that this would be our last dance. The music ended and he led me back to the bar, oddly sober, leaving me to feel like a hot potato, hastily disposed of. Had he remembered? Or was he concerned about having said too much about a fellow officer to a Russian? He nodded a token thanks and disappeared into the crowd.

"Ah, good, you've ditched the Yank," said a very Brit RAF officer at the bar. "Can I buy you a drink, love?"

"Actually, *he* ditched me. Didn't want to dance with me again," I said. "It must be something I said."

"Sensitive, isn't he? For a Yank. It certainly wasn't that he didn't find you pretty enough." He signaled for the bartender. "What're you drinking? This American bourbon is damnably good. Still prefer Scotch whiskey, or even Irish, but it's not half bad."

"I usually drink wine."

"Ah. Bad luck. Grapes are still hard to come by, love. Hard to grow them with vineyards still surrounded by mines. You don't sound German. East European?"

"Yes." I extended my hand. "Kira Voronova. And yes, I'd like a drink. Perhaps a small beer."

"Geoffrey Parker," he said, shaking my hand longer than necessary. He was attractive, a bit older than most of the servicemen I was meeting. "You're Russian, aren't you? Not many Russkis come over to the Bizone."

"Perhaps we don't feel welcome over here."

"Well, we'll have to fix that, won't we?" He raised his glass. "Here's to better Soviet-Bizone relations."

It wasn't long before we were on the dance floor, moving feverishly to the Dixieland band. He tried unsuccessfully to teach me the Lindy Hop, and was keen to "jitterbug," a bizarre twisting and kicking dance he'd learned from American WACs stationed in England. Breathless after a couple of sets, I excused myself and followed the makeshift signs indicating a restroom in the basement. The circular metal staircase was treacherous in Angela's heels; lighting was poor, and air quality bad, reeking of sewage and decay. Two men were talking at the foot of the stairs. I proceeded with caution, one hand on the clasp of my purse, ready to take out my gun. The other clutched the rickety railing.

I picked my way down quietly until the voices became clear. Russian? Our servicemen rarely ventured into the Allied zones for entertainment. They needed a permit from their superior officers. The Soviet government didn't want personnel exposed to Americans, to be seduced or corrupted by their affluence; or risk them being bribed with cigarettes, cameras, fountain pens, and cheap wrist watches.

I slowed my step, and as I did, the power went off. Having lights go was endemic in Berlin. Rather than continue down in the dark, I sat on the stairs to eavesdrop.

"*Fuck. There go the lights,*" said a deep male voice.

"*God, I hate this city,*" said his companion. "*Anyway, my answer is the same. These things take time. It's risky. We should cool it for a few months."*

"We can't. Hey, I know the risks. I also know what'll happen if we don't move forward. We have to do it soon. I may not have much time."

"You know what our people will want in return."

"I'm prepared for that."

The voices were vaguely familiar. The Kommandatura? A conference? The Belenkos' party? One of them sounded like Igor Fomichov, but I couldn't be sure. Or was it the voice of the clerk in the next cubicle in my office? A Leningrad accent, but I'd met a number of people with that accent in the Russian Zone.

The music upstairs stopped, and the door opened above me. People headed down, complaining of the darkness. As if on cue, the lights flickered back on.

The voice continued, *"Let's go. There's a fire exit down here that leads to the parking lot. My car's right outside."*

From my perch midway down the stairs, I tried to rush down to see who they were, but the stampede to the restrooms impeded me, and I only managed to glimpse the backs of the two uniformed male figures hurrying through a dark hallway. I dashed after them, but when I opened the exit door, all I saw was a car driving off in the darkness. A dark-colored Horch.

CHAPTER 28

"When are you going to tell me about when you met up with Maxim again?" Angela asked one day, not for the first time. I had teased her with only part of the story.

"It was a long time after I met him as a child in Ukraine. As he had predicted, a good six years. As soon as I reached my sixteenth birthday, I'd signed up for flying lessons in Moscow, but I never thought he, of all people, would turn up as my instructor! It was quite a shock. The very last thing I expected.

"The classes were taught at a small airport outside the city, in an old rundown hangar. The only furnishings were a lectern for the professor, a desk, a telephone, and uncomfortable chairs. Lighting was poor, and the hangar smelled of fuel, dust, and mold from a roof that leaked. But I thought it was wonderful.

"I'd just graduated from secondary school. My mother had insisted I enrol at the Moscow State University and I applied to please my parents, but my dream of taking to the sky was more vivid than ever. So, much against their better judgment, they also allowed me to apply to the *People's Flying School*."

"With the caveat that you had to keep your grades up at university, I'm sure," interjected Angela.

"Oh, yes, there were strings attached! But a lot of people took up flying in those days. Aviation was always important to us Russians."

"Because of the size of the Soviet Union?"

"Yes. So much of it is inaccessible by road."

"Did you know then you'd become a night bomber?"

"No! I thought my pilot's license might complement my engineering degree. That I'd work in some area of aircraft design. I never thought I'd be in combat."

"In fact, nothing was farther from my thoughts. It was the summer of 1939. We weren't at war; Stalin and Hitler were about to sign a treaty of nonaggression. Life seemed good. More or less. And I wanted to fly for the sheer joy of it."

"Was it unusual for women to take flying lessons in the Soviet Union?"

I shot her a wry smile. "No, but you'd have liked the odds, Angela. There were twenty students in my class. Only six were women. We herded together as women do when surrounded by all that testosterone, pretending to ignore all the men around us."

"Good odds," agreed Angela. "But tell me about Maxim!"

Moscow, 1939

Yes, the odds I mentioned were great if you were a teenaged girl. But I only had eyes for the professor, Maxim Dubkov, the man I recognized as the pilot in my grandparents' field in Ukraine when I was ten. Maxim wasn't even from Moscow. I could never have imagined that he'd turn up six years later at the People's Flying School in the Capital.

Much was expected from Russian girls of my generation. It was understood we'd learn homemaking skills by osmosis, but we were still encouraged to enrol in fields like physics, mathematics, medicine, or engineering.

Living in a patriarchal society, we were realistic about which of the sexes was destined to be the deferred-to elite. Despite our career choices, we knew where we stood—subordinate to men.

That first day, though, negativity was far from our thoughts. The other girls in the class and I were dreaming of flying planes. We herded together, sitting with our notebooks and sharpened pencils poised as we awaited the arrival of the instructor. Chatting in low tones, we immediately stopped when our lecturer—confident and handsome—strode in and took charge of the room.

Shocked, I caught my breath. I dropped my pencil. Yes, he was older now; he even had the promise of a little gray in his blonde hair. He still had his mustache, but was otherwise clean-shaven and wore wire-rim glasses. His name hadn't been announced ahead of time, but he was unmistakably my Russian flyer, Maxim Alexandrovich Dubkov.

After circling the sky together that day in Ukraine, I'd had a pre-pubescent fascination, a schoolgirl crush, on Maxim, fantasizing about him for those six years. He'd become the hero of my childhood, remaining at the ragged edge of my consciousness ever since. Rarely had a day gone by when I hadn't thought about him, or at least glimpsed the fading vision of him.

When I recounted our meeting and the idealized memory of our flight to friends my age, the story, overlain with new sheen and color, took on aggrandized proportions, some I almost believed myself. As time went by, my feelings for him evolved from a childhood crush to teenaged yearnings.

Now, at sixteen, I was craving experimentation. When he stood there at the lectern, handsome, slim, and muscular, stirrings and desires surfaced that had not been there when he descended into the field.

What I wanted to know now was what he would be like in bed.

With charismatic authority, Maxim wrote his name on a blackboard and then positioned himself at the front of the class before a large illustration of a glider he'd placed on an easel.

"Gentlemen. And of course, ladies." He tossed our row a condescending smile. "Welcome to the People's Flying School."

He went on to conjure a mesmerizing mystique about gliders. "Before you fly airplanes, you must understand the principles of gliding. In this course you will learn about gliders inside and out." A groan of disappointment went through the group.

"Never underestimate the glider, comrades."

Using a pointer and an enlarged photo of the interior controls of a glider to illustrate his lecture's highlights, he tapped on the illustration for emphasis.

"These extraordinary vessels are more versatile than planes. They can be powered by gravity and air currents only. Consider the opportunities this provides in warfare, ladies and gentlemen. If the last war with Germany has taught us anything, it's that victory in future wars we fight will be won in the air."

We weren't expecting that. A young man in the front row muttered something to his friend next to him and they both snickered. Maxim drilled him with a stern stare.

"We have some scoffers among us," he said sharply. "Don't be so quick to dismiss the possibility of war, my friend. You need to become better informed. There could be a conflict with Finland soon. And our Motherland is anticipating confrontations with the Baltic States in the near future. To the west of us, there is always Herr Hitler of Germany lurking on the sidelines. So do not be lulled into thinking we are at peace."

We were all anxious to hear about flying airplanes, not listen to a lecture on gliding or war tactics. But Maxim was methodical, feeling we needed to understand the principles of flying small aircraft before we tried to operate one.

The mention of Germany caused a restless stir among the young men in attendance, and one of them shot up his hand.

"And yet, Professor, is it not true that Germany is no longer a threat to us? At this moment there are talks between Soviet Foreign Minister Molotov and German Foreign Minister Von Ribbentrop to ratify a nonaggression pact between the Soviet Union and Germany."

Maxim shot him a dark look. He hadn't expected his lecture to be hijacked in another direction by deluded students, but he was quick to steer it back on track.

"I don't know the answer to your question, Comrade. Only what I read in *Pravda*. This is not a course in political science. I am merely stating the obvious. We cannot ignore the lessons history has taught us. We must be prepared for aggression from neighboring countries at all times and know how to take control in the air. Which means you will want to pay close attention to what I teach you in this course, instead of interrupting. Now if I may continue ?"

There was a moment of silence and a thickening in the air as the men—most of military conscription age—considered what he said. They were no longer snickering.

"As I was explaining," Maxim resumed, referencing the illustration, "with engines off, gliders can move silently through the sky, often for hours at a time if you can hit the right thermals. An experienced pilot can shut engines off at a thousand meters, and glide over enemy-held positions. Apply this tactic to any small aircraft and it can be deadly."

He paused meaningfully. "While I'm not here to give you military training, I urge you to imagine for a moment the advantages of such stealth. Without lights or the roar of an engine, you can attack at night in silence. Get in fast before those searchlights and anti-aircraft on the ground get a bead on you, destroy the lights, attack, and then get out in time to avoid the fire-works. Fast."

There was silence in the lecture room. Seduced by the underlying message of his talk, the men were hanging on his every word.

"In this course, I'll teach you to do that," he continued. "You will learn about gravity, lift, angles of attack. You will learn about Bernoulli's principle. You will learn...."

As we scribbled furiously, he went on uninterrupted about the frenzy of information coming our way, and I had to fight my inner thoughts about him and our past encounter to concentrate. I wanted so much to learn, to excel, to be the star of his class. As a young woman in a man's field of interest I knew I would have to work harder; I couldn't miss a word.

He spoke for almost an hour. Finally, he said, "And that's it for today, ladies and gentlemen. You all have your textbooks. Study the first thirty pages. And pick up a workbook from that pile at the back on your way out. Do the first three lessons."

A hand shot up and a young man asked, "When can we actually do some gliding or flying, professor?"

"None of you will see the inside of a glider or plane for a while yet. Master the principles first. I'll see you one week from today." And with that, he was done. He lingered a few moments to tidy up his lectern.

I was blushing as I seized the moment to approach him. Leaving the coterie of girls I'd sat with, I dug into my pocket for the little pin he gave me all those years ago.

"Mr. Dubkov," I said, "May I have a word?"

He glanced up, curious, but didn't stop what he was doing.

"Yes, what is it, Miss . . . ?"

"Voronova. Kira Sergeyevna Voronova."

"Yes? What can I do for you? Was something not clear?"

His voice thrilled me as much then as it had the day I first met him. It was a deep voice, throaty from years of smoking; husky, very male.

"You don't remember me, do you? We met six years ago."

"And why would I remember you?" His bold eyes took in my blossoming figure as he rolled up a map.

His brusqueness didn't deter me. "Has your sense of direction improved?"

He glowered sharply. "What do you mean?"

"Six years ago you lost your way in Ukraine and landed in a field where two children took you to their grandmother. You had some borscht with them, then took the little girl up in your airplane. Remember?"

A slow smile crept over his face and his eyes crinkled in amusement. "Yes, I do remember that. Has it been six years? You were that little girl?"

I grinned at him and touched the site where his lips had briefly touched my forehead. "You kissed me, right here, tickling me with your mustache." Showing him the pin, I added, "And then you gave me this."

He took the pin and his smile grew broader. "The pin from my flying club! So that's what I did with it. Yeah, I remember. It was a little piece of junk, but you were clearly taken with it."

I reached out and snatched it back. "It's still important to me. It's been my inspiration."

He laughed then, a charming laugh displaying nice straight teeth. "To answer your question, yes, my sense of direction is much better now. That was only my second solo flight; I had no idea what I was doing. Thank goodness your grandmother fed me and set me on the right path. How is she?"

"She passed away last year," I said. "My grandfather had to move to Moscow. He lives with my parents."

I didn't need to explain that my grandfather had

moved to Moscow in fear of his life, and that peasants on collective farms often vanished. He nodded in understanding. Picking up his briefcase, all he said was, "I'm sorry about your grandmother. A kind lady."

"Yes. She was strict, though." I came clean and confessed the lie I'd told my babushka that day he landed in the field, and how I'd brought down the wrath of her wooden spoon.

He threw his head back with laughter. "And I believed you! I'm lucky she didn't go after *me* with her spoon. You deserved that paddling."

"It was worth it. Every whack," I said. "That flight was the highlight of my life at the time."

A few students and another instructor were filing in through a side door.

"There's another class," he said. "Come join me for coffee at the café around the corner. You can tell me what you've been doing all this time. What was your name again—Klara?"

"Kira."

"Sorry. Kira."

He was soon to get my name straight.

I was delirious with joy. He had to remind me to pick up a workbook as we left.

What he called a café was a grotty little *stolovaya* near the airfield, a canteen frequented by airmen and students, but I couldn't have been happier if it'd been the glamorous Metropol on Red Square. I only had eyes for Maxim, whom I addressed deferentially. At his insistence, we soon slipped into a casual informality, using the informal pronoun as we sipped our 'coffee'—a tasteless beverage, mostly chicory.

"*Lastochka*, stop calling me, professor," he said. "It makes me feel old."

To me, he *was* a little old—I was only sixteen, after all—but I thought his twenty-nine years conferred sophistication, knowledge, and experience, while in no way diminishing his good looks. It became clear after about an hour and two cups of the awful stuff we were drinking that we didn't want our time together to end.

I finally said, "I have to go. I have homework for school tomorrow. First year engineering; not an easy course."

"Good girl. I did the same thing. Gliding lessons while I attended Lomosov. I took mechanical engineering." He finished his beverage and got up to leave.

I couldn't wait for the next lesson.

CHAPTER 29

Berlin, 1947

W hen Petrov's secretary, Inna Gradska, next summoned me for my debriefing with him, I was tempted to mention to her that I'd seen her in the West. Something told me not to.

"He's happy today," she remarked.

I tried to imagine what would make Petrov happy. A whole carton of American cigarettes, or Napoleon brandy. Perhaps a black market Mickey Mouse wrist watch? They were selling for as much as $500 U.S., and in big demand among Red Army troops.

"Come in, come in!" he called out to me when he saw me at the door. He was grinning as he fingered a file folder. "I've been doing more research on our friend, Major Victor Moran. I've found out some interesting things.

Had he found the elusive major?

"Sit," he ordered.

He beamed at me. "It turns out your American, Victor Moran, is a talented linguist. His White Russian father was named Moranov. He speaks flawless Russian. His German is excellent, too. His mother's parents were German."

"But that's impossible," I protested. "His German was barely passable when I met him in London."

Then I recalled how Moran had told me about a German grandmother in Pennsylvania who'd insisted on speaking to him in some dialect of German. At the time he said he didn't remember any of it. So, another lie.

"The man has mastered a few German accents, including a low Viennese dialect," Petrov went on. "His French is excellent, his Spanish and Italian quite fluent, and he makes himself understood well in Turkish and Arabic."

I shook my head. "I find that hard to believe. The U.S. airman I met was a linguistic dolt."

"A cover. He's clever. Which makes him all the more valuable if we could bring him over. We've waited too long for him to make the first move. We have to find out more of his recent activities. He's got to be in West Berlin somewhere. I'll get some of our people over there on it."

"He hasn't been around," I insisted defensively. "I've asked everyone I met in the West."

"If he's back in Berlin, we'll find him. Then you can step in."

I nodded, hoping Moran hadn't left Berlin for good. He was still my ticket to the flying instructor's job Petrov used to lure me.

"I was planning to tell you . . . I spoke with a friend of his who said he had been in Istanbul recently."

Petrov sat up straighter in his chair and glared at me with reproach. "Ah. Why didn't you say so? Istanbul. Now we're getting somewhere! Did he happen to mention why he was in Turkey?"

"No. Just that Moran had gone there on business for a while. He'd been in Incirlik, near Istanbul."

"Interesting. So the Americans are working deals with Turkey. Probably to build an air base; to launch missiles, more than likely. Did you ask him what kind of business?"

My face grew hot. "No," I said, examining my hands. "I didn't want to appear too eager. I was going to wait till I saw Moran and coax it out of him in person."

He stood up. "Incirlik you said? Incirlik…" He strolled over to a large map of Europe on his wall. "Yes, here it is, near Adana." With a red pencil, he circled the city. "Southeast of Ankara, not far from the Syrian border. Perfectly positioned for a missile base." He looked back to me. "This is good. Valuable information, Comrade."

He sat down and looked speculatively at me. Finally, he nodded.

"Well done."

I breathed out. Petrov could frighten me with his dark stare as much as any German pilot shooting at me from a Messerschmitt. Perhaps more. In wartime, I was too young to value my life and I'd been willing to risk it. Maturity had taught me that a beating heart was more relevant than a brave one.

I left his office feeling, if not appreciated, at least that I'd accumulated a few points toward getting the position I wanted. I was still aching to take to the air again. There were days when I didn't think I could spend one more day at the Kommandatura.

CHAPTER 30

Berlin, Summer, 1947

On weekend visits to the American side that summer, I was well-equipped. My gun was easily accessible in my purse. I wore my summer uniform when I crossed over, medals on full display. In my clunky army shoes, I resembled any soldier on parade.

One Friday, I was late getting away. It was after the rush hour stampede of workers returning to the East on bicycles, and I was alone as I headed west along the Unter den Linden. The sky was clear as I walked at a comfortable pace toward the Gate and the British Zone. It was eerily quiet.

Always vigilant, I thought I saw something stir. Leisurely sprawled on a park bench in Pariser Platz were two of our soldiers, eyeing me as I passed. Since our troops had burned the Adlon Hotel at the conquest, there was no activity at that juncture of the boulevard. Nobody was around to help me if things turned sour. The scorched trees in the area were struggling back, but still not vernal enough to offer cover. A chill of fear. I clenched my teeth as my latent anger resurfaced. Would they dare? I doubted they'd have the nerve to attack a decorated woman in a Red Army uniform in broad daylight, but this time I was ready.

Dipping my hand into my purse, I caressed the reassuring shape of my pistol. Head held high, I passed them without a glance, vowing to kill without remorse if necessary. Then I heard the expected footsteps. They were on the move and following me. I sped up my pace, walking faster, to almost a jog. I still had about a hundred feet to go before reaching the Brandenburg Gate demarcation line. Beyond that, there would be people around, as black marketers and tourists were numerous near the destroyed Reichstag.

My worst fear was not another assault. What worried me was that Petrov had, in a moment of whimsy, changed his mind about allowing me to cross because my past performance was unsatisfactory. That he might have sent troops to pull me back to the dreary East, doomed to stamping forms all day—perhaps for the rest of my working life.

As I was getting close to the demarcation line, a Moscow accent pierced the air. And the voice was familiar.

"Captain! Captain Voronova! Wait. Please wait."

I whirled around. With a firm grip on my pistol, I stopped and put down my grip. There was only one man behind me.

"Who are you?" I demanded.

"Captain Voronova, Kira! It's me, Boris. Nadia Harlamova's son. From the apartment in Patriarshy Ponds."

An unexpected jolt into the past. Back to Moscow before the war, when my family's paradise was irretrievably lost; when we stopped living well and had to share our home with strangers.

I took a deep breath. Boris. The snotty, messy kid who filled the apartment with cigarette smoke, noise, and body odor; who thought farting contests were the height of entertainment, and created havoc by wrestling with his younger brother Anton while I struggled to complete my homework. *That* Boris. He'd been sixteen and I was a little older. He was working at the Tula Armaments factory when the war broke out.

With time, Nadia had managed to burrow her way into my grandfather's affection, and we'd all become fond of her. We had even taken to Anton, who turned out to be a reasonable kid, devoted to his mother. But we found few redeeming qualities in Boris. I disliked him on sight when he moved into our home, the more so when I had to repel his pathetic attempts to flirt with me. On his days off work, his smoldering dark eyes would follow me around, a cigarette dangling from his mouth —an affectation he borrowed from a Humphrey Bogart movie. The last I heard, Boris had been conscripted and sent to the front in Stalingrad. Nobody but Nadia was sorry to see him go.

"You almost got yourself shot following me, Boris," I said sharply. I was about to put my gun away when he said:

"Yes, I know. And I would deserve it. I'm sorry."

He was acting guilty about something. I kept the weapon firmly in hand.

"Kira, please put the gun away."

"Why are you following me? What are you doing here?"

"They assigned me to Berlin after the conquest instead of sending me home to Moscow. I'm working at Special Camp Number Seven in Oranienburg."

"Sachsenhausen? The Nazi concentration camp?"

"Yes. We're using it now; as a prison. I work there as a guard."

His voice stirred recognition in my memory. Not in Moscow. Here in Berlin. More recently.

"Listen, Kira ... I just wanna talk ... I wanted to apologize." He paused, still willing me to put my pistol away. He hung his head. "That night on Französische Straße—I know you recognized me. I'm sorry. I was hanging out with other guards from Sachsenhausen. We were out of our minds with vodka, looking for Schatzies."

So, that was it. He'd been one of the priapic soldiers who attacked me after the Belenkos' party; the Muscovite who believed me when I said my name and rank. He'd done up his pants and skulked down the alley when I identified myself; when I screamed for them to stop. Yes, someone *had* called him Boris.

Memories of the attack came flooding back to me in quick cuts, each one a painful stab. My recollection of the incident filled me with so much anger I was nearly choking with rage. With no one around, it would be so easy to shoot him point blank, with no regret. In the dark, I hadn't recognized him back then. The whole assault was a blur.

"I would have killed all of you," I hissed, grinding the words out between clenched teeth. "You're lucky I wasn't armed with a gun that night. Have you any idea what it's like for a woman to be attacked by four predatory animals assaulting in a pack?"

"I know. We fucked up. That's why I'm apologizing. I don't want it to get back to my commanding officer. Or to my mother." He might have said *especially* my mother. He'd be as much afraid of Nadia Harlamova as a court martial. I could recall her blasting angrily from her room armed with a hairbrush or umbrella, or a belt, to break up noisy sibling squabbles.

Seeing Boris brought back painful memories of that awful period when my family's life changed so much.

Unreasonably, I found myself laying all the blame for our altered lifestyle on him. With renewed fury, I glared at him now.

"The war is over, you idiot. Yet, you and your friends are still disgracing our army."

"Hey," he shot back defensively. "It was a hard war."

Thoughts of Frau Schuman's story reinforced my fury. "It was hard for everybody, asshole. That didn't give you and your pals an excuse to go after every female in sight."

Boris glanced away and shrugged. "They were Germans."

"German or not, they were women—human beings."

He kept his eye on my gun. "It's just that, well, when our troops first took Berlin, we thought we deserved to, you know . . . have some fun with the women. A lot of them wanted it."

As though our troops had been doing the women a favor. I thought of Steffi's 63-year old grandmother, just waiting for Russians to arrive and violate her!

"We'd been at the front; we finally got paid after three years, and the vodka was flowing. We'd earned it. Even Stalin said it was okay."

"Well, it wasn't okay," I snapped. "And Stalin has changed his stance on that. Last year you were ordered to stop. What you and your friends are still doing is criminal. Imagine what other countries think of us. Or do you not care?"

"Won't you please put that gun away?"

When I didn't, he added, voice cracking, "Look, Kira . . . Captain. I did try to talk the others into leaving you alone, didn't I? You remember that, right? We were drunk."

"Being drunk is no excuse. I was injured in that mêlée. I had a black eye for weeks. I *should* kill you," I said, raising the gun as though taking aim.

"Well, that's why I'm apologizing," he said rapidly, pleading his case. "I knew you recognized me."

His hands were trembling. I'd made him feel fear as I had that night last spring. I hoped he'd need a change of underwear.

Having accomplished what I wanted, I put the gun away. Wheeling around, I picked up my grip and turned back to my path over to the British side, leaving him to believe that I'd recognized him. He didn't follow.

"Well, they did it to us," he called out behind me. "The Germans were no better in the East."

He wasn't wrong, but it had to stop somewhere. With a sigh, I kept walking. Now that I knew he was one of them, I could report him, but I knew I wouldn't. I might despise Boris, but Nadia had saved my father from Siberia, a certain premature death.

I could never forget that.

CHAPTER 31

When I arrived at Angela's this time, my bag held not one, but three of the pretty dresses Beatrix Belenko had given me. Putting aside the inflamed feelings my discussion with Boris had roiled up, I focused on how I could share my bounty with Angela to repay her for past generosity.

She was impressed with my new clothes, but appeared distracted. I'd seen Angela in these moods before, but she'd never been willing to share her dark moments with me.

"What's wrong?" I asked.

She shook her head; her eyes were rimmed with red.

"Angela," I said firmly as I touched her shoulder. "We're friends. Please share what's going on. I've noticed your unhappiness before. Perhaps I can help?"

"I doubt if you can, Kira. It's about my sister. Ingrid."

"You have a sister?" I remembered the photo on the dresser. "Is that her—the girl in the photo?"

"Yes, she's two years older than I am."

"You've never mentioned her. She lives in London?"

She shook her head. "No. In Germany. I recently found out she's in Berlin. In the East."

"The East?" That was a surprise. "Does she work for us? For the USSR?"

She shook her head, choking back tears. "I can't talk about it."

"But if she's in Berlin, isn't that something to be happy about? You'll get together often."

Angela clammed up, making it plain that any more discussion about Ingrid would be out of bounds. She'd tell me about her when she was ready. We had the whole weekend.

She opened the grammar book. Because I'd brought dresses we could talk about, this time she integrated many words that related to clothing into our lesson:

"A jumper is a sweater in the U.S. and for Americans a jumper is a tunic," she said in a voice devoid of her usual enthusiasm or interest. "And what I call knickers, the Americans call panties."

Useful information I'd never found in engineering manuals. "Which should I be learning?"

She managed a smile. "That's up to you. British is more universal. But then, you might meet a generous Ami and want to run off and live in the United States."

"That has never entered my mind," I said. "I'm Russian. I love the Motherland."

It was the wrong thing to say. Her smile disappeared.

It was nine o'clock when we walked into the "Marching Saints." The club was coming alive and the band was blasting dance tunes to the rafters. The atmosphere was smoky and congenial. We found two free barstools and sat down. After ordering drinks, Angela, now more like her old self, was acting happy and animated. A British officer she knew sat down next to her, chatting her up over the din.

A hand on my shoulder. "*Ah, guten abend Fraulein,*" said a male voice in German—poorly accented German. "*Capitaine Voronova, nicht wahr?*"

A chill went through me. I whirled around and caught my breath.

Finally.

CHAPTER 32

There he was. The mysterious Major Moran, standing behind me. With no eye patch this time, I got the full piercing effect of his blue eyes twinkling with amusement.

"*Wie geht es ihnen, Fraulein?*" he queried politely.

I caught my breath. At last, I'd be able to report something to Petrov. I answered Moran in the same bad German accent, pretending to struggle with words. I indicated his right eye, where the patch had been, feigning concern.

"So, is your eye truly healed?"

This threw him. He'd forgotten about the patch. "Uh … yes, it's fine. It was a metal filing. Microscopic. But they got it out."

How glib he was! "It's a little swollen."

"It is?" He hid his surprise at my equally glib reaction. "There's so much crap in the air—"

"And no cane, I see. Your leg is better as well."

"Oh, yeah. That too. It's fine." He flexed his leg.

"It was the other leg," I pointed out.

The smile he returned told me he knew I was making fun of him.

"Your recovery is miraculous, Major. And you're very tan. Have you been away? A vacation?"

He did look good. In his summer uniform he was handsome; more so than I remembered. The early part of the summer had been cool in Berlin, heating up only in mid July, so few Berliners were sporting tans. His deep color belied the possibility that he'd been in Berlin all this time.

"Not exactly a vacation. I was away, though. Military business."

"Where did you go?"

"A warm country."

"North Africa? Italy? South of France?"

He grinned. "Keep trying, Comrade."

I could not keep the charade going without laughing, so I switched to colloquial Russian. "Why the games, Major? And in such terrible German! Why did you pretend not to know Russian when we met in London? It would have made our conversation much easier."

He affected a sheepish mien, shrugged, and then carried on in impeccable Russian. "Okay, so maybe I do speak a little Russian. You're not mad at me, are you?"

"Should I be?"

He shrugged.

He'd called me at the boarding house in the spring. But why did he avoid me after that, and why step out of the shadows now?

My worry was that he might have taken up with a pretty Schatzie during that time. If he lost interest in me, I'd be of no value to Petrov. No more visits to the West; no more hope of a promotion to flying instructor. The position had become my all-consuming grail. I had to keep Moran interested.

"Hi, Vick," Angela said, turning her attention to us.

"Angie," he switched to English and kissed her cheek. "Haven't seen much of you lately."

"Well, you haven't been around." With a quick glance in my direction, she added, "Besides, I've been teaching."

He nodded knowingly. There was an easy familiarity between them. Then she introduced us. "Vick Moran, aka Viktor Moranov."

"But you knew that," he said to me. "You've been checking on me. I must have made quite an impression on you."

I gave him an embarrassed smile. "Don't flatter yourself."

"Frank Marcus said he saw you here and you asked him about me."

"Only because you told me you lived in the American Zone when we met in London," I said. "I've been coming over to learn English from Angela."

"I've been thinking about you. I called that number you gave me. A cranky German lady answered. Said you weren't home."

"Frau Schuman, my landlady. She told me you'd called. You told her you'd call again. Good thing I haven't been waiting by the phone. That was months ago."

"As I said, I've been out of town. On and off."

"Where did you say you've been?"

"I didn't." Turning to Angela, he said, "I saw Bob Fletcher scarfing down bratwurst at that table by the window with a pretty schatzie hovering over him. You might want to go and stake your claim." Fletcher was an RAF pilot—a hot dancer— Angela sometimes dated.

"Perhaps I'll do that," she said, taking her cue. To me she said, "If this bloke becomes a bother, give me a sign.

I'll straighten him out. And be careful. He has a bad reputation." She stood up. "Let me know when you're ready to leave."

"That was easier than I expected," he said, slipping onto her seat. He switched from Russian to German to order himself a lager and an American hamburger, rattling off what he wanted on it.

"How about you?" he asked me. "What're you drinking?"

"I have a drink."

"Want to try one of their burgers?"

I shook my head. "Your German has improved," I observed.

"I've been studying."

"Studying Russian, studying German. Commendable. But I understand you hardly needed to do that."

He shot me a bemused glance. "You know a lot about me. Sounds like your Russki friends have been checking me out. A bad sign, Comrade. They'll be gunning for me next." He faced me then. "So, what's the deal? Are you the lure to bring me over to the dark side? A little honey for the trap? A bit of *Kompromat*?"

In a few short disarming sentences he'd stripped away my subterfuge.

"Why would they do that? Are you someone of interest to the Soviet Union?"

He took a sip of his beer. "I could be."

We were quiet for a moment, before he said, "You want the truth about our encounter in London? Okay." He put his hamburger down. "I'd heard of you, the famous Russian "night witch" with all the shiny medals, stationed in Berlin. I wanted to meet the legend. Frank Marcus pointed you out to me at the hangar—he remembered you from Potsdam."

So they had tracked me right from the hangar where I'd hallucinated about Rufina.

The quirky idea that he might already be working for our side occurred to me, not for the first time. But if that were so, Petrov would hardly have assigned me to spy on him. Unless they were testing me? Like a chess game, the moves were infinite.

"Why didn't you simply introduce yourself to me?"

He shrugged. "I figured you'd regard a wounded warrior more favorably."

"A silly practical joke, then."

"If I'd come up and put the make on you, you'd have thought I was just another brash, pushy American."

"And are you? 'Putting the make' on me?" I felt a rush of vitality. I was enjoying our flirtation.

"I'll let you figure that out."

"I thought I saw you here one night, but it turned out to be another officer. He offered me six cigarettes for my favors."

"I hope you didn't take it," he said with a grin. "You're worth at least a whole pack. Maybe even a carton!"

I pretended to hit him with the back of my hand. And he, in turn, pretended to duck.

Resuming his narrative with a chuckle, he said, "When I saw you in the viewing gallery at Drummond Hill, I grabbed a buddy's cane. Somebody else lent me his eye patch. Russians *were* allowed in that gallery, you know. I made that up about it being restricted."

"I should have guessed. Do things always come easy to you?"

"No, some things are harder to earn than others." He gave me a lazy, sexy smile, and inched closer to me.

"You had me fooled," I said, feeling the heat of his presence, but not backing away. "What a clever fraud you are, Major."

He moved closer. Our faces were almost touching and I could feel his breath.

"So, am I forgiven?"

"Why did you really want to meet me?" I peered at him flirtatiously, enjoying the game. "There's no shortage of women around here."

"Isn't it obvious? To get you roaring drunk and take you to bed, so I could learn all your state secrets and topple the USSR!"

"Very funny," I said.

"Serious answer? I wanted to meet you because I admire a woman with smarts and guts, especially if she's also pretty."

I had no retort for this.

"Of course, if you *are* selling state secrets, we'd be more than interested."

"You're wasting your time, Major. I work at a low-level job in the Kommandatura. I stamp job applications of former Nazis who want to be part of a new Soviet-controlled Germany."

"Want to be? Or have to be?"

I shrugged. "It doesn't matter. It's all about finding work—and extra rations."

"I'm sure they have big plans for you, though," was his cryptic reply.

When the music began, we leaned in closer to hear each other, within kissing distance. His after-shave, a lemony, sandalwood fragrance was definitely having an effect on me.

CHAPTER 33

After this playful exchange, I was pretty sure Moran wasn't one of our agents. Transported to the short time we spent together in London, I tried to recover the magic of our first encounter. Had I known I was to come under Petrov's scrutiny later, I would gladly have skipped our little coffee klatch that day; never have risked scribbling down my phone number. For one foolish moment, I'd speculated that it might result in a mild flirtation when I returned to Berlin. A reckless thing to do. I should have used my head.

But I was in it now, stuck having to ingratiate myself with Petrov. The way to do that was to find out more about Moran's activities and figure out a way to get him interested in changing loyalties. An impossible—even ridiculous—task. The man was an important asset in U.S. Intelligence. Why would he want to bother with the Soviet Union? I had to wonder how far our side would go to win him over. An offer of money, perhaps? My assignment was to find out how corruptible he was. If he was.

I had to make it work. I was so desperate to get out of the Kommandatura and into the sky. Not a day passed now that I didn't picture myself in the flight instruction job Petrov dangled as a reward for finding out information. At work, chafing at the monotony of it, all I could think of was my "new job," already seeing myself dressed in a flight suit; giving orders as I had before. Mentoring young girls wishing to fly.

Two G.I.s Vick knew interrupted us, and they exchanged a few matey words in English. It gave me time to collect my thoughts and regroup. I needed to recover from my surprise at Moran's apparition; to learn something about him I could relay to Petrov. Moran turned his attention back to me. Because he'd been speaking English to them, he carried on.

"You know, your English isn't bad," he said after we'd chatted for a few minutes. "I can tell you've been hanging out in the Bizone. You just need a little practice."

"Angie's a good teacher."

"Yes, the best. She's been helping me with my Turkish. Quite a linguist."

"Turkish? Yes, you'd need that in Istanbul," I said.

He stared at me in surprise. "So...you've managed to collect information. Yeah, I was in Turkey. Didn't get much time in the city, though. A business venture."

"You seem to do a lot of 'business.' "

"Probing for my state secrets?"

"Do you have any to tell me?"

He lowered his voice and whispered in my ear. "You'd have to get *me* drunk and take me to bed for that!"

I laughed—nervously, because the idea wasn't lacking in appeal. It had been a long war, an eternity since I had been with a man. And hadn't Petrov given me the go ahead to have a good time while I carried out my assignment?

"You know the cliché about loose lips sinking ships," Moran said.

"You're laying down ground rules?"

"Just sensitive areas we can't talk about. Tell me what you're doing these days, Comrade, apart from sitting at a desk stamping things?"

"Nothing." I said. "Nothing productive or interesting."

"Wouldn't you rather be doing what you do best?"

"Meaning?"

His chuckle was deep and throaty. "Well, I meant flying. But perhaps there are other things you do even better than that?"

I shook my head. "No, I'm not flying. I wish I were."

Moran ordered himself another beer. "Sure you don't want a drink?"

"No, thanks."

"I'm back in the cockpit," he said.

"You are? Lucky you." I felt a pang of envy.

After a few minutes, he said, "Full disclosure, I never stopped flying. I did lie to you about being grounded when we met at Drummond Hill. I'd flown to London from Berlin that morning, piloting a C-54."

"I should have guessed." I could visualize the C-54 from photos. It was one of the planes America had provided Russia in the Lend-Lease program. A good, reliable plane.

"Listen, maybe I can make it up to you; all those fibs. Would you like to see what I'm flying these days? A little spin, maybe?"

"You're offering to take me up?" This was better than I could have hoped. I could fill my report to Petrov with descriptions of the controls of an American plane, hopefully, some exciting new design. "Except for my brief trip to London as a passenger, I haven't been in the air since 1945."

"I'm not sure if I can get clearance, but it's worth a try."

"I understand."

"To take a Russian officer up in a US military plane . . . I'll need permission from top brass for that. It's a long shot." He was quiet for a moment, toying with the idea. "But rules are meant to be broken. I'll see what I can do. You free next weekend?"

"Yes, I think so." *Yes, yes, yes!*

"I'll call you if I get the go ahead. We'll set something up. Maybe on Saturday?"

"Yes, I believe I'm free. Call me—even if you can't."

The band was easing into a nice slow song, "Near You."

"Dance?" he asked, touching my hand as he gestured in the direction of the band.

My head was still buzzing from his invitation to fly. "I'm not very good," I said.

He shot me a sexy grin. "That doesn't matter. It's not the steps that make it fun."

I felt the tattoo of his heartbeat as we nestled together cheek-to-cheek and I breathed in his scent. He was a good dancer, light on his feet, and he led me across the floor with ease.

I had to keep reminding myself that I was there to spy on him. Nothing more. Petrov's warning—"*He deliberately sought you out*" echoed in my head. All these months I'd been searching for him, had he been playing hard-to-get, calculating the precise moment when I'd be exasperated and eager? Planning when to pounce? If so, he had timed it right.

I knew I had to be careful. Vick Moran was not intense and tightly wound like Maxim; he had an easy charm, a way of making a woman—this woman, at least—

feel special. To allow myself the luxury of getting involved with him would be all too easy. But I was no longer a moonstruck teenager. Maturity had taught me to control my impulses. Much as I liked the feel of his smoothly shaved face touching mine, the secure feeling of his arm around my waist as he held me, and the gentle touch of his hand as we swayed to the music, I reminded myself I was only with him to collect information. Period. To forget that would put my life in grave danger, and I'd already had enough danger to fill two lifetimes. No, too high a price to pay; nothing was worth that.

Still, for now—in this place, in this moment—moving in rhythm to the music was lovely. The nearness of him. We danced several slow Glenn Miller numbers. Finally, I saw Angela check her watch, the signal that she was ready to leave. With regret, I pulled away.

"I have to go," I said.

"Too bad. We were just getting started. I've got a jeep outside. I could drive you home."

I shook my head. "No, thanks. I'm staying the night at Angela's."

"Okay, then," he said, disappointed. "Rain check."

I didn't understand what that meant, and glanced outside the window nearest us to check for rain.

He leaned over and kissed my cheek. "You're cute, Comrade," he said with a grin. "It's just an expression."

I touched my cheek. The kiss—no more than a peck —caught me by surprise. What surprised me most was that I wanted more. Much more.

"I'll be in touch," he said. "Oh, I almost forgot."

He fished into his pocket and placed something in my hand; then he was gone. It was Luba's pearl earring.

CHAPTER 34

A week or so passed.

Frau Schuman covered the telephone with her hand and mouthed: "The American who speaks German."

"Do you still want to check out what I'm flying, Comrade?" Vick Moran asked. He took delight in calling me by our Russian honorific. "How about Saturday morning?"

I made no attempt to be coy. It astonished me that he'd so quickly secured permission to take me up in a U.S. military plane. I'd told Petrov it might take several weeks.

"Of course! I'd love to. So, you got the go-ahead to take up an enemy of the American people?"

This was met with a low chuckle. "I got clearance for a short hop. Do you have a flight jacket? If not, I can lend you one." There was hesitation before he said, "After we land, we can have lunch. I might even show you where I live."

I detected a slow inviting smile in his voice.

A bonus, I thought. Not only would I tell Petrov about the inside of a newly engineered US plane, but I'd also have a potential spy recruit's home address and personal information to give him. What happened after we got to his place—well, I'd figure that out.

Saturday was a perfect day for flying, cool and clear, almost cloudless. Vick was waiting for me in a jeep in the British Zone outside the Brandenburg Gate. With his tan, his aviator sun glasses, and an informal beaked cap, he was as handsome out of uniform as he was in it. He jumped out of the jeep and helped me into the vehicle, planting a chaste kiss on my cheek. "Welcome back to the good sector of Berlin, Comrade," he said.

"I thought the American Zone was."

"Same difference. It's the Bizone; the Brits are our best allies." Then he added, "We know where we stand with them. No games or dirty tricks."

I got his little jab. We Russians were no longer to be trusted—if we ever were.

A sidelong glance, and then he broke into a grin. "Think about it. Are there any nice Russians on your side of this city? Besides you?"

"Nice ones? Sure. They're mostly women, though."

"They keep them well-hidden, from what I've observed. But with your rowdy troops hanging around, I guess they have to."

I didn't rise to the bait.

With fuel shortages, there was no needless driving around. Vick Moran knew the best detours and the most accessible streets in West Berlin. As he snaked his jeep past rubble, juddering over debris to Tempelhof, he spoke casually about flying in general, and we chatted about non-controversial things.

I told him my perception of his country, cobbled from Busby Berkeley song and dance musicals—Hollywood movies I'd seen, mostly shot in California. They portrayed America as a beacon of glamour in an idyllic Technicolor world of sunny skies and swaying palms; romances of beautiful women and handsome men. In this fantasy Eden, spontaneous music and singing broke out without preamble, often with choreographed dancing or synchronized swimming. Much more fun than dreary films based on novels by Sholokhov or Solzhenitsyn.

We both laughed at my perception. "I can't vouch for all that synchronized stuff, or palm trees. But I can tell you it's a pretty nice place to live. A huge, prosperous, self-sufficient country. We're free to move around. And no shortages or rationing."

I knew it was an overly simplified view. America had plenty of problems, and our side made sure we were all aware of them. But an abundance of food in itself would make it a paradise for me. No rationing ever? A twinge of envy as my stomach growled from the paucity of Frau Schuman's breakfast. Food fantasies continued to tease my mind.

Soon, we heard the roar of planes taking off and landing. Tempelhof airfield came into view, the baleful Nazi artwork outside a reminder that it had once been a stone's throw from Columbia Haus, a concentration camp. Vick parked the car and turned off the engine.

"There she is," he beamed as we strolled toward the planes from the parking lot. "The Gooney Bird. C-47."

My face contorted with ill-concealed disappointment. I'd expected some marvel of American engineering with state-of-the-art features, a new model designed to show off post-war Yankee know-how. But few aircraft were as well-known, so widely used, and in service for as long as the C-47. Every branch of the U.S. military and all the major allied powers had flown them.

He gestured toward the plane. "You've been up in one

of these?"

"Never."

"No? She's a great little plane. As troop transport, she carries twenty-eight in full combat gear. But I'm sure you knew that. You're up on all our equipment."

I acted like I was.

The sight of the large number of C-47s on the ground took my breath away. "There are rows of them! I had no idea they were still so much in use."

"If you Russkies keep threatening to cut off West Berlin, you'll see a lot more of them."

"Cut off West Berlin? That's news to me."

But I knew perfectly well what he was talking about. The rumors of a possible blockade to force the Western Allies out of the divided city. Petrov had hinted as much. We Soviets thought the time was coming to sever ties with some of our former allies; time for the USSR to take over all of Berlin and cut it off from the West.

Additionally, it would help us control our East Berlin population. No way in; no way out. West Berlin was accessed from the rest of West Germany by a single, easy-to-barricade road. Boat traffic on the rivers would also be easy to divert. Only air corridors would remain open.

In terms of human cost, such a blockade would be catastrophic, a humanitarian crisis leaving nearly two million people in danger of starvation. They'd be cut off, facing not only the prospect of hunger, but the winter cold, unemployment, and misery. Would our side do it? Stalin wouldn't bat an eye. He'd done it in Ukraine, creating the infamous *holodomor*. Whether the rest of the world would let him do it again was another issue. An improbability.

But Berlin itself was an improbability. A fractured city, deep in the communist-held part of the divided country —only one hundred miles from the West German border, yet so far away.

We Russians could'do it. To blockade the Allied-occupied side and choke off communications and supplies to West Berliners would be like taking the proverbial candy from a baby. Yes, the baby would scream blue murder, but in the end, what could it do? And who would stop us? They'd get used to the idea. Nobody was ready for another war.

To avoid such a move by us, the Allies would have to relent and allow Berlin to be united under our Soviet hegemony. Would they? Or might they find some ingenious way to avoid such a scenario?

"Do you think West Berlin would survive if our side did what you're suggesting?" I asked.

Moran didn't answer. Instead, he redirected my attention to the aircraft with his hand.

"Yeah, we sure love our Gooney Birds. They're the perfect little cargo plane. We have plenty of them," he said, then added meaningfully. "And the manpower to crank out more. A lot more. As many as we need, even if it means keeping production lines going around the clock for the next decade."

This jolted me. So, the Americans were not only expecting a blockade—they were already preparing for it and planning ahead. Finally, here was something I could report on: the U.S. was still building C-47s with the same enthusiasm it did during wartime. Or was that disinformation Vick wanted me to convey? He was too smart to blurt out information he didn't want our brass to know. I would let Petrov and Belenko figure that one out. My job was to report on what I saw and heard.

"We keep these beauties outfitted for light transport, aircrew training, navigation and gunnery, and—in spy parlance—for photo-reconnaissance," he said, in a lighter tone. "You can tell that to your friends in the East. But they know it already."

"I'm not a spy."

"Sure you are, Comrade. You all are over there. We get letters every week from people on your side with 'information to sell'. *Geheime Informatoren.* 99% of it is bullshit. If they don't have real information, they're happy to make some up. They don't usually ask for money; just passage to somewhere in the West, like Frankfurt if they want to stay in Germany. England, or the U.S. Some other place overseas, like Australia or Canada. New Zealand. South Africa. Or follow their old friends to South America."

I said nothing. I well remembered neighbors or tradesmen in Moscow lingering in stairwells or doorways; people hanging around subway stations; all in the unofficial service of the NKVD, getting dirt on fellow citizens to ingratiate themselves. With money, rations, or their own self-preservation at stake, people would say anything. Not surprising that the ignoble practice would flourish here where spying was a ubiquitous hobby.

"Such devotion you all have to your Uncle Joe," mused Vick. "But Stalin was every bit as bad as Hitler. Even worse. The full body count isn't in yet. And I'm just talking about the war—not the purges."

Abruptly, the memory surfaced of my father being dragged off in the middle of the night by the NKVD. The innocent people dispatched to the gulag—or executed. The dreaded purges of the 1930s. Our leader had a lot to answer for.

There was an awkward moment of silence between us. Perhaps he was waiting for me to defend Stalin. But the looming image of the man dominating the area of Unter den Linden in front of the Adlon Hotel choked off any attempt to do that. I could say nothing in Stalin's defense. Accustomed to lowering my voice when his name came up, I kept quiet.

"For Berlin right now, Kira, *It's the best of times; It's the worst of times.* The good news is, the war is over. The bad news is, the Cold War has begun. Will we end up with the "spring of hope", or the "winter of despair"?"

I got that he was quoting someone, a writer or philosopher whose work I was unfamiliar with.

"Our two powers are now locked in a conflict to win Germany's soul," he continued earnestly. "A delicate balance."

"The Soviet Union has a firm hold on a large part of Germany," I said. "So, which side will win this cold war, Mr. America?"

He chuckled. "Nobody knows that, honey. It's anybody's guess. But this I do know: We're living in historic times. What happens here in Berlin now will have an effect on this country for a generation—perhaps a lot longer."

I couldn't disagree with that.

He offered me a mint, then popped one in his mouth.

"Enough about politics. Shall we fly?"

Happy to leave off the serious implications of what he said, I nodded as I peeled away the candy wrapper. But his words lingered.

Moran strapped a parachute to my back. Then he put on his own; a ritual of mutual patting and strapping, helping each other. Political differences aside, we were two pilots working together.

He assisted me in boarding, then lost no time explaining the inner workings of a C-47. My eyes ran over the control panel. I took in its shiny newness and smell of the interior, marveling at the relative comfort of the seats as I compared it to my Po-2.

I said, "How spoiled you Americans were during the war."

"Spoiled? Ha. You should see some of the planes we fought in. B-24s, B-17s. And even the Gooneybirds we flew in combat. Crude benches, no comforts. This particular one is new; a sports car."

"What I fought in for three Russian winters was a biplane with an open cockpit. I'm sure what you flew was more substantial aircraft than that."

He laughed and shook his head. "Well, okay, admittedly what we had was a hell of a lot better. I'm surprised you never got to fly one of these, though. Plenty of them were sent to Russia. They're one of the aircraft Stalin ordered for the Lend-Lease program."

The name 'Lend-Lease' was a euphemism. Despite Stalin's inclination to play it down, it was a known fact that the United States had sent us about eleven billion dollars' worth of war materiel: tanks, fighter aircraft, ships and trucks, jeeps, weapons, and munitions—virtually everything needed to defeat Hitler. After the severe battering the equipment took during the war, the Americans didn't want any of it back. An American senator had said it would be like getting back used chewing gum.

"None of your fancy American planes reached the women's regiments," I said.

"Yeah, I keep forgetting. The best equipment went to the guys. I guess you ladies were considered expendable. You got to fly the noisy sewing machines. Those rickety little trainers." He smiled at me in admiration. "I don't know how you survived up there in those crop dusters with Messerschmitts shooting at you. But you're still here to tell the tale!"

"Yes, they were death traps. It sometimes happened that the engines would conk out halfway through our missions, and the navigator had to climb out on the wings mid-flight to restart the props!"

Moran shook his head.

"Our other two female regiments flew PE-2s and YAKs. They weren't much better. We lost about one third of our female pilots. Thirteen in my regiment alone."

"How many sorties did your pilots fly?"

"All three regiments? Around thirty thousand in all."

"Tough gals," he chuckled. "The famous Night Witches."

"Only my regiment—the night bombers—were called that. Why not call us pilots? We were just flyers defending our homeland, too young to know the danger we were in. Is that so different from what you were?"

"No. You sign on for crazy stuff when you're young."

He was quiet for a long moment. Then, "Listen, how would you like to learn to fly a decent plane?"

I caught my breath in surprise. "This one? Are you serious?"

"Dead serious. You up for it?"

"Your superiors would never allow me to fly it. A Russian military officer."

He shrugged. "Who's going to tell them?"

CHAPTER 35

M oran spent the next hour or two teaching me the basics of the aircraft. I was in my element, full of questions, and couldn't get enough of his instruction. To be back in a plane again was heaven; the prospect of flying it, seraphic pleasure.

What he was doing was a security breach I'd never have dared risk had our positions been reversed. Strange that he'd bother to take so much time teaching me. Afterward, he quizzed me and when I answered everything correctly, he started the engines, called for clearance from the control tower, sat me in the pilot's seat, and moved to co-pilot.

"Take her up."

A rush of terror. If I made a mistake and we crashed, it would be difficult to explain what went wrong after we bailed. *If* we were able to bail. I began the cockpit procedures meticulously. As he called the tower for taxiing instructions, I gently coaxed the throttle into position and lifted off. Only then did my fear abate. The engines hummed efficiently, their sound almost musical to me. Slowly we lifted off the ground, and before I knew it, we were up eight thousand feet.

For a nostalgic moment, I was a child again, flying for the first time with Maxim over a Ukrainian landscape. But Vick Moran and I were sailing the skies at speeds I'd only dreamed of. This time I was too high up to see much of the view. No target commanded my attention, and nobody was shooting at me.

About forty-five minutes later, lathered in a stress-induced sweat, I asked Vick to land the plane, but he refused. "Come on, Comrade. In for a penny, in for a pound. Get her down. You can do it."

I had to fight off a wave of panic. I stiffened my back and, following my instincts and instructions from him and the tower, brought the Gooney Bird safely down to the tarmac. Weak in the knees from the exhilaration of the flight and the apprehension of landing it smoothly, I was breathing rapidly by the time we parked it in the area we'd started from. After I turned off the ignition I stood up almost in tears, unsure on my feet, wobbling on rubbery knees, my stomach queasy.

We took off our parachutes and quietly headed for the car park. I was disoriented, limping feebly toward his jeep. I couldn't believe I'd flown it. And flown it well.

"You done good, Comrade!" Vick said with a matey slap on the back. "Real good. C'mon, you need a stiff drink."

I did. My nerves were tingling; my hands still shaking.

"Shall we go to my place? I've got some good bourbon, and scotch whiskey. We also have wine--some nice Bordeaux and a bottle of white Burgundy. And we can raid the ice-box for something to munch on. I've got French cheeses and some cold cuts. Some good bread. All thanks to the Frenchies setting up in the Trizone. We do a lot of bartering. They love American cigarettes."

"I'm not sure I can eat. But I could sure use that drink."

Vick's apartment was small, but amply furnished with mismatched pieces scrounged from the Army's concession warehouse. He shared it with another U.S. Army major, a man named Jack Reilly who, after shaking my hand and murmuring a few niceties, tactfully took his leave.

"Gotta go, kids. We're cleansing the records of more Germans," he said as he exited. Vick explained Reilly was doing work similar to mine: processing the papers of Germans who were former Nazis.

The difference was that we in the East regarded fascist training an asset because their efficient, brutal methods made for great secret police and guards. On the American side, they were far more single-minded. They weren't seeking out brute force talents. If applicants were scientists or professionals, every effort was made to wipe their records clean. The much coveted *Persilschein.* Valuable assets were de-Nazified so they could work with the U.S. government.

Vick poured me a glass of pre-war Chardonnay, and selected some jazz records to play on the gramophone. We sat on the sofa listening to the velvety vocal tones of Billie Holiday as we sipped wine and nibbled snacks, and before long, my tensions eased and my body relaxed. Replacing my stress was a new feeling, gratitude mixed with another kind of excitement. I waited for him to make a move, calculating how I would handle it if he did. When he did nothing, I finally spoke:

"The earring."

"What about it?"

"Thank you."

"What for?"

"It was you, last spring, wasn't it?" After those troops attacked me near my apartment. You were in the car that stopped?"

"Yeah. That was me. It was the night I tried to call you. I happened to be in the Russian Zone. I was going to tell you it was me, but there was no time. You were in trouble."

"I didn't recognize your voice because you were speaking Russian. What were you doing over in the Soviet Zone?"

"I was meeting someone. When I saw what was happening I thought it was a German woman they were assaulting. I stopped my car to help and I heard your voice, screaming in Russian. What a potty mouth! Where'd you learn all those cuss words?"

I smiled. "From the men training at Engels."

"I'd have seen you home, but I had to deal with those guys first." He shot me a stern look. "You shouldn't go out alone at night. Hasn't anyone warned you about that?"

"Everyone."

"I get it. You're not good at taking advice."

"I appreciate what you did."

"You don't need to thank me."

"I do," I said quietly. "You came along just in time. Those troops—they didn't believe me when I said I was Russian."

"Didn't matter to them one way or the other, honey. They were drunk; you're a woman. End of story. They weren't thinking with their brains. I'm glad I could help." He lit a cigarette. "Your troops have been doing that since the war ended. Not so much now. At first, Stalin sanctioned it—thought his boys deserved to cut loose. But venereal disease and complaints from the Allied powers finally reined them in."

"And your American troops? I suppose they were

angels?"

"Not angels. But this was extreme. A million and a half Russian troops stormed Germany after the conquest in April of '45. They had little food and no place to billet. Hadn't been paid or had much sex for two or three years. And their hatred for the Germans ran deep. Very deep."

"And your soldiers?" Even after Frau Schuman's account, my knee-jerk reaction was to defend our side.

"By the time we arrived in July, things had cooled down. Our G.I.s had gotten paid all along. The war had been hell, but here in Berlin they were adequately housed and well-supplied. They had no love for krauts either, but they could be more subtle. They could offer goodies like lipstick and nylons or cigarettes to the ladies.

"And don't lay it all on us Amis. The Frenchies and the Brits wanted female company too. But they'd been through tough times. They didn't have as much to offer."

He thought about it. "Women don't fare too well in war-time. Especially when they end up on the wrong side."

"Because they came offering food and trinkets, I suppose that excused your men from exploiting hungry women?"

"Whoa! Listen, I'm not condoning the system. Just sayin'; 'twas ever thus. But Americans were offering quid pro quo. Your Russki troops thought they could steamroll the place."

He paused, pouring us more wine. Then he said in a concilliatory tone, "I know. It's not right—women still can't venture out of their homes at night. You found that out the hard way. Women need a curfew."

"A curfew?" I was incredulous. Bristling, I said: "Tell me you're joking. A curfew for the *women*?"

He was taken aback. "I meant...for their protection..."

The wine was having its effect and I was like a dog with a bone: "Since the aggressors are men, isn't it the men who should be under curfew?"

He looked at me, startled. Then he roared with laughter. "You have a point, Comrade. You have a point. But don't expect *that* to happen. Ever!"

If nothing else, I'd made him think. I thought of Steffi Bauman carrying unwanted Russian babies and I said neutrally: "The after-effects of all this will live on. With the children."

"Yes. Ironic. Hitler virtually wiped out a white, culturally German people—the Jews—in the interest of ethnic cleansing; but the next generation of Germans will have Russian, Mongol, Moroccan, British, French, and American fathers."

"So much for his German Aryan ideal."

"Diversity wasn't his thing."

He moved a little closer to me then. He brushed my cheek with his lips and took my hand, about to say something.

The phone rang. Frowning, he hesitated. Then answered it, glanced at his watch, and had a terse two-minute conversation in a language that sounded Middle Eastern.

After he rang off, the song stopped, and silence settled over the room. The record had come to an end and he removed it, but didn't replace it with another. The whole ambiance had changed.

"I just found out I have to be out of town for a few days," he said. He was serious and preoccupied. "I have to get back to Tempelhof."

He slipped the record back into its sleeve.

I don't know what would have happened if the phone hadn't rung. Any flirtation we had going abruptly evaporated. The call transported him to another place and he was distracted. He threw some things into a bag while I put away the food. When he drove me home we spoke only of trivial things, then parted with another chaste kiss on my cheek that only left me feeling empty and cheated. Despite our scrappy repartee, I'd been more than ready to take things to the next level.

"Will I see you again?" I asked.

He smiled then. "Sure. When I get back. I'll call you." Then he was gone in a cloud of Berlin rubble dust.

CHAPTER 36

T he following Monday I told Petrov about the C-47s on the Tempelhof air field, my flying lesson, and our conversation about the blockade. I related how Vick Moran claimed the Americans were going to deal with it, their plans to build more planes; how he had bragged about their capacity to produce. I reported on the phone call that interrupted us, and Moran's departure.

Gleeful, he hung on my every word. "So they're hoping to air supply West Berlin with their C-47s if we blockade? Ha! We'll see how long they can keep that up."

Forthcoming I might be, but when he asked for Moran's address, I clammed up.

"I couldn't read the street sign," I lied, surprising myself. "It was charred, and there was no number on the door. Sometimes numbers are hand-written on little signs stuck in the ground, but his place didn't have one." A plausible explanation, if untrue. I hoped nobody had been following me. Petrov did not push me on the address; instead, he focused on the phone call.

"So he was speaking what? Turkish?"

"It could have been. I don't speak Turkish, so I can't be certain. He was fluent, whatever it was."

"Has he offered to take you up again?"

"Yes, he said something about another spin. After he gets back."

"That's good. Excellent. You enjoyed yourself?"

"Oh, very much. To be flying again, and piloting a plane like that was great fun," I said, hoping to deflect attention away from my attraction to Vick Moran, while reminding him that I was a competent pilot.

A blush settled over my face as I recalled the moment before the phone call interrupted us. What might have happened; the fantasies of possible scenarios I basked in afterward . . .

Petrov was silent for a moment. With a meaningful smile he said, "I'd remind you, though, not to think of flying away like an American eagle, Comrade Voronova."

"I serve the Soviet Union," I said, allowing indignation to color my voice. "It would never occur to me to do such a thing. My only desire is to teach our enlisted women to fly. As you promised to help me accomplish."

"Yes, yes. We'll get to that. But I feel I must remind you that the West plots to lure our people. To work against us. That's why he approached you in London in the first place. We need to be careful dealing with former allies." He stressed the word "former."

"I understand," I said.

"Was he on track to seduce you?" he asked abruptly.

Something I'd asked myself. "I couldn't read his mind. He had to leave. He became distracted, focused on some problem. So it turned out to be a friendly encounter. We ate lightly; had a glass of wine. That's all. Then he drove me to the Gate. He was rushing to make his plane."

Petrov raised his eyebrows with interest and said evenly, "This is all good. Next time, find out more. Whatever way you can. Get him to tell you details about what the Americans are up to in Turkey. And exactly how they plan to deal with the blockade. I want details. Get his phone number and address. You're doing well,

Voronova. Carry on. Dismissed."

I quickly left his office and headed toward my cubicle, asking myself as I usually did if our meeting had been successful. Had I told him too much? Too little? And why had I withheld Major Moran's address?

The truth is that, as loyal as I was to our Motherland, I had learned to be wary. My father's ruin had stamped me indelibly, and governed all my future faith, or lack of it, in the regime.

With his address, our secret police could appear at Moran's door and arrest him on a trumped up charge. Such kidnappings were common. And I wanted nothing to do with such a scenario.

Now less than ever.

CHAPTER 37

M oran traveled sporadically the rest of that summer, but when he was in Berlin, we'd go flying in the C-47 on Saturdays. To my surprise, he was usually business-like afterward. Always friendly, even mildly flirtatious, but increasingly he was withdrawing from romantic involvement. Sometimes we'd stop at his place for a quick drink and a snack, but with Reilly usually around, we'd taken to driving over to the area designated as the future French Zone for coffee and croissants. Very public. Impersonal. We'd talk about war experiences, our families, future plans.

We were getting along, becoming good friends, and enjoying each other's company, but that was all. Very platonic.

I was confused. Had I had misread his signals the first time? I was sure I'd seen a meaningful look in his eyes as he'd handed me my wine during Billie Holiday's sultry rendition of "All or Nothing At All." But that look disappeared. Why was he bothering to help me log hours in a C-47 if he had no ulterior motive?

Petrov had even begun to yawn during our debriefings. "Is that all?" he'd say, betraying that he'd been looking forward to descriptions of lascivious scenes between us.

Finally, I discerned a subtle shift in Moran's attitude. On this occasion, he had given me no instruction while we flew the Gooney Bird. I'd been completely on my own from take-off to landing, and I was feeling chuffed. It was a kind of graduation. He too was pleased. A toast was in order.

"Reilly's in Washington," he said. "We could go to the apartment—if you like."

We'd toasted my accomplishment in three languages and we were both feeling happy and mellow. A lovely bottle of champagne sat half-empty on the table near the sofa. Sinatra was singing "Someone to Watch Over Me." We were both feeling relaxed and happy. As usual, I had taken off my flight suit—which we now kept at his apartment—and donned a skirt. Vick Moran was extolling my talents as a pilot when he abruptly paused to observe, "You have beautiful legs, Comrade."

He moved closer to me on the couch and took my hand. I could feel his warm breath on my neck and a frisson tickling my spine.

"The rest of you isn't bad either." He said this as though he was only now discovering my attributes.

I'd been still basking in his praise of my flying talents; now he was lauding my looks. It had been a long time since a man had paid me such unabashed compliments; a soothing balm to my ego, so battered during the war, and since my arrival in Berlin.

Putting my glass down on the coffee table, I finally said: "This is such a cliché seduction, Vick."

He chuckled at this. "You mean getting you roaring drunk so you'll tell me secrets to topple the U.S.S.R.? Are my intentions so transparent?"

The champagne was kicking in. I gave him a tipsy smile. "Yes. I've suspected your attentions. From the day I met you in London."

He paused to put out his cigarette. "Seduction hasn't been much on my mind, Kira. What happened during the Blitz put a damper on my love life for a long time."

"Are you saying you haven't been with women since?"

"No, I'm not saying that. There have been plenty of girls, but none of them had to be seduced. And never anything serious."

"It takes a long time to recover. After I got the letter from the War Department telling me about my husband, I felt the same way." I was touched by the look of compassion that crossed his face as it edged closer to mine.

I added, "But life has to move on." Even as I said it, I knew that I was ready to put the past behind me.

He nodded. His lips were grazing my cheek, my throat, my chin, caressing my ear as he buried his face in my hair and neck. I all but purred with pleasure.

"That first day I saw you in London," he said, his voice low, "all that gray—the fog and rain—you were the only bit of sunshine in that place, with your smile...your blonde hair." He kissed me lightly on the lips.

The champagne, the music, and his proximity awakened a strong, reckless urge in me, much like the time I scribbled my phone number on his cigarette package.

"I want you," I said bluntly.

He grinned at me. "You're very direct."

"Life is short. Why waste it?"

"You have a point."

"I miss you when you're away."

"Are you sure it's not the flying lessons you miss?" he teased.

I shook my head. No, it wasn't. The truth was, I had missed *him*. Missing him had morphed into desire, and now we were here together. We had so little time, I didn't want to be bothered being coy.

"I miss you too," he said, fingering a strand of my hair. "I keep thinking about that day in London. How I wanted to take your clothes off, unravel those braids. Spread them out on a pillow . . ."

"And?" I asked as I reached up to unbutton his shirt, he took the pins out of my hair and ran his hands through it. His breath was warm and perfumed with wine.

"And do what I plan to do now," he murmured.

"You talk too much," I said.

"Yes, ma'am."

He began to undress me. "Cute undies," he observed as he slid them off.

Thank you, Beatrix Belenko.

Everything was 'for now,' I told myself. Our relationship was temporary. And potentially adversarial. One day soon he'd go back to America; I'd be returned to Moscow. Or better, stay put in Germany where I could work and—if I did things right—be teaching and flying again, perhaps with another risible ribbon or medal for service to the Soviet Union. Whatever the outcome, we'd never see each other again. The ground rules were clear in my mind.

If the war had taught me anything, it was to live for today. Life could be snuffed out like a light bulb. I was determined to enjoy the moment.

An ephemeral interlude; pleasurable, and something that would advance my standing with Petrov. That's all this was. All it could ever be.

CHAPTER 38

Galina was going to Moscow. One of the higher-ups at the Kommandatura was heading there for an important meeting—something to do with currency changes in Berlin—and the male pilot selected to fly him over was recovering from a foot injury. Having completed logging the hours required by Aeroflot, Galina was fingered to replace him.

"I'm very excited," she told me as she rushed into my bedroom. "It will be so good to get away from this shit-pile for a few days. And to fly a decent military plane! Put my new skills to work."

While I would have loved to see Moscow again, with Vick back in Berlin I was more than content to stay, at least for the moment. Vick and I had made plans to go flying that Saturday, and with our relationship taking a new direction, I lived for the excitement of my weekends with him.

"Could you do me a favor?" I asked Galina. "Drop in on my father and grandfather?"

"Of course."

"And could you find out what Zinaida Sebrova is up to? You remember her?"

"Zinaida? Our mechanic? Of course. Do you have an address?"

I nodded, withdrawing a letter from the top drawer of my nightstand. "She wrote me a year ago on my birthday. This address is probably still good."

Luba had a letter ready for Galina to deliver to Zinaida as well. "I have so much to tell her!" she said. She'd found a boyfriend and wanted to share her good news with the whole world.

"Who is this mysterious suitor?" I teased her. "Anyone we know? A Russian bigwig?"

"No," Luba said, blushing. "No, not Russian."

"American, then? Or British?"

"Neither. He's Polish. A refugee. Stanislaw Kurzeszyn. I'm quite mad about him."

"Bring him around so we can meet him. Perhaps when Galina gets back. Then we can all look him over."

That weekend, I was surprised to see Angela waiting for me at the Gate. "Vick's been delayed. He asked me to meet you, and to tell you, 'Reilly is home.' You'll be staying with me."

My anticipation sagged.

"It will be nice to spend more time with you. I've missed you," said Angela, taking me by the arm. She appeared troubled. "You take my mind off things."

"Is something wrong?"

We were ambling past the tattered ruins of the Reichstag and had to walk past tourists and visiting media still wandering through the former fortress of power with ghoulish curiosity, taking pictures, hoping to find souvenirs in the rubble.

"I'm worried about my sister, Ingrid," Angela said. "During the war, in London, she worked as a cipher clerk for the S.O.E."

"The British Special Operations Executive?"

"Yes. They sent her to Berlin after the war. She was working for the British at first. Then she became a private contractor and was recruited by the Americans, handling sensitive material."

"Ingrid told you this?"

"No. She kept it to herself. I was so naïve, I thought she was here doing general office work. Vick Moran was her boss. Her Russian is perfect, so he arranged it in such a way that your people believed she was one of theirs. She secretly reported to someone at the Kommandatura. That person reported to the G.R.U.—the Main Intelligence Directorate in Moscow."

It was the Soviet Union's largest foreign intelligence agency.

"And what was her job description exactly?"

Angela hesitated, as though remembering which side I was on.

"I shouldn't be talking about it."

"Tell me. It won't go any farther."

"Well, her job was to encipher outgoing messages and decipher incoming ones. The Americans—Vick and his group—gave her bits of useless disinformation to pass to the Russians—to your side. You don't want to know too many details."

"I do," I insisted. *At least Petrov does.* "You can trust me, Angela. I want to understand why you're worried about your sister. Who was her contact at the Kommandatura?"

I had crossed the line. Perhaps I was pushing too hard. I sensed a clamming up, her trust ebbing away. She drew back and let go of my arm. "I have no idea. But even if I did, it would be safer for you not to know it."

We both knew that nobody could hold out against the

torture methods used in interrogation.

I tried another angle. "You and Ingrid spent time here together?"

"No, I was a radio operator in London while she was here. She was very secretive. Only Vick and the mole at the Kommandatura knew what she knew."

A mole at the Kommandatura. A nice bit of intelligence for Petrov—unless he was the mole. For the first time, I wondered about his loyalty to the Soviets. Anything was possible during these unsettled times. He was the first to point out that the Cold War created strange bedfellows.

"So, what happened?"

Angela thought for a moment, then decided to trust me. "Ingrid got caught. Within a few months of her arrival in Berlin, she uncovered valuable information about Stalin's efforts to steal nuclear secrets and about Russian sleeper agents. She passed on a wealth of information to the Americans through a Canadian spy in Ottawa. The Russians—your side—found out and she was arrested."

My heart sank for Angela. "She was killed? I'm so sorry —I thought you were troubled because there was some way you could still help—"

"She wasn't killed. I thought she had been. The Soviets' secret police kidnapped her. Grabbed her off the street. We searched for her a long time; finally, we accepted that she was dead."

"But?"

"But Vick Moran recently found out that she's alive. They're keeping her in East Berlin. Conditions there are terrible and I'm sure she's been badly treated. They won't let me visit her."

"That's the way it was when my father was arrested. My brother and I weren't allowed to visit him, either. My mother saw him only once a month."

"Your father was arrested?"

It occurred to me how little we knew about each other. In all the time we'd spent studying, I hadn't mentioned my father's brush with the NKVD. "Yes, but he was later released."

"He was lucky, then."

"Yes. A family friend helped him to get out. Do you know where Ingrid is?"

"Moran traced her to Sachsenhausen, the prison in Oranienburg on the Havel River."

"Sachsenhausen?" It was where Boris and his fellow guards were employed. I wouldn't let myself imagine how Ingrid was being abused by that bunch.

A thought struck me. "Is that why you came to Berlin? To find your sister?"

She nodded. "My parents are broken-hearted; they sold all their jewels and icons to pay for lawyers. Vick tells me that if we don't free her soon, she could be executed. Or shipped to Siberia, to some gulag camp. They've only delayed her trial because she might have some propaganda value. They've been hoping to use her for some political gain."

I didn't say it, but I thought death would be preferable.

Angela's eyes filled up. "She's a British citizen. The lawyers tried to make a deal with American OSS operatives and MI-6 contacts in London. We hoped there'd be an opportunity to exchange her for a Russian spy the British have in custody, but nothing has worked out. And we're running out of time."

I pulled her into a hug. "I'm so sorry," I said again. I was genuinely miserable on her behalf.

Later, when I saw Vick I said, "I'm worried about Angela's sister in Sachsenhausen."

He shot me a wary look. "She told you about Ingrid?"

I said she had.

"She shouldn't be talking about it. Things are pretty dicey right now," he added. "The less said the better. It's a bad situation. Ingrid is a pawn. I understand her health is deteriorating. If she doesn't get out of Sachsenhausen soon . . ." He shook his head. "They don't treat spies well."

I nodded. I was being exposed to the strange world of spycraft; unfamiliar to me, but I was learning.

He said, "You Russians love to latch onto a story like this. Hold her up as an example to other potential traitors; spin out lots of anti-west news stories, and create an international incident over it. "

"And yours don't do that?" I demanded. I continued to surprise myself with the loyalty I felt to Russia.

"Trust me, we're not playing roulette with this poor girl's life. She was working for us. We're doing our best to negotiate something."

We were silent for a moment while I considered this. Finally I said, "Vick, I know a guard at Sachsenhausen. Know him well, in fact. He worries about what I'll tell his mother about . . ."

"You know a Sachsenhausen guard's mother?" he

interrupted.

"Yes. Nadia Harlamova. She and Boris and his brother Anton lived with my family communally in our Moscow apartment. Nadia and Anton still do. I didn't know Boris was in Berlin until recently."

He looked thoughtfully at me. I could sense he was spinning ideas around in his mind.

"When you saved me from those louts that time last spring? Boris was one of them. After I yelled at them in Russian and told them who I was, he's the one who took off, so you didn't get to knock sense into his head."

"A deferred pleasure. Maybe I will yet," he said. "Call him."

I wanted to help. Yet, I shuddered. If Petrov knew that I was collaborating with Americans to interfere with a Russian prisoner, I'd be sharing a cell with Ingrid. It could mean immediate execution for both of us. I had a difficult decision to make. I was going to have to choose sides. And there was a lot at stake.

Could I count on Vick and Angela to play straight with me? As lovers now, Vick and I were sharing intimate moments, but I had no illusions. He could end our relationship with abrupt ease at any time. I was beginning to love Angela like a sister, but I'd learned to be suspicious of everyone. I was still Russian, and they wouldn't forget that any more than I could.

Yet, I couldn't bear to picture Angela's sister caged in Sachsenhausen. Going forward, the idea of Ingrid—of any woman—going through the horrors she was, would gnaw at me if I did nothing.

I hadn't taken any big risks since my night missions

over German-occupied territory. It was time I put aside the intimidation of people like Petrov. Time to take a leap of faith and do what I could.

CHAPTER 39

When I returned to the East Zone on Sunday night, Galina had come back from Moscow. She and the others were in Frau Schuman's living room sipping black market hot chocolate contributed by Elena, a gift from her mysterious Brit.

"Kira, I wish I had good news for you. First of all, I couldn't find Zinaida Sebrova. I went to the address you gave me, but she had moved and left no forwarding address."

Luba and I were both crestfallen. Zinaida had moved without notifying either of us. It was becoming clear that our mutual friend wanted to cut ties with her friends.

I was digesting this when Galina added, "Your grandfather had a massive stroke—"

"Dedushka? Oh no! Is he dead?"

"No, not dead, but he's in the Moscow General Hospital."

She grimaced and shook her head, and I understood. His situation was hopeless; he was not going to recover.

"There's more, Kira. The woman, Nadia, from your apartment? The NKVD has picked her up. It sounds like she had a black market scheme going with someone, a lover. They've both been arrested."

"Nadia? Oh, no!"

"They were selling gourmet foods and medicine," continued Galina, shaking her head at the foolishness, the risk.

I was reminded of the time I came home to Moscow to recover from pneumonia, seeing the kitchen table overflowing with plenty; Dedushka putting her groceries away. He'd mentioned Nadia's black marketeering then. No wonder her side of the pantry was so full. As a hairdresser, she had many customers who were wives of Party members. They would often pay her with luxury goods and food, keeping her larder filled. And there was all that food and medicine she got from her lover. She must have had a profitable operation.

"By the way, there are eight people living in your family's apartment now, all of them paranoid about their quarters being bugged—I couldn't get much out of your father."

"But you saw my father? Is he well?"

"As near as I could tell, yes. He couldn't talk much, but he appreciated my visit and sends his love."

"What about Nadia's younger son, Anton?" I asked. With Nadia's arrest, Anton would now be an enemy of the state. As would Boris. "You saw him?"

"Anton? Yes, he's still there. He and your father have forged close ties."

"What will happen to Nadia?"

Galina shrugged. "Black marketers are being dealt with harshly, Kira. She could be executed."

Why hadn't I said something to convince her to stop? We should never have encouraged her, eaten her food, without reminding her of the dangers. Not that she would have listened.

"It will depend on which judge she draws," continued Galina. A tough one could put her through the wringer

—a show trial to make an example of her, and possibly execution. A kinder one might send her to a gulag work camp for twenty years."

"Kinder? Given that choice, I'd opt for the firing squad."

Alone in my room, I thought of Nadia. How my feelings toward her had changed over time: Hostile when we first met, but after a while, a softening, a mutual respect, and finally, a friendship. She had even helped my mother deliver my precious Pavel; was the first to wash him and hold him, to tuck him, tenderly swaddled in a blanket, into my waiting arms. That made her almost family.

It was all too much to absorb. With the weight of what I'd offered to do for Vick and Angela still heavy on my mind, and now Galina's depressing news, I needed to think, to move, to walk.

To welcome Galina back, we'd planned a little dinner party. I was put in charge of dessert, and to make Galina's favorite noodle pudding, I headed for the grocery store to buy flour, sugar and eggs—as always, buying extra in case I saw Steffi Bauman. Luba shyly announced that she'd bring her new boyfriend, Stanislaw Kurzeszyn as we all wanted to meet him. As far as we knew, Luba never had more than a date or two with anyone she met. No boyfriend of any duration.

When I gave Trudi the store clerk my order, she handed me a note.

"From Fraulein Bauman," she whispered. "Her mother asked me to give it to you."

I had a terrible feeling that I knew what the note would say. You didn't deface a photo of Stalin with impunity, especially if you were German. My heart sank. Steffi was in the Women's Detention Center of Sachsenhausen, and needed to talk to me about "a matter of great importance."

I thanked Trudi, pocketed the note and went home to call the prison. They told me that as a Russian officer, I could be admitted on visitation day, but for no more than ten minutes. I shuddered to think of what Steffi was going through at the prison—all for a childish prank.

Sleepless that night, I cursed the ongoing brutality of Stalin. The terrible purges. The state of my country. My father's arrest, the fate awaiting Nadia and Ingrid, and now poor Steffi—all these things kept me awake when I wasn't brooding about my last mission with Rufina.

I'd spent my life being loyal to my country, all the way back to my days of singing the "Internationale" hymn as a schoolgirl in Komsomol meetings. I knew it better than the new State Anthem introduced during the war. Now, I had to ask myself—could I ever sing either again?

CHAPTER 40

After yet another flight at Tempelhof, Vick and I were having lunch at Le Rendez-Vous, a grotty little makeshift café in what was to be the French Zone, I told him about Nadia's situation as reported by Galina, hoping he might have some answers.

"I wish there was some way to help her," I said.

"You think Boris knows what's happened to his mother?" he asked, taking down Nadia's full name as he munched on a baguette.

"I doubt it. Nadia was arrested very recently."

"Then we have a good quid pro quo situation," he said. "That's great. I might have friends who can help get Nadia released. But we'll have to do it soon."

I was genuinely astonished. "Who do you know that can work out a deal like that? She was arrested in Moscow by the NKVD, not Berlin," I stressed, in a whisper. "For selling on the black market! We aren't like you—no rap on the knuckles or short term jail sentences there; we *execute* black marketers."

"Yeah. But Boris's mother isn't important."

"She may not be important to you," I said. "But she means a lot to my family."

"What I meant was, she's not politically important. She's only important to Boris. So my 'friends' can probably arrange to spring her without attracting unwelcome attention."

We were silent for several minutes.

"I have an idea," he said finally.

Vick explained the details of how to realize his scheme. He had access to the dollars that would take care of necessary bribes. Boris had to cooperate, and that's where I came in.

CHAPTER 41

It was around this time that Vick hinted that, for him, our relationship was more meaningful than a casual weekend affair. We'd been seeing a lot of each other; had been enjoying a loving intimacy. I had to admit to myself that he was special. There was no longer denying what I felt at the sight of him, the happiness that filled me; the joy that surged in me when we made love. I was falling for him, and the thought terrified me. Consequences of an affair in Berlin, tangled with political allegiance, could be fraught with danger.

"Have you ever thought what it would be like to live in America?" he asked me.

We were sitting on the couch at his apartment after a particularly heated session of lovemaking and Vick reached over and took my hand.

"When I'm through here, I'm going to Washington to work at the Central Intelligence Agency. It's a new division of the U.S. government, replacing the O.S.S."

A new spy agency? It was something Petrov would want to know, I thought idly; harmless information that would soon be common knowledge. I could share that. I was being selective now, sifting such information from the more confidential things I sometimes happened on. Something in me had broken over the past few trips to the West—since I'd sensed the depth of my feelings for Vick.

He leaned toward me. "It's quite likely that it'll relocate to Langley, Virginia later on. You'd like Virginia, Kira. It has a beautiful seashore. That's almost as good as having the synchronized dancing and swaying palm trees you were on about."

I laughed. He was playing back my vision of his country, but raising the idea of being with him in the U.S.

I admit the idea of living with Vick thrilled me. I could imagine us in a little house with a white picket fence somewhere in America; a place we didn't have to share with anybody. Our own garden, a bathroom and a kitchen, a telephone, no listening devices planted in walls. A home where we could be free; be together in peace and privacy. I was even ready to have children again. We sat quietly for a few minutes as I visualized Vick's version of America.

Vick spoke first: "Kira, Berlin is a dangerous place right now."

I laughed. "You've just discovered that? It has been for quite a while, Vick."

"Yes, but now, for you, it's particularly dangerous." There was concern in his voice.

"What are you saying?" I asked. "Trying to scare me?"

"No," he assured me. "But...well, it's worse than you think. It might be a good idea for you to leave Berlin."

He said this as if I had any place to go and the freedom to leave. Or resources. I tried to brush off his concerns.

"Why are you bringing this up now? Do you know something? Am I already in trouble?"

Stroking my hand, he ignored my question. "Virginia has a nice climate. We could swim in the ocean, lie on sandy beaches, have picnics, clam bakes, eat soft shell crabs; there are mountains for hiking, caves to explore, we could get bikes... rent horses."

I liked that he said 'we' could do those things. He was seeing us as a couple. A splendid plan. Or a dream. But I couldn't help thinking that underlying all this description of life in Virginia there was a warning, one he was not ready to tell me. That he was being more concerned for my safety than anything.

Yes, I thought. And where would I go from there? What he seemed to be suggesting was a loose arrangement without commitment. Nothing lasted forever. If Vick grew tired of me, what then? I would be in a foreign country with no family. No friends or support system; the taint of communism on my record in a country increasingly hostile to communism. A place where Russians were despised.

On the other hand, what would I have if I stayed in Berlin?

CHAPTER 42

I telephoned Boris at the prison and asked him in my friendliest voice to meet me in the Tiergarten near the zoo the next day. He was curious, and as it happened, it was his day off. He managed to get a pass to cross over. I arranged to have Vick arrive about five minutes after I did.

"Bring lots of cigarettes," I told Vick.

"Have you heard from my mother?" Boris asked as soon as he saw me. "Is that why you called?" Nadia had told him we kept in touch.

He sat down next to me on a park bench. I noticed he had doused himself in cheap cologne.

"She hasn't written to me. Not for a while," I said.

"I haven't heard from her in two or three weeks, Kira. It's not like her. Mail delivery is bad, but . . ."

"And Anton? Have you heard from him?"

"He never writes. But I suppose if things weren't going well he'd let me know."

So Anton had not yet given him a heads up.

"Boris," I said, "I'm afraid I have bad news for you. About your mother." I told him what I'd learned and watched his composure dissolve.

"Fuck!" he screamed, jumping up—once again the irritating teenaged boy of our youth, bad-tempered and whining.

"I told her, Kira! So many times, I told her this would happen. She wouldn't listen. The stupid bitch! Had to have her caviar, and ham, and fancy cheeses. And always ready to hustle a little money on the side. The cow. The stupid cow!"

He looked at me in anguish. "With her arrest, do you know what this makes me? Anton and I are both enemies of the people. Fuck!" He stomped on the ground for emphasis, kicking a rock.

I sat him down on the bench and tried to calm him. After all, he was already in active service stationed in another country. It wasn't likely they'd do anything to change that, at least not right away. It might impede promotions, but I didn't see Boris as a likely candidate for leadership anyway. As for Anton, he was already at the bottom rung in a dreary factory job, working to produce armaments. There wasn't much more they could deprive him of.

Vick joined us then, and I introduced them. Boris was uneasy. An American military officer—one who spoke perfect Russian?

"Boris, this Ami officer thinks we can help your mother," I said. "Once she gets sent to Siberia, nobody can get her back, but right now, she's still in Lubyanka; Major Moranov has a plan to free her—if we act fast."

Boris darted anxious looks at both of us. "What's the catch? Nobody does anything for nothing."

"Right. In exchange, I need a favor," I said.

Vick extended an open pack of cigarettes. With unabashed venality, Boris grabbed a cigarette and placed it over his ear. Good for a treat or a trade later. Then he took another one to enjoy, and lit it.

"Keep the pack," Vick told him.

Boris lost no time pocketing it. His interest was

perking up.

Vick laid out his plan. At first, Boris was so aggrieved at the suggestion of helping to free Ingrid, he got up to walk away, justifiably terrified of going before a firing squad for treason.

"Are you crazy? I can't do that," he shouted, before glancing over his shoulder. He lowered his voice. "Bad enough that my mother has dealt me a load of shit, making me an enemy of the people. What you're asking me . . . Fuck, I could get killed!"

"Not if you don't get caught," I said. "And think of your poor mother, what she's going through. Do you want her to be raped and beaten by guards? Frost-bitten in Siberia. Starved and worked to death?"

A guard himself, Boris knew what I meant.

His reluctance to help was understandable. The firing squad was a fate that crossed my own mind. I visualized Boris and me, blindfolded, standing against a wall at dawn as new recruits from the Red Army used us for target practice. Vick cajoled him into sitting back down and continued to sweeten the deal, assuring Boris he had contacts who would protect him. Boris's interest was heightened when Vick offered him his wristwatch, then handed him a whole carton of American cigarettes he had brought along.

After a lot of wrangling and reassurance, Boris agreed. We worked out a plan to free Ingrid from Sachsen-hausen, smuggling her out with cooking staff when they changed shift at the prison. It involved bribing, and cutting electricity at the prison at the right moment. We assured him that Nadia would be set free in Moscow at the same time as Ingrid.

Finally, Vick handed him an envelope. "There's a thousand bucks in there, Boris. Yankee dollars. You'll need it for bribes. I'll give you another four thousand when you deliver Ingrid Taylor safely to us."

Officially, it was neither U.S. nor British policy to pay for the release of people of interest, but Vick said he had private contacts, both in London and Washington, with hidden resources he could draw on. With the right connections and enough money, anything is possible. It was the least the Allies could do for Ingrid.

For Boris, this unexpected windfall was a lottery win; for Vick, it was a pittance. Boris could have insisted on a lot more, but he didn't know that. His defiance melted away and he warmed to the plan.

"When will my mother be released?"

"As soon as Ingrid Taylor is," said Vick.

"Done," he said. "You'll have her here at this time next week."

"What? You can't do it sooner?" I asked. The longer it took, the more time a drunken Boris would have to brag about his new source of income, leaving me dangerously exposed. And the longer Ingrid's life would be at risk in that stinkhole. Each day that passed in Sachsenhausen had to be a day of unspeakable agony for her, one day closer to the time when her body could endure no more.

"That's the best I can do," he snapped. "Be sure to have the rest of the money."

He was learning fast.

CHAPTER 43

Luba had begun to concern us. She was away a lot now, coming home only to bathe and change her clothes.

We all loved Luba dearly; she'd been a pillar of strength and bravery during the War, and with her engaging smile and cheerful outlook, a companionable roommate these past months that we'd all been together at Frau Schuman's. We met Luba's Polish refugee boyfriend, Stanislaw Kurzeszyn, at the little homecoming party we had to celebrate Galina's return, and we came away with mixed feelings about him.

On the one hand, he was quite handsome. Frau Schuman, Galina, Elena and I were quickly won over by his demeanor, politeness, good table manners, and education. It was almost too good to be true.

"I don't trust him." said Elena. "He's a little too charming."

Galina agreed: "Charming like a snake. Did you see how he orders Luba around when he thinks we're out of earshot?"

"Yes. And how she jumps up to wait on him." I chimed in, recalling her compliance. "She's afraid of him."

As Russian women of our time, we were used to catering to the men in our lives. We'd come of age in a patriarchal society, and while we might have resented it, tradition dictated that we never question our subservience. I'd watched my mother, a brilliant physician, wait on my father after a twelve-hour shift at the hospital, even when she wasn't feeling well. But this was different, somehow. There was something not quite right in Luba's relationship.

Our concern for her was validated when we caught glimpses of Luba's bruises one evening. She was on her way back from the bathroom wearing only a towel.

"Luba!" I exclaimed. "What's going on? Those bruises on your arm..."

"It's nothing," she answered dismissively. "Nothing. I fell at work while I was working on a plane. That's all."

I wasn't going to be put off. Gently I took her by the arm. "That bruise, Luba. It's clearly the mark of a hand."

She hastily pulled her towel up over her arm, and the resulting shift revealed some bad discoloration on her right leg and hip.

"Those aren't recent bruises ... or injuries from a fall," observed Galina, who'd been watching us.

Elena put down the needlework she'd been working on. "Luba, tell us the truth. We're your friends."

Luba became agitated. "I have! I told you, I fell. You should all mind your own business!"

"If you ever want to talk about it, we're here for you," I said, my hand around her shoulder. Luba shrugged me away and burst into tears as she hared off to her room.

"Leave me alone!"

"I've seen bruises like that. Many times," said Frau Schuman, who appeared like a revenant out of nowhere. Listening to our conversations was her main form of entertainment. "Men are pigs!"

Then she expanded this thought: "Russian men are pigs; Poles are pigs. American men are pigs, too, but at least they have money."

CHAPTER 44

V ick and Boris had it all set up. Vick wouldn't explain, but I was sure the mole at the Kommandatura was working with them behind the scenes.

With our plans to save Ingrid and Nadia simmering in place, Vick and I stole away on borrowed bikes the following Saturday morning after a flight in the C-47. We'd brought an insulated bag with chicken salad, crudités, some foie gras, and a picnic basket with French bread he'd bartered with Daniel, his chain-smoking chef friend in the French Zone—his usual contact over there. Food for cigarettes.

We set up our picnic on the river bank of the Spree in a hidden corner of the Tiergarten, away from the bicycle and walking paths, and spent a few hours relaxing in the sun. Eating, drinking champagne, cuddling under a blanket, and yes, making love *al fresco*.

I won't lie. I was scared. Our plan to save Ingrid could go terribly wrong, especially with Boris involved. But lying there with Vick, I'd managed to block out the worries I had, at least for this one carefree interval of time.

"These are moments I'd like to capture and remember forever," I murmured in his ear after I'd collapsed, drowsy and happy in his arms. "I'd be quite content to spend the rest of my life like this."

Vick laughed and kissed me. "Is this the gutsy pilot who took on the German Luftwaffe? All dewy-eyed and romantic?"

I stretched like a lazy cat, enjoying the moment. "Hmmm. Yes. The same."

"You'd get pretty bored with all this idyllic decadence," he said with a grin, "A woman like you."

I shot him a contented smile as I reached up to kiss him. "How well you've come to know me. No, you're right. There has to be something else."

He'd been chewing a blade of grass. Removing it, he kissed me. I thought it would lead to more, but he wanted to talk.

"But we could, you know, have a lot of happy moments together, like this."

"You mean if we lived together in Virginia?"

"Uh huh. Though I was thinking of something a little more permanent."

I waited. My English was good now after all these months, but I wanted to make sure of what he had in mind.

"If we were to get married, I could make you happy. You know I love you Kira."

It was the first time he said it, and the conviction that he was sincere reawakened my desire for him. Reinvention of my life in the U.S., becoming Mrs. Victor Moran, was a whole other thing to think about.

While many of the vanquished German girls dreamed of finding an American to marry them and sweep them off to the U.S. to be removed from their misery, for us Russians, indoctrinated by the Party since childhood, it was different.

We had won the war, and those of us young enough to enjoy our victory had an eye to the future. Even though Vick and I had talked about Virginia and the life we could have there, the idea of never seeing my own country again still stuck in my throat. I thought that before answering, it might be time to clear out the ghosts that haunted our relationship.

I was leaning into him in an intimate, happy embrace. "Tell me about your wife," I said gently.

"My wife?"

Thinking of the future, he hadn't expected to be drawn back to the past. An expression of pain momentarily crossed his face. He took a minute to think about it, deciding what to tell me and what to leave out.

"My *late* wife. I met her in London. Her name was Lorraine. I called her 'Sweet Lorraine,' like the song. A beautiful person. Physically pretty, yes, but I mean, she was a great lady. Sweet. Very English."

A pang of jealousy made me sorry I'd dredged up the subject.

He picked up the story. "I'd gotten banged up in a car crash around that time—cracked ribs. My driver was an American GI who wasn't used to driving on the left hand side of the road. Lorraine was my nurse at the clinic they brought me to."

"How long before you married?"

"Not long. I'm not a guy who hesitates when I want something, and I usually know pretty early what that is."

He looked at me meaningfully.

"I'd known her about six months when I asked her to marry me. We were together just a short time. One of your typical whirlwind romances so common in wartime. A lot of hasty marriages took place in those days; guys going off to war."

"When was that?"

"It was early in the conflict. I was working Security out of the American Embassy in London at that time. Joe Kennedy was still our Ambassador.

"Things were great for a while. Until the U.S. entered the war and I got my orders to go into active duty. Lorraine was pregnant by then. I'd convinced her to move to the States, where she'd be safe, but her mother, a midwife, talked her into staying in London to have the baby —babies, as it turned out—our two little girls. She cancelled her plans to move to the U.S."

He stopped and took a sip of champagne.

"This was during the Blitz?"

"Yeah, just before it ended. The babies came early." His expression changed to anger. "Those goddamned doodle-bugs were deadly. Lorraine, the babies, her mother, a visiting aunt and a cousin. Wiped out. Imagine, sixty thousand innocent people killed in that Blitz. Fucking Hitler."

I was silent, reproaching myself for my pettiness, my moment of envying poor Lorraine.

"Too bad she didn't go to America."

"Yeah. Hindsight."

He brooded over the results of the Blitz for a few minutes before speaking again.

"The War has made me a fatalist, Kira. I've seen a lot of horrendous stuff, as I know you have; so many killed. Situations where death was all around us. Luck has everything to do with it. Sometimes it's a matter of centimeters. Being in the wrong place at the wrong time —yeah, I know it's a cliché, but it's true."

I nodded. He was echoing my own thoughts. Rufina . . .

We lay there for a minute or so, holding hands.

"Your turn," he finally said.

"My turn?"

"Your husband. I want to know all about this guy who won your heart."

"More like I won his heart," I said with a smile. "I chased him shamelessly!"

I paused to gather my thoughts.

"We met in 1933 when I was just a kid. I was staying at my grandparents' in Ukraine and he landed in their wheat field. He was in his early twenties then, and I was in awe of him. He took me for a short trip in the air, and I was hooked on flying for the rest of my life. Afterward, he gave me a little pin to wear; a metal airplane from his flying club. A cheap little thing, but I treasured it. It became my lucky charm; got me through the war. Like you, I believe that survival is only a matter of luck.

"When I went to flying class in Moscow six years later, it turned out he was my instructor—I was sixteen then, a silly child still—I was infatuated with him and hounded him endlessly."

"I've had girls like you in my flying classes. A royal pain in the ass."

We laughed. "Yes, that was me. A terrible pain."

"So how did it go down?"

"He eventually saw the error of his ways, and I got him to marry me. Then he was killed at the front. End of story."

Amazing, I reflected, how by omitting the details of

sorrow, we could reduce the sum of our lives in so few words. *Some tragedy.*

During the war, survival was everything. If you didn't survive, you fell into a big black hole of nothingness. Adieu hopes and dreams. I believed then—and still do—that if two people love each other, they can get through anything. As long as they can remain alive.

We were quiet for a moment.

"Neither of our past relationships have had a happy ending," he said finally. "Ours will go a lot better."

"I hope so," I said.

He kissed me and smiled. "I'm looking forward to a lot of great times together."

He looked thoughtful. But then his mood changed and he became playful. He took my hand. "Let's go in for a swim."

I'd already had a quick dip, but had come out right away. "You're crazy! It's October," I said, shaking off his grip. "The water's too cold for me. You go ahead. I'm going to lie here and soak up some sun."

"Afraid of a little cold water? A Russian girl?"

Laughing, he dived in and thrashed around sputtering in the water. Alone on the beach, I lay back continuing to dry off in the fading gentleness of Indian summer sunlight. And my thoughts drifted to that romantic time with Maxim . . .

CHAPTER 45

O ver the friendly coffee with him after that first lecture, Maxim was astonished when I told him how his words had influenced me. How they'd inspired me to take up flying. He was pleasant; he was cordial. Nothing more.

Soon after, I approached him after classes with some facile question I knew the answer to, hoping he would suggest another encounter. No invitation was forth-coming. Undeterred by his reserve, I insinuated myself into his presence as much as I could. Pretty soon, I stopped socializing with the other girls and sat in the front row. My hand would shoot up for every question. I provided correct answers, spoiling all his attempts to engage the class as a group. Lingering after class, I'd ask him trivial questions. We were both aware that this was a ruse to get his attention.

At first, he tolerated my behavior. Then he ignored me and called on the boys by name. Worse, he'd rush away after lectures to prevent me from buttonholing him. Unfazed by his indifference, I continued to pursue him.

Prudence and maturity, two qualities I eventually had to cultivate, did not play a big part in my private life at that time. Zinaida had always advised me to exercise caution, but after she moved away there was no one close to me to rein in my exuberance in matters of the heart, and I'd become reckless.

Finally, Maxim stopped me as I was gathering my things after class:

"Miss Voronova, I need to speak to you," he said.

I expected him to steer me to the café, but instead, he led me to a park bench in a small birch grove near the hangar, shielded from the other students. He'd been silent as we made our way there, ignoring my attempts to converse, but after we sat down, he finally spoke.

"Klara," he said tersely. "You must stop this."

"It's Kira," I said.

"Kira, then. You must stop."

"Stop what?"

"This...this fixation you have...with me."

"Aren't you flattering yourself? I'm simply being a good student."

"Bullshit. I've had women like you in my classes before."

I refused to be cowed: "Maxim, stop pretending."

His tone softened and he sighed. "Okay. Look. You're cute and you're smart, and I like you, but you're becoming a distraction in my classroom."

"You're saying you're not attracted to me?"

"Of course, I'm attracted to you." His eyes quickly scanned my body; "But you're being a pain in the butt. I'm way too old for you. I met you when you were a little kid. I'd feel like a child molester if we were to . . ." His voice trailed off. "Kira, find someone your own age."

There was nothing I could do about our age difference, but I still believed that determination could solve all problems. I allowed my eyes to fill. "Maxim—"

"Professor Dubkov to you," he interrupted sternly. Gone was the friendly informality he'd encouraged that first time.

I edged closer to him on the bench. "Maxim," I continued, "Please. Can we go someplace else, somewhere we can be alone?" I shot him my most seductive smile.

He was taken aback. He stared at me and I watched a full range of emotions cross his features. Exasperation. Surprise. Incredulity. Then it changed to one of interest. Interest and something else. Desire.

"Alone? You aren't exactly subtle, are you?"

"Subtlety doesn't work with you."

"You're so young." he said.

"Not that young."

"Well, I'm too old to play games."

"Ha. All this resistance, pretending to forget my name, this playing hard-to-get . . .you *are* playing a game."

We were quiet for a minute or so. Then he reached over and casually touched my hand, sending an electric bolt through me.

"That's not true, Kira. I want to do the right thing."

"Well, don't. I don't want to play games either."

He looked thoughtful. There were a few minutes of silence. "If you're serious...my brother and his wife are at work. We could go to their apartment? They're on a street off the Arbat. Their communal neighbors all work, too."

I leaned forward and touched his arm, smiling up at him. "I'm very serious."

Once he gave in that first time, I behaved in a more appropriate way in class, but afterward, I had no trouble getting Maxim to bring me to his brother's place, and I knew from the first day we made love that I wanted to marry him. Did I mention he was my first?

Maxim was everything I wanted in a husband. He was intelligent, a graduate engineer, and an expert pilot. He was a loyal Party member and expected his fealty to help him advance in whatever field he chose. A bright future lay ahead of him.

Maxim wasn't only handsome and smart, he was cultured, and well versed in history and literature. And music. With a smile, I recalled that while we made love, he would play classical music and control his thrusts to harmonize with the music. His favorite piece was Tchaikovsky's *1812 Overture* and he would time his joyful release to the boom of the cannons.

"I want to make love to you all the time," Maxim said one time as we snuggled after a particularly lovely afternoon. "In class, I look at you and lose track of what I'm saying. I'm explaining Bernoulli's principle and I'm thinking about sex. Taking you to bed. All the things you like me to do. But we should take things easier. I'm worried you'll get pregnant. I'm careful, but . . ."

"Would that be so terrible?"

"Be serious. In the first place, you're barely more than a child yourself. Secondly, we're not married and we'd have no place to live. In the third place, the Germans may be planning to invade us."

"Don't be ridiculous. They wouldn't dare. We have the biggest army in the world. And we have a non-aggression pact with Germany."

Maxim said, "Some say Stalin expects a war; sees it as an opportunity to grab a piece of Poland."

"How do you feel about that?" I asked, knowing that it

would mean certain conscription for him.

"What I think isn't important. Stalin has to decide what's best for the Rodina. For our Motherland. He's in charge. German fighter planes are a force to reckon with and this war—if there is one—will be fought and won in the air by our Falcons. They'll need all the pilots they can get."

A popular notion, left over from WWI. At that point in time, none of us knew about the brutal power of Hitler's panzer tanks.

A chill ran through me; a premonition of some terrible cataclysm lying in wait. I'd heard stories about the Great War from my father. Only twenty or so years had passed since then, our brief peace interrupted by a Civil War and two revolutions that overthrew and then murdered our tsarist rulers. We'd had ongoing terror unleashed from 1934 by NKVD henchmen like Yezhof—and later, Beria. And Stalin wasn't finished with us. He continued to purge our population.

"Another war?" I whispered to Maxim. "Must we be crushed even further? Haven't we suffered enough?"

"All I'm saying is, we don't know what's in store for us," he whispered back. "We're the products of our history, and our history in the making. Things will probably get worse before they get better."

West Berlin, 1947

Vick snapped me out of my reverie. He'd emerged from

the water, shivering. His hair was drenched and he playfully shook his head like a big shaggy dog, spraying me with water.

"Stop it!" I shouted. "You're getting me wet. Stop!"

"You deserve to get wet. You wouldn't come in and let me make love to you in the water." Naked, he quickly toweled himself dry. "Christ, that water's like melted ice!"

"What do you expect this time of year, *dummkopf*? Summer's over," I chided, laughing. "Come here, I'll warm you up."

He cuddled up to me under the top blanket. His body was damp and cold. I had removed my swim suit to dry in the sun, and recalling the days I was discovering the joy of sex had put me back in the mood. I put my arms around him, rubbing his now pebbled skin to renew the natural heat of his body, feeling the wet hairs on his arms, legs, and chest as he continued to shiver.

"Mmm, you're nice and warm," he said cozying up against me, absorbing the heat of me like the apricots in Dedushka's orchard seeking the sun to ripen; a puppy warming itself by the hearth.

As his body heat returned to normal, so did his desire, telegraphed by the hardness and vitality of him. "What happened to your swimsuit?" he asked.

"I took it off."

"Good girl."

"Bad girl," I corrected him.

"I hate to say this, bad girl, but we should be getting back," he whispered in my ear. When neither of us made a move to get up and pack our picnic things, he smiled slowly.

"Maybe a little while longer." he said, voice husky. "I can see you're in no rush.

We reached our peak of exhilaration and emotion together—like climbing to a mountain top and skiing downhill—leaving us satisfied, exhausted, and breathless.

Relaxed and happy, we exulted in each other's animal presence as we lay there for a while longer, holding each other, kissing and gently touching: Both hating to get up and move; neither of us wanting to pack up. Apprehensive about the near future—what was ahead of us the following Saturday—yet living in the moment, we were looking down the long road to a possible happy life, not alone, but together.

A different kind of love, I reflected. A warm glow now as we basked in the sweetness of mature feelings for each other. No *1812 Overture* cannon blasts. No raging hormone-driven teenage passion. Not the wild, heedless, carefree loving of my younger years, so frequent and wildly experimental. That wasn't what I needed or wanted right now. I just wanted Vick. Some genuine passion, satisfaction, caring, and contentment.

The sun was about to set, and a cooling stirred the autumn air. "You haven't given me an answer," said Vick as we packed up to leave.

I hadn't. As much as I wanted the life he described, I hesitated. When I was younger, I wasn't afraid of the unknown. But now I was more conflicted. It was such a big life-changing step. A frightening one.

"Can I have a little time to think about it?"

He frowned. "Not much. Remember what I told you.

It's a dangerous world out there. I need your answer soon."

"Give me a couple of days."

Even as I said it, my mind was made up.

CHAPTER 46

"We're worried about Luba," said Elena over breakfast on Monday. "She's been away since Thursday."

"She must be having a good time," I said brightly. "Are her clothes all here?"

"Yes. But I don't trust this Stanislaw boyfriend of hers."

"That refugee is too good-looking for your friend," Frau Schuman interjected maliciously as she poured the watery chicory drink she called 'coffee' into our cups. "I don't know what he is finding attractive about her."

"Perhaps he appreciates her kindness of spirit," said Galina, a caustic hint that our landlady should acquire some of Luba's sweetness.

After breakfast, Galina confided to me that the K-5 secret police had been around on Friday to talk to Luba, as well as Stanislaw Kurzeszyn.

This raised alarm. I equated the newly-formed East German secret police, K-5—later called the Stasi—to our brutal NKVD, later the KGB. If anything, the K-5 were worse, determined to show Moscow they were up to the task. Concerned, I called her station at the airport, but nobody could, or would, tell me anything.

My appointment to visit Steffi in prison was the next afternoon. I took time off work and rode the U-Bahn to the Women's Detention Center at Sachsenhausen. I hadn't seen Steffi since after I'd delivered Beatrix's maternity clothing to her via Trudi the grocery store clerk.

At the door of the prison, they took away the foodstuff I'd brought her. I doubted she'd ever see it. Dressed in oversized prison garb and now extremely pregnant, a subdued Steffi met with me in a dreary, heavily-guarded meeting room with high barred windows. One side of her face was swollen, her lovely long blonde hair had been shorn, and she was almost unrecognizable.

"What did you want to tell me?" I asked. "No, please— don't cry. We only have ten minutes. Just talk to me."

She blinked away the tears threatening to flood her eyes. "I'm so glad you came. They won't let my mother visit." She wiped her nose on her sleeve. "Captain, they've sentenced me to eight years in prison."

My heart sank. "Oh, Steffi. I am so, so sorry."

Sorry, yes. But at the same time, I was relieved. At her age, prison was a better alternative to execution—as long as she had the stamina to survive it.

"It's to be served right after I deliver my baby. I'm due any day."

Eight years. She would be twenty-five when she got out. Still young enough to start over. She could do that. But the lost years, without her children or family, the misery of the gulag—she had no idea what was ahead of her.

"What can I do to help?"

"Nothing. Nothing for me, but ..." Her face was pale and serious. She had grown up overnight. "It's my babies. Lorelei, and this one. I know I said I hated them, but I don't. They're still my babies. I can't bear to think of them in an orphanage, Captain."

"Can your mother help?"

"My mother works long days; she's a Trümmerfrau— she can't care for them. She gets double rations, the second highest classification, but she has no money or time to take on a couple of children, especially a newborn. And she has to work. Hard work. She's tired when she gets home. Could you contact her for me? Perhaps someone in the family could take them."

She thought about it for a moment, then added, "We had some cousins, a young couple with children living in Dresden."

I'd been about to write down names, but I winced when she said Dresden. The shattered state that city was in after the Allied bombings just before the war's end stayed my hand.

"Please," she begged.

"Yes, I can do that for you," I said to humor her. I took down her mother's contact information.

"Even if I have to sign them away for adoption ... I can't let them go to an orphanage."

I was about to leave when she had another thought. "Captain, if my mother can't find anybody in my family, could you please ask around? There are so many orphans, I know. Authorities are sending babies to the East to be raised as good communists. And I've heard of unscrupulous people buying our babies on the black market, selling them in places like America and Australia.

"But I thought, if you know of someone? My little Lorelei is beginning to walk; she's cute, and a well-behaved toddler. She's with my Aunt Hannahlore now. But my aunt's not well. She was injured in the bombings. She can't keep her. And this baby is due any day."

I did not want to raise her hopes. But to reassure her, I told her I'd check it out. They wouldn't let me hug her as

I left, so we had to be content with a sad wave.

"I'll write to you," I whispered. "*Viel Glück.*"

She'd need all the luck she could get.

I knew I couldn't get in to see Ingrid Taylor while I was there, but before heading for the U-Bahn, I inquired of one of the matrons if a Luba Golyakova might have recently been brought in. It was a long shot. I made a mental note to check hospitals next.

I waited as the matron disappeared to verify records of recent inmates brought to the facility. When she returned, she said Luba had been held there briefly, but had left two days ago. I had to ask—of her own accord? Was she okay? Where did she go? But I was met with a shrug and stony silence.

Galina was horrified when I told her: "Arrested? And we can't find out why or where they've taken her? I'll ask my boss, General Vorobyev. He may be able to find something out."

CHAPTER 47

The next evening, the apartment was eerily silent. Frau Schuman and Elena were out, and Galina was alone in her room. She was crying; rare for her. After all she'd been through she often said she had no more tears, but there were always fresh ones to be found —as long as there was tragedy in our midst. I saw that she'd been packing a suitcase.

"What's wrong, dear?" I asked.

"It's Luba," she said, sobbing. "Oh, Kira, she's dead. Luba's dead!" She covered her face with her hands.

"Dead? Oh my God, Galina! Are you sure? What happened?"

"I don't know all the details. Just what General Vorobyev could find out. She should never have gotten mixed up with that Stanislaw guy. There was something shifty about him. And we didn't like the way he treated her... those bruise marks . . ."

I clenched my fists with fury, ready to avenge her death on the conniving Pole. "What did he do to her?" I demanded.

Galina shook her head. "It's not like that. He's dead, too, Kira. They were caught stealing aviation equipment. The General told me Stanislaw was shipping it to some resistance group in Poland, smuggling it to Polish anti-communist partisans. He was using Luba. She had access to a storage area at the airport where some aviation aids were kept—I don't know what they were—aircraft parts, anyway. He got her to steal them and then sent them, via a truck driver he knew, to his contacts in Danzieg ... well, Gdansk, now. The authorities lost no time, apparently. Luba and Stanislaw were both in prison for only a day or so. There was some kind of sham trial, and they executed them the following morning."

I was overcome with grief. The swiftness of it. The complete lack of mercy. For Luba to have survived the war at the front, risking her life, only to come to this.

"Poor misguided Luba," I said softly as tears gathered in my eyes. "She wanted so much to have a boyfriend. So lonely, she let that smooth-talker get her into trouble. I never liked him."

"No, none of us did. I grabbed his arm one time when he was waiting for Luba in the living room. I told him if I ever saw a bruise on her again, he'd have to answer to us."

"What did he say?"

"He told me to go to hell."

"Too bad I wasn't here. It would have been a show of strength."

"It was a weekend. You were in the West."

I shook my head, still coming to terms with what happened. "Luba must already have been dead when I was at Sachsenhausen. When I inquired about her."

"Probably."

"That's why they were so evasive. Have you told Frau Schuman?"

"Yes."

"What did she say?"

"She said she was glad she'd gotten Luba's rent money last week."

I rolled my eyes.

Indicating the open suitcase on her bed, I looked at her inquiringly. "Why is your suitcase out?"

She lowered her voice to barely a whisper as she put

her finger over her lips.

"Shhh. I was planning to tell you tonight. I'm leaving."

"Leaving?" I sat down. "Where are you going?"

"To Palestine. That trip I took to Russia convinced me. I didn't like what I saw, Kira. If I go back to Moscow they'll never let me leave."

"Probably not. I understand things have tightened up."

"And Anti Semitism has long existed in Russia."

"True." A shameful page of our history.

"Not only that, Kira. But I overheard General Vorobyev and another Russian officer saying that Russian women will be banned from 456 jobs."

I wasn't sure I heard her correctly. After my own experience there, I should have seen it coming. "That many? Are you sure? Which jobs?"

"Russia lost so many people during the war, they want us to become baby machines to repopulate for the next war. They're saying it's for our safety; to protect our reproductive health. No heavy lifting, nothing involving electrical tools, carpentry, home repairs, and . . . you won't believe this, Kira, driving a tram or piloting a plane!"

I gasped, bursting with anger. "So *now* piloting a plane is too dangerous? It wasn't when we were dropping bombs in the Crimea' with the German Luftwaffe shooting at us?"

Galina shook her head. "Ridiculous, isn't it? It means flying for Aeroflot was just a pipe dream for me. With this new ban, they'll never let me fly."

"This is such bullshit! It's so we won't take jobs from Russian men."

"Of course."

"Will that ban be in effect here in East Germany?"

"No. Not enough men came back to put in a ban like that. The destruction was so bad here and so many people have fled to the West, they need women to work and rebuild. They'll even start opening up the country to *Gastarbeiters*—workers from other countries, like Turkey."

"That will certainly change the face of Germany."

"So, there's nothing for me in Moscow," she went on. "Anti-Semitism in Russia could easily rise up again. And Stalin's oppression—I can't look the other way anymore. What they did to Luba was so terrible."

The day was shaping up to be one full of awful surprises.

"How will you get into Palestine? With the quotas the British have slapped on, there are long waiting lists for Jews."

"Yes, I know what the British are doing. Their game of obstruction. But a friend in the French sector is helping me. He has important contacts. You don't want to know more than that. There are exciting things happening there. Like Jewish statehood. And he thinks I can get a job with EL AL, a new airline starting up next year. He knows someone in Tel Aviv who can help me."

It hit me like riding crop. "Galina, have you been working with the French?"

She was quiet for a moment as she mulled whether to confide in me or not. Finally, she admitted that her friend was a French Jew.

"Is his name Marcel Levy by any chance?"

I remembered my encounter with Levy in "Marching Saints." How he he'd tried to buy information about our ex-Nazi applicants from me. The British Mandate in Palestine would expire in May. Levy was most likely spying for the Jews from various countries working to establish and develop a Jewish state there. And Galina—who better to spy for Levy than a Jewish driver for a Russian general in East Berlin? A driver who could eavesdrop all day?

"Marcel is picking me up tomorrow," Galina whispered.

"He's a Nazi hunter, isn't he?"

Jews were seeking revenge on Nazis, especially the lesser known war criminals who'd escaped the scrutiny of authorities. Feeling that justice delayed is justice denied, they were in no mood to wait through more lengthy trials. Their strategy was to find them and dole out punishment that would fit the crimes. Now. Not later.

Galina said nothing.

"Is he a follower of Abba Kovner?" I asked.

Kovner was taking retribution to a whole new level. A Lithuanian Jew demented by the war, he had vowed to poison six million Germans in retaliation for the six million Jews murdered in the Holocaust. A nation for a nation. His group was called *Nakam*, Revenge in Hebrew. He was also helping to smuggle Jews into Palestine in defiance of the British through a network he called *Aliyah Bet*.

Galina still didn't answer. She took a bottle of wine out of her cupboard.

"Another gift from General Vorobyev," she smiled. "Shall we have a proper farewell?"

I nodded and she poured us each a full glass.

"I can't talk about this, Kira. And you mustn't tell anyone what I'm doing. Please promise me—not a word."

"Of course."

"How did you guess?" she asked as she handed me a

glass.

"I told you, I've met Levy in the West. He wanted me to sell information about ex-Nazis I was processing. Are you two romantically involved?"

Galina took a generous sip. "Well, sort of. Marcel is smart and attractive. And he's nice. I'm not sure where it's going. It's early days. Romance isn't uppermost on my mind right now."

"Galina, I hope you know what you're doing. Kovner is a terrorist."

"Don't worry, Kira. I do. Anyway, Kovner has left off his outlandish ideas for now. He's taken a more moderate stance. Let's not talk about it. Here's to the future."

"Promise me you'll be careful, Galina. These are dangerous times."

She nodded, raising her drink. *"Za vashe zdorovye!"*

I joined her in clinking glasses. *"Za vashe zdorovye!"*

"You've been a good friend to me, Kira. I'll miss you."

The feelings were reciprocal. We'd probably never meet again. Overcome with sadness, I savored this brief time together before we went our separate ways.

I wanted to confide in her about my own plans. Vick's proposal; and that I might be living in the United States. I wanted to tell her if her flying career ever took her to the U.S., to visit me in Virginia—but I couldn't do that without divulging secrets. I wasn't sure if any of my plans would even materialize. And talking about them might jinx them. Nothing was sure in this world.

"We've been through so much together, Galina."

"Yes." A smile came over her face. "Remember that time we ran out of fuel? I'd given you the wrong compass reading on the way back to base."

Could I forget it? The fear. The bitter cold.

"I had to make an emergency landing."

"A *belly* landing! It was so scary. In the middle of winter, sheer ice on the ground. Landing was like tobogganing; skimming over glass."

"Yes. No brakes on our little Po-2s."

"You were brilliant. You never lost your nerve," Galina said with genuine admiration. "You always had a reputation for being a daredevil."

"Was I really known for that?"

"Yes. That, and for flying the most sorties. I learned a lot from you."

"We learned a lot from each other. But that time, it's a miracle we made it back. Luckily I finally hit that brush and rocks poking through the ice. It slowed me down so we could come to a stop."

The wine was taking effect and we chuckled at the memory. "Those villagers with broomsticks and shovels ... they came at us out of nowhere."

"I don't know how they could have mistaken us for German fliers the way we were screaming for help. But the red star on our plane was covered with frost. And it was dark."

"Yes. They were rocking the plane on the ice. No matter how much we yelled at them in Russian to stop!"

"They probably had trouble with our accents," I suggested.

"In that open cockpit, we could have been seriously hurt. They were swearing at us, shouting and denting the aircraft. It sounds funny now ..."

"Finally, one of them believed us. What was his name?"

"Mikhail. He shouted at the others to hold off. Once they realized we were Russian, they couldn't do enough for us," recalled Galina.

"Yeah. They smothered us with bear hugs. Mikhail took us in and fed us; vodka all around. Extra logs on the fire; their rations of candles lit; and he put us up overnight in clean beds."

"Mmmm. Yes. With feather duvets. Such luxury! I didn't want to go back to base. We were so used to napping on the cold ground. I had a sprained ankle and Mikhail bandaged me up. He turned out to be the village veterinarian and the head of their local soviet."

"Thank goodness he had access to some petrol." I said.

"In the morning, we went out to the plane and saw that you'd come to a stop on the crest of an ice-covered cliff."

"Yeah. That's why the peasants were rocking the plane; they were trying to push us over the edge!"

I shook my head. Thinking about it in the isolated reflection of present day memory was more terrifying than when we actually went through it.

Galina picked up the bottle and gave us another generous pour.

"Those villagers sure banged up our plane, though," I said. "I thought we'd be sent to the Guard House when we brought it back."

"Instead, we found out we'd earned a medal because we saved it!"

The absurdity of it. We laughed out loud. Perhaps it was the wine. "Luba and Zinaida put in a lot of work repairing the damage. Remember how they scolded us? Luba went on and on; a dog with a bone."

Luba's name brought us back to the present; our laughs silenced, smiles faded. The wine was making us maudlin. We were quiet for a long minute as we both contemplated those moments of danger from the past, and Luba's tragic end in prison.

While her execution was a grim reminder to me how vulnerable we were when it came to ignoring rules and laws of our government, talking about our brush with death reinforced how courageous we were.

If I could manage to get out of a situation like that, I reflected, I could handle my involvement in saving Angela's sister. The lives of Nadia and Ingrid depended on it. Galina was probably making the same equation about her journey into an uncertain future.

"Poor Luba," Galina finally said. "She deserved so much better."

"She did."

"I'll miss you, Kira."

Tears had replaced our laughter. We fell into a silent hug.

"*Zhelayu oodachi*. Good luck," I said.

The wine bottle was empty.

CHAPTER 48

Monday mornings, the thought of shuffling papers was painful as I landed back in the real world of the Kommandatura. It was like returning from a distant planet. This particular Monday, a red-eyed Inna Gradska wore a glum expression.

"Is something wrong, Inna?" I asked.

"He's being sent back to Moscow."

"Who? Not Senior Lieutenant Petrov?"

Her news hit me like a rogue ballistic missile. I'd always thought Petrov would be promoted up the ranks in East Berlin. This signaled a major career change.

My immediate thoughts were not of Petrov, but of how this would affect me and our arrangement—my easy access to the West every weekend. His transfer to Moscow had to impact my situation.

I'd decided to marry Vick and move to the U.S., but in the meantime, I needed the freedom to come and go on weekends.

"I'm going, too," Inna said, interrupting my thoughts. "He's asked for me. Vasily and I—Senior Lieutenant Petrov and I—we're close friends." She turned away.

"Doesn't Comrade Petrov have a wife in Moscow?" I asked, inviting her to elaborate.

Inna faced me, her expression bluntly hostile. "That's none of your business, Comrade."

Since Inna had been crying over his recall, he was possibly in trouble, getting blamed for some problem in Berlin, with no idea what faced him in Moscow. The direct line from Petrov buzzed and she picked up her intercom. She murmured what sounded like assent, and hung up.

"He'll see you now."

Petrov was at his desk, a bottle of brandy in front of him. A hefty portion of its contents were in a snifter. He hadn't shaved.

"Hullo, Captain," he said. Without getting up, he gestured for me to sit. There were circles under his eyes and he appeared listless under his dark shroud of day-old beard.

He'd been looking at something on his desk. Following his focus, I discerned it was a photo of a rather plain plump woman with three young children. It explained Inna's tears. He put it away as I sat down.

"Good morning," I replied after saluting him. "Is it true, Sir? You're returning to Moscow?"

He sat straighter in his chair, an attempt to recover his old authoritative demeanor.

"Yes. Yes," he replied grandly. "The high command wishes to brief me on some career moves. I'm quite looking forward to going back." His words sounded hollow.

"That's wonderful," I said, playing along.

We both knew that a summons to Moscow inspired fear. Whatever fate the government had in store was not usually explained, so it was highly possible Petrov would be delivered to the NKVD, never to be heard from again. Everything in his manner told me he had no idea what to expect on his return. It could be a promotion—or a firing squad for some trumped up charge under Section 58 1(b). The catchall. Any number of crimes could be manufactured if Stalin wanted a scapegoat for something. And uncertainty was half the torture.

I waited for him to ask me for new information gathered on Vick Moran.

Instead he said, "I'm leaving the day after tomorrow. I have a pilot to fly us out. I want you to co-pilot—now that you're a U.S.-trained hot shot flyer."

This caught me off guard. "Fly to Moscow?"

"Yes. I said I'd have you flying, didn't I? We'll leave from Schönefeld first thing Wednesday morning at 6:00 hours."

A fear popped into the wary territory of my mind. "And the plane, sir? Will it be returning to Berlin?"

"Yes, the following day. You'll be flying several high-ranking officers in Moscow back here. Tell Inna to clear you for an overnight stay in the female barracks at the Karl Marx airfield."

It was a small airfield near the military base used mostly for training.

"Yes, sir," I said, taking a deep breath. While I had an uneasy feeling about this, there was a bright side to it. If I planned it right, I could visit with my father and Dedushka in Moscow. Perhaps I could find Zinaida, too. It might be the last time. Once I married Vick and moved to the U.S., who knew when I'd get back. If I'd ever get back.

"Inna will give you the departure and landing details," he said, interrupting my thoughts.

"Sir, my present assignment in the West? And your promise to have me instruct—will that all be the same as before?" Though not optimistic, I was curious to see if he had given me any consideration.

He avoided my gaze and waved his hand at me in annoyance as he reached for his telephone. "We'll discuss all that later, Comrade. Dismissed."

His attitude telegraphed what I suspected. It had been an empty promise all along, a ploy so I'd do his bidding.

I wasn't about to let him off the hook so easily. "But, sir, our arrangement? The English lessons, the position..."

He ignored me and dialed his phone. I opened my mouth to speak again, but he was already in conversation on the phone and he turned away from me. I saluted his back and left.

CHAPTER 49

F or privacy, I called Vick from a phone box on the way home to tell him I'd be flying to Moscow.

"What? No!" he shouted. "Don't go, Kira. Find a way to get out of it."

"You know I can't do that. I'm in the Army. I have to go."

"Trust me, Kira! You can't. Tell them you're sick."

"I'll be back in time for the weekend," I assured him, but the anxiety in his voice forced me to acknowledge the nagging fear burrowed in the back of my own mind.

"I leave early Wednesday morning and fly back to Berlin Thursday with replacement personnel," I said, hoping that saying it could make it so. "You're worried for nothing, darling."

Unconvinced, he emitted a long sigh. "Be careful, Kira. Please. I love you."

I knew he did, but it was good to hear him say it again at that moment.

"I love you, too."

"I'll be thinking of you the whole time."

◆ ◆ ◆

Moscow

Fond memories of flying over Moscow with Maxim as his student revisited me as our pilot lowered altitude a few miles from the Karl Marx airport.

The view below brought me back to the first time Maxim said I was ready to take to the air and we flew over Moscow together. It was in the spring of 1941. We were flying a Po-2 trainer with me at the controls. For all my bravado, I was only confident because he was seated behind me, coaching me, directing, and correcting with the dual controls. Still, it was *my* flight. My first of a great many.

Barely able to contain my excitement, I'd attached Maxim's little pin to my flight jacket with great ceremony before we got into the plane.

"Don't depend on that for luck," Maxim had scoffed. "Either you know your stuff or you don't. We'll soon find out."

"You said yourself I was ready," I sassed him as I put on my flight helmet and adjusted my goggles.

Drinking in the regal majesty of Moscow from the air that day, I asked myself how any foreign nation could bear to disturb the city's powerful beauty, her stately elegance. Yet, armies continued to try throughout the centuries of Russia's turbulent history.

Moscow was not the most beautiful city in the country, but for all the faults of our government and the things I hated about Russia at that time of my life, the capital still held me in its grip. Moscow had been worth fighting for, and there was a time I'd gladly have died to preserve it.

"You have the makings of a fine pilot," Maxim finally said to me as I landed back at base.

I lapped up his praise. Ironically, I had never bothered getting a driver's license, but I was about to become a legal bomber pilot in a brutal war. Throughout my nine hundred and forty two sorties, it was Maxim's reassurance that sustained me.

◆ ◆ ◆

This trip for Petrov couldn't have been more different. We were flying a large plane—nothing like the trainer. My weekend air time with Vick in the C-47 had done much for improving my skills, and throughout the flight I was happy and comfortable about spelling the pilot whenever he needed a break.

After staring at rubble in Berlin for so long, Moscow—at least from the air—still had a unique magnetic attraction. Thanks to our numerous antiaircraft gunners, the capital had been largely spared during the war. Though some bombs had managed to find their way to the city, there was little visible war damage from our vantage point. It looked much as it had six years earlier when Maxim and I soared over it during my first solo flight.

This time, as the co-pilot to a Captain Valentin Kuzmich, I was in a good position to admire the sight of the glittering Moskva River as it gracefully swept its way through the city. St. Basil's Cathedral and its colorful fairy-tale domes, the vastness of Red Square, and the imposing Kremlin fortress all brought back feelings of pride and duty.

Strangely, I felt Russian again, as Russian as a *matryoshka* nesting doll. Like the dolls, I had reached out from a core of insignificance, expanding in stature from student pilot to a captain in the Red Army Air Corps. Growth I was proud of.

We landed in Moscow without incident, and as Petrov gathered his belongings at the airport, I shook his hand and solemnly wished him all the best in his new position, whatever it was. I had never liked him—fear of what he represented did not allow me to—but I didn't wish the NKVD on anyone.

"Good-bye, Comrade Voronova," he said. "I hope you'll always serve the Soviet Union proudly."

"Thank you, sir," I said. "I'll make every effort."

Then he added, "Be careful."

I was startled. "Yes. Good luck, sir," I said.

As an afterthought, I asked him, "Do you know who will be replacing you in Berlin, sir?"

"Yes. A Major Anatoly Sinyakov. An old friend of mine from Moscow."

Major Sinyakov! Like a thunderbolt, my memory of the time I had pneumonia at Engels swirled into my head: the major's refusal to let me fly with him to Moscow. He was the heartless pilot who disapproved of women in combat; the chauvinistic officer who thought we should be home minding children, and didn't want a woman anywhere near his precious plane. Now I was supposed to work for him? His arrival could only throw a huge spanner into my plans. Until they were firm, this was the man I would be dependent on for all the privileges I now enjoyed. Vick was right. I had to get out of Berlin. Fast.

I didn't react, but thought I should say something: "I don't suppose he'll want me to instruct new pilots, as you and I discussed."

Petrov smiled. No doubt he knew the major's aversions well. "I think not, Comrade. I'm sorry."

He wasn't sorry. We both knew he was never going to let me take on the instructing position. Had such a position opened up, a man would have gotten it. He and Sinyakov were cut from the same cloth. Men who only used women, either as lovers in bed or as subservient housewives to birth their children and wait on them. Women like me, with credentials as leaders and ambitions, they would use to further their own political ends. Then toss us away.

Two men in NKVD uniforms were waiting for Petrov next to a black Mercedes parked just off the tarmac. Tentatively, he approached the car.

I expected to see him frog-marched to the vehicle and shoved unceremoniously into it, NKVD style. Instead, one of them saluted him, relieving him of his briefcase as he led him to the car.

Life was full of surprises.

It was still early in the morning. After checking into the women's barracks with a silent, inscrutable Inna, I ordered a taxi and headed to the hospital to visit Dedushka.

The state of the hospital was deplorable. Few repairs had been made to war damage from stray salvos. There were cracks in the plaster, dirty linoleum floors, and soiled bed linen on the cots. The appalling ward my grandfather shared was foul-smelling. I counted two rows of beds, twenty-four in all, sheltering elderly men, many of them veterans and amputees. Their hopelessness filled the space with an unsettling fog of despair; they were waiting to die.

Dedushka was thin and gaunt, his complexion gray under a week's growth of beard, and there was an aura, a yeasty smell about him that told me it would not be long. I took his hand in mine, and kissed his thin, sunken face, exacerbated by the absence of his dentures. I fingered the scar below his eye near the cheekbone where my mother had stitched it, an ugly reminder of the assault by the NKVD thug the night they came to arrest my father.

I said, "Dedushka, it's me, Kira. How are you feeling?"

He showed no sign of recognition. Hoping something, a stray word, my voice, a shared remembrance might spark a conscious thought somewhere deep in his mind, I said: "The other day I was remembering how you taught me to play chess at the farm in Ukraine. You always let me win. I still play with my friends, and I always think of you."

No reaction, but filled with grief, I persisted, stroking his hand: "I have such good memories of the farm, Dedushka, time spent with you and Baba . . . when you took Yuri and me to a friend's stables and put me on a horse for the first time. I was afraid, but I loved it and you told me I'd be a good horsewoman some day."

Dedushka stared, glassy-eyed, his expression flat. I babbled on a few more minutes, but it was no use. Dead organic brain tissue can't be restored to life with words of affection. He had no idea who I was, and I was overcome with sadness. A nurse appeared by his bedside with a cart, and told me my time was up.

"Good-bye, Dedushka," I whispered finally as I kissed his unresponsive hand. Recalling how my mother had flirted with the concept of an afterlife, I added, "Give my love to all of them: to Baba, Mama, Yuri, my little Pavel, and Maxim."

Who knew? Perhaps Mama's vision of the world beyond this life was more correct than I had let myself believe. Dedushka would soon find out.

CHAPTER 50

From the hospital, I boarded the subway and headed to our old apartment at Patriarshy Ponds in the Presnensky district. So much had changed in such a short time, I thought, observing the shabby, war-weary people seated around me on the train.

My life in Moscow with my family and the special chapter of it with Maxim was over. Only nostalgia remained for what I treasured so deeply. What would my life have been like had the war not claimed Maxim? Would our youthful love and devotion have lived on, or fizzled out with time?

And our baby boy, Pavel. What would he have been like had he survived the war? What kind of husband and father would Maxim have been? Sometimes I pictured him as a strict paterfamilias; the disciplinarian who'd keep our son in check. I'd be the indulgent parent, slipping Pavel the few rubles I could spare, extra helpings of food, and sweets.

Other times, I saw Maxim out in a field playing soccer with our son, or teaching him to play ice hockey. Later on, he'd instruct him to fly. Would we have had other children? The answers were hidden in an evaporating cloud of possibilities.

Such were my thoughts as I traveled on the Moscow subway among the mid-morning crowd.

I got off the train at the elegant Pushkinskaya station and walked toward our apartment building. Strolling through the once lush allee of trees and gardens of the Ponds—of which Mikhail Bulgakov had written so eloquently in his novel, *Master and Margarita*—I was saddened by their woeful neglect. No source of inspiration to anyone now; the few people sitting on benches were mostly veterans and beggars. Old women dressed in rags, with burlap sacks containing their worldly possessions, fed crumbs to the ubiquitous pigeons. Construction equipment littered the paths. One of the buildings had been recently torn down, and the air was full of concrete dust, reminding me of Berlin.

Fortunately for me, my father was not at work. He met me at the door in his pajamas, coughing and covering his mouth with an oversized handkerchief. I was taken aback at how he'd aged.

Galina had been right. Our home was now inhabited by more people than I'd have thought possible, and inside the apartment there were mattresses and laundry strewn in unlikely places. I could barely get through the former dining room, where one tenant had set up a large rack for drying clothes. My father was living in the cramped space that had once been his study. Getting past his shock, he welcomed me with a hug and a glass of hot tea, sharing his meager supply of cheese and some stale bread. I watched him swallow a pill from a small container he kept in his pocket.

"I had a spell at work yesterday," he explained.

"A spell?"

"I have a problem with my heart. My mitral valve. They sent me home." His voice fell to a whisper. "It wouldn't do to have me die on them on the factory floor. Too much trouble."

I knew no pill would heal a heart valve.

The wild idea of stealing a Red Army Air Corps uniform from the base and smuggling my father onto our return plane trip sprang to mind. I said, "If I could get you to Berlin, Papa, I have a friend—an American officer —who might be able to help get you to the United States. They'd be able to repair your heart there."

"Lower your voice," he commanded in a harsh whisper. Then his tone changed and he reached for my hand, slowly shaking his head. "My darling girl. My smart, sweet Kira. Always thinking. But no. I'm too old to start over in a new country."

My enthusiasm was unbridled. I leaned in toward him. In a low voice, I said, "But in the United States you would get proper care, Papa. They have the latest medicine, modern hospitals, cardiologists—"

"Kira," he interrupted me. "Kira, I can't leave Anton. With Nadia arrested, I'm all he has now. He's become a son to me."

Nadia's younger son? Did he see Anton as a replacement for Yuri?

"Anton's a good boy, Kira. Not like Boris at all."

"But you must think of yourself, Papa."

"What you're suggesting—smuggling me—would put us both at risk for execution. Let's speak no more about it." His low tone was kind, but firm. "For my sake and yours."

"Well, what if we could do the proper paperwork and do it legally?" I whispered back. "It would take longer, but—"

The hopelessness in his face was chilling. "Kira, you don't understand. They'd never let me go. You don't know what's been happening. Things are much worse here now. We're not free to leave."

Surveying the apartment, crowded with other people's belongings—odors from kicked-off shoes, dirty laundry and body sweat—I recalled when our home was clean, private, and peaceful. I peered at my father more closely. He'd never recovered the weight he lost in prison. He was thin and sick, his face deathly pale.

Papa was right: he was not well enough to go through all the bureaucracy of leaving the country legally. Though still in his early fifties, he might not have the years left. Confined to a tiny, tight space like a cage, he had accommodated himself to it, considering it better than the gulag. He knew full well what it was like to be a guest of the NKVD, and nobody cherished freedom more. At times, he'd probably thought what it would be like to leave Russia. If he said it was impossible, chances were he'd looked into it and it was. My shoulders sagged with discouragement.

He was very tired, and yearned for bed, so I took my leave. With heart-breaking clarity, I knew that I would never see my father again. Tearfully, we embraced for a long moment and I said, "Good-bye, Papa. I'll miss you so much."

"Good-bye, sweet girl. My love goes with you."

"I'll write to you."

He whispered in my ear, "Be careful what you write. And learn to read between the lines."

CHAPTER 51

It was mid afternoon when, tired and dispirited by both visits, I hailed a taxi and headed to a new address I'd found for Zinaida through an association for women veterans. There was no telephone number. Her apartment was on the fifth floor of a run-down building with no elevator in a slum neighborhood.

The stale smell of boiled cabbage and garlic choked the air in the stairwell; I swallowed hard to repel the nausea in my throat. I climbed to her floor, where I stood for a minute or so to catch my breath. The screams of a baby echoed through the decrepit space. A male voice shouted *"Zatknis! Bud' spokoyen,"* ordering it to shut up.

My knock on the door summoned the sound of thumping: a cane or a crutch. After a minute, the door was cautiously opened, and an elderly, one-legged man leaning on a crutch appeared in the doorframe. One of his arms hung uselessly at his side. His eyes grew wild as he took in my uniform.

"Yes? What is it? What do you want?" The baby renewed its howling.

His disheveled gray hair was thin, his scruffy white beard yellowed from nicotine. Beyond his parched lips some of his darkened teeth were broken and others were missing. An odor of alcohol and cigarettes tainted his breath. The voice was gruff and gravelly.

I had to raise my voice over the screaming child. "I'm looking for Zinaida Ilyinichna Sebrova," I said, peeking past his shoulder for some sign of her.

"Who wants her?"

"We grew up together, and served in the same regiment. During the war."

He opened the door a little wider.

"Kira?"

Silence.

I gasped. I knew that voice.

"*Maxim*?"

"Is it really you, Kira?"

I nodded, so shocked I couldn't speak. A ghost, surely. The blood drained from my face. Light-headed, I grabbed the doorframe for support and closed my eyes. My heart was beating rapidly and my hands began to tremble.

"Come in, come in," he muttered as he ran his good hand through the tangle of his greasy hair. "Zinaida's at work. She's back on the line at the Tula Armaments factory. Her old job."

Her old job? So, her years of military service had done nothing to remove the taint of her father's legacy. She was still an enemy of the people. I wondered how long she'd be allowed to work, given that so many jobs would soon be denied to women.

I remained standing at the door. I wanted to turn and run down the stairs as fast as I could. Distance myself from this phantom; from the whole situation.

The baby continued its despairing cries. Maxim motioned for me to come in and sit on the shabby, stained couch, held up on one side by a sturdy book to replace a missing caster. He picked up the wailing child and collapsed onto the couch, propping his crutch within easy reach. I eased my way inside.

"Sit, Kira. Sit. My God, what a shock! I never expected . . . you're the last person I . . . How long are you here for?"

My mouth had gone dry. "Just for the day," I managed to say.

"Sorry about the mess." He made a feeble attempt to clear a chair. With reluctance, I sat down.

"Zinaida will be so sorry she missed you."

Somehow I was beginning to doubt that.

The small room was cluttered with clothing, laundry, a smelly diaper pail, a few hand-knitted baby toys, and yellowed copies of *Pravda*. For lack of shelving, books had been piled against walls, and dirty dishes were stacked on a small table. A makeshift clothesline was sagging with the weight of diapers and damp baby clothes. Buckets of water, presumably brought in from a communal kitchen, took up a lot of the space, as did a few shelves of pantry items. A second toddler sat in a play pen, clutching a blanket while it sucked a soother, probably too steeped in misery to cry. The screaming child smelled foul, and I suspected a soiled diaper as the source of its discomfort.

We were shouting to be heard, and finally after several minutes of this mayhem, I could no longer stand it. I took off my coat and rolled up my sleeves.

"Here, Maxim, let me take him."

"It's a girl," he said. "Name's Sophia. That's the boy, Kirill, over there. Twins, we had. They're a year old."

"Where do you keep your baby changing things?"

He handed Sophia to me and indicated a corner of the room equipped for diapering.

Sophia stopped crying when I picked her up. My mind was rapidly taking stock of the situation, the past mingling with the present in a whorl of emotion. Still in shock from Maxim's unexpected apparition, my hands continued to tremble as I changed her and I was afraid I'd stab the poor child with a safety pin. An angry rash covered her little bottom. I busied myself cleaning her with water from one of the buckets and I applied some cream I found at the changing table. Once she was in a fresh diaper, I kept her on my lap and soothed her, my head still buzzing with the reality of the situation. During all this, Maxim sat on the couch and stared at me, as shaken as I was.

Sophia continued to shudder and hiccup as children do in the aftermath of a good cry. She was a pretty child, with Zinaida's big intelligent blue eyes and a thick jumble of reddish blonde hair that curled with perspiration from her tearful outrage. A lovely baby, she awoke all my maternal feelings. Despite the tension in the room, a rush of affection went through me as I kissed her chubby cheeks and her forehead, while rubbing her back. She was my beloved Pavel's half-sister, after all, and this alone endeared her to me.

As Sophia calmed down and her brother dozed off, the room became mercifully quiet and my brain cleared. I looked at my husband—he *was* still my husband—once handsome and healthy and strong, now reduced to a shadow, a stranger I hadn't recognized. At one time, he'd been my whole world. I shook my head. Having gone through the pain of mourning Maxim's death, I now had to deal with the fresh anguish of knowing he was alive.

Finally, I broke the silence. "Well, Maxim?"

He nodded. "Where to begin?"

"Begin at the end," I said. "The end of the war."

"The end. Yes, it finally did come to an end. So...when I returned to Moscow, you weren't back. You were still in Berlin after our army took the city. That was in '45. I was a wreck."

"Your leg...?"

"Wounded in the field. It became gangrenous in Majdanek, a Nazi camp near Lublin in Poland. A Russian doctor—also a prisoner of war—amputated it."

"How long were you there?"

"About a year. I think. You lose track of time. Anyway, I survived the Germans, they were releasing some amputees because we couldn't work, but when I arrived back here, I was put in prison again. First Lefortovo, then Lubyanka. For a 'check-up' they called it. It was an interrogation; I was tortured."

Maxim had lowered his voice, and I followed suit. "You were tortured by *our* people? Who? The NKVD?"

He nodded. "Yes. They knocked out some of my teeth, crushed my arm. By the time they let me go, I was unfit for any kind of labor. I was destitute, homeless. Look at me. I'm like an old man."

"Why were you put in prison? What had you done?"

"Done?" He stared at me, incredulous. "Nothing. I'd served our country. But I'd survived. We weren't supposed to come home, Kira."

"But that makes no sense!"

"Stalin wanted us to die," he continued. "Millions of

our troops died in prisoner of war camps, Kira. Not thousands. *Millions.* Unreported. The statistics you read about? They're only the fallen troops."

Stalin's adage came to mind. I said flatly: "The death of one man is a tragedy..."

". . . 'And the death of millions, a statistic' " he said, finishing the quote. "You may be in the Army, Kira, but you've led a sheltered life. Military women weren't held to the same standard."

"You think that?" I bristled with indignation. "We were told it was better to crash and burn than be captured. A third of us got killed. We were given cyanide capsules to take if we were caught. Otherwise, we'd suffer unimaginable abuse by the Nazis."

"And there is the difference between us. For men, it was understood we'd be put through unimaginable abuse—but *by our own people!*" His smile was bitter. "You'd tell your friends at the front: 'If I fall and I'm captured by the enemy, say that you saw me die.' If you were declared dead, at least your family wouldn't suffer." He clenched his jaw. "I was thinking of you."

He shifted in his seat to get comfortable. He said in a low voice: "Stalin calls troops taken prisoner "traitors to the Motherland." Your brother Yuri was lucky. All he lost was his life."

Thinking of Yuri brought a lump to my throat. "But sometimes, a soldier has no choice but to surrender."

"There's always a choice, Kira. The choice is to keep fighting and be killed. And it's the only course of action our leader considers honorable. Die and you die with honor. Then you're a hero, and earn a useless, posthumous medal." He added, "It's all in Order #270, delivered in 1941. Check it out. Stalin's words: *No state allowance or relief for veterans and their families.* Officers, like me, who survived a camp, were treated even worse; we were called "malicious deserters," a separate category, and our families were mistreated accordingly. No rations; nothing. Some were sentenced to hard labor; many were shot. Sometimes their wives were imprisoned."

This was all a revelation. An appalling one. "How could our country treat its veterans with such cruelty?"

He shrugged. "I've never understood the reasoning behind it. It's what happens when you have a leader . . ." he stopped, then lowered his voice. "The walls have ears."

"How long were you in prison?"

"In Moscow? I was in Lubyanka for about a year. '45 to '46."

"But Maxim, I was back here for two years after the war ended! In Moscow, finishing my engineering degree. I came back in '45, right after the conquest. Why didn't you contact me? I had no idea you were still alive."

"I was barely alive. Skin and bones. I didn't want you to see me . . . emaciated, broken, starved." He coughed, then looked up at me. "It didn't have to be like that. The Swedish Red Cross tried to distribute food parcels to us in the camps. Hitler said he'd allow it; *Stalin* refused. He let our men starve to death."

"As punishment for being caught." I said.

"Yes. As punishment for being caught," he echoed. He shook his head, wincing as he absently rubbed at the stump of his missing leg.

Only then did I bring up the obvious: "You and Zinaida...?"

He hesitated. Then lapsed into a fit of coughing

"Zinaida traced me through a clandestine veterans' group where she volunteered. When she saw I was in a bad way, she offered to help."

"So, let me understand you. Zinaida found you, but she didn't tell me."

Zinaida and I were seeing each other socially back then. We'd gone to the cinema or met for tea sometimes. She was job-seeking at the time.

"Zinaida never told me you were alive, or that she was helping you. And then…two babies?"

I thought of the loose clothing and ample coats she favored. Later on, she was always busy with something. She'd call or write to me instead of getting together.

"Don't be hard on her," he said. "It was better that way. You were busy picking up your old life. She'd give me reports. How you were finishing your degree. Keeping an eye on your father and grandfather. Mourning Yuri. She didn't want to burden you."

"Burden me? You're my husband!"

We were silent for a moment while the realization of that declaration sank in for both of us.

With an abrupt shift in his train of thought, he said: "I often think about landing in that wheat field, the day I met you, Kira. Before Stalin. You were a teenager. The pure air of our Russian countryside—"

"That was in Ukraine, not Russia," I corrected him. I was still bristling from his deceit. "And Stalin *was* in charge. It was a collective farm, a *kolkhoz*; my grandparents were indentured servants to the state. And I was ten, not a teenager."

This brought on more coughing. "My injuries affect my memory, Kira. I did take you for an airplane ride, though, I remember that well."

He looked at me, and for a long lingering moment, I saw in his eyes the Maxim I once knew and loved. I looked past his frail body; the pinned fold of his trouser leg, his useless arm. His skin beneath the beard was pale but unwrinkled.

He said, "I know you're the one person—I'd never tell Zinaida this—the one person who ever made me truly happy. I loved you so much."

Noting his use of the past tense, I repeated the word: "Loved."

"You will always have a special place here." He placed his hand over his heart. "You were the reason I survived the war, Kira. Why I fought to stay alive, even after I was injured. When I was in Majdanek, and later at Lubyanka, thoughts of you were what got me through. I dreamed of coming home to you and Pavel, of having another child, teaching pilots again, finding an apartment in a nice neighborhood, not like this shit-hole."

I glanced around the shabby room and the bleak view outside. It *was* a shit-hole. It seemed to close in on us, the odor from soaking diapers and baby sick; the tape over cracked windows, the ugly furniture; water marks on the ceilings. . .

"I've come to love Zinaida," he was saying. The wind rattled the windows as his words sank in. "She helped me a lot. At first I was grateful. And then she got pregnant."

He glanced in the direction of his slumbering babies, brushing Sophia's damp hair back off her face with his hand as she slept. Maxim had been at the front when I had Pavel. He never even saw him. The fantasies I had of them together, the hockey, the soccer—they'd forever be figments of my imagination.

"The babies have been a joy to me. They make it all worthwhile. Do you have someone, Kira? In Berlin?"

I hesitated. "I have been seeing someone in Berlin. An American."

"An American?" He digested this information. "They're all rich. No wars on their turf. So, you've landed on your feet. An American can give you a good life."

We sat in silence. How could I tell him it was Vick, the man, who made me happy, not the good life he could offer me?

"It's all for the best then, isn't it?" he said abruptly. "Everything changed at some point."

He took a home-rolled cigarette from a box with his good hand, worried by a tremor I hadn't picked up on. Threads of tobacco hung from the paper and when he lit it they showered flame. Tiny burn holes in his clothing told me this happened frequently.

"I'm sorry, Kira," he said. "I could never leave Zinaida now. She and I...we need each other. We're a family."

"I understand. Things can never be the same," I said quickly.

"No, they can't. The war...it screwed up all our lives. If you need me to sign anything, Kira, for a divorce, I'll help you any way I can."

"I appreciate that."

"Zinaida's a terrific girl, Kira. She takes care of me, sees to my needs. A good mother to our babies."

Was the implication that I had not been a good mother to Pavel? Maxim had never approved of me going into combat.

"Yes," I said. "It's good that you have her." We were both nodding.

The pale little boy in the play pen had been dozing, but now he was awake and crying, nose runny. I'd gently placed little Sophia on the couch, but she awoke to her brother's cries and their shrill duet was deafening.

I remained long enough to help Maxim bathe the twins, diaper them, and give them their bottles, all the while thinking that this could have been my life—our life together. Now, it was Zinaida's.

I cuddled their babies one last time, kissed them goodbye and, shrugging into my army tunic, I said, "I must go. I fly back to Berlin early tomorrow."

"You look smart in your uniform, Kira. So important. All those fancy medals."

I buttoned up my overcoat, determined to act with magnanimity, while inwardly raging at Zinaida's duplicity. And Maxim's. But what was the point?

"I'm sorry to have missed Zinaida. Give her my love."

"You're not angry?"

"Of course not. Zinaida helped you when you needed it. You love each other, and you have two beautiful children. That's all that matters."

He nodded, then leaned forward as though to kiss me on the lips. I smelled the sourness of him, his musky body odor, and alcohol. I moved away.

As I reached into my pocket, my hand touched the little

pin he gave me all those years ago, the good luck charm that got me through the war. I took it out and placed it in his hand. "Here. Give this to the twin who grows up to be like you, a great pilot."

His trembling hand reached out. "Ah, yes. My little pin. I can't believe you still have it. Thanks. I'll put it away for Kirill."

"It might well be Sophia," I challenged. Hopefully, the ban on women flying wouldn't last forever.

He laughed then. "Sophia? Yes, why not? It might be Sophia. She's a determined little thing. She might turn out like you."

"Good-bye, Maxim."

I blew him a kiss. Then I closed the door, and made my way down the darkening stairwell to the street. Outside, I gulped fresh air, taking deep breaths, relieved beyond measure to be out of the fug of their claustrophobic apartment. I walked at a fast clip toward an area where I could find a taxi.

I had not gone thirty feet when a tramway car stopped behind me. I turned around to watch it disgorge its passengers and saw Zinaida stepping down from the car in an overcoat too long for her, a kerchief tied over her hair. She carried a bag of groceries, and glancing both ways for traffic, she crossed the street; resigned, careworn, and prematurely old in the early twilight.

I did not call out to her.

CHAPTER 52

*Z*inaida. How could you?

I'm exhausted after my stressful afternoon. I sit back in my seat in the taxi, an emotional wreck.

Being back in Moscow, I find myself mired in images from the past, and they come at me in rapid succession. Snapshots. Flashbacks of things that I want to forget. I'm swarmed by them; propelled to the surface of my mind by my visit to Zinaida's and Maxim's apartment—the home of the two people, outside my immediate family, who had meant the most to me in the world.

The shock of seeing Maxim again, a sadly transformed Maxim, reminds me of the time I was sent home to Moscow with pneumonia . . .

Moscow, 1943

Plenty of hot soup, a warm bed, Nadia's black market penicillin, and lavish coddling by my mother had quickly worked their magic. I confessed our elopement to my parents, and once they recovered from their shock, they accepted the situation with equanimity. The war had made us all fatalists.

Once I was feeling better, Maxim and I got together as often as we could, squeezing in as much time as his schedule would permit. For several ecstatic days, we relived the joy of our previous trysts, renewing our promises to each other, our determination to make each other happy once the war ended. We vowed we would survive, each for the other. Our parting was painful and bittersweet, spun with hopes and dreams against the grim reality of an ever-escalating war.

I returned to Engels, more in love with my husband than ever, if that were possible, missing him beyond anything I could describe.

But I was to pay dearly for my trip home. It didn't take me long to realize I was pregnant.

I was determined to stay on, flying and bombing, as long as I could hide my condition. Because I felt so deeply about Maxim, I couldn't consider termination, even though that option would have been available through Doctor Kamanev, the doctor at Engels. No. It was *our* child and I would cherish it. When the war was over, everything would be normal again, and we'd be a family. As we planned.

I kept my pregnancy a secret from the authorities. My sisterhood, sworn to silence, helped whenever they could with extra food from their own rations. Zinaida and Luba would take their time servicing my plane to give me more rest between sorties. No one leaked a word to our commander, Colonel Drobovitch. Finally, around five months in, I had to admit my condition to my superiors. After securing a permission slip from Dr. Kamanev, I managed to get on a repositioning plane back to Moscow to give birth, piloted by one of the female aces in another regiment.

My mother and Nadia delivered Pavel together; I hired Nadia's cousin Masha as a nanny, and I was given two months off before I turned my adored baby over to them and returned to the front. Motherhood on hold: One of the most painful things asked of any mother.

The day at the Moscow train station when I returned to

base after Pavel was born, I had a terrible premonition. From the train window, I saw a large black dog in the snow outside. The emaciated animal, mangy and listless, appeared to be there for a reason, to warn me about something. For a moment I seriously considered getting off the train. I wanted to run away with Pavel, to take refuge in the woods, and not report for duty at Engels.

In the taxi, my thoughts of Zinaida wrench me back to that time at Engels. The excruciating memory that I always suppressed insists on resurfacing, and I'm forced to confront the day when my world collapsed:

My baby was a few months old. I had a hammer in my hand, about to nail a few photos of Pavel—posed with Masha and my mother—to the wall behind my army cot. He was such a lovely baby, photogenic, but oh, so serious. Staring directly at me, he seemed to be asking why I wasn't in Moscow to take care of him. I often asked the question myself.

Zinaida appeared by my side.

"Kira, dear," She said, a gentle touch on my arm. "Could you leave off doing that?"

"Why? What is it?"

"I've . . . had a letter from your father."

"Papa? He wrote to *you*? Why?" My voice dropped to a whisper as I put down my hammer. "What did he say?"

Zinaida couldn't answer. It was only then I saw some girls approaching—Luba, Elena, Galina, and others. Dorm-mates that she had assembled for support.

"Is my baby all right? What's wrong? Give me that letter," I ordered, extending my hand. "Give it to me now!"

She didn't extend it, but instead allowed the letter to be snatched from her hands. She continued to stand there, eyes blinking tears. The other girls also stayed in place, frozen and unmoving, like models in a tableau posed by an artist for a painting.

The preamble of the letter from my father heralded my worst fears:

"Zinaida, I'm writing to enlist your help. I cannot bring myself to write to Kira directly. I'd like you to be there to take her hand when she hears this terrible news."

Zinaida's red eyes and the tears flowing out of control down her cheeks told the story. Impatiently I shuffled through the pages for immediate answers.

"What's happened? What is it? My baby! Is he sick?"

Zinaida covered her face with her hands. Commander Drobovich, appeared. She stepped forward with authority. "You must be brave, Voronova," she said softly. "We have all had to endure many hardships during this war."

"What is it?" I shrieked frantically. "What?"

I continued reading:

"It was another stray bomb, Zinaida. When the sirens went off, everyone ran to the shelter, my wife carrying little Pavel. They stayed there until they thought it was over, about an hour. They should have stayed longer. Another few minutes would have made the difference. Nadia, and Masha, the babysitter, begged my wife not to leave. But the neighbors who had also taken shelter with them told me later the baby was crying and my wife wanted to hurry back to the apartment to feed him. They were almost home when they were blasted by an incendiary bomb."

They tell me I fainted into Zinaida's arms at that juncture. I don't remember. I just recall Dr. Kamanev giving me a sedative.

That scene, repressed for so long, plays back in my mind. The pain . . .

I watch the fleeting view of Moscow outside the taxi through the pale blur of my tears. The driver hears me crying and turns to ask if I'm all right. I can't answer.

My maternal urge that day at the train station, the desire I resisted to hide with my sweet angel, my need to keep him safe, the baleful black dog. None of it had been wrong. It had been prophetic. I close my eyes, still tasting the sorrow.

For the next couple of months at Engels, I continued to function, but with a vengeance, hating the Nazi fascists more than ever. I took unnecessary chances in the sky, scaring my navigator. I wallowed in the sympathy of my sisterhood. I cried; slept little. And ate hardly at all. My life had turned to hell. Without Zinaida, I don't know how I would have gotten through that time in my life. Zinaida. My steadfast friend.

My thoughts drift to the two years, after the war when I was in Moscow finishing up my engineering degree.

I was always delighted when Zinaida would get in touch to have lunch or tea in that interim before I re-upped. I'd mourn my mother and baby and she sympathized; when I routinely bemoaned Maxim's presumed death, she'd listen patiently.

"I can't bear that he's gone," I told her, tears in my eyes. "I think of Maxim every day."

Zinaida had only nodded, the soul of empathy.

"I'm sorry you didn't meet before he left for the front. You two would have really taken to each other," I said.

She merely smiled.

The hypocrisy! I recoiled with disgust at the whole situation. All that time Zinaida and I had gotten together after the war, she'd been living with Maxim—a damaged Maxim—making babies. The thought is mind-blowing. I'd been through a lot during the war. But this? The thing I least expected was the ultimate betrayal by the two people who'd meant so much to me. She had her reasons; reasons I'd never know. I simply have to accept that.

Still, whether I like it or not, the visit to their apartment was cathartic; it gives me closure. I'm ready to turn my life around with Vick. A new life, with someone I love. I'll give him my answer as soon as I get back to Berlin.

I dry my tears.

CHAPTER 53

After wending its way through Moscow in a tangle of undisciplined traffic, the taxi stopped at the guard house of the Red Army barracks for women near the Karl Marx military airport. The driver smiled at me and wished me good luck. Noting a few missing fingers in his waiting hand, I tipped him generously.

I was directed to the Marina Raskova Dorm. With the war over, female troops had vacated the area. The building sat pretty much empty, and the silence was chilling. In appearance, it was much like the facilities at Engels, bleak, grey, utilitarian, and wrapped in coils of barbed wire. Inside, it was unheated and in disrepair, with no background hum of chirping young women to give it life.

The Marina Raskova Dorm held twenty cots, with an enclosed toilet and a sink at one end of the dorm area. A communal shower in the outside corridor was large, intended for groups; basic, and in need of a good cleaning. Grateful that I would be there only one night, I unpacked my small grip and, tired from the trip and my three stressful visits, thought about finding something light to eat, and getting some sleep on the iron cot with its thin, lumpy mattress.

There was a clatter at the metal door, echoing throughout the dorm and I jumped up in alarm. In walked Inna Gradska, wearing a smug smile.

"Senior Lieutenant Petrov wants to see you tomorrow morning." she announced. "You're to be at his new office inside Lubyanka in the Meshchansky District at ten o'clock."

The headquarters of the NKVD. I knew where it was.

"At ten? But Inna, I'm supposed to fly back to Berlin at 6:00 tomorrow morning! Captain Kuzmich, the pilot, is expecting me."

"He'll be fine. The plane is transporting Russian officers to Berlin. There's bound to be a few pilots or navigators among them," she said. "You're not indispensable, you know."

"But I was told . . ."

"You're not leaving Moscow, Comrade."

"I'm not?" There was a tremor in my voice. Her words were like a sharp spear plunging through me, piercing all my dreams.

Did this mean I was never going to leave? Surely not. Any moment now I would wake up. This nightmare would go away; return to some hidden recess of my subconscious, instead of scaring the hell out of me in real time.

"But why, Inna? My understanding was that I'd return tomorrow, early."

"Maybe you're too valuable." Her voice dripped with sarcasm. "After all, you're an engineer. And you speak English. Perhaps he thinks you'll serve the Red Army better here in Moscow."

My legs had gone rubbery and weak; I sat on the bed. I thought I'd be delivering Petrov to the nefarious forces of the NKVD, but I was mistaken; he wasn't in a prison cell—he had an office at the prison. It occurred to me that Vick might have known about this. It would explain why he was so insistent that I not take the trip.

A shudder of despair. I thought about the deal Vick

and I had contrived with Boris. I had so many questions. Had Boris told people about our scheme to free Ingrid while he was drinking? The wrong people? Had a spy been watching me? Perhaps word had gotten to Petrov—the revelation that I was not the loyal soldier I professed to be. Was my former boss now in an influential Intelligence position at the NKVD? Was he bringing me in for questioning? Had they decided I wasn't suitable spy material and should be terminated—perhaps for treason? I cringed when I thought of the tortures Maxim had endured. Another worry—were they also going to go after Vick?

"I'd prefer to go back to Berlin—" I ventured tentatively.

"You'd prefer?" She laughed.

"To pack up my personal things," I continued. "Tie up loose ends. Then I could come back on another military plane, like the one we came in on this morning."

Her laughter was genuine. "You're too funny, Voronova. Are you missing your pretty trifles? Your French perfume and American lipsticks and nylons from their PX? Forget them. You've had your fun in the West. Amateur hour is over. You're in Moscow now. For good. Get used to it."

For good! The chilling finality of her words hit me like a metal vault door clanging shut.

Was she right? If so, it meant I would never see Vick again. In a rush of emotion, I realized how deep my feelings for him were. I hadn't planned it this way. He had ferreted his way into my life. Now I couldn't imagine living without him.

Tears welled in my eyes, and I turned away. Like an ill-fated sable caught in the woods, legs gripped by iron teeth, I had fallen into a trap.

I straightened up. "Tell him," I said in a voice as clear as I could muster, "Tell Senior Lieutenant Petrov that I serve the Soviet Union. Ten o'clock. I'll be there."

"A car will come for you at 9:30. Be ready."

She sounded disappointed that I'd not reacted with more grief. She picked up the leather case she'd left on one of the other beds, hoisted her purse over her shoulder and made to leave. "I won't be sleeping here. You'll have this place all to yourself."

"You're not staying?" It was not that I wanted her company, but the prospect of being alone in these cell-like barracks was discomfiting.

"You're a silly fool, Voronova. You know that?" she said, laughing. "Did you think I was "just a secretary"? That I was in Berlin to do the filing? And that I'd be staying here, in *barracks*?" I thought of her effortless English; the brief sighting of her in the West with a British officer; her relationship with Petrov. Clearly, there was more to Inna Gradska than the image she presented. She knew what she was doing, like any highly trained professional.

Horrified, I heard her lock the door with a clunky key after letting herself out. There was no doubt; I was in lockdown. A prisoner. The dorm I was stuck in was merely a large cell, with Inna as my jailer.

I thought about her phrase, "amateur hour is over," and it hit me. Unless they were going to execute me, the bastards might have plans to educate me formally in the art of spycraft. I might be slated to become a properly trained Intelligence Officer.

I'd heard of our government operating a school near

Moscow that educated women in the art of seducing men. Its purpose was to toughen and de-feminize women with instruction in the various ways of performing sex; luring unsuspecting men for Intelligence purposes. *Kompromat.* I'd be subjected to lessons in tedious spycraft, like following people, listening to bugged phones, brush-bys, and dead drops. These were taught along with various courses in torture methods, weaponry, self defense, bomb making, and assassinations. Inna was likely one of their graduates. I didn't want any part of it.

Was it better than being shot by a firing squad? Arguably, life was always preferable to death. But it was a distasteful, repugnant fate nonetheless, well beyond what I'd signed on for. Even if I later managed somehow to defect, going through such a brain-washing education would inevitably change me. I would become someone I despised. A hardened, amoral woman like Inna. Spy work was the last thing I'd ever wanted, and I regretted getting involved in any of it, at any level. Vick had probably seen this coming. Why hadn't I?

Alone, I allowed myself the luxury of tears. Then fear turned to anger and I pounded my pillow furiously, sending dust and feathers in all directions. Getting a grip on my emotions, I scanned the area for windows or fire exits. I checked for hidden cameras. I gazed up at a tiny window high above the beds, and considered it as my way out. But there was no way to reach it. The bathroom cubicle had no window at all.

I could see no escape from the compound either. If by some miracle I managed to get out and sneak past the guards and barbed wire, I had no means of getting back to Berlin. Or even Moscow, for that matter. If I were apprehended by the sentries, I saw myself condemned to hard labor in some gulag.

What saddened me most was that I'd never see Vick again. The cottage with the white picket fence, children; all our plans, our life together in the U.S.—beaches in Virginia, clam bakes, spelunking in caves, riding horses on peaceful trails—I would never get to experience any of it with the man who had become the great love of my life.

To preserve sanity, we try to order our lives so we can plan for things. We reach for life buoys to grasp in un-settled times. But there was none of that in Russia. It was impossible to plan under a dictatorship. Everyone was vulnerable. You did what you were told. And even when you did, the rug could be pulled out from under you. I was a pawn, one of many. My life no longer be-longed to me—if it ever did.

I had no choice but to follow orders and meet Petrov the next day.

CHAPTER 54

Without undressing, my shoes still on, I lay down on the bed. Eventually, overwhelmed by a great sadness from events of the day, I cried myself into a fitful sleep. I don't know how long I was out, but it was uneasy slumber, badgered by one of my recurrent nightmares: this time I was in Moscow, at home with my family, and the NKVD were at the door to take my father away. Pounding on the door . . . pounding, hitting my grandfather . . . pounding . . . grabbing my father . . . my mother pleading . . . the pounding ... pounding ... pounding . . .

The pounding on the metal door in real time woke me up with a start. I snapped on the light and looked at my watch. It was 5:45 a.m.

"Open up!" A man's voice. More pounding.

Not a dream, then. This was real. The NKVD were arriving to arrest me. They would escort me to Petrov's office. But Inna had said to expect them at 9:30. Petrov wanted to see me at ten. It was much too early.

Executions usually took place at dawn. Around this time. I grew panicky. There would be a quick trial and then . . .? I thought of Luba and Stanislaw, and tears gathered in my eyes. Tears for Luba; tears for myself. I was overwhelmed by a deep sense of loss. I was to die now, at not yet twenty-five, before my new life was even to begin.

"I'm here for Captain Kira Sergeyevna Voronova! Open up."

I made my way to the door. "I can't open it. It's locked

from the outside."

The man muttered something like "Shit!" and left.

What new, damning evidence had they found? Did Inna say something to incriminate me? It would be easy for her to invent some malicious report. She may have been spying on me all along. Alone, I waited in a paroxysm of weeping as the events of the past year in Berlin ran through my mind like a cinematic newsreel, pointing out mistakes I'd made. Clearly, I should have guessed early the power Inna wielded; should have been more friendly to her.

I suspected I might have Boris to thank for my predicament. A few drinks out with his buddies, and he must have spilled out all the information Petrov would need to nail me. One thing was clear: I would never see Vick again.

The voice was back. A key turned in the lock and the door creaked open.

He was in his late twenties, an NKVD corporal, tall and lean, with a thin black mustache and military bearing. The NKVD worked in pairs. Why was he alone? A flashback to the time Boris and his friends attacked me. Was this another gang rape attempt? I glanced over his shoulder, expecting a few others to appear and shove me back into the dorm onto a cot.

Instead, he quickly saluted in deference to my rank and lowered his voice. "Hurry up, Captain. Get your bag. They're waiting."

"Who?" I asked.

"Hurry," he repeated.

Petrov. It had to be. I quickly threw my few things

into the little case on the bed next to mine. Chest pains were shooting through me; I hoped that I'd have a heart attack before we arrived at Lubyanka. I thought about possible ways I could kill myself in a cell, wishing I still had the cyanide pill they'd issued me at Engels. Now would be a good time to take it.

He took my bag and led me down the long dark corridor; tossed a lazy wave to the sleepy soldier in the gatehouse, who motioned us through. Then he quickened his pace. There was a military transport truck parked outside the barracks, with nobody in it, engine running. The corporal helped me up into the cab. Something was fishy. NKVD would never be so polite.

"Where are we going?" I asked.

He put his finger to his lips, a conspiratorial shush.

"Please tell me. I was told to see Senior Lieutenant Petrov at 10 o'clock."

"New orders." He dimmed his headlights to the lowest setting and brought his foot down on the accelerator to speed away. "A change of plans."

I was becoming impatient with his terse answers and this Kafkaesque arrest, but I said nothing. I assumed he was transferring me to a holding cell somewhere to await trial.

We'd gone about two miles before I sensed we were moving away from the city center and its prisons. A few more miles, and lights from the airfield sifted into the dark. We were speeding along the tarmac toward the plane I'd co-piloted the day before. The cockpit was ablaze with light, beckoning like a lighthouse to a desperate ship-wrecked sailor.

"It's about time," barked Captain Kuzmich, when he

saw me—the same pilot I'd flown in with. Already ensconced in his seat, wearing earphones, he looked at his wristwatch, "You're fifteen minutes late, Voronova. I was about to leave without you."

"I'm sorry," I said. "I was told my orders had changed —"

"No time for excuses," he snapped over the sound of the engine. "Hurry up. Our runway's been cleared for take-off."

Lowering my eyes to accept the reprimand, I struggled to hide a smile. I threw my bag inside and one of the Russian officers sitting on a bench caught it and stowed it away. Then he offered me his hand to help me scramble up the top steps of the moveable stairs. Dizzy with joy, I was in the co-pilot's seat in a second, earphones on, and the officer who had helped me up closed the hatch as the stairs were rolled away.

Crackling chatter on the radio to the pilot stuttered from the control tower; a roar of the engines as the aircraft struggled to take off in the chilling wind. I willed it all to move fast and have it behind me, to be air-bound and safely away from Petrov. In the distance, about a mile off, I saw my driver speeding away.

But traveling toward us from a different direction, the brightly lit headlights from another car appeared out of nowhere. I froze. Our pilot taxied down the runway and we lifted off. In minutes, he had turned and we were heading west. I was leaving my homeland behind for the last time.

Soon after, Captain Kuzmich went to the back of the plane to speak to one of the officers, leaving me in charge. I heard a crackling in the earphone and a voice from the airport tower came on, ordering our plane to turn around and await landing instructions. I caught my breath.

Then I reached over and turned it off.

CHAPTER 55

"I fully expected a double-cross from your friend Petrov." said Vick.

He had met me at the airport. We were in his apartment, and he was nuzzling his face in my hair as I leaned my head on his shoulder.

"He was never my friend," I said, "He was using me." Then I admitted, "You've no idea how scared I was. I never thought I'd be so happy to be in this ash-pile again."

"Yeah, you appreciate Berlin when you know the alternative." He brushed a strand of hair off my face and kissed my cheek. "God, I don't know what I would have done if they'd kept you there."

"My worst nightmare, Vick. All I could think of was that we'd never be together again."

I'd poured out all the details of my horrendous trip— the visit with Dedushka, with my father. My brief but frightening incarceration in the barracks, and my miraculous rescue. The one thing I held back was the visit to Zinaida's and the revelation that Max had survived the War. I didn't know how he'd react. And I was still taking it in myself.

He put his arm around me then and we kissed, a long meaningful embrace. He was a soothing balm, my refuge from the surreal day I'd had in Moscow, and I clung to him, not wanting to let go. To think how close I'd come to losing him.

Finally, he said, "You look exhausted."

"I am."

"I have food in and a nice bottle of wine. Reilly's in Frankfurt."

There was a breezy insouciance about him that I couldn't put my finger on. It occurred to me that Vick Moran had never doubted I'd return as planned. I thought about the way my rescue was handled in Moscow—the young man in the NKVD uniform who drove me to the plane; how breezily the sentry waved us through. It was all too easy.

Had Vick somehow pulled strings to get me out? And how would he have that kind of clout? I looked to him for an explanation, but none was forthcoming. Recalling the car speeding toward us as we lifted into the air at the Karl Marx airport and the message from the tower afterward, I cringed. The whole course of my life could have changed in that one moment.

Later, after a decadent hot bath, a bout of glorious love-making, and sleeping soundly for a few hours, I awoke. He was staring out the window.

"Can't sleep?" I asked him as I propped my head on my elbow and patted his pillow. "Come back to bed, and I'll tire you out."

"You're awake," he said. "Good. Listen, honey—we need to talk." Instead of getting back into bed, he sat in a chair next to me and turned on a lamp. He'd already made coffee and poured us each a cup.

"Vick, what is it?" I blinked as the light flashed on and glanced at my watch. "It's four o'clock. Can't this wait until tomorrow?"

"Kira, promise me you won't get upset."

"I can't promise that." My fear was that he was being

shipped out, leaving me in Berlin, unprotected. *Not now!* It would spell disaster for my safety, and for our plans.

"It's time for me to level with you," he said. "I haven't before because I thought the less you knew, the better—and the safer you'd be."

I sat up and faced him. "What's going on?"

"Remember asking if the U.S. government minded me taking a Russian military officer up in one of their planes?"

"Of course. You said it would be our secret. Is that what you're worried about? The only person I told was Petrov. But you knew that."

"I lied to you."

"Lied? About what?"

"Did you believe I was important enough to cut through the bureaucracy of our military brass? Get a pass to take a Russian officer up for weekend jaunts in a military plane *just for fun*?"

I found myself shaking my head. I had wanted to believe it, but deep down, I didn't think it was possible. Even Americans wouldn't be so naïve.

"I was carrying out orders. I was training you to fly that C-47."

"Training me? What for?"

"We were hoping to bring you over to our side."

"That's no secret, Vick. Petrov said that was why you approached me in London. To recruit me. I told him then, and I've told you since—I don't know any state secrets or any of the workings of Soviet Intelligence. I was trained as a pilot and an engineer, not as a spy."

"Petrov was wrong. In the beginning, my interest in

you was strictly personal. I told you—I thought you were pretty and smart. I wanted to see you again. But then our people started thinking." He said nothing for a full minute while I waited. "You're the kind of person we like to recruit. You'd have made a great Intelligence operative for us."

"What makes you say that? I've had no training in spycraft."

"No, but that can be learned. You've proven you have guts under pressure; you're bright—most important, you know the workings of the Kommandatura. You keep your own counsel. And aside from your German and Russian, you're fluent in English. I was never fooled by your early attempts, by the way."

We were silent for a minute or so.

"I guess I knew," I finally said. "I didn't know it, but I knew, if that makes sense." Russians liked to consider Americans reckless and inept, but I had seen another side of them. "I don't think I ever bought that your government would let a Russian officer get *near* one of your planes, let alone fly one. And certainly not for recreational purposes. Not unless they had an ulterior motive."

"They did have. Frank Marcus figured you'd be a useful addition to our spy stable in East Berlin, but for what he had in mind, you'd have to be able to handle the Gooney Bird."

"And when were they planning to approach me with this job offer?"

He reached for my hand. "It doesn't matter. It's moot now. It all changed after you and I became involved. Once that happened, I didn't want you in harm's way.

I've made that clear, so that ship has sailed."

I withdrew my hand, annoyed that a man would try to take control of my career path, even if it was Vick. "Not so fast! Why would you make such a decision for me? Perhaps I would have wanted to—"

"Trust me. It's risky business. And now you couldn't, anyway, after your escape from Moscow." He waved the idea away. "They'll be looking for you. Let's think about *now*, Kira. I wasn't kidding when I said Berlin is going to become an even more dangerous place for you. I'm staying on because I'm needed for one last important job. Reports are it will be early next year."

"Next year? I thought your tour of duty was up in a few months?"

"It would have been, but for the blockade. Access between the Russian sector and the Allied Zones is going to tighten up real soon. They're planning to secure the border. They're even talking about building a wall—"

"A wall? That's just a rumor. Or are you saying you know for certain it will happen?"

"I'm not sure about the wall. That may take some time. But the border will be strictly controlled. And soon. You won't be able to come and go the way you have. And with Petrov gone, even if you could justify how you left Moscow and were to continue in your old job—a remote possibility—his successor may not let you leave your sector at all. They may shoot people who cross over. You'll be a virtual prisoner over there."

I knew he was right on all counts. And I was all too aware of what the management style of Petrov's successor would be.

"You don't know the worst of it, Vick. I found out who

my new boss is. His name is Sinyakov. A hard-nosed bastard who doesn't like women in the service. He and I have a bit of a history, going back to Engels."

"All the more reason." said Vick. "But it doesn't matter. You'd have been on a tight leash by whoever took over. Worse, now that Petrov knows you've escaped, he'll be gunning for you. You've got to leave, Kira."

"Vick, are you responsible for my return from Moscow?"

He answered only with a slow smile.

"Seriously. Level with me."

"We'll talk about it later."

"Well, answer me this: Has Boris reported me about helping Ingrid? If so, I'm in even more trouble."

He took a big swallow from his coffee. "Kira, listen carefully. On Saturday morning, I want to get you on a C-47 going to London."

"You want me to fly it?"

"No. I'll get one of our off duty pilots. One of the passengers going with you is a navigator. Another one is a pilot, but he has no clearance to fly one of our planes."

"I want to fly it," I said. "Can you get me clearance?"

"You? No. I doubt they'd go for that."

"I insist, Vick. I've logged the hours. I've been up with you so many times. All I need is a decent navigator who can act as co-pilot."

Vick thought about it. "It could be dangerous. You'll be flying over Russian-controlled East Germany."

"Vick, you're talking to someone who flew 942 combat sorties during the war! I know how to dodge anti-aircraft flak."

"Well, I'll talk to them. Logistics-wise, it could work out. A lot of our other pilots are on a rotation, slated to take off on other flights. The others may need a break."

He kissed me then. I patted his pillow again. I didn't have to pat it twice.

Vick was back to me that afternoon. We were sitting in the living room of his apartment.

"They've agreed, Comrade. By default. There's no one else available."

A grin crept over my face.

"You'll be bringing several people with you."

"Several? Who?"

He shook his head.

"Can't you tell me who they are? At least some of them?"

He thought about it. "Well, Boris is going to deliver Ingrid tomorrow. She and Angie will be on board. A few other people. A British operative in East Berlin, someone I've never met. Other operatives we owe protection to. Trust me, Kira. The less you know the better."

I did trust him. And it didn't matter. I was determined to go, no matter who would be along with me. "I hope Petrov hasn't ordered a warrant for my arrest. If he has, I may not be around on Saturday."

"That's why it has to be Saturday. No later. We can't drag our feet on this, for your sake, and for Angie's sister. By then, they'll be scouring Berlin for her. We're moving her here from Angie's apartment. The others need to get out right away, too."

"If I do this Vick, I can never return to Berlin."

"Having second thoughts?"

"No, but it means I won't see you until your tour of duty is up."

"I'll be back stateside before you know it. Keep our bed warm in the meantime."

I saw the happy and eventful years ahead for us, but I was haunted by all the unknowns in the short term. For one thing, I was still legally married. A major hurdle.

Before I went to Moscow, the future path had stretched out with astonishing clarity. But my visit with Maxim had introduced a whole new problem. I had to come clean with Vick.

"There's something you need to know, Vick," I said. "I'm not sure how to tell you this. I'd planned to tell you that I wanted to marry you, but when I was in Moscow, I found out that my husband is alive. He's in a new relationship. But it means I'm still married. I was going to tell you this weekend. I'm sorry."

I poured out all the details of my visit with Maxim in Moscow. "He's willing to sign divorce papers," I concluded. I looked up at him miserably, expecting the worst. Expecting him to be angry that I hadn't told him right away. But he was wearing a smile.

"Give the U.S. Office of Security Service some credit, Comrade. You thought we hadn't researched your background when we considered having you work for us? We knew about your husband. In fact, we took the liberty of drawing up divorce papers for you. Sign them and we'll get them to your husband via diplomatic pouch. Once we get Maxim to sign off, you'll enter the U.S. as a tourist with a special visa, and as soon as I get home we'll get married. Then you can stay in the U.S. You'll qualify to live under the War Brides Act of 1945 until you get citizenship."

"A war bride," I repeated, trying out the label, still reeling at the fact the U.S. government had known about Maxim being alive when he'd been dead to me.

When I'd said good-bye to Moscow on Thursday, I knew I was leaving my life there behind, but there was no doubt now in my mind which side I belonged on. The West wasn't perfect, but it was infinitely better than what I was leaving. Besides, I loved Vick and was committed to following him wherever his career led him.

But I admit the logistics frightened me. Where would I go once I got to America? All I knew was I'd be safer in the West, and free. I was depending on Vick to clarify what he had in mind.

My other worry was who knew about my flight out of Berlin. "The other passengers," I said. "I know you can't tell me their names. But if they're leaving Berlin, I'm assuming they're all in some danger."

He hesitated. "Yes. They are. There's one asset who's been passing on valuable information. Thanks to this person, we know all the details of the blockade planned for next year. We don't have much time. The controls at the border will be put in place soon."

The specter of another Leningrad flashed before my eyes. Without help from the Allies, thousands of Berlin residents could die.

"This intelligence has given us time to organize the

airlift," Vick continued. "We'll have to bring in supplies to over a million people every day. We have a lot of work ahead of us. That's why I can't leave with you. Believe me when I say I'd like to, but I'll be needed here."

"How will you be involved?"

"The airlift means expanding and improving Tempelhof's landing facilities and infrastructure well ahead of time."

The numbers he rattled off boggled my mind.

"You'll have planes coming in and out of Berlin every few minutes!"

"Make that every thirty seconds!"

"Half a minute?" I shook my head in disbelief, imagining the constant overhead roar and the prolonged pollution of air already contaminated by the war. "How long can you possibly keep that up?"

He shrugged. "As long as it takes. It's going to cost a shitload of money. We'll be flying into Tempelhof from Frankfurt, and to Tegel in the French Sector from Hamburg. They'll exit by taking off from Gatow in the British sector, heading for Hanover."

I was stunned. They had it all planned and coordinated. "Realistically, how long might it go on for?"

"We're hoping it won't be more than three weeks to a month. Long enough to negotiate with your side."

"The Nazis lost Stalingrad because they couldn't continue to supply their troops by air," I said.

"The reason the Nazis failed was because they were far from home base and had to supply the whole eastern front at the same time. We're close to West Germany and we're only coming into Berlin—one city. Half a city."

"True. But what you're describing—"

"It'll be a widespread, international effort, the biggest humanitarian effort in history."

"It sounds impossible."

"We can't do it alone. We'll use the resources of *all* our Allies, not just the occupying forces. Eight thousand tons of food and other necessities will be brought in per day. Every day."

My only hope—a naïve one—was that the blockade would get cancelled so Vick could come home sooner.

"Is there any chance it won't happen?"

"Not much. We're introducing a new currency, the Deutsche Mark, in West Berlin to replace Occupation Marks. Your side is furious, for reasons I won't go into. It's complicated. Blocking off all our transportation and communication lines is their way of getting back at us. They're closing down the Autobahn 'for repairs.' Flexing muscle. A step closer to taking over the whole city of Berlin."

He'd continued to refer to the Soviets as "your" side, and I had to ask myself, which was truly "my side"?

My mind had been in turmoil for a growing period of time. I'd begun my position in East Berlin and the spying on Vick in good faith. I was Russian and a committed Communist, indoctrinated since childhood. I'd even temporarily exulted in my Russian-ness when we landed in Moscow a few days before. But so much had happened to shake my faith in the system. Like a crack in a seawall buffering a hurricane, the breach in my thinking had been growing. It was about to burst through, like rushing flood waters.

I had come to accept a moderate socialist approach to government, but I could no longer accept totalitarian rule by dictatorship, enforced by brutality. Much as I loved my idealized Rodina, like Galina, I couldn't look the other way at the toxic methods our Communist government used to destroy lives. The lives of people like my father, like Maxim. And yes, Zinaida. Ordinary hard-working people who just wanted a good life.

"Vick," I said, "Once I fly these people into London, I can't come back. Where will I go from there?"

He was silent for a moment, and my heart pounded in anticipation of what was coming. He took my hand and kissed me.

"I have all your papers ready, Kira. In the States you'll be safe till I get home."

My mind was buzzing. "What do I do with the plane when I get to London?"

"After you drop off your passengers, you'll leave the plane at Drummond Hill, in London. Then you'll board a commercial BOAC plane from London to Washington, and from there, a car to Virginia."

A wave of panic. "How will I do that? How can I manage on my own in America? I don't know anyone there!" My father said he was too old to assimilate a new culture. Was he right? Perhaps I was, too?

"My sister Katie will meet you at the airfield in Washington, and she'll drive you to her place outside Washington. You'll stay with her until she has everything set up and finds a furnished apartment for you till I get back stateside. Katie works as a contractor for the Navy, a smart lady. You'll like her. She'll help you open a bank account, find a job—something in aviation. Your English is good now. Don't underestimate yourself. You're a resourceful woman, Kira. Bright and strong."

His faith in me helped quell the panic rising in my chest. Knowing that I could never come back was staggering. Cutting ties, leaving people I loved. But at the same time, I was buoyed by his confidence; excited about our prospects for the future. I felt a motivating jolt of determination. Yes, I could do this; I *would* do this.

"Not a word to anyone. Pack only essentials. Your landlady and housemates have to believe you're going to Angela's as usual."

"How is Boris getting Ingrid out?"

"You shouldn't know all the details. Let's just say he hit us up for more money to pay off kitchen help at Sachsenhausen. And an electrician to cut the power. Angela will be here, waiting. And at five a.m. on Saturday, I'll drive the three of you to Tempelhof.

CHAPTER 56

With Petrov gone, I had no one to answer to. I remained in West Berlin the next day so we could firm up our plans. This included calls to his sister and a telephone introduction. She sounded lovely. And efficient. Before I left, Vick produced a bottle of champagne and we treated ourselves to a few glasses to celebrate. I was feeling light-headed and giddy. The end was in sight and I was excited.

"I hope we're not jinxing things by celebrating now," I said.

"Well, I won't be with you to celebrate afterward," Vick pointed out. "I'll drive you to the Gate this last time. Do your packing, get a few hours sleep, and come back here really early tomorrow. Remember—talk to nobody."

I admit I was worried when I left him at the Gate that evening, though the champagne helped calm me. I walked quickly, half expecting to be shoved into a car. My concern increased when Frau Schuman greeted me.

"There have been K-5 officers around looking for you this morning. They woke me up," she complained, disgruntled. "I told them you were in the West."

"I can't imagine what they want with me," I said. "Perhaps it has something to do with Luba."

"I thought when I took in Russian women that I wouldn't be bothered by authorities," she grumbled.

She waited for an explanation, but I said nothing. For a moment she looked as though she wanted to confide something to me, but then she pursed her lips.

"I'm going to bed," I announced, yawning for emphasis. "I need an early night."

So Vick was right. Petrov had put out the word. I acted cool, but my heart was hammering in my chest. I couldn't sleep, tossing and turning as I remembered my father's arrest in the middle of the night. I could only hope the K-5 were not as efficient as the NKVD. I dozed for a while, then woke up at 3:00 a.m.

The champagne had dulled my inhibitions, and I still felt both restless and reckless. An idea came to me, and I got up, dressed in my uniform, put my gun in my purse, and stole out of the apartment, heading for the Kommandatura.

There were a couple of our guards posted there, outside the front door, laughing and engaged in a conversation about women. One of them was drinking from a flask. I still had my key to a side door used for afterhours overtime. Furtively, I took advantage of sporadic cloud scatter to sidle around the building and let myself in unseen. I stumbled through the offices, guided only by the pale light from a street lamp outside until I came to Inna's desk. I'd once seen that she kept keys in her top drawer, and was gratified they were still there. As I reached into the drawer in the dark, I knocked over a stapler and it crashed to the concrete floor with a metallic clang. I shuddered, froze, and waited.

An inside door opened, and quietly, I slid under her desk. A light flashed around the office.

"Hullo? Anyone there?" A man's voice. Russian. A watchman doing the rounds.

He wandered around the cubicles in a haphazard fashion, finally directing his light in my direction. His footfalls got louder as slowly, his legs came into my view from where I was scrooched under the desk. I reached into my bag and fingered my gun, hoping I wouldn't have to use it. What had I been thinking, coming here? I held my breath. He'd most certainly be armed. A gunfight would attract the two guards. It could not end well.

"Bloody rats," he muttered.

Would he stoop to pick up the stapler? If he did, we would come face to face. Instead, he paused a foot away from me to light a cigarette. I slowly released my breath. His feet moved on, heading the way he came.

He closed the door and I waited a few minutes. When he didn't return, I hurried upstairs, and with Inna's keys let myself into Petrov's old office, locking it behind me. I lit the low voltage lamp on Petrov's desk, then removed my file and Vick's from the drawer where he'd kept them. I couldn't prevent Major Sinyakov from knowing so much about us, but I could slow him down.

I was about to leave when I spotted the chair I'd so often occupied in a sweat while answering questions. A crazy idea came to me and I set it down at the back wall where Stalin's picture hung. Standing on the chair, I removed the loathsome image from the wall. At Petrov's desk, I worked rapidly. Unclipping the encasing glass, I slid it from the frame, and slipped the photograph out. Gleefully, I took an eyebrow pencil from my bag and drew a big smile on his face.

"For you, Steffi," I whispered.

As an afterthought, I took my lipstick and gave him a red bulbous clown nose. I replaced the glass carefully over the photo to avoid a smear, set it back into the frame and clamped it down. Then I re-hung the photo and admired my handiwork before turning off the light.

I left the way I came, chuckling all the way home as I thought of Major Sinyakov's reaction when he arrived to replace Petrov. If I were later sent to a gulag, I'd at least have something to laugh about. Then I headed for Frau Schuman's and threw a few things into my suitcase.

Blame the bubbly.

CHAPTER 57

I'd seen photos of Ingrid and knew she had once been lovely. The woman I met at Vick's apartment on Saturday was a wraith: hollow-cheeked, with missing teeth, and bruised, blemished skin—a grayish hue with rivers of blue veins at the temples. Her hazel eyes seemed huge and shone too brightly.

Angela said Ingrid was sleeping badly, and she started at the least sound.

"She's showing signs of sleep deprivation," said Vick. "A favorite form of torture over there. The disorienting effects from it can last a long time."

The Indian summer weather was warm, but Ingrid shivered with cold. She also showed signs of suffering from venereal disease. Angela had bathed her and washed her hair, applying antiseptic ointment where her scabby skin showed lacerations, and bites from rats, bedbugs, and lice.

Angela's eyes alternated between joy and sadness. In the pre-dawn hours of Saturday morning, before we left with Vick, she spent the time cradling Ingrid in her arms and soothing her as she continued to discover marks on her body. It was obscene, what they had done to her. We kept assuring her we'd all be heading for London and leaving Berlin behind for good. Repeatedly, she would doze, startle awake, and ask us, child-like, where her parents were.

Angela had asked me to pick out clothing for her, and I'd packed an outfit I inherited from Beatrix. The slacks and jacket hung shapelessly on her too-thin body, but anything was better than her prison garb.

Recalling how my mother had nursed my father on his return to us from prison, I asked, "Do you have any light soup? Biscuits or crackers, maybe? Give her a very little, the lighter the better. She's probably dehydrated, among other things." I lowered my voice. "I hope she's up to the trip home."

"She can't stay here. Once we get her to London, Colonel Francis Marcus will meet us with an ambulance and we'll take her to hospital. My parents will meet us there."

"Shouldn't she see a doctor or a nurse here first?"

"Vick doesn't trust anyone enough. And there isn't time."

"Let me help you with the soup. I'll spoon it to her."

Ingrid accepted our slow spoon-feedings of broth like a baby bird, and to our great relief she kept them down.

When Vick picked us up, we headed for Tempelhof, where the C-47 was ready, an engine humming. A cot had been found for transporting Ingrid, and we immediately settled her on it in the cabin, strapping it down. Angela brought a blanket and picnic basket with a thermos of broth for Ingrid, some biscuits and sugary juices from the PX. Vick had tucked in some water and MRE ration packs for the rest of us.

He placed a revolver 'just in case' between the pilots' seats and then quickly left the aircraft. I doubted I'd need it, but it was reassuring to have the weapon there while we were still on the ground. I hadn't met my copilot, but I hurried to take my place in the cockpit to go over my checklist of pre-flight details.

"*Guten Tag, Frau Voronova,*" said a child behind me.

I turned in surprise.

Little Achim Belenko, bright-eyed and happy, stood clutching a well-used stuffed bear as he sucked a lollypop.

"This is my first airplane ride. I'm really excited!"

"Achim!" I exclaimed reaching for his hand. He planted a big sticky kiss on my cheek and I ruffled his hair.

His sister Liesel joined us in the cockpit. "*Guten Tag, Frau Voronova,*" she echoed her brother. "Have you met our new baby sister?"

Vick had returned and was boarding the plane. My eyes went from the children to Beatrix and Dmitri Belenko who were right behind him. Beatrix was holding a baby in her arms.

"Beatrix!"

"Hello, Kira," she greeted me warmly, kissing me on both cheeks. "Now you know why I was clearing out my wardrobe. I didn't know that you'd be leaving, too."

"Neither did I," I said. Still stunned at the turn of events, I indicated the baby. "You received my letter."

"Yes. We picked her up a week ago. Thank you so much. She's such a good baby. Steffi's grateful to you, too. We've named her Isolde Steffi Belenko."

I smiled. "Steffi would like that."

"Yes, I thought it would be nice to honor her. I wanted to take little Lorelei as well. But Steffi's mother was too attached to her and has managed to make some arrangements for her care. She hadn't yet bonded with Isolde, so it was easier to let her go."

Beatrix kissed the baby's forehead. The two of them were well-matched physically. Little Isolde had the same blonde hair and blue eyes. Sad as it was that the sisters would be separated, at least one of Steffi Bauman's daughters would have a chance at a better life.

Vick was back in the cockpit and slid into the co-pilot's seat. He smiled, "Your first international flight in an American plane, Comrade. Ready?"

"You're coming with us after all?"

"I wish I were. I'd love to fly with you—maybe to Paris or some nice beach in the Caribbean," he said with a grin. "No, I have to clear things with the tower."

Dmitri Belenko entered the cockpit and greeted me over the sound of the engine: "Good morning, Captain." To Vick he said in Russian: "Excellent choice of pilot, Viktor."

"General Belenko, good morning," I said, trying not to act surprised.

Vick turned and said something to him. Hearing them speak together in Russian jogged my memory: the same two voices I'd heard plotting in the basement of the Marching Saints bar. The conversation that I didn't report to Petrov. So, it was Belenko's exfiltration they'd been plotting.

Belenko returned to the cabin to speak with his family and when he was out of earshot, I asked Vick, "How long has this been in the works?"

"Dmitri's been our man for a long time. I've been handling him since he took over at Karlshorst and moved his family to Berlin. He knew a German wife was a liability, and it would blow up in his face eventually, but he adores Beatrix. He was afraid Petrov was beginning to suspect him, so Dmitri arranged to ship Petrov back to Moscow to get him out of the way while he got ready to defect."

"Belenko was responsible for Petrov's transfer?"

"It was the last official duty he discharged; with his cover about to be blown, his family was in immediate danger; he had to get out. Pronto. I agreed. It was time."

"Will he continue to work with you?"

"He'll be working in London as consultant to MI-6." A glance at his watch. "You've been cleared to fly out. Dmitri hasn't, so he'll be your navigator. Just waiting for one more passenger."

There was a scuffling sound of footsteps on the metal stairs. Our last passenger stepped into the cabin—breathless, disheveled, and flushed.

"Sorry I'm late," she said, gasping for breath. "I had to dodge a few secret police following me."

My mouth was open in a surprised 'Ohh.'

"Did you manage to lose them?" Vick asked her.

"I hope so. I was on the back of a friend's Vespa. They ordered us to stop, shooting off bullets into the fog. I had him slow down so I could slip off and I hid behind some trees near the airfield. Thank goodness it was misty. I ran the rest of the way."

I was on my feet, my arms stretched out to welcome her.

"Elena! Oh my God. I can't believe it. We're leaving Berlin together."

"Don't tell me *you're* the pilot of this plane? I'm getting off!" She pretended to head back down the stairs. Then we fell into each other's arms, laughing.

"My, we've come up in the world since our Po-2 days," she said, with a quick glance around the aircraft. "And with a Russian general for a navigator, no less!"

"I can't believe it." I said, still reeling. "You never let on. I didn't expect to ever see you again. With Luba gone, and now Galina off to Palestine via Paris—you and I going to London . . . Frau Schuman must be in shock."

"Oh, you haven't heard? Her husband, the doctor? She found out late last night. He wasn't dead, after all. He's been a POW all this time. He's been admitted to Charité Hospital. He's sick. And he isn't right in the head." She tapped her temple. "There's no way he'll ever practice medicine again. She'll need our rooms for him and possibly a care-giver, if she can afford it."

Perhaps that was what Frau Schuman had been about to tell me. I was sorry for the *gnadige Frau*. We'd shared friendly moments. She had been kind to me when I was attacked. And generous about lending me her shoes. Recalling Maxim's disabilities after imprisonment, I could imagine what was ahead for her husband.

"So much for her finding another Russian General," I said.

"Oh, I don't know. She's pretty resourceful," Elena said with a sly wink. "I have a feeling she'll do all right. And she'll inherit Frau Belenko's clothes to work her wiles."

"And you, all this time, you've been working for the British. How long?" I asked.

"About two years. A few months after the conquest. I'd met a British officer on an errand in the West, and we hit it off. I speak good English, by the way. My mother taught me English along with German."

I recalled Elena thumbing through my English work-books and homework.

"You were just pretending with my textbooks."

"Yes," she laughed. "My British officer . . ."

I interrupted her. "Stephen Carter?"

"You know him?"

"I met him at the Belenkos' party."

"Yes. Well, I took up with Stephen for a while after the British opened their Sector. His wife hadn't arrived yet. When she came, we eventually broke it off. Then he asked me to spy for him.

"I had no choice, Kira. I was in exile. I couldn't go home to Moscow without getting sent to the gulag for stealing that damn parachute. And I was never at home in Ber-lin. East Germany is shaping up to be as brutal as Russia —if not worse. Only the brand name has changed."

I nodded. We'd come to the same conclusion.

"Besides, I want to be free—to travel—to see Paris. New York. London!" Her eyes were shining. "Now, at last, I can visit all those places."

"And you and Stephen?"

"Well, it's over between us, I have no ties. No regrets. No regrets about anything. I did what I had to."

CHAPTER 58

"Time to go," Vick called out.

The magic words, "Runway 1, cleared for take-off" resonated through my headset and I reached for the throttle.

"Okay, Comrade," Vick said to me over the sound of the engine. "This is where I get off. By the way, you should thank Dmitri for your escape from Moscow."

"*He* arranged my escape?"

"We both tracked you from the time you left. All it took were a few calls on his part. The pilot of the plane in Moscow? Captain Valentin Kuzmich? He's an old friend of Belenko's. He would have waited for you. The Corporal who delivered you to the plane was his son."

"And Nadia? What about her?"

"Belenko saw to it that Nadia was released, too."

"So Nadia is safe?"

"She is. He couldn't help your friend Steffi, though. That picture she defaced? She picked the wrong guy."

Yes, she had. I nodded sadly, watching little Isolde, cuddled in Beatrix's arms. I couldn't save everyone. Then, thinking of my silly pre-dawn caper at the Kommandatura, I repressed a smile.

I should have been tired; I'd had little sleep. But I was used to that from my combat years. The events of the last couple of days had energized me. I watched the sun, creeping above the eastern horizon, as it burst through the vivid brush strokes of violet and gold painting the sky. Vick kissed me good-bye; another long, lingering embrace—though they were never long enough—a bittersweet moment. Would it be our last? After what we'd both gone through, the war years, it was logical to speculate. Being Russian, I'd learned instinctively that if something could go wrong, it just might.

Heading for the exit, he had to shout over the roar of the second engine. "Good luck, Comrade. See you stateside!"

I offered him a hopeful smile.

"No worries," he reassured me. "It'll go by fast."

With a gentle touch to my shoulder, he left the cockpit, waved to our passengers in the cabin, and disembarked, leaving Belenko to close the hatch, and the ground crew to remove the mobile stairway.

"We have a good day, Captain," Belenko said, taking his seat beside me. He buckled up and placed earphones over his head as we began our taxi down the runway. "Clear skies from Berlin over France to England. Light showers in London, but that's norm—"

He stopped mid-sentence and grabbed the gun Vick left between our seats. I followed his gaze. The pale light of the autumn dawn was burning its way through the morning mist, enough that I could see the silhouettes of two large cars speeding along Tempelhof airfield, heading in the direction of our runway. Not far behind them, a patrol wagon, with ominous flashing lights, sounding a klaxon—set for a major arrest.

"Get ready to duck, Captain," said Belenko calmly. He turned and shouted back to the others: "Get down!"

Elena was out of her seat in a second, pistol drawn, ready to assist us if she had to. Beatrix was on the floor hugging all three of her children. The baby whimpered, barely audible. Angela's head was down, a protective arm flung around her sister as we all held our breath.

A bullet grazed our left wing and an unwelcome image of Rufina flooded my mind: the look on her face when I turned to urge her on that fatal sortie. Her terrified eyes. The bloodied scarf . . .

I forced my mind to focus on the present: The K-5 henchmen sent to arrest the Belenkos and Ingrid. Elena. And me. Technically we were all on American-controlled soil, but that wouldn't stop them. The reality was, if they managed to cripple the plane we'd be in Soviets hands, and it would be Sachsenhausen for all of us —regardless of jurisdiction. Nobody could help us once we were in the grip of their secret police. It would be just one more international incident to remain unresolved.

I thought of Luba facing the firing squad. Was this icy fear how it had been for her? And was it how I would end my days—ignobly? Shot as a traitor? We all would be. With luck, they wouldn't torture us first, but that wasn't likely. I thought of what Ingrid had already endured, and I shuddered to think of how the General's family would be treated. Their poor children . . . and now Steffi's baby, abandoned to fate yet a second time.

The wail of a siren, then sounds of fire being returned. I glanced down and saw several U.S. Army trucks with troops in helmets, shields, and protective gear emerging from a hangar. They too were racing toward us, returning the K-5 fire with automatic weapons. I had to bring the plane to a halt.

The K-5 police—eight men in total—ceased firing on us, forced to turn their full attention to the military vehicles. It was sheer Pandemonium. The sirens continued to shriek and lights flashed and glared. Deafening cacophony of gunfire drowning out the sound of our engines as more American troops joined in, blasting their way into formation surrounding the K-5. It had become a déjà vu war zone. I was back in the Crimea.

For the next ten minutes we all kept down with guns blasting, klaxons, and tension all around us. Ingrid was sobbing; little Isolde was wailing. Liesel and Achim were too terrified to react; their mother bravely comforting them. A scene the children would never forget.

A grenade was thrown from the Allied side and one of the cars turned into a fireball. An explosion followed, and I saw bodies thrown from the inferno. The surviving shooters got back in the second car and the patrol wagon, as they abruptly turned and sped away in the direction they came from, automatic weapons still blazing from shattered back windows. Had Vick been in one of the U.S. Army trucks defending our aircraft? Was he injured?

As I raised my head, a glance below revealed Vick, standing on the tarmac in an army helmet, frantically waving us on. I gave him a thumbs-up sign. I was already set to speed down the tarmac and raise the nose skyward. I lowered the flaps and pushed the throttle as far as it would go. Over the roar of the engines the plane began its trajectory.

"Vick expected something like that," said Belenko, his face bathed in perspiration despite the chill of early morning. "The troops were standing by." He grinned at me, but he was shaken. He had been their prime target.

When we were in the air, he looked at me in admiration. "Well done. But I don't imagine those clowns fazed you, Captain. You've seen that kind of action before."

"Yes, I've been shot at more than once," I agreed. "But not by our side. And having passengers, kids to protect? That's a first."

We continued our rapid rise and I banked toward the west above Steglitz and Lichterfelde. Despite our getaway, tension prevailed in the cockpit. Belenko and I both knew that anti-aircraft fire was still a possibility over East Germany, where a Russian fighter plane could be hiding in innocuous drifts of cloud. We had to reach as high an elevation as we could, as fast as possible. Belenko sat in rapt attention, searching the skies with a navigator's practiced eye.

To be shot down now, when we were well away from Berlin, was my greatest concern. It wasn't until we had left Russian-occupied territory, soaring through safe air space over Western Europe that I allowed myself to appreciate how blue the skies were; how beautiful and welcoming. I was leaving everything I knew behind me. Family, friends, and the country I had risked so much for. Who knew what lay ahead?

I took a deep breath, and then spoke into the microphone: "Good morning," I said to my little band of frightened passengers. "This is your captain speaking, Captain Kira Voronova." I was smiling. Everyone on board knew who I was, but I took pleasure in saying it.

I considered adding "Former 'night witch'," but instead I told them that our worries were behind us, that we were quite secure and they could all relax; to be sure to stay buckled up in case of turbulence. Like any commercial flight captain, I reported on our altitude, flying time, our speed, visibility, ETA in adjusted zonal time, and the weather in London. Then I told them to make themselves comfortable and have a good flight. We all knew we were heading in the right direction.

EPILOGUE

R ufina's death haunts me sometimes, more than two decades later. I've learned to accept that it's only through fate that I'm still here now in my middle years while Rufina, a year younger than I am, is not. A power beyond our own decided who would survive that war. Any war.

Even after all this time, on rare occasions I still relive my night sorties in clear detail under the cloak of sleep. The sirens and the searchlights; the shrapnel and the flak; the stress and the extreme cold—they flash like roman candles going off in my slumbering mind.

And always, there's the blood streaming down Rufina's face.

When that happens, I waken in a bath of tears and sweat. This morning, when I opened my eyes I was in a highly disturbed state after a variation on that nightmare. I'd been dreaming I was bedded down on icy hard ground under the wing of my plane. It was beginning to snow, and I was at a temporary base in a Crimean cow pasture, hungry and shivering, hands and feet numb as Luftwaffe planes roared overhead, strafing the airfield.

Instead, I wake up in a comfortable bed in a sub-tropical climate, wrestling with bed-clothes. A damp sheet is wound around me like a shroud. Shards of sunlight warm my bones as they slant through sheer curtains, stirring in the island breeze.

A strong, familiar hand reaches over to hold mine as he clears away the sheet. I feel the strength of his body beside me, warm breath on my cheek. Solace and calm drift over me with the gentle, reassuring feel of Vick's touch, the light tactile feel of wiry hairs on his forearm and bare chest teasing my skin. His unshaven cheek grazes my smooth one as he whispers through a smile: "It's okay, honey, you were dreaming. You're safe. You're here with me. In Key West."

Relief floods through me. I lie back, basking in the serenity we all take for granted when our safety isn't threatened.

It wasn't always easy for me in America. Raised in the Communist Party, I arrived amid Americans' fears and dread of Communist subversion, promulgated by Senator Joseph McCarthy, that peaked around 1950. But the carapace I'd taken refuge in over the difficult years in my homeland had toughened me, and my happiness in being reunited with Vick helped me to survive it all.

We lived in a Virginia suburb while he worked for the CIA. Between the births of my children I opened a small training school there, instructing future flyers of small aircraft. So, with no help from Petrov, I did teach flying again.

Like Elena, I've never had regrets about my defection. As predicted, there *is* a wall in Berlin separating East and West. K-5, the East German Secret Police is now called the Stasi. The dreaded NKVD has morphed into the KGB. Only the names have changed. I know that with my willful, reckless character, I would have run afoul of them at some point if I'd stayed.

After Vick retired from the CIA in the 1960s, he was offered a job instructing at Boca Chica, the U.S. Navy base outside Key West, Florida—very much a Navy town.

Now, post-Cuban missile crisis, a couple of years after a presidential assassination, we again live in difficult times. Security is tighter; the Vietnam War is revving up, and there is a need for more and more pilots. And instructors.

When he told me we were moving to Key West, Vick said, "So, at last, you'll get all those palm trees you used to talk about. And your white picket fence."

Yes, there are palm trees everywhere; our small Southard Street property is surrounded by them. A mango tree towers over our house at the back, but the front garden is sunny. Several different colors of bougainvillea vie for growing space with a passion fruit vine, as they struggle for dominance in a climb over the fence's pickets. The only conflict I ever want to see.

Most evenings, we watch the setting sun in almost reverent silence as it dips below the horizon. In balmy trade winds off the ocean in the Florida Straits, we bathe and snorkel; kayak and sail every chance we get. It could not be more different from what I left.

Today is Sunday, and our teenaged children are moving around in the kitchen. It's Mother's Day—I'd forgotten. I'm to have breakfast in bed. The normalcy of it offers a sharp contrast to the grim details of my dream of Rufina.

My eldest daughter is almost the age I was when I joined the Red Army and flew in combat missions taking on Messerschmitts and Focke-Wolf fighter planes. Her biggest concern right now is the dress she will be wearing to her prom as she listens to the Beatles. And that's as it should be.

With age comes wisdom. You can't stay angry forever at people you've loved. After lung cancer claimed Maxim, Zinaida reached out to me, more than once, begging my forgiveness. She was a precious tie to the past, to my family, and my country. A tie I couldn't sever completely. I miss her. Recently, she sent me a photo of the twins. They're nineteen, both handsome children. Kirill, now the picture of Maxim, has become a professional ice skater. Pavel might have resembled him.

And Sophia? Because of the ban on women flying in Russia since the war, that profession—her first choice—is denied to her. Instead, she has become an aeronautical engineer. She favors Zinaida, but it sounds like she is a lot like Maxim. Attached to her collar in the photo is the little airplane pin I left with him that day in Moscow when I held her in my arms to quell her cries. I only hope her father's amulet brings her the luck it brought me.

ABOUT THE AUTHOR

Joanna Brady

Night Witch in Berlin was the winner of the Florida Keys Council of the Arts award in 2015, and the Anne McKee Artists Fund in Key West in 2020.

Joanna Brady is author of the Key West historical novel, *The Woman at the Light*. She divides her time between Key West and a stone cottage in a medieval village in Southwest France.

joannabradysite.com

PRAISE FOR AUTHOR

"Joanna Brady, author of the elegantly written The Woman at the Light, has created a new masterpiece with Night Witch in Berlin. Historically based, each chapter propels you to the next. Her writing is superior, and the story leaves one bewildered at the bravery and skills of these astonishing female pilots. A must read!"

- RUSTY HODGDON, AUTHOR OF SIX NOVELS. PAST PRESIDENT OF THE KEY WEST WRITERS GUILD

"An exciting story, beautifully told, about an aspect of women in war that has not received the attention it deserves. Joanna Brady tells the story of a Russian female flyer during WWII who becomes a spy in West Berlin after the war, involved in activities which are still relevant today."

- LEWIS M. WEINSTEIN, AUTHOR OF A FLOOD OF EVIL, A PROMISE KEPT AND SEVERAL OTHER NOVELS

Made in the USA
Columbia, SC
09 December 2024